The

Crystal

Parts 1-3

By J. A. Daniel

Published by Books for the Nations Publishing

ISBN 979-8-9919089-0-0

Part One: An Instant
"An amount of time so small, it is immeasurable, yet in it, your life, your world, can change forever"

Chapter 1

The bright evening sunlight shone through the window on the far wall of the classroom. It struck the board from which my chemistry teacher was attempting to explain the effects of quantum entanglement. I couldn't focus. This time of day, the light reflected in just the right way to shine in my eyes for the entire class. Between the blinding sunlight reflecting off the white board and the complexity of the subject, my mind drifted from the topic at hand, thinking over the past few months...

So much had happened in just the past six months. I didn't even know who my mother was until my Dad died in February. I would often ask questions about her when I was younger, but always got the same answer, "She was an amazing woman, but she passed away." He never gave me any more than that, so I eventually gave up asking.

The day after he died though, she just showed up out of nowhere. She went to court and claimed that My father had never divorced her. This was, of course, true because she was supposed to be dead. She was then able to take over his estate without regard to the will because he never made a new beneficiary. She was entitled to the entire estate, and apparently a part of that estate was me.

She didn't want me, only the money I brought with me. She blew through that money in just two months, drinking, partying, and who knows what else. After the money was gone, she was forced to sell the lake house, the house I grew up in. I went from my nice house by the lake on the east side of town, to an apartment in the slums of the west side of town.

It's quite the downgrade, especially seeing that in his will, my father left custody to the parents of my best friend, Blake Vale. They lived only a few houses down from me when I lived on the lake. It could

5

have been so much better. But Instead, I was ripped from everything I knew and drug off to be with my mother.

I wish I didn't, but I hated her for it. She was selfish, greedy, and deceptive. I didn't even know her. I had no desire to know her. She is so… No, I better stop. I try not to let my anger get the better of me. I can't change it. Being angry only makes it harder.

I'm one of the few kids who would rather be at school. I stay away from my house as much as possible. It's old and dirty- basically falling apart. She never took care of it, and despite my best efforts, there's not a lot that I can do with it. I'm a pretty handy guy, but even with my job at the local hardware store it's just too much to fix. I keep it standing though. I fixed all of the leaks and drafts. The floors are vinyl and are covered with staines. The walls used to have holes. I was able to fix those, but my mother wont let me paint because she says she "can't stand the smell".

Blake's Dad, Mr. James, offered to help my mother with the rent so we could get a better place, but when he refused to give her cash and only pay for it directly, she refused his help. I guess if she couldn't use it to party, she didn't want it.

Her only source of income is some sort of government benefits, which should be more than enough to get a better place, but any money over the bare minimum is spent on her lifestyle which includes only three things, binge watching cringey soap operas, partying, or sleeping off a hangover – or all three at once.

I do have some things to look forward to though. On the weekends she lets me stay at Blake's house. That place is my true escape. I usually get to spend Friday and Saturday nights there and go to church with them on Sundays.

I couldn't be more thankful for my Dad and the Vales taking me to church. If it were not for my faith, I don't know what I would have done in all of this. God keeps me grounded. He has shown me favor by giving me a true family in the Vales. Sometimes, life gets to be a lot for me lately, almost too much to bear, but when it does, I know to pray. It is the little answered prayers here and there that keep my faith up. They make me hope that one day He will see fit to answer the bigger ones:

getting away from my mother, having the power to help others like me, to be adopted by the Vales.

The Vales are my true Family. Blake and I have been like brothers for as long as we've been alive. His parents and my Dad were very close friends growing up, and that friendship continued until he died. Dad always had to work long hours and go on long business trips, so I spent about as much time there as I did at my own home.

As I was thinking, I realized that today was Friday, the one day I was actually excited for school to be out. I would be leaving to go over to Blake's any minute. This realization pulled my mind from its daydreaming. I looked across the room to see Blake, also half asleep. It was no wonder; this teacher had the most monotone voice I think I had ever heard.

"Quantum entanglement is something only now being understood. In 2034, a scientist by the name of Alfred Henry unlocked the secret to understanding…" he paused to turn the page of the work book he was reading from "this Phenomena. His experiments allowed for the first teleportation, the most substantial feat of the twenty-first century thus far. Does anybody know what the first object to be teleported was? Anyone?"

Everyone knew the answer, but no one was going to answer.

"A Pebble." He continued, "He later would experiment on mice, but found that they would reform after being transported, however, there would be no life in their cells. The stress was simply too much. While he discovered that it was impossible to teleport organic matter without killing the cells, he changed the way energy would be transferred forever. This is because in learning how to teleport atoms, he also discovered how to entangle electrons.

His experiments allowed for power lines to be rendered obsolete and brought about the first energy boxes that could transport energy right from the source. Batteries no longer run out, cars no longer need gas, planes no longer need fuel. Now a battery the size of a tic-tac can power a jet engine so long as it is properly entangled with the energy source"

7

I have to admit, it was a breakthrough that I was very happy for since it made energy so cheap. I don't have to buy gas for my car or charge my phone. It's only been ten years since the discovery, but basically everything has switched over to quantum batteries. It does make me a little nervous about what weapons there could be now. It's something that is always a topic of the news. I try not to buy too much attention though.

"His life's work ended abruptly when he attempted to entangle himself with an energy source. The purpose of this experiment was never discovered, and the energy source was never disclosed but..."

RING!

He was cut off by the bell. The entire class was jared from their boredom induced sleep. They gathered their things, and headed for the door.

"Remember, Your projects on Alfred Henry are due as soon as you come back on Monday" the teacher said as the last students scrambled out the door.

Blake and I walked out into the hallway, headed for the parking lot.

"He was even more boring than usual today," Blake sighed.

"He made about as much sense too. I got the history part, but the science is beyond me," I complained.

"Well, seeing how he was just reading it all off of the book and never looked up, I don't think he does either."

"True" I admitted, "I'm not sure anyone really does. I mean, weren't they only able to replicate Alfred's stuff? I don't think they ever had any other breakthroughs. Didn't they just use his notes to duplicate the quantum batteries?"

"You know more about it than I do. I'm just glad my car runs on it. I was not looking forward to having to buy gas. I was born at the right time!"

"Wonder what happened to the guy?" I inquired.

"I don't know. Scientists can be strange people. Probably tried to give himself super powers or something," Blake joked.

"Yea, Let me know when they figure that out." I remarked, "I'll be first in line."

We exited the school and walked about two miles to get to Blake's house. We always just walked home this time of year. We both had cars, but when the weather was nice, we preferred to walk. It gave us time to discuss our day.

As we entered the neighborhood, Tullahoma Lake came into view. The Sun was positioned in the west, but it was not yet low enough for the colors of the sunset to break through. Its bright rays reflected off the water making the lake mirror the puffy white clouds and their blue backdrop. On the far side of the lake there were no houses, just trees, their branches waving in the muggy afternoon breeze.

Once we reached the home, Blake went upstairs to his room to finish some homework and I, having nothing pressing to take care of, walked down to the edge of the lake. Their house sat about halfway down an inlet, or as we call them in the South, a slue. It was about 100 feet to the other side of the slue. To the right was the rest of the lake. It wasn't very large, but large enough that you couldn't see the whole thing from any one spot. In the distance, the dam holding back the water could be seen. The sun would set in line with the dam, making its reflection visible over the water until the very last ray had dipped over the horizon.

I sat in a reclining wooden chair on their boat dock overlooking the water, enjoying the peace and quiet. The dock was made of wood and rather than floating, it had supports that went to the bottom of the lake; I guess it acted more as a peer than a dock.

Fish gathered around the posts waiting to be fed. There was a metal can in which the Vales kept fish food. We would throw some out every time we went down there. A fishing pole with a lour attached was laid down on the side of the pier. Just as I thought about grabbing it, Blakes mom, Mrs. Cassey, called from the house telling me it was time for supper.

9

She had such a soft voice. I never noticed until I had to spend time with my mother. My mother's voice wasn't exactly gruff, but always had a miserable undertone. She was never happy. For that, I sometimes felt bad for her. My life wasn't great, but I had people who could make me happy, no matter how down I was. My mother had no one, no one who could put a smile on her face, not even me.

I shook the recurring thoughts of my mother from my mind, left the comfort of my chair, and walked up to the house. I walked in through the sliding glass door which led right to their dining room and kitchen. The driftwood style, oak dining table was to my right. Around it sat Mr. James and Blake's little sister Kinsie. She was younger than us, about 8 years old at the time; just old enough to be sassy, annoying, and somehow still adorable all at the same time. They never let each other see it, but Blake and Kinsie were deeply fond of one another. There's nothing Blake wouldn't do for his little sister, even if they did like to fight. I guess the bickering was a way that they showed each other they cared, without having to show it.

In the kitchen, Blake was fixing himself a plate. On the stove there were green beans, rolls, and mashed potatoes. Mr. James had cooked steaks on the grill which sat on the island, positioned in the middle of the kitchen. I went to the right of the island to the refrigerator, and grabbed myself a bottle of water. Then I took a plate from one of their cabinets, fixed myself a plate, and joined the rest of the family at the dining room table.

We said grace and began to eat. Blake's mom started off the dinner conversation as she always did, "How was school today boys?"

"Fine."
"Yea, pretty good"

"Anything exciting coming up?" she asked.

"Well, If you count the projects on Alfred Henry that are due on Monday as exciting…" I said sarcastically.

"Yea, That guy always has to be giving us some kind of project. I can't believe I'm saying this, but why can he just give us tests instead?" Blake chipped in.

10

"Probably because he wouldn't know what the right answers are," I joked, sort of.

This made the family chuckle, well all except for Kensie. Not because the joke was all that funny on its own, but we had all had this same teacher, Mr. Johnson. He had to be long overdue for retirement, and he hadn't changed a bit since Blake's parents had him.

Mr. James spoke up looking in my direction, "Me and your Dad had that class together. Daniel already knew everything there was to know about chemistry. Between that, Johnson's voice, and your Dad's mischievous side, we knew something crazy was going to happen every day in there. One day, he just kept asking Johnson questions. Well. the poor guy didn't have a clue what to say. Your dad would just answer his own questions. He would ask it and then give the response to himself. Well, that got the whole class going so they started to ask questions and before Johnson had the chance to even think of the answer, Daniel would answer them. Well, the guy got fed up with that and got Daniel sent to the principal."

I always liked it when Mr. James told stories about my Dad. It always made me feel close to my Dad. I could imagine him doing it and it was like still getting to make memories with him even though they were Mr. Jame's memories.

"What did the principal do?" Blake asked

"Well, he never did much of anything to Daniel. They were pretty good buds and most of the time, the principal would find his schemes funny. He would just keep him up there for a little while and chat, then send him back to class.

"Wouldn't that be a nice deal," I said.

"Yea, He had it pretty good" Mr. James agreed.

Dinner was delicious, as always, and soon gone, but we stayed around the table and talked for a while longer, then Blake and I went down to the lake to swim. It was the end of August and summer still had a firm, humid grip on Tennessee just as it did every year. It was

11

always annoyingly hot this time of year. Even at this hour (about 5:00) it was about 90 degrees, but it was perfect lake weather.

Blake was always more athletic than me. I could never beat him in much of anything. I was just naturally skinny and he was naturally more athletic. He was good at every sport he tried, and I... was not. But there was one thing, one competition that I stood a chance in, and that was swimming.

On these hot summer evenings we would often find ourselves competing in countless races, swimming across the lake. I would win some, and he would win others. He usually started to win more toward the end of the evening because I would wear down quicker.

Tonight was no exception. It was just normal. It was fun. Those were two things I found myself cherishing more and more. Blake used to not like to swim with me. He would never admit it, but he didn't like that I could beat him. But after my Dad died and everything happened, he did it more out of pity for a while, to make me feel better. Then, as we did it more often, I believe he truly grew to like our weekly "swim meets".

The sun began to set on the far side of the lake. Still, the sun lasted longer than we did. Both of us got tired and hopped up on the side of the dock. Blake grabbed the fishing pole I had spotted earlier and began to catch all of the "pet fish" that lived under the dock. He would get one about every cast and would throw them back just to catch another.

For this day and age, it was rare to see kids our age just taking time to sit. Most could be found gaming or watching Television, or in some virtual reality program, but the Vales didn't really keep TVs or anything like them in their house, something about it "rotting the Brain". They did keep one in the living room to watch the news or have a family movie night. Though, they mostly encouraged their kids to read, or go down to the lake, or other things like that. My Dad was never quite that way, but I found that it was peaceful and centering just to sit back and watch the sunset. Reality, though not always ideal, is still better than a made up one to me.

I know Blake never really understood what it did for me, coming over to his house, how much it helped me. Just being around them was rejuvenating. I knew I probably seemed boring sometimes. I

12

could be content just sitting looking at the wall of their house, just because of how good it felt to be sitting there. Of course, looking at the sunset was even better than the wall.

I outlasted Blake. He stood up and announced that he was headed inside.

"Well, I guess I've done enough sitting for one night," I conceded, "I'll head in too. I'm ready to get into some dry clothes anyway,"

I lifted my feet from dangling off the side of the dock and followed Blake up to the back door. Mrs. Cassey had towels waiting for us. We were mostly dry from sitting out of the water, but we still took the towels to wipe our feet and legs.

The white tile floor was cold on my bare feet as I walked by the kitchen, through the living room and up the stairs. At the top of the stairs there was a long, carpeted hallway. To the left was Kinsie's bedroom and to the right was mine and Blake's. I had my own room there on the far end of the hall, connected to Blake's through a Jack and Jill bathroom. It used to be their guest room, but they gifted it, and everything in it, to me as my own room in May, for my birthday.

Blake and I parted ways in the hall. Since we shared a bathroom we had to stager taking our showers. I let him take the first, and headed to my room.

On the left wall of my room I had a queen bed, nightstand and dresser (stocked with Buckle jeans, my favorite shirts, and other nice clothes). In the corner was my guitar, (which I left at the Vales' to make it more convenient to bring to church on Sundays, since I play on the praise team).

On the right was my closet, complete with shoes and a few choices for Sunday suits. Beside the closet was the bathroom that connected to Blakes room. Everything I had here, the Vales gifted me. I lost most of my things when my Mother took over my Dad's estate.

All of the bedrooms upstairs had two windows on the far side of the room, both overlooking the water. In my room, between these two windows, I had a shelf displaying many things I had acquired over the

13

years including a collection of unique pocket knives and some of my martial arts equipment, including my bō (a wooden staff used for martial arts) and a katana, which I was never brave enough to use.

I had tried, and been successful at martial arts for years. I had my black belt (also displayed on the shelf). Some friends from church, including Blake, and I had taken classes since we were about 4. That is until February when my dad died. After that, life was just so crazy that I had to stop. Now, I could start them back, but I'm just trying to make do. Blake stayed with it though; he still goes every Tuesday. We were actually a pretty even match when I quit. I could beat anyone who challenged me, except for him. It was still one of those things in which he always seemed to win.

I went to my dresser and pulled out a fresh pair of jogging pants and a T-shirt. I tossed them over to the bed and took my phone out of my pocket (I know, don't worry it's waterproof). I sat down on the floor and leaned against the wall.

I pulled up my mom's location. She didn't know that I tracked her phone, but when she didn't come home for three days one week, I decided I needed to keep an eye on her. One day, while she was drunk, I put an app on her phone and removed it from the home screen. I'm sure she'll never find it.

It showed that she was at home, I'll have to admit, it's a good change from the bar. I then looked up some information on Alfred Henry. I was planning on making a slideshow presentation for my project. For him to be so well known and to have such a big, world-changing discovery, there was surprisingly little information on him. I was only able to find one picture of him, a black and white copy, cut out from a newspaper. It's the 21st century! How are there not more pictures of this guy? My research was interrupted by Blake poking his head out of the bathroom door.

"Shower's empty" He said

"Finally! I was beginning to wonder if you fell asleep in there." I joked.

"Just be happy I left you some hot water"

"How gracious" I said with a laugh.

I grabbed my fresh clothes off of the bed and headed for the shower.

I closed the door behind me and hurriedly jumped in, turning the water on as I stepped over the side of the tub. The hot water ran over my chilled body. I didn't realize I was shivering until I got in the shower. I guess the air conditioning and the cold lake water didn't mix well. I lost track of time, the peace of the home and the warmth of the water caused my mind to clear as I enjoyed reflecting over the good day I'd had, and planned for another one the next day.

Once I felt fully relaxed, I got out and dried off. The clock on the vanity read 8:00 pm. I put on my fresh clothes, brushed my teeth and walked over to Blake's room to see what he was up to. His room was laid out almost exactly as mine was but in reverse. He sat on his bed reading a book. I couldn't make out what it was.

"And you said I took a long time in the shower," he said sarcastically.

"Well, I figured I should figure out if you were justified or not"

"Right…"
"Right!"

Blake's face gained a more serious look. He scooted to the edge of his bed. "So how are you doing?"

I knew what he meant, but for some reason my heart wouldn't tell him right off. "I'm feeling pretty good from that shower at the moment."

"No, I mean *you*. We haven't talked about… everything, for a little while. I just want to make sure you're okay"

Blake often had to squeeze information out of me when it came to stuff like this. I didn't like to talk about my feelings, or my life. I knew it was good for me to talk about it, but for some reason I tried to deal with stuff on my own.

15

Reluctantly, I opened up, "Well, my mother came home drunk twice this week. That always makes her yell. I try to stay away from her, but there's only so much room in that stupid little apartment. It's falling apart, Blake. The roof sprung a new leak on Tuesday. I have to work every weekday until 10 just to support myself and keep that place liveable. I don't even have time to breathe until I come here."

I didn't feel it happening until it was already too late. I was beginning to rant. "And that woman is so filthy, I can smell her stench coming down the hall. Take a shower lady! There's a new hole in the sheet rock, from her little party friend Kathy, I'm sure. Why do I have to babysit my own mother!? You know how she didn't come home last week for like three days? Well I found out from Kathy that she got drunk and just started driving. She got lost in Kentucky! How did she even get to Kentucky?"

And then I felt them, tears, streaming down my face. This made me aware of the overwhelming rage that had come over me and with this realization, it quickly turned to sadness. Somewhere in the conversation Blake had gotten off the bed. He put his arm on my shoulder then pulled me into an embrace. The hug grounded me. I began to come back from my anger and find reality again.

I had to be strong at school, and I didn't really have anyone to talk to at home. Blake tried to get me to talk about it often. It helped me get it off of my chest, and he worried about me so he wanted to hear it. It had been about two weeks since my last break down, so this was long overdue. I felt another tear, this time on my neck. It was Blake's. He wasn't completely crying like I was, but his own tears began to shed as he empathized with my situation. I'm not really sure how long it took me to get a hold of myself, but eventually I did.

I pulled away, wiping away my tears and, in a more collected manner, I continued, "I just don't know what to do Blake. We tried the police, they won't help me. I tried getting her to let me just stay here but then she threatened to call the police on your parent's for kidnapping, and she's crazy enough to do it!"

"Well, Dad probably wanted to have this talk with you, and that's probably why he didn't tell me, but I heard him talking to Mom. He got you a lawyer. This guy thinks that you have enough information on your mother and that you're old enough that you may be able to take her

16

to court. They think you can either be emancipated or have guardianship turned over to my parents."

"Didn't we already try that a long time ago?" I asked, trying not to get my hopes up.

"Yes, but that was right after it all happened. I think it's an evidence thing. You didn't have any against her then, but you do now."

I was speechless. If this worked, my life would finally be everything I had wanted it to be since my dad died.
"I need to talk to your dad."

"I think you should wait," Blake said, "I'm not even supposed to know this. I just heard them talking. He may still be working on stuff."

I tried my hardest to keep my hopes down. I didn't want to be disappointed again. I calmed back down and conceded, "Well, I guess you're right. I just can't hardly wait"

"I figured you could use some good news"

"Yea, next time maybe lead with that before you make me cry."

"I'll do my best," Blake smiled.

We talked for a while longer, mostly about how much evidence I could get against my mother, and then about Mr Johnson's class project. By the time it was about 9:30, I decided to call it a night and headed back to my room.

I knelt down next to my bed and began my prayers. They started out the usual, praying for forgiveness, Praying for my church, my friends, my family, and my life, thanking God for being able to be at the Vales' house, even if it was for just the weekend. Then I ended them with a special request.

"God, I know I ask for a lot lately, but I am gonna ask for just a little bit more. Please, help this lawyer to know what he is doing and to get me away from my mother. Help there to be all of the evidence that the courts need and help me to be able to live here. Help what Dad would have wanted to come to pass. Give me the strength to stand up to this evil and empower me to defeat it. In Jesus name, Amen"

Chapter 2

I was gently called to consciousness by the morning sun shining through the window. I rolled over to see that the clock on my nightstand read 7:00 am. It may seem early to some, but I never really liked to sleep in too late. I sat up and raised my pillow, wedging it between the wall and my back. I grabbed my phone which was sitting next to the clock. I looked to make sure there were no messages and then opened it to make sure I hadn't missed anything on social media. After a few minutes of this, I slid out of bed and walked over to look out the window over the lake. The water was smooth in the still morning air. A gentle fog drifted across the surface water, illuminated to a radiant gold by the first rays of sunlight.

I saw off in the distance what I thought was a bird, but then I realized it was a personal aircraft. They were becoming more and more common. With the invention of quantum batteries, a large amount of energy could be stored in a small space. This allowed for hover and antigravity technology to be perfected in recent years. Relatively small and affordable personal aircraft had just recently become available and legal to the public. I was still getting used to seeing them. But even the local supermarket had a parking zone just for them. It was not unusual to see two or three every time you went to the store.

I watched until the craft was out of sight and then decided to head downstairs. Mr and Mrs. Vale were the only ones up. Mr. James sat reading the newspaper on the couch in the living room and Mrs. Cassey was cooking breakfast: bacon and scrambled eggs. It smelled delicious.

"Good morning, dear" greeted Mrs. Cassey

"Good morning!" I replied

I walked over to the couch and sat down on the opposite end from Mr. James. I couldn't help but think about what Blake had told me the night before, but I heeded his advice and kept my knowledge to myself- for now anyway. I grabbed the remote and began to flip through the channels. Nothing good was on so I finally just settled on the news.

The reporter was talking about some sort of attack on a government conference in Africa. Apparently it killed some leaders, presidents of some nations over there

A man's voice played over images of the scene, "Out of the 195 countries in the world, 40 have lost one or more of their leaders in the past year and that number is expected to go up to at least 65 after this recent attack. Is this just a coincidence or is there a pattern? Jill?"

The screen cut to a young woman, standing outside the rubble of the destroyed building, "Well Steve, It may seem suspicious, but each death of these leaders over the past year has been confirmed to be by different organizations with different intentions, or simply just pure accident. Local police are saying that this 'bombing' is likely just an untimely gas line explosion. Many suspect that there may be foul play, but according to the records, this is all coincidence."

I noticed Mr. James had put down the newspaper and became interested in the world news. "Kind of strange, isn't it?" I asked.

"World's in bad shape, but I guess it's been that way for years," Mr. James answered.

"Valid" I admitted, "What do you think? Gas leak or foul play?"

Mr James' squinted at the TV, almost angrily "Anytime there's politics involved, it's foul play"

Mr James was never too serious about the news, but this subject seemed to have him on edge. I assumed, or sort of hoped, it was because he was stressed about the court case coming up.

The screen cut back to the male reporter in the newsroom. He continued, "Thank you Jill. In other news, the three year anniversary of the disappearance of two children in rural Kentucky is today. We will be interviewing the parents and receiving new revelations of just how cold the trail went, as well as looking at other cases like it, right after the break."

They cut to commercials. I heard someone coming down the steps. Just as I turned to see that it was Blake, Mrs. Cassey said, "Breakfast is ready boys!"

20

We all fixed our plate and sat down at the table as we had last night, only now Kinsie was absent.

"So what do you boys have planned today?" asked Mrs Cassey, turning her attention to Blake and I.

I had tried to come up with something, but nothing really stood out to me. I was just glad to be around, so my plan was whatever Blake's was. And thankfully, he had one.

"I was thinking we would go down to the basement and pull out some of the old disks," Blake said, "It's been a while since we've been disk golfing."

Blake and I went through a spell where we were trying all kinds of lesser played sports, him hoping to find more to master, me hoping to find something I was good at. The only one we ever stuck with for any time was disk golf. For a while, about two years ago, we would go every Saturday afternoon. There was a course right next to the lake, not far from the house.

"Do we still have those?" asked Mr James.

Hopeful, Blake responded, "I'm not 100% sure, but I thought it would be worth a look. I don't remember ever getting rid of them"

"Well, just be careful. I haven't been down to that basement in ages and last I checked, there were boxes stacked very... *interestingly*" Blake's dad turned to look at Mrs. Cassey.

"They are only stacked *interestingly* because *you* did not want to help." Mrs. Cassey said, folding her arms.

"*I* didn't help because *I* wanted to throw that junk away."

"That is my mother's *junk!*"

"Ok! Well, before I witness World War III, I am headed to the basement." I interjected standing up from the table. They weren't actually fighting, but I was done with my food and it was a good time to excuse myself.

21

"I'll second that" said Blake standing up from his spot.

"Ok, you boys have fun!" said Mrs. Cassey, "I'll have your father straightened out by the time you guys get back."

"What she means is, she's gonna make me do the dishes" sighed Mr. James.

"Precisely! Now get to work!" Mrs. Cassy said with a smile, shooing him from his seat.

Blake and I put our dishes in the sink and headed to the basement. There was a door to the right of the stairs that opened to a separate spiral staircase which led to the basement. We went down and began our search.

"So where would these be?" I asked.

"How am I supposed to know?" Blake shrugged.

"Well, it is your basement."

"No, it's Mom's basement where I keep a few things. The real reason Dad didn't help is because she has to keep this place 'organized'." Blake said in air quotes, "Which is Mom for, put everything where no one can find it but get mad when they don't put it back."

"I see his dilemma."

"Yea."

Some time passed with us rummaging our way through boxes, some of which (mostly in the back corner) were stacked to the ceiling. There was a zig zagging row of shelves going down the center of the room, and on the far side of the basement, a door that led to the outside. Kayaks and an aluminum boat took up the space closest to the door, to make them easy to reach when going out on a lake day.

Eventually, I made my way to the large, ceiling tall stack of boxes at the back of the room. On the bottom was a box marked "Outside Toys".

"Hey Blake!" I called, "I think I found it." He was on the opposite end of the room looking on the shelves closer to the door.

"I'm coming!" He said as he snaked his way through the row of shelves.

"I'm pretty sure it's this one," I pointed.

"Outside Toys?" he asked

"Yea, sounds like something your mom would label it. See if you can hold the ones on top while I pull this one out."

"I'm stronger, let me pull it out." Blake boasted.

I rolled my eyes, "I'm shorter. You just hold those"

"Fine"

I pulled the box, and it began to scoot out. I pulled a second time. Now it was about half way out and all of the boxes on top, about four, were wobbling.

"Last time, hold 'em"

"I've got it"

I gave it one final tug. When I did, I elbowed Blake who was right beside me. He let out a sharp exhale as the air was forced from him. This caused him to lose his grip on the boxes. I tripped over Blake's leg, causing us both to fall backwards as the boxes fell on top of us.

For a moment, we laid on the ground stunned. Blake looked at me. I looked at Blake. We both looked at the mess, then back at each other. All over the floor there were photo albums, christmas decorations, and disks.

"Boys, what was that?" Called Mr. James from the top of the stairs.

"We found the disks" I yelled back, standing up, then helping Blake to his feet.

"Sounds like you found more than that" he called sarcastically, "Just don't let Cassy see."

"Will do" Answered Blake. Turning to me, he said, "You should have let me pull it."

"And had your superior strength elbowing me in the gut?" I smirked, "I personally think we made the right decision."

Blake rolled his eyes, "I can tell you are not rusty on your martial arts. That's the best hit you ever got on me."

"Is that so? I recall almost beating you that one time we had to go up against each other at regionals."

"I recall letting you almost win. I didn't want to embarrass you."

"Just like you're going to let me almost win disc golf?"

"Oh No, I'm going to stomp you in that." Blake said playfully.

"We'll see about that." It was probably true, but I didn't want him to think so, "First... let's get this cleaned up before your mom comes and investigates."

"Agreed"

We threw all of the disks in the box they rolled out of and put it to the side. Then, we somewhat separated the Christmas decor and photo albums into separate boxes, and hurriedly stacked them back where they were. It wasn't quite like we found it, but good enough to fool Mrs. Cassey. At least until Christmas anyway.

Blake grabbed the box and toated it upstairs. I went to follow him but then noticed a box slid up under one of the shelves.

"Oh, we missed something," I said.

"Just sit it on the shelf. It'll be fine." Blake said passively.

I reached under the shelf and raked it out. The box was about five inches thick and about as long and wide as a laptop. It had two latches on one side and two hinges on the other. What was striking about it was that it was covered with metal work. The design formed a central ball in the middle of the case with jagged ridges spreading across it from there. The metal was shiny, resembling silver but it had a white hue. In one corner was a tiny pendant with some sort of bird in it.

My curiosity got the better of me. I unhooked the latches and opened the box. When I began to open the box, a rush of air came from it, startling me. A wave of blue light coursed throughout the metal work. As soon as I cracked it I could see a soft blue glow coming from the inside. I was honestly nervous for what I would find, but I built up the courage and opened the lid.

Surrounded by a bed of foam padding was a glowing crystal. It was about four inches long and two inches wide. It was uncut, but seemed to be naturally pointed on two ends. It wasn't bright, but did give off a soft blue light, the source of which was spread throughout the crystal. Brighter lights flickered back and forth through the inside of it. Wires, made from the same metal that was on the outside of the case, ran over the top of a solid foam bedding. The wires radiated with a faint blue glow, with the light moving out from the crystal.

"Blake!" I called up the stairs, "Come look at this!"

"What is it?" He called back.

"I'm not sure. Come look!"

He circled down the spiral staircase and walked over to where I was.

"What is…" He stopped as the crystal came into his view. "Woa! I don't remember seeing that down here. Where was that?"

"I found it under that shelf" I gestured to the shelf in front of me, "I guess it fell out of one of the boxes."

"I never had anything like that. Maybe it's one of Mom and Dad's old toys or something."

25

"I mean, it looks cool and all, but I don't think it would be much fun to play with."

"Maybe it does something. Take it out and see if it still glows like that."

I reached in and plucked the crystal from its perfectly cut out resting place. Its composition was intriguing. The light it gave off surrounded the chrystal and almost seemed tangible- almost like a blue fog encompassing it. It was heavy; heavier than it seemed it should be. I bounced it in my hand feeling its weight. As I did, it became lighter. Just before I could comment on this fact, it flew out of my hand. It came to rest in the air a few feet in front of where Blake and I were standing. It sat still in mid air for a moment and then began to spin.

Blake and I both jumped as the sudden motion startled us. My mind was racing, analyzing what was going on, but failing to find an explanation. Could an old toy be doing this? Blake and I took a step back. "I guess that's what it does." Blake said with a bit of worry in his voice.

The crystal began to make a humming noise and a sphere of the same blue energy I had seen on the wires appeared around it, this time brighter and more volatile, mixed with flashes of purple. Waves and arcs jumped across the surface of the sphere of energy. The humming grew louder.

Smaller blue lights shot out from the crystal and began to orbit the sphere until they were moving so fast, they formed three rings of light, all at different angles around the sphere of energy. There was no way of escape, the crystal was blocking the way out. We were trapped in the back corner of the basement. The humming grew louder.

My interest in the crystal had now turned to terror. Blake and I backed up more. His face mirrored my emotions. Fear gripped us both. An arc of blue electricity leaped from the sphere and blasted one of the shelves behind it, sending the shelf and its contents to the floor. We each let out a startled "Woah!". We threw our hands up to protect our faces and took another step back. The humming grew even louder. We were now about as far away as we could be without being pressed against the wall.

"Boys!" Mr James yelled as he was coming down the stairs, "What's going on down here... Gwoa!" He saw the same scene we did, but we were cut off, helpless. The humming had now reached a roar. There was nothing anyone could do but watch and pray.

Suddenly, a bright flash and a loud *CRACK* filled the room. I felt my back hit the wall as I was blown backwards. Searing heat, that started at my chest, covered every inch of my body. Then everything went dark.

Chapter 3

"I did it... He finally found it...Now we have a chance..."
Dad. Was that...? Dad!
"Dylan"
Dad! How can I hear you?
"What happens now is up to you, son"

"Dylan!"
"Is he ok? Dad?!"
"Go get your Mom. Now!"

I came back to consciousness abruptly, taking a gasp of much needed air. My eyes widened. I could only see light at first, then shapes. Then, I realized that Blake and Mr. James were standing over me. Blakes face and eyes were red. I couldn't tell if he was crying or just in a panic. Mr. James wore the look of relief more than anything.

"Oh thank God," sighed Blake and he sat down on the floor next to me.

"You gave us a scare, son," said Mr. James.

"What happened?" I asked, sitting up.

"You don't remember?" Blake's voice was shaky.

"I remember being thrown into the wall when the crystal exploded." I replied

They stared at me, then Blake said, "The crystal didn't explode. It shot you." Blake pointed to my shirt.

I looked down to see a baseball sized hole in my T-Shirt right over my heart. I reached up to inspect it. The skin was red. There was also a raised pattern left behind on my skin by the energy. It seemed to be a scar, though, I wasn't sure how that would be possible. That design, I knew it, but from where?

"How do you feel? Nauseous? Does anything hurt?" asked Mr. James.

28

I took a moment to think about it. Actually, I felt just fine. "No sir, I think I'm ok."

Blake and his dad gave each other a look. It wasn't worry, more like confusion. "I'm gonna take a look at your back," said Mr. James.

"Ok" I agreed, slightly confused.

He walked behind me, knelt down again, and lifted up the back of my shirt. He ran his hand down my spine. "Does any of this hurt?"

"No sir," I answered.

"Incredible" murmured Mr. James.

"What is it?" I demanded, getting a little annoyed by the strange looks and vague comments.

"It's just..." Mr. James paused.

"Look at the wall Dylan," Blake said squarely, pointing behind me.

I looked. About half way up the wall there was a chunk busted out in the cinder block and cracks spread from one side of the wall to the other. I was finally beginning to understand. They had thought I was dead. I should be. I was blasted hard enough to hit the wall with the force to break it, and here I sat, without a scratch.

"I did that? How?"

"It's a miracle," Mr. James shook his head in near disbelief.

I saw the crystal on the floor in front of me. It appeared to sit where it had fallen. Blake, seeing my line of sight, asked "What is that thing?"

Mr. James took a long pause, seemingly thinking of how to word his answer, then said, "I'm not sure. Daniel gave that case to us the week before he was killed in the accident. He told us to keep it safe for him. He said it would be a gift for Dylan one day and he didn't want him to find it, so he gave it to us. I never thought anything else of it, with everything getting so crazy." Mr. James stared at the odd case sitting on the floor, next to the fallen shelf.

I sat there puzzled. Why? Why would my dad give them something this dangerous? How did he even get something this dangerous? And the week before he died? Could there be some correlation? And that voice... Didn't I hear his voice? Then I realized, the case! That's where I had seen the pattern! "Blake, hand me that case!" I asked with urgency.

Blake looked puzzled but didn't argue. He picked it up from beside him and handed it to me.

I knew they were confused. Of course the story of my Dad was startling, and I'm sure they expected some sort of comment on that, but I wanted to start answering questions before I asked new ones. And the case had the answer to at least one.

I took the case from him and held the front of it next to my chest. Every element, the central ball in the middle and the jagged lines leaving it, matched my new scar exactly. Each line was turned in the exact same way. The metal work on the case and the scar were perfectly identical.

"Well that is strange" said Blake with a puzzled look on his face.

"It has to mean something, right?" I said excitedly, "This means that the crystal was meant to do that, that the pattern was predictable!"

"Well let's not jump to any conclusions." Mr. James stood up "It is interesting, but I think it's important we get you some rest. Let's get you upstairs"

"But don't you think it's important that we get some answers?" I said as Blake helped me to my feet.

"In time, yes. But if I have to take you to the ER this is going to be very hard to explain to the doctors, let alone your mother, so let's get you some rest to make sure we don't have to do that."

I knew I was ok, but the thought of *that* situation made me want to be sure as well. Blake wanted to help me walk, but I assured him I didn't need it. I really did feel fine. We stepped over the mess and went upstairs to my room. I sat down on the end of my bed. Blake took a seat next to me and Mr. James stayed at the door.

"Now Blake, you keep an eye on him. You'll be staying in here tonight. I don't want Dylan alone. Anything happens, you call me before you do anything"

"Yes sir," said Blake

"I'll be fine Mr. James" I assured him.

"I'm sure you will, just want to be *extra sure*" And with that, he left to go back down stairs, I assume to fill in Mrs. Cassey, who must have been outside during the whole thing.

For a while we sat in silence, processing what we had just witnessed and what we had heard from Mr. James. The emotion from hearing his story had just begun to set in. The week before? Really? That can't be a coincidence. All of the business trips my dad went on, what if they were something else? I don't think it would have been anything sinister, I can't imagine it, but what if all of his time away, his long hours at the office, were because of that thing. He always told me he was an accountant for the military base about an hour from here. But, now that I think about it, why would an accountant go on business trips?

As I was thinking about my Dad, I remembered a voice. The voice I heard just before I woke up. It was my Dad's. I knew it. How though? A memory? I decided to run it by Blake.

I broke the silence, "While I was out, I heard my Dad's voice."

"What?" Blake looked at me, his eyebrows scrunched, "What are you talking about?"

I realized how random and insane that must have sounded, but I continued, "Just before I woke up I heard my Dad say something like 'I did it. He finally found it'"

31

"Dylan, I don't know what you heard, but you know how crazy that sounds, right?"

"Yes, yes I know. It sounds like I hit my head, which I did. But, I don't think I was hearing things. Especially knowing that somehow my dad was connected to that crystal." Blake said nothing and had a strange look on his face. I couldn't place it. "What is it?"

He paused then said, "Dylan, your heart stopped. You were dead... and like, not just for a second, like five minutes" he teared up, "We thought you were dead."

I could see it had been traumatic for him- more so than it was for me. I mean, I guess he did just watch me die. I did the only thing I could think to do. I stood up off of the bed, put my hand on his shoulder and pulled him into an embrace. "I'm still here" I said. He began to cry. Of course, this caused my emotions to swell. "You know we sure do a lot of this lately." I somberly joked.

"I wouldn't mind doing it less" Blake replied, through his tears.

Once we composed ourselves, I realized I was hungry, starving in fact. "Let's go grab something to eat." I said.

Blake agreed and we walked downstairs. Mr and Mrs Vale were on the couch. "Dylan, honey, how are you feeling?" asked Mrs Cassey.

"Just fine actually." I said, "It's kind of crazy."

"Yes it is. Well, thank the Lord! You let me know if you need anything. Blake, how about you sweetie, you okay?"

"Yes ma'am. Just a little shook up is all."

"I'm sure."

She walked over and gave us a long, group hug and then helped us find some food. She made us each a turkey sandwich. I finished mine and then heated up some leftovers from the night before. Then, I made some ramen noodles. Then, I ate a few candy bars,

32

prepackaged cakes, then a bag of jerky, then a protein shake, and some granola bars. Then I realized I was eating everything they had and even after that, I was still hungry. I just thought maybe I hadn't eaten enough that week and It was catching up to me. But this worried Mrs Cassey so she began to look up problems I could have on her phone.

I think Kinsie must have been ordered to leave because I never saw her and I thought I heard Mr. James on the phone, asking someone if she could come over to their house. It made me slightly uncomfortable. It seemed like they might know something they weren't telling Blake and I. Especially because they were so calm about the whole thing. But I shrugged it off and decided to watch a movie with the family.

The four of us sat down in the living room and ended up watching a whole trilogy of action movies. They were low budget and I had never even heard of them. But once you looked past the laughable CGI they were actually good. We would all make jokes and made eachother laugh. And, now that I think about it, the company is probably what made the movies good. By the time we finished the trilogy, we had eaten lunch and dinner, and walked around the neighborhood. It was about 9:00 pm. I think I had finally convinced them that I was okay, but Mr. James still wanted Blake and I to stay in the same room, just in case anything were to happen.

We went up and started getting ready for bed. While Blake was in the shower, I sat on the bed re-thinking the whole event with the crystal. I had questions, and I wanted answers. I knew that Mr. James knew more than he was saying. But whether it was anything important to me, I didn't know. There had to be more to the story of that case.

The way the chrystal spun, the lights that began to orbit it, It had to be some sort of technology, right? Could something like that be natural? I had never seen or heard of anything like it. How would you even make something like that? I saw no evidence of wires. It just looked like a solid crystal to me. It looked natural, not manufactured.

A whirlwind of questions began to fill my mind until I could no longer focus on one question without being interrupted by another. Before my mind could think too deeply into the events of the day, I was interrupted by Blake telling me He was done with the shower

Blake and I traded spots. I got in the shower and for the first time began to examine my scar. This led to all new questions. I wasn't exactly sure what it was, but a scar seemed the most accurate description. I washed it and ran my hand over it. The central ball of the pattern was directly over my heart, so close that when my hand was on it, I could feel my heartbeat. The ridges were smooth and seemed to even have blood vessels running along with them. How could my vascular system reroute to follow them? Did it or did it run along blood vessels I already had? If so, how did it match the design on the case?

The lines that ran from the central ball went no higher than my collar bone. No one would ever see that I had it since it could be completely covered by my shirt. This was good. I wouldn't have to explain it to my mother.

I got out of the shower. As I was getting dressed, I could see in the mirror something else strange: my muscles. They were much larger and more defined. Each muscle, once unremarkable, now stood out with heightened definition.

"Wow" I whispered as I ran my right hand over my left arm. Somehow I hadn't noticed till now. I had no explanation for how this could happen. With all the things that had happened that day, this was one change I welcomed. After a while of admiring my transformation, I decided to take this change as a win but keep it to myself. I was worried it may only be some sort of temporary side effect that would fade away as the days went on.

I got dressed, now noticing the snug fit of my clothes. I walked back into my room to find Blake already in bed. He had taken the left side so naturally I took the right. I wasn't sure what his dad wanted to accomplish by having him in here. His room was right next door and he sleeps so deeply, he would probably be oblivious to any disturbance.

I knelt down on my side of the bed to say my prayers. Along with the usual, I thanked God for sparing my life and the lives of those with me. I thanked him for the amazing transformation. Then, I climbed into bed and drifted off to sleep.
***

My eyes opened. I looked around my room. I wasn't sure what woke me up. I rolled over to see Blake on the other side of the bed fast asleep. I realized that I needed to use the restroom so I got out of bed, careful not to wake Blake, and headed to the bathroom. As I made it about half way across the room, I saw a shadow out of the corner of my eye. I turned back toward the bed to get a better look. Nothing.

Now paranoid, I attempted to tell myself it was just my imagination and moved on. Then, I saw it again. This time, coming straight for me. I dodged out of the way just as a shadowy figure lept toward me.

They were wearing all black. Their clothes were tight fitting but thick- tactical. They wore a metal helmet. It was rigid and had lots of plating. Across where their eyes were was a black, glass like strip, which I assume allowed them to see. On their waste they wore a utility belt, but I couldn't make out what was on it. Now spotted, they stood there in a stand-off.

I reached behind me and took the katana from its display and unsheathed the sword. I tried to reach back in my mind and remember the forms I had learned in martial arts. "Blake!" I yelled as loud as I could. He jolted awake and then at the sight of the intruder yelled, "Waaa!"

I decided to make the first move and swung my blade at the figure. They dodged and landed a punch in my gut. It didn't phase me. I was able to counter and kick them in the helmet. This wasn't the best move, since I was barefoot and their helmet was metal.

"Oww!" I yelled, grabbing my foot. The intruder took their chance and lunged at me. They hit me with such force that we smashed through the window. I dropped the katana and we rolled down the side of the house. The tar shingles scraped my bare arms as I rolled. Just before we fell off the roof, two small flames appeared on the back of the intruder. It seemed to be a jetpack. He flew just enough to land safely on the ground below.

I was able to catch the gutter. It bent and strained under my weight but I was able to pull myself up. It didn't take the figure long to fly up to where I was. The jet pack was very slender and sat flat on his back. It was so small that I hadn't even noticed it until he used it. Its flame was small and orange, and would change sizes as the figure moved around.

"Dylan!" Blake called. I turned to see him throw the staff out the window. I caught it just as the figure landed back on the roof. "I'm gonna go get Dad!" Blake yelled, and he disappeared from sight.

The Attacker pulled a small cylinder, about 5 inches long and the width of my staff, off of his utility belt. He thrust it out in front of him. When he did, it expanded to about 5 feet. It reached its full length in a fraction of a second and when it was fully extended, a blue blast of energy shot out from each end in a flat circular pattern.

It had been what was quickly beginning to feel like forever since I had dueled. But the challenger wanted a fight, and I wasn't going down without one. I swung and landed a blow on their shin and progressed after that. Swing after swing they blocked with their staff. He countered, but I was able to keep him moving backward until he was on the edge of the roof.

Then, the figure grabbed my staff. His jet pack activated and thrust him backwards, pulling me off the roof. I fell to the ground, landing on my back. The fall knocked the breath out of me. The shadowy figure glided down between me and the house. "Where is the crystal?" He asked. His voice was disguised by a modifier. It was gruff and deep.

I lay there for a moment gasping for air, then stood up and sucked in as much air as I could. "I don't know... what you're talking about." I lied.

"It is here!" He called my bluff, "You can't win"

"Maybe," I confessed, "But I can fight until I lose."

As he advanced toward me, all I could think was that I was about to die. He would hit me with that thing and probably cut me in half. I backed up. I knew I was outmatched. I couldn't run faster than he could fly and I couldn't defeat him with just a stick. The figure walked toward me. He swung and I dodged, then again. Then, Mr. James' voice rang out. "Hey! Is this what you want?" The figure turned from me to look at Mr. James. He was holding the case open, facing it toward us. The glow of the crystal could be seen shining out of the case. "You can have it! Just leave him."

36

"Unfortunately, you are in no position to bargain, and I need them both." Growled the attacker.

He spun around, jabbed his staff at me, and hit me in the center of the chest. There was a blue flash and I was blown backwards, losing consciousness before I hit the ground.

Chapter 4

My eyes fluttered open. I couldn't see well, but I could hear voices, so I closed my eyes again and attempted to listen.

"How did we not know that he left one behind"

"We only searched his house, not this one. We didn't feel there was a reason to." There was a pause.

"He's coming back around."

I wasn't sure what all of that was supposed to mean, but since they knew I was waking up, I opened my eyes. I wouldn't be getting any more information with them closed.

I was strapped into a chair. Cuffs bound my wrists and ankles. I was still in my clothes that I had been abducted in. The room I was in was dimly lit by one fluorescent light which gave off an electrical humming noise. On the far side of the room, there was a one way mirror set within a cinderblock wall. I must have been in some form of interrogation room. On the wall adjacent to the window, was a door. It was open and the two men which I heard talking were standing in the doorway, one on the outside of the room and one on the inside.

I could see into a white, well lit hallway on the other side of them, but that was all of the context I had to know where I was. I had no clue how long I had been out or what had happened after I was knocked out.

The man in the hallway wore the same tactical gear as my attacker, but his helmet had retracted, forming a metal ring around his neck. I could see a staff like the one which had been used to defeat me, contracted and hanging on his side. My vision was blurred. I couldn't see his face very well, and I had no way of knowing if this was the man who attacked me or if he was perhaps just another person like him.

The man standing inside the room was wearing a suit. It was dark gray and his back was turned to me. The man in the hallway pointed toward me and tilted his head down, causing the helmet to form. The man in the suit turned around.

"Welcome," He said, opening his arms, "Are you comfortable?"

I said nothing

"I'll dispense with the pleasantries then," he clasped his hands "Where did you get the crystal?"

I knew I didn't have any information for him, but I didn't want him to know that.

"What did you do with my family?" I asked, trying to be as detestable as possible.

"Oh you mean your friends. If I recall, your only *family* is your mother... whom you hate. Correct?"

What? How did he know that? I was taken aback by this. I said nothing in response. I only glared back at him.

"Oh, we have been watching you for a long time." The man was very animated in his talking, making flailing hand movements, pointing, and pacing back and forth "I know everything about you. I simply thought you were no threat, until yesterday, when we picked up a large energy reading, matching that of a very valuable asset that was stolen from me a few months ago. Now, you are going to tell me everything you know, or your friend will suffer."

He gestured to the one way mirror which went clear and I could see Blake on the other side. He was strapped to a chair just like mine and facing the glass.

"Blake!" I yelled uncontrollably. I didn't know what had happened to the Vales. I was glad to know he was okay, but I didn't want or expect to see him here. Blake didn't acknowledge me. He stared blankly at the glass, his face ridden with worry and confusion.

"Oh, he can't hear you, or see you, but you will be able to see and hear every ounce of his agony as he is slowly killed by that chair. Unless, you tell me everything you know about this." He gestured to the man with the tactical gear and he brought over the case that contained the crystal.

I was terrified. I didn't know anything about the crystal, nothing that was worth anything to these people. I was helpless to save Blake. My demeanor changed. I was no longer worried about being tough, I pleaded, "I don't know anything. I promise. My father gave it to Blake's parents in February just before he died. We found it yesterday and it almost killed us. That's all I know. I promise!"

"How unfortunate" The man shook his head, "Not unfortunate that I don't believe you, but that I do. If you have nothing to offer me then you and this hostage are of no use to me." The man turned to the soldier, "Kill *Blake* first, then this one."

"No! No!" I screamed, "Please!"

I heard a wail of anguish. Red energy leapt across Blakes body. They were still going to torture him, eventhough neither of us had anything to tell them, and they knew it.

"No!" I began to pull at the binders holding me to the chair. I could see blue energy as it began to surround my body. Just as I thought I was out of time and the chair was about to kill me, the cuffs broke from off my wrists and ankles, and I leapt from the chair. I was caught off guard by this and almost fell, but I regained my balance and stood in the middle of the room, free.

I still didn't understand what was happening. Did they let me go? Did the chair malfunction? I noticed the soldier draw his gun and point it at me. "Stay back!" He said through his voice changing helmet.

"How did we not know he was gifted?" the man in the suit asked frantically as he was backing out the door.

Gifted? What are they talking about? As I was trying to figure out what was going on and how to save Blake, I noticed a blue light being reflected off of the glass. I looked at the chair I had leapt from, but it wasn't the source. Pieces of the metal binders sat broken on the floor, reflecting the blue light as well. Then, I realized the light was coming from me.

I held my arms up and looked down in disbelief. Blue energy radiated down my arms in graceful patterns- like streams flowing from the scar on my chest all the way to my fingertips where it would circle back toward my body.

My disbelief was put on hold by the growing urgency of Blake's screams. I didn't know what I was now capable of, but since I was glowing and I was able to break the metal binders, I thought I could probably break the wall that separated us. I turned, clenched my fist, and punched the wall. When I did, blue energy spread out from the impact. The blocks that made up the wall left their resting places and the glass shattered.

The soldier fired his gun at me, but somehow, I sensed the moment he was about to pull the trigger and the trajectory that the blast would take. I moved out of the way just as a red bolt of energy flew by my head. I spun around to face the men. When I did, a blue bolt of energy lept from the ends of my fingers and struck the armored man in the chest. This knocked him off his feet and sent him flying out into the hallway.

The blast that came from my hand knocked me backwards. I stumbled over the rubble of the wall and fell into the room where Blake was. I looked up from the floor and saw that he was convulsing in the chair as the red energy arced from the arms of the chair and ran across his body.

I scrambled to my feet and grabbed the shackles holding his wrists to the chair. Some of the energy lept from the binders to me. It was an excruciating cessation, but my adrenaline allowed me to continue. I ripped them open, breaking the latch that held them shut. This must have broken the circuit because the chair turned off and the energy ceased. Blake's body relaxed. He slumped down in the chair. I could see him breathing shallowly.

I knelt down and ripped the shackles off of his ankles, then asked, "Can you walk?"

He didn't acknowledge me. I put my hands on his shoulders and shook him, "Blake!" I said, trying to rouse him. Blake opened his eyes and realized who it was standing over him, "Dyan? You're alright… I didn't know what they did to you." His breathing was labored and his voice was weak.

41

"Yes, I'm fine, but we have to move," I said with urgency. I was sure that they had more than just one soldier and I didn't know how many I could take.

"Yea, yea. I think so." I helped Blake out of the chair. He was a bit wobbly at first, but he gained his balance. He seemed to be mostly ok. It seemed his body was just in shock from whatever the chair had done to him. I hoped the effects would wear off soon. "They, they didn't even... ask me any questions," he said between deep breaths.

"That's because they were asking me all the questions."

"I guess they thought you looked smarter... I owe you one" I was glad to hear his banter. I figured if he could still do that, he was going to be fine.

Once I was sure he could walk, I went to the door of the room. The door to my room was open, but I didn't want to wait for Blake to hobble over the rubble of the wall. I punched the door the same as I had the wall. The blue light radiated from the impact and it flew off of the hinges, into the hallway.

"Woa!" Blake stopped, "How did you do that?"

Honestly, I hadn't taken much time to think about how I was doing it. I only had one, somewhat logical, answer, "I think the crystal must have done it to me."

"Is that why they brought us here?"

"No, They were just as surprised as I was."

An alarm began to sound. We ran down the hallway. Neither of us knew where we were, but we were hoping to find a way out.

As we rounded a corner, we met four soldiers in their uniforms. Before they had a chance to react, I stretched out my arm and blasted one of them as I had earlier. I didn't know what all I could do, what powers I had, so I didn't try anything new. I just envisioned what had already happened and was able to make it happen again. Two of the soldiers drew their guns and the other activated his staff but this time it projected a flat shield that went from the top of the staff to the bottom and was about as wide as it was tall. It was just big enough for the three to get behind.

They began to fire, and Blake and I retreated back around the corner. Their blasts missed and blew holes in the concrete wall behind us. I could hear one say through their helmet, "We have engaged the enemy, send reinforcements to hallway 23A"

I didn't yet understand how to use the powers fully, but they had come through before. There was no other way out but for them to work again. I built up the courage and lept around the corner. I blasted the shield with a bolt of energy. It didn't do anything to the people behind it, but it was enough to overload it. The shield turned off and I charged at the soldiers, sensing the trajectory of their shots and dodging them.

When I got near, I punched one in the stomach and he slammed into the wall. The one with the staff jabbed it at me but I grabbed it in the middle and snatched it from his grip, quickly redirecting it to jab the soldier still holding a gun. I landed the blow right on his sternum. A blue wave of energy spread across his body as he was thrust, with great force, into the wall.

I turned back to the last remaining soldier just as he drew his gun. He would have gotten the drop on me, but before he could pull the trigger, a red blast came from over my shoulder and struck the gun, knocking it from his hand. I took my chance. With my right hand I swung the staff and hit him across the side of his helmet, throwing him off balance. As I followed through, I lifted my left hand. I visualized the energy leaping from my hand in his direction, I could feel it flowing from my chest, down my arm and finally, to the tips of my fingers, where it leapt and struck the soldier in the abdomen. He was tall and I was at a lower angle so the blast caused him to hit the ceiling with his back, then fall face down onto the floor.

I turned around to see that Blake had picked up on the other soldier's guns and was the one who shot him. "I may not have powers, but my dad taught me how to shoot a gun."

"I'm glad!" I exclaimed, "Looks like we're even now."

Our victory was short lived. I heard the sound of people running, coming from behind us, and, judging from his look of worry, Blake heard it too. "Let's get moving!"

We ran down hallway after hallway. The place was a maze, but we managed to stay ahead of our pursuers. I didn't say anything, but I didn't see us finding our way out on our own. We took a turn and ran through a pair of double doors, above which read "Strategic Sciences Division". When we got to the other side, I used the staff that I stole to jam the doors shut.

This looked like every other hallway we had been down, but something felt different. As we ran past one door, I stopped. "What are you doing?" asked Blake as he stopped just ahead of me.

Something felt strange, like something calling me, something familiar. "There's something about this room."

"Something good or something bad?"

"I can't tell"

"Well you better tell quickly because they're gonna be coming through that door any minute."

Blake was right. We didn't have time for this, but I had to see what it was. The door looked as though it was made from the same metal as what was on the case that contained the crystal. It didn't have a door handle but beside the door was a key pad with a large screen. Something told me to put my hand on the screen. I listened. When I did, the whole door radiated with blue energy. I stepped back and the door opened on its own.

"That has to mean something." I said, hopeful.

"It means we're wasting time" Blake was getting agitated and nervous. I knew if this turned out to be nothing then I was endangering our lives, but we were getting nowhere by just running. And I couldn't shake the feeling I was getting from this place. It was like a memory, but not my own.

I walked into the room and Blake reluctantly followed. As soon as he was in, the door closed behind him. "See, we're safe in here" I said to Blake, only half paying him attention. I was inspecting the room.

"We must have different definitions of safe."

The room appeared to be a deserted lab. There was a lab table in the middle of the room and a chalkboard with formulas written on it in the back. There was a counter that lined one wall which was covered with miscellaneous parts, glasses, and chemicals.

"Welcome!" a voice rang out

Blake and I were both startled. Blue energy radiated down my arms and around my hands as I drew up my fists. Blake held up his stolen gun, ready to fire. We both looked around the room for the source.

"Sorry. I seem to have startled you. Allow me to introduce myself." A blue projection shown down from the ceiling, creating a hologram above the lab table. The hologram was not elaborate, but rather just a ball made from about ten vertical lines.

"I am ALI, An artificial intelligence that is completely Autonomous, hence Artificial Living Intelligence or ALI. You are Dylan I presume." The lines of the ball moved up and down as it spoke.

"How do you know me?" I asked coldly.

"Well you have caused quite the stir around here for one. I would say most people in this building know who you are."

"So you work for them?"

"Oh no, of course not. I am just in their system, monitoring them. I work for no one but you."

I was becoming very confused, and a little creeped out. I did not trust whatever this thing was. I wanted answers, "You work for me? Why?"

"Because that is what your father instructed me to do."

"And how do you know my father?" This was only getting stranger.

"He created me. I was his lab assistant for years. After his first lab partner, Alfred Henry, was killed in an accident with the very crystal you have come into possession of. You've probably heard of him"

"A time or two. " Blake chipped in, becoming more intrigued, just as I was.

"You're just giving us pieces. I want the whole story, everything you know about my father and the crystal.

"Well, your father was a brilliant scientist. Right out of high school he got a job working with the prestigious scientist Alfred Henry as a lab assistant. Of course, He was not as well known at the time. Their objective was to study a strange red crystal, much like the one you have now.

Together, they discovered that it was entangled, on the quantum level, to a star in a distant galaxy. They were able to study the star through the crystal and found that the composition of the star was of substances never before seen or even thought of. In their studies, they unlocked the secret of Electron entanglement. This led to discoveries that Alfred Henry is famous for.

Then, your father stumbled across another crystal - the one you have now. It was sealed in a wooden box in a secret room of Alfreds lab. When he opened the box, a powerful blast, like the one that gave you your powers erupted from the crystal. Due to a mutation in his genetic code, your father absorbed the blow and became entangled with the crystal, giving him the ability to tap into the power of the star, just as you can. Alfred never knew that this happened.

Not long after this, he and Alfred were experimenting with the red crystal when it did the same thing. There was an explosion and Alfred was said to have died, but we later found out that he didn't. It seemed he had the same mutation.

Then, The Organization found out about the red crystal. They confronted your father and claimed to be the US Military. They asked

46

him to continue his research on their base, conveniently located close enough for him to commute from the house that he already had. They gave him the lab of his dreams in exchange for him continuing his research on the crystal. He was also removed from anything that had him credited with Alfred's discoveries. He was to be unknown to the world. He wasn't allowed to have a lab partner, so he created me, an AI so advanced that it gained autonomy as though it were a living being. He named it ALI.

Then, one day, he found a loophole, something very small, a mistake on the behalf of the Organization that he thought was the US government. He sent me into their files to investigate, and what I found was disturbing.

I found records with detailed reports about five crystals (Red, Blue, Yellow, Green, and Orange) of similar composition each showing up throughout history. Countless wars including the Holy Crusades and the World Wars have been fought in order to possess them and yet they still remain a secret to most.

Over the past 200 years the organization has rooted its way into governments attempting to cripple them. In recent years, under the new leadership of one who can wield the red crystal, they have found a new direction. Your father realized that their intent was to take over the world in order to enslave the population. Their goal in mind was to create a worldwide workforce set on colonizing the galaxy.

Your father and I found that with all five crystals, they would activate 5 armies complete with airships, advanced robot soldiers, and their highly trained operatives. There would be one army for each quarter of the globe, then one to protect the capital of their empire. One crystal could more than power the whole thing, but they needed all 5 crystals so that if one was ever stolen or somehow destroyed there would still be 4 armies active. They had all but one. Your father immediately stopped making weapons and researching the crystal and spent all of his time trying to figure out how to stop them.

He created a resistance using files that detailed the whereabouts of enemies of the Organization. There were cells all around the globe. They made weapons and were almost ready to launch an operation to steal all of the crystals, but then the group fell apart.

47

Now we reach February of this year. The Organization was about to acquire the fifth crystal. They penetrated Russia's most heavily armored vault and captured the Yellow crystal. They were on their way back over the Atlantic ocean when your father learned of this. He used a fighter jet to board their airship from which they conducted the operation. He used his powers to fight them off, steal the crystal and destroy the ship. He used a new device he had invented to jam all of their transmissions. The ship was unable to call for help and crashed into the Atlantic. They didn't know who did it then, but once they pulled security footage from the wreckage, they would.

He came back to the states and sealed up his lab with Unitum, an impenetrable alloy that he discovered, so that only one who was entangled with the crystal could open the lab without destroying it. He gave the crystal which he was entangled with to the Vales and the other he took with him. He had been preparing an impenetrable fortress somewhere in the US. His goal was to take you and the Vales to this fortress if the Organization succeeded in taking over the world.

But his plan changed. He started to think of a way he might be able to destroy the crystals. Realizing he could postpone their takeover or even stop it, he took the crystal he stole up to the fortress and from there he has fended off the Organization ever since. He is trying to come up with a device that can un-entangle the crystals with the star. If he can succeed, the crystals can be stripped of their power.

He faked his death in order to keep the Organization from going after you. If you knew nothing and you thought that he was dead, then you would mean nothing to them until you found the crystal, at which point he would connect with it, and use it to give you powers, sending you here for us to have this conversation"

I stood in stunned silence. I couldn't even say it was the craziest thing that had happened in the past 24 hours. As a matter of fact, this was the first thing that made any sense. I wasn't even mad at my father for not telling me. I was just glad to know what was happening and even more so to know he was possibly alive! All of the dots were beginning to be connected. Except for one, "Why was I drawn to this room?"

"Since you and your father are both entangled with the crystal, you were detecting his memories. You...wait" He stopped. The blue hologram began to ripple then paused and said, "They've found us. Since you've opened the door, the seal is broken. They will be able to break in. It's time to go. I will explain more later. Under the lab table there is a button, press it"

I followed his instructions without hesitation. I slid my hand under the table until I found a raised spot on which was the button. When I pressed it, a ring of white light spread from it and began to make its way across the room. In its wake formed two cabinets and a weapons rack along the far wall and a stack of books and a helmet on the table.

"Woa, how did that happen?" Blake asked.

"It's teleportation from a secret room far from here," ALI answered swiftly. "Now, go to the cabinets, each of you. When you open the door, Take the puck off of the inside of the right door and slam it onto your chest. Quickly!" Commanded ALI.

We ran over to the cabinets. I didn't understand what he was talking about exactly until I opened the door. There were plates of armor made from the Unitum metal and a jetpack hanging neatly on the back wall of the cabinet. A disk about the exact dimensions of a hockey puck was stuck to the inside of the right door, just as ALI had said. I followed his instructions and when it hit my chest, A white light and black mist spread across my body. Left behind was a tight fitting black material with some small blue lights on my arms, chest and thighs. On my feet were tall, black tactical boots.

Once the light had ceased, the armor flew from the cabinet. Vambraces slid over my hands and onto my forearms. They were outfitted with some sort of technology, but I wasn't sure what they did. Next the Tassets came off and affixed to the blue lights on my thighs. Last was the Chestpiece. Once it was in place, the black material morphed to cover them. The armor was incredibly thin and fit perfectly.

I stepped back from the cabinet. I looked next to me and saw that Blake was wearing the same suit. I moved around a bit, testing it out.

It didn't restrict my movement at all. I looked back at ALI and the helmet on the table. Acknowledging me he said, "The helmet is yours, A gift from your father. Put it on."

I did as he said. When my back was turned, the jetpack flew off the rack and attached to my back. I guess that was its command for it to attach. It pushed me forward slightly, but not enough for me to lose my balance.

The helmet was very similar to the ones I had already seen on the other soldiers, but it's visor was wider than the others, I imagined for better visibility. It also had a more elegant look, less edgy, more rounded and smooth.

When I put the helmet on, it connected to the collar of my suit and a puff of air came from it as it sealed. A heads up display was projected on the visor. In the top left, I could see all of my vital signs and a diagram of the crystal's energy flowing through my body. There was a large concentration over my heart, then it seemed to spread pretty evenly across my vascular system, with concentrations in my hands. In the bottom right corner, I could see the same ball that was projected on top of the table.

ALI's voice played in the helmet, "Since I'm sure you don't know how to fly, I am going to have to put this in training mode. I will have the controls unless you take them away from me so don't press anything on either of your vanguards."

"Are those the wrist things?" Blake asked.

"Precisely" said ALI, "This channel will be for all of us to communicate. Blake, tilt your head down to put on your helmet."

I turned to look at him. He tilted his head and gave me a nervous thumbs up. There was pounding at the door and it began to slide open. Then, a port hole opened in the ceiling. It was quite small. It didn't look like we would fit.

"We gotta go through that?" I looked at the lab table to where ALI was, but the projection was gone.

50

"Yes sir. It is better than staying in here and I assure you, we will fit" I could see the blue ball on my heads up display moving as ALI talked.

"Whatever you say"

Both of our jetpacks ignited just as the soldiers broke open the door. We flew up, me going through the port first and then Blake. We made it out just as the first red shots were fired behind us.

Chapter 5

We flew out of the building into the dark night sky. Sirens blared as we climbed higher and higher. In the top left corner of my helmet's display the altitude was projected. We were nearing 1,000 feet off the ground.

"ALI, I think that's high enough," Blake said nervously.

"No! We must get higher than the shield! If the shield is raised before we get above it, we will be trapped in here." There was almost a hint of emotion, urgency, in ALI's voice. Maybe it had been there the whole time and I was just now noticing it. Still, it was surprising for something inanimate.

As he spoke, a purple pillar of light rose from the ground in the distance on the other side of a tree line, then another off from it, then another. The trees were blocking whatever they were coming from. As I watched these in the distance, one shot up right in front of us. It caught me off guard. My arms flailed as the jet pack jerked me to the left. Blake and I were split up as the pillar passed between us.

I looked up. The pillar was purple but composed of red bundles of energy shooting up to the top. When the pillar reached its final altitude it paused for a moment and then began to spread out in a wide domed pattern, moving toward the ground just as the others were. The dome was red and would have patches with a darker tone moving fluidly across the surface. Red energy arced from near the top of the pillar to the domed surface they were creating. The pillars on the other side of the trees were beginning to do the same thing. At a distance, they seemed to be moving slowly, but with this one so close, it became evident that they were moving quite fast and covering a very large area.

We came back to flying side by side. "New plan" ALI said, "We are going to have to get low. Lean down the lean up when I tell you. Our timing must be precise."

ALI lined Blake and I up, side by side. I did not like the vagueness of this plan. "Why are..."

"Lean down now!" ALI interrupted.

52

A force from the jet pack tipped us over. Still, we each did as he instructed and began to swoop toward the ground. My stomach rose to my throat. I tried to scream, but was unable to push air from my lungs. The passing air roared in my ears and we cut through the night sky.

I managed to turn my head to the side and saw that the shield was quickly moving toward the ground out in front of us. I saw no way that we could beat it. My heart was pounding.

"Lean up in 3"

The shield was now right in front of us and we were racing along the surface.

"2"

We were even with the edge-only about five feet from it. Its edge was a fiery red line that spit ambers from it as it tore through the darkness.

"1, Pull up!"

I leaned up just as a powerful blast came from my jetpack. It thrust me forward enough to dip under the edge. As soon as I was clear, I crashed into the tree canopy. I hadn't realized how close to the ground we were. My jetpack sputtered and attempted to slow me down. My feet were facing the ground and my arms were flailing trying to catch a tree branch. I couldn't catch one but between my attempts to slow down and my jetpack, I was able to land somewhat safely. My feet hit the ground with a thud and my momentum thrust me forward. I rolled to a stop.

I stood up. Only one thing was on my mind, "Blake!" I yelled, "Blake!"

ALI spoke in my ear, "There is no need to yell, we all have one coms channel. He is to your right."

I turned and saw Blake about twenty feet away, gaining his balance after falling through the trees. "I'm good," he said, giving me a thumbs up.

I sighed with relief. I looked behind me to see the soft red glow of the shield. It was almost invisible next to the black backdrop of the night sky. I waited a moment to catch my breath and to let my brain process. Then, I walked over to meet Blake and discuss what to do next. The more I thought, the more I realized I was clueless. I didn't even know where I was. I didn't understand what was going on. I didn't even know what day it was.

"ALI, where are we?" I inquired, hoping to find answers.

"We are on a remote part of what is known to the public as Arnald Airforce Base. Where your father used to work. Were you not paying attention back in the lab?"

"I was, it just didn't register. I have been through a lot today... or... this week, month, whatever it is. What day is it even?"

"It is 10:24 pm Sunday, August 24, 2042"

"I was out that long? I was taken Saturday night."

"Technically early this morning." ALI corrected, "They wanted to make sure the entire family was captured before they woke you up. It took a lot of work to locate Blake's sister."

The Vales! I hadn't even had a second to consider the rest of the family! I had just been focused on getting out of that place. They had them all!

"We have to go back!" Blake insisted, "They're still in there!"

I didn't have time to respond. ALI broke in, "They are not here. And even if they were, we could not save them. They were transported to a more secure facility in Montana. They never keep one group of prisoners together."

"Well then we have to go there." I said.

"No. You are not understanding. They were caught off guard by your powers. If they had time to prepare, you would not last long. On top of that, the Montana base is the location of another crystal. It is much more heavily fortified. You wouldn't make it past the front gate. That's not important right now. They will be sending more after us. Right now, we must focus on hiding."

"So you want us to abandon our family? You're just some program," I insulted, "You don't even understand."

"I understand your attachment to them. I also understand that you need my help to work the equipment you have. I am not suggesting you abandon them. I am suggesting that you work on your abilities, that you learn more about this weaponry and yourself. Then, you will be powerful enough to run a rescue mission."

This was reasonable. Having the rest of the Vales was leverage for the organization… or bait. Either way, they likely would not harm them.

There was one problem. Blake saw it first and said "So you want us to train? With what? You can teach us the technology and you can teach him about his powers, but without a person to spar against, how will we know if we are good enough?"

"Dylan's father always intended for him to find me and this technology, and his powers. He also suspected that he might not be here to teach him. So he created a program. The material that what you are wearing is made out of can morph into any form, just as you saw it do when you put it on. It can make a humanoid opponent for you to spar with of increasing difficulty."

This plan was sounding better by the second. I saw our time running out and spoke up, "Sounds like a good deal to me. I want to talk more about it, but we need to get out of here no matter what we do. It won't take them long to see that we aren't inside that shield. I know a place we can lay low. Unless you have a better place ALI?"

"Well that depends on your place. We can talk and fly."

Our helmets rose from our collars and formed over our heads. Our jetpacks ignited and we lifted off the ground and through the trees. "Now what is this place, Dylan?" asked ALI

"Yes, I would like to know too." Blake asked, confused.

"Across the lake from my old house, there are woods. There's an old homestead there. The whole thing's fallen in but there is an old storm cellar there. I used to swim across the lake and play there when I was younger."

"What? You never told me anything about that!" Blake said, slightly offended.

"I found it while we were mad at eachother that time. After we made up, I decided to keep it a secret in case we were ever upset at each other again. Then, I forgot about it... until now"

"What, when were we mad at each... OH! You mean when we were fourteen, you and Anna got together, and you stopped spending time with me? That time that we were mad at eachother?"

"First of all, I did still spend time with you, just not all of my time. You got Jealous and stopped hanging out with me."

"Oh really? Well..."

ALI stopped us, "BOYS! Let's not get stuck in the past."

We weren't really fighting. I wasn't sure if ALI had picked up on that though. I went on as though he thought we were fighting, just to make him feel better, "Well, we did make up"

"And I got my own girl now," Blake boasted, "So I guess it did work out."

We flew for only about twenty minutes until I could see the lake. The moon reflected off of the still surface of the water. I could see the entire lake. Every curve and inlet. The water poured over the spillway of the concrete dam. Its cascading water could be seen shimmering as it went over the edge and down the creek on the other side.

I looked at the row of houses where the Vale's house was. It sat as though nothing had happened. There was no evidence of police involvement that I could see. The whole neighborhood sat quiet, oblivious to what had just happened.

"Where is our destination?" ALI asked.

"See my old house?" I pointed, "Straight across, about a mile into the woods."

"Your Dad let you go a mile into the woods?" Blake inquired, "That does not sound like him."

"My Dad didn't know everything I did." I smirked.

"I can't read anything on my scanners. Are you sure?" ALI asked.

"There's not much to read. It's a concrete box in the ground with a pile of wood beside it."

"Ah, it's a concrete cellar. Good. They won't think to scan for that." He paused, "Found it."

We slowed down over the woods and lowered down gently onto the forest floor. The display on my helmet swapped from allowing me to see natural light, to a night vision. It wasn't like the green kind I had seen before. It was blue, and created a very crisp image.

To my left I could see the fallen in house. All that remained recognizable was the deck that was in front of the rest of the house and the brick chimney that stuck up from the middle of the rubble.

"Where is the cellar?" Blake asked.

"It's over here. I covered it up when I found it." I walked over to where I remembered it to be. I found the pile of brush that I had stacked on top of it and pushed it to the side. This revealed a mostly solid wooden door with a concrete frame.

"See, I told you. Right where I left it"

I lifted up the door to reveal a set of stairs that led down into the cellar. Blake and I walked inside. It wasn't very large, only about eight feet by eight feet, about the size of a bathroom.

"It is a shelter," ALI said.

"It's not going to be fun to sleep on that concrete." Blake complained

"I never said it was great. I just said I knew a place."

"I can help with the comfort." As ALI spoke, a black fog began to come from the puck that I had placed on my chest earlier. It flowed down and spread out on the ground, then condensed, forming two pads, side by side. The same fog came from Blake's puck. It ropse up and began to spin. After a moment it began to glow, illuminating the room with a soft white light. "Better?"

"Yea"
"Good enough"
"When you are ready to take your armor off, just reach for the puck and pull it off."

Blake and I reached it at the same time. The puck was buried under the black material but it moved away as I reached for it. I took hold and pulled it off of my chest. As I did, all of the material converted back to a fog and entered into the puck. The metal components of the armor released, the helmet retracted, and the vanguards loosened and slid off my arms. The armor sat suspended in the air and I was left standing in the same clothes that I had on when I put on the puck.

"Now put the puck on the wall next to your bed." ALI instructed.

I put mine on the right side of the cellar and Blake put his on the left. It attached to the wall. Then, the armor moved to the wall, attaching itself where it would be in relation to my body.

It was amazing technology, but I don't think either of us had enough energy to be amazed. We said goodnight and a short prayer. I thanked God for keeping me and Blake safe, mostly, and then gave into sleep, promising to finish praying in the morning.

Chapter 6

Rays of light peaked through the holes of the wooden door to the cellar. I sat up. My eyes were heavy from my deep, dreamless sleep. I looked over to see that Blake was still asleep. We had made it through the night. I hoped this meant we were safe for now.

I stood up and took my puck from off the wall. ALI had talked of training and I wanted to learn all that I could, not just to help the Vales, but to be able to protect us after we saved them.

I eased open the door of the cellar, careful not to wake Blake. The sunlight trickled down through the thick canopy of hardwoods. The sun was already high, I guessed it was about 10:00 or so. I pressed the puck to my chest and the black suit covered me once again. The armor was not on me this time so it was more fitted and more maneuverable-much more comfortable.

I nodded and the helmet constructed itself around my head. "Good morning, sir." ALI's voice said

" 'Morning ALI. I'm ready to start that training."

"Well, you're getting right to business, aren't you?"

"I just don't want to be helpless when the Organization shows up again."

"Well, that I can understand. Now I guess the first thing we should address is your power, what *you* can do. Your power, as you know, comes from the star with which the crystal is entangled. This means that the entire power of the star resides within the crystal. You are entangled with the crystal, which means that the power flows from the star, to the crystal, to you. Since the crystal is a conduit for this power, the closer you are to the crystal, the more powerful you will be."

"But we don't have my crystal."

"Well, that is true, but it doesn't mean that you can't get it back."

"And how am I supposed to do that? The Organization has it. Even if I could steal it, I don't even know where they are keeping it."

"You have a special connection to the crystal. You can summon it no matter where it is. But they will also be able to track it. Therefore, that is how we will conclude your training. For now, you can draw its power at a distance."

ALI paused. I looked to the corner of my display. His bubble was doing something I had never seen it do. It had turned into a cloud like emblem and was moving in a circle.

His voice returned, "I am looking at the security footage from the base. It seems you have figured out how to make a crud plasma blast already, that's really just instinct. You have found your super strength, again, instinct. Now this is impressive, I have a recording here that shows you using a shock-blast a couple times. That is slightly more advanced. Your instincts seem to serve you well. But discipline will serve you better."

A black fog began to come from the puck on my chest. Then I noticed more mist coming from behind me. I turned to see the same mist coming from the cellar, I assumed it was my bed. The mist joined to form a cloud in front of me, just like the one ALI's emblem had changed to.

"This is the training program your father created. It will create opponents for you to fight against. No field mission will ever be fair, so neither will these fights. They will increase in difficulty until you complete the course."

I was confident that I could beat this. I had made short work of the operatives at the base. How could this be any different?

This mist formed into a human shape. It was completely black, shadow-like, and was not completely stable. I could see the mist flowing up and down the artificial body. I didn't know exactly what it could do, but it's appearance was formidable.

I reached down to the utility belt where I hoped to grab the staff, but there wasn't even a belt there. Had it not appeared when I put on the suit this morning? "Hey, where are my weapons?"

"Lesson one, you are a weapon," my helmet retracted on its own, "While your suit is an extension of your powers, there will not always be technology to help you. Feel the power of the crystal within you. Call it to your aid. You control this power, it is not a reflex, but a muscle. Breath, envision what you want to do, then do it."

ALI was right, I needed to learn to trust my powers. If they really were as strong as ALI was making them out to be, maybe I wouldn't even need weapons.

I closed my eyes and clenched my fists. I thought of my powers, of the night before when I had used them. I waited. Nothing. "ALI, this isn't working. Why isn't it working?"

"You must breathe, relax. Think of your purpose. Your why. Why do you need your powers to work? You are connected to them now through your sub conscience. You must connect with them there to bring them to your conscious self."

I looked at ALI's emblem, then at the shadow man in front of me. My "Why"? My why is to save the Vales, to protect Blake, to break The Organization.

"Relax." ALI coached, "Your vitals show that you are using anger. You can reach them through anger, yes, but they will be unstable. Reach your power through love, compassion, determination"

I opened my eyes and threw up my arms in frustration. Why was it this hard? I had just used them! I didn't want to think about love. All I wanted to think about was war. War against the Organization that had succeeded in ruining my life.

I stopped myself. I took a step back. I needed these powers to work. I needed to save the Vales. But I didn't need to lose myself. I took a deep breath. I held my arms down at my side and opened my hands. I began to think of the time I had spent at the Vales house. I thought of church. I thought of them giving me my room. I thought of the fun we had and the love I had for them. Then, I thought of them sitting in a cell, captured, scared. That was my "why", to stop that, to return to the good times.

I gritted my teeth, relaxed, then reached out. I thought of the blue energy surrounding my arms, flowing from the scar on my chest.

Suddenly, I felt the energy come alive within me. I felt it flowing through me and cover my arms just as I had commanded it. I opened my eyes, feeling good about myself for finding my power, but also having a new determination and understanding for what I was doing and how I would do it.

I looked at the opponent in front of me. Rather than standing there blankly, he was now in a fighting stance with his fists raised and what appeared to be a replica of my powers surrounding his arms and fists.

I raised my fists as well and assumed a fighting stance. "Very good" said ALI, "Begin!"

The figure stretched out his arm and sent a blast of the black mist hurtling toward me. It caught me off guard. I dove to the ground as it flew over my head. It hit the remains of the porch behind me, sending boards flying into the air.

"What was that? That would hurt!" I yelled at ALI, "I'm not trying to get killed in training!"

"Mistakes in battles have consequences. So will they in these simulations. If you mess up, the consequences will be painful, but you will be ok."

I stood up and called the energy to appear back on my arms. I thrust my arm forward and sent a blast of energy back at the figure. He dodged with a simple swerve and began to charge at me, sending a blast of black mist as he ran. I returned his hostility by running at him. I dodged each of his blasts.

When we met, I called my power to concentrate at my fists as we threw punches at each other. I was able to block some. He felt real, tangible, very human like. It wasn't long before he landed a punch right in my chest. This was accompanied by a hard blast which sent me flying backward.

I hit the ground on my back, flipped over, and slid to a stop. It hurt, but not as much as I was expecting. I looked back at the figure. He was running toward me once again, but stopped mid-stride, stuck in the air.

"It seems you are in need of assistance. You have more than one way to use the power of the crystal."

"And what is that?" I asked.

"Well, many ways I am sure have not even been discovered yet, but one that I will teach you now is the shield."

"You mean like that thing that almost killed us last night"

"Not quite, more like the one which that soldier you fought had."

"How do I do it?"

"Well, that only you can truly figure out, as I have never had these powers, but I can describe to you what it was like when your father would use it. Now, concentrate just as you did before. The shield is a flat, condensed energy field. It is able to absorb plasma with the same polarity, and deflect plasma with opposite polarity. It should start at your fingertips. From there you can control the size."

I listened to this but then began to tone ALI out. I could see exactly what I needed to do. I held out my hand. I envisioned the energy flowing around it condensing at my fingertips, turning from a wild flame, to a solid state. I allowed the energy to flow down my arm, to my fingertips, and then to the air around them.

I watched as the energy began to create a surface. It was blue with darker ripples of purple that would flow through it. I stretched out my arm but kept my hand flat in front of me. I grew the shield until it was a wall in front of me.

"Very good" ALI congratulated, "In time you will learn to further controle its shape, but this is good for now. There is one more thing I would like to teach you before we move forward. You also can move objects through telekinesis. This is a simple trick to learn once you know how to make a shield. It is the same concept, only, invision the energy surrounding the object and then lifting it off the ground"

I set my sights on a fallen tree sitting just a few feet away. I followed the same process as before. I held out my hands toward the log. I watched as the energy fill the air around the old tree and condensed in streams along the surface. The streams were blue with darker tinges flowing through them, just as the shield.

I lifted my hands as though I was scooping the tree up. There was resistance. I sent more energy through the air, to the tree and lifted harder.

"The power is like a muscle, the more you work it, the more you can lift."

I focused and lifted once more. It began to shake and then lifted off the ground. I held it until it was about five feet off the ground, then I was forced to let go. I was out of strength.

"Very good," said ALI, "In time, lifting trees will be simple. You must work with it. Resume."

" Now?" I choked. I was out of breath from the struggle of lifting the tree.

I received no answer. The figure resumed its course, charging at me. He shot a bolt of his black mist at me, but I raised the shield to intercept it. Then, I quickly countered with my own blast. He dodged it, but I used my new ability to grab a board from the rubble of the old house and flung it at his feet.

He jumped over it and continued his charge. I brought back the shield to block another of his blasts just as he reached me. The shield gave me just enough time to bring both hands in front of me and release a blast much bigger than I ever had before. This blast didn't look like lightning as the previous ones had, rather, it was a solid stream of plasma that was uniform and bright.

When it hit the figure, he dissolved and the black mist disappeared.

I smiled, still out of breath, and sat down on the ground. The mist came back and formed ALI's original emblem (the ball made of columns). "Congratulations" ALI said from the ball, "You delivered a fatal blow and finished your first task."

"Fatal blow?" I was still catching my breath, "I'll fight these fake things, but I'm not killing anybody"

"Dylan, I understand the loss of human life is tragic, but we are at war now. It is an unfortunate consequence. Any life you take within the Organization saves thousands."

This did not sit right with me. I would not be killing anybody, "God chose to put them on this earth and God will choose when to take them off. That is not for me to decide. And we are not at war. I just want to take back what they stole from me."

"Dylan..."

"No, you work for me. That is how we will fight. If I am skilled enough, I can complete any mission without the need for me to take any lives."

"And what if you are able to get an army on your side?" ALI inquired, "Will you tell them not to take lives? They don't have your powers. Following a directive such as that could get them killed."

"I'm not planning on commanding any armies and even if I did, the choice to take a life or not would be one they would have to make, just as I have."

"Very well. If these are your orders, I will modify your training to deliver non-lethal, incapacitating blows. But this is not ideal."

"Thank you."

ALI's mist returned to the puck on my chest and I turned back toward the cellar to see Blake standing behind me. "You did pretty good," he said, folding his arms.

"Thanks. How much did you see?"

"I got out here after I heard the tree fall"

"Oh, the tree didn't fall, I dropped it."

"Well, I guess nothing surprises me anymore." He stopped and looked at me awkwardly for a moment.

"What is it?" I asked.

"What you said about not killing, are you sure?"

This caught me off guard. My initial response was to be angry. Why were we even discussing whether it was ok to kill or not? Then I took a step back. War was common all throughout history. Killing was common. I needed a better explanation than "killing is wrong". "What is my Why?" I thought.

I responded "The people who work for this organization are just like you and me. They were born into a side of the conflict. Many likely never even knew there was another side worth considering. They are real people. I guess the reason I know I couldn't kill, is because after I did, I wouldn't be able to live. I would die on the inside, the guilt, knowing that they may have had a family, knowing that God may have given them one more chance to change and I took that away."

Blake stood for a moment "I know you're right. It's basic Sunday school. I just don't if it's possible"

"What do you mean?"

"I don't know if it's possible to win, how can we defeat them if we can't fully fight them. If we go all out in our fighting, there's no way not to. Especially with you. I know that it's right to fight them and that it's wrong to kill them. So what's the solution?"

"We just have to learn how to control ourselves."

"I know. And I know it's the right thing. I just hope we don't lose lives, our lives, other people's lives because we are trying to save lives," Blake said, hanging his head.

He was right. I didn't know how we could do it either. The idea of winning a war without killing. It's antithesis.

"I know." I said, " And I don't know how we'll do it. But we just have to keep doing what is right. We just have to take one step at a time."

Chapter 7

The training went on for what felt like a month, but in reality was just a week. ALI didn't teach me any more new abilities, but he taught me to be proficient in the ones that I had. I became stronger, faster, and better at fighting.

ALI initially gave much protest to my "non-lethal" training style even after he altered the training course. But I believe it was Wednesday when he finally conceded that I was doing good enough for the strategy to be effective.

With ALI's help, we modified all of our weapons to be non-lethal. Our Plasma phasers were changed so that the blast, rather than being confined to one spot, would spread out like the blast from a staff, causing the nervous system to overload, and the recipient to black out (possibly for hours at a time). ALI also instructed me on a way to modify my staff. I gave it a function so that it could shoot forward like a missile, and when it made contact, it would send a shockwave from it. This shockwave would not only cause damage, but overload the nervous systems of those close by, before returning back to me.

Blake trained alongside me. We grew as a team. He was better at fighting, but because of my powers, I far outmatched him.

ALI also taught me how to hone in on my senses. He taught me that the crystal gave me a sort of echolocation. I could fight in the dark or even with my eyes closed, so long as I learned to use this ability. And I did.

I could even sense the moment before the shadow figures would make a move, the moment before they pulled the trigger, where they were going to swing their weapon. ALI told me that it was because I could sense the electricity in the nervous system, allowing me to sense people's intentions and emotions.

And then finally the day came. It was early Sunday morning, the week after we had been taken, the day we would complete our training, and the day I would summon the crystal.

***

"Duck!" I yelled to Blake.

Blake dove to the ground as I turned around and intercepted a blast of energy with my shield. Then, Blake quickly fired back. It was a direct hit to the chest and the shadowy opponent faded away.

Two more formed behind him. One carrying a staff and one carrying an atomizing sword - a blade that ALI said could cut through almost anything (of course these were just replicas created by the black mist). Supposedly, they were the traditional weapon of The Organization, but they had been using staves to fight me because they wanted me alive.

They charged toward us. "You got those?" I asked Blake, turning my attention to the five figures in front of us.

"Yea, easy money" He said with a smirk as he stood up.

I held the shield up in front of me, blocking the barrage of blasts coming from the firing squad. As I was thinking how I would advance on the five opponents, three more appeared behind them, each sporting an atomizing blade.

"When you are slow, you give the opponent more time to regroup and send more troops. If you are pinned, they will send melee troops to finish you off." ALI coached.

"Thanks ALI. We can see that." Blake said as his staff clashed with the blade of one of the troops he was fighting.

I lowered the shield and sent a burst of energy with both hands toward the attackers I was dealing with. I hit the fallen tree which they were taking cover behind. It splintered the trunk and sent three of the figures flying backward. I used my telekinesis to pull my staff from my waistband and extended it mid air. I grabbed the staff and leaped at the three melee attackers.

I clashed with the one leading the three first. My staff met his blade above our heads. I used my left hand to shoot a small blast of energy at his feet. This caused him to fall, but before I could incapacitate him, the other two reached me.

I backed up, deflecting each of their strikes, and the occasional blast from the remaining two gunners. I knew that the other three would be getting back in position soon, and then we would be outmatched.

I could sense Blake fighting behind me. He had his hands full but he was holding his ground. Another melee with a staff appeared at a distance in front of Blake, just as he landed a blow on the attacker with a blade.

"Blake, how's it coming?" I asked over my shoulder.

68

"It's comin'" he said out of breath, "Just keep those guys off of me.

"That is my job." I said as I lunged at the attacker on my left.

I landed the blow in his abdomen and he dissipated, but he was replaced by more gunners who appeared behind the tree. Now there were eight gunners and the three that had been knocked back were taking their new positions along the fallen tree.

I turned my attention to the attacker on my right and advanced. I was able to hold a shield large enough to protect both Blake and myself from the shots of the gunners. It took a lot of focus, but I was able to fight these troops without having to deflect shots in between.

The troop that I had knocked down was now up and coming for me once again. I advanced on them both, pushing them back toward the gunners. They tried swing after swing but they couldn't touch me. I had them right where I wanted them.

Just as I had them about half way between the tree and Blake, I raised my left arm and caught the swing of the opponent on my left with my vanguard. The fake blade hissed as it attempted to cut through the impenetrable metal. I took my staff and jabbed it under my arm, landing the blow right in his chest. Before he had even completely faded away, I jabbed the staff to my other side, and caught the other attacker with the butt of the staff.

I emerged from the mist of the two defeated opponents and set my sights on the gunners, who were cowering behind the tree, trying to shoot through my shield.

I held out both hands in front of me, my arms fully extended. I caused the shield to dissipate and put all of my focus on the tree. Before they had time to react, I lifted up both pieces of the tree, and thrust them back toward the gunners. This knocked them all back and caused about three to fade into mist.

The remaining ones scrambled trying to gain their footing. I saw a group of four to my left. They were close enough together for me to try out the new feature on my staff. I lifted my staff and gave it a sharp clockwise twist. This caused rutters, similar to the fletch of an arrow, to jolt out on the back. On the butt of the staff, the push peg (the weapon part of the staff which throws the opponent backward) retracted and was replaced with an engine.

I released the staff and it shot forward with the speed of a missile. It hit right in the middle of the group, sending each one flying in a different direction, as they dissipated in mid air.

I sensed a blast about to come from my left. I spun around and lifted my right arm to the place I knew it would strike. It hit the vanguard just as the staff returned to my hand. I used the momentum the staff already had to lunge it at the figure, who was sitting on the ground, still recovering from being hit by the tree.

The staff hit him in the chest and he faded away. I grabbed the staff as it returned to my hand, then turned back to Blake ready to help him. Just as I did, he delivered a blow on the last opponent. He turned to see if I needed help but realized that we had beat the course. He retracted his helmet.

"Let's go! Finally got through the last one!" Blake said, pumping his fist in the air.

I smiled, glad to be done, but feeling the weight of what we were stepping into. I retracted my staff and attached it back to my waistband, then nodded my head to deconstruct my helmet. ALI returned all of the mist to our pucks, but left just enough for him to make his emblem in between Blake and I.

"Very good boys. You've both done very well."

"What's the likelihood of deaths from that round?" I asked.

"1.34%. That's only from you throwing the tree, and assuming that it might be something heavier in an actual battle. From this round, there would have been zero deaths."

"That's what I like to hear." I said back.

"Now you each know that that was all of the training I have for you. You are ready to go up against the best The Organization has to offer. All that is left now is for you to summon the crystal, go after your family, and to find out where you fit into all of this. Are you ready?"

Blake and I walked toward ALI. "No" I said as I reached him, "But that's not what matters, what matters is that we are prepared."

"And we are that." Blake said.

"Yes we are," I affirmed.

"Then Dylan, now is the time. Reach out, connect with the crystal, call for it, feel its power and command it to come to you."

I closed my eyes. I could feel the crystal. I turned around so that I was facing away from ALI. My heart jumped. The energy within me intensified. I held out my hand in the direction of the base. I was drawn to its warmth, but I commanded it to come to me. I waited.

I could feel it traveling toward me as my power grew and the blue glow around my body brightened. I opened my eyes and looked up. Through the trees, I could see a fiery streak in the sky. It was the crystal. In an instant, faster than I could see, it tore through the trees and stopped about an inch in front of my raised hand. The blue energy raced down my arm turning into an aurora across my entire body.

I pulled in my hand and turned it over to get a good look at the crystal. It looked just as it had the day it shot me. Three rings surrounded it going in different directions, resembling the diagram of an atom. Smaller lights flowed through the rings just as they had done on that day, only now it looked more stable, almost calming.

The rings and lights retracted back inside the crystal and I closed my fist around it. "What do we do with it now?" I asked as I turned back to ALI.

"Your suit was designed to hold it. Put it next to your chest and the suit will form to it."

I did as he instructed. When it got just a few inches from my chest it lept from my hand and attached to the puck which sat on top of the black material and metal armor. It just happened to be above the scar as well.

I was sure that was no coincidence because as soon as the crystal was in its place, the pattern of the scar appeared on the surface of the suit, recreating it perfectly. Cascades of the soft blue energy flowed down the lines of the scar. It honestly looked really cool. I was impressed. It felt like being a real superhero, like something out of a movie.

With that thought, I was overcome with a wave of new emotions on the whole thing, a new perspective. I wasn't a superhero. I was just a kid, a kid who a week ago was just trying to graduate. Then, all of this happened. My life was wrecked and I was expected to be a soldier in a war that hadn't started yet and that the world didn't know about.

I pressed a button on my vanguard and activated my jetpack.

"Where are you going?" Blake asked, confused.

"I just need a few minutes alone." I answered as I lifted off, "I'll be fine. I'm just going down to the lake."

I just needed to take it all in, and not that Blake wasn't a big emotional support for me, I just needed to be alone with my thoughts to get my mind right before we took on this endeavor.

I broke through the trees and landed next to the water. It was still early. The sun was rising on the other side of the lake, but was not yet high enough to be seen over the hill and houses which sat on it. I looked across to my old house, thinking of what life used to be like, and would never be like again.

"God, how am I supposed to do this - be this?" I looked down to the crystal, "I just want to be normal. Is that too much to ask?" A tear slipped down my cheek. "Let someone else fight this war."

I heard a rustling in the trees behind me. I turned to see Blake breaking through the canopy. He landed beside me. "What's going on?"

I don't know why but I didn't really want to tell him. I don't know what had clicked in me. All week I had been focused on getting to this moment, to save the Vales, to maybe even save the world, now I just wanted to hide.

He waited patiently for my response as I tried to find words. "I guess it all just hit me at once, the realization of what we are about to do."

We stood in silence for a moment, looking over the lake.

"I've got an idea," he proposed, "It's Sunday; It's still early; Let's go to Church."

That was the first idea in a long time that really sounded good, no fighting, just a little normalcy, "I actually think that would be nice," I said, now glad he hadn't listened when I said I wanted to be alone, "But, umm, what are we gonna wear? All we have are these suits, and they aren't exactly the kind of suit you wear to church."

"I think I can help with that," ALI said from a speaker on my collar. The suit began to change. The armor and jetpack detached themselves and floated over to the side. The crystal retreated inside the puck (I'm not quite sure where the puck went, but it was out of sight). The suit changed into an all black, very formal, dress suit, complete with

72

a tie and a pin sporting the shape of the scar (a symbol recurring more and more).

"How long have you been able to do that?" Blake asked.

"This material can change into almost any form, it is simply limited to one color." ALI replied.

"Well, it might be just a little too formal, but it'll do" I said, "Now put it back to normal so we can fly there.

He did as I said, but only reattached the jetpack. The armor would stay behind. We flew back and stashed it in the cellar and then flew off toward the church.

The church sat on the highway on the edge of town. It was a beautiful building which seated about 250. The white steeple towered over the building and could be seen at quite a distance away. Just the sight of it made me feel better.

The parking lot was full since church had started already. Thankfully no one really parked in the back. We flew over the church and landed in the back parking lot. As soon as our feet hit the ground, our suits morphed and our jetpacks detached. "ALI" I said, "Stash these somewhere safe."

"Yes sir" He responded and the packs floated off toward the field at the back of the church.

Blake and I walked around to the front, opened the front door and walked in. The doors were large and opened up into the foyer. The ceiling was tall and from it hung a large chandelier. In front of us was the door to the sanctuary. We could hear songs coming from inside. The sounds filled the foyer. It felt good to hear music. It had been a while, felt like it anyway.

To the right was a lounge area where people would often sit and talk. A couple was sitting there, watching the service on a TV screen. They were the greeters for the day.

The couple stood up. It was Brother and Sister Brinkley. They used to be my Sunday school teachers when I was in third grade. "Oh, good morning boys!" Sister Brinkley said waving, "How are you two doing today?"

The answer was truthfully, not so great, but I knew everyone would be oblivious to what had happened. I was sure The Organization had seen to that. I decided to give the customary response, "Oh, we're doing fine. How about you?"

"I'm doing pretty good." She said with a smile, "We've missed you and your family lately. Is everything ok?"

Blake decided to respond to that one, "Oh, they haven't been feeling very good lately. We just got over it last Sunday. Family's still got it rough though. We just decided we needed a little church before we went back to take care of them."

It wasn't a lie. In fact, It was the complete truth. "Well bless your hearts! I'll be praying for all of you." said Sister Brinkley

"Thank you, we could really use it," I replied as we began to walk toward the sanctuary.

We opened up the doors and walked into the sanctuary. There was always such peace there. We took a seat in the back row. We were the only ones on it. We sang along with the songs. My mind, for the first time since all of this started, was at ease.

The Worship set ended; Pastor took his place behind the pulpit and began to preach. His message was simple and exactly what I needed. His title was "Do What Needs to be Done".

"You can't wait for someone else to do what needs to be done. If you do, you will wait your entire life. Many Jews knew that their leadership was corrupt, but it took Jesus entering into the temple to clean some of the mess up. He went in and flipped over the tables of the corrupt.

Jesus was our ultimate example on how to live. Just as he did, sometimes we must flip over tables. We must stand up for what we believe in. If Jesus had waited for someone else to cleanse the temple, it would have never been done. If he had waited for someone else to die on the cross, you and I would have no remission of our sins. Sometimes we must lay down what we want, and take up the burden of others. It is the only way they will be saved"

The message ended. Rather than going up to the altar to pray, Blake and I decided it was best to go. We didn't need lots of questions, and we had heard the message we needed to hear. As we began to walk out of the sanctuary, we were met by Pastor. This was strange as he would usually stay up at the altar to pray until he dismissed church.

"Boys, it was good to see you today."

"It was good to see you too." Blake and I said almost simultaneously.

"Are you doing alright?" Pastor asked. I couldn't evade the question.

"Pastor, I..." I opened my mouth to tell him we needed to talk, but something caught my attention. A feeling. An instinct.

I broke eye contact with him and looked behind him, out through the foyer. Through the glass of the front door, I could see six figures, dressed like the soldiers at the base, walking across the parking lot. Around their waist were all kinds of weapons. They looked different though. Their helmets, their suits, everything just looked better, higher budget, more effective and sleek.

"ALI, we're gonna need those jetpacks and armor. Now!" I said, "Pasor, keep everyone in the sanctuary. Please!"

He stared at me with a confused look. I just hoped that once he figured out what was going on, he would listen. I looked at Blake. I don't think he saw them, but he knew I sensed something. We ran toward the entrance. As we did, our suits changed back to their tactical version. The crystal reappeared on my chest. We flung open the doors and stood face to face with the soldiers.

They stood, unmoved, looking at us. The soldiers were in a line with one, standing in front of the rest, who spoke up, their voice modified by the helmet, "We only came for the crystal and its wielder. Give it and yourself up and not only does everyone here walk away, but we will return the Vales to their home."

I would like to say I took a moment to think before I spoke, but I didn't. I was just angry that they had shown up here and a bit over confident from my week of training. "It would be tempting if you actually posed a threat." I taunted, "New terms, You walk away now, we don't hurt you." Just as I finished speaking, our jetpacks returned and attached to our backs.

"No deal," he replied.

"Then I guess we hit a gridlock" I nodded my head and my helmet constructed, hopefully hiding the bit of fear on my face. I knew this would be our first real fight. Blake constructed his helmet and drew his staff. I summoned my powers. Blue energy radiated down my arms and the crystal began to glow a bit brighter.

75

They each drew their weapons. Four carried atomizing blades. They ejected the metal blade from its hilt and white energy radiated up and down them.

The leader and one standing next to him carried staves. They extended them. Everyone stood there in silence, waiting for someone to make the first move. I discreetly began to move my fingers, using my power to grab hold of a car behind them.

All at once, the six of them rushed forward. Two going to the left, two to the right, and two straight at us. I lifted the car and yanked it toward the two on the left. It hit them from behind, knocking them forward and to the ground. I allowed the car to pass over them, then dropped it just as the other four reached us.

They were highly trained and better than most of the simulations we had done - better than the soldiers we had fought at the base. Blake was trying to handle two at once, but was being pushed back toward the church.

I was fighting the leader and the other who carried a staff. I was able to deflect their swings and dodge their jabs, but I was outmatched in close combat. I leaped backward and used my powers to push them away from me. I then thrust my staff at one who was attacking Blake.

It hit him in the side. The blue energy spread across his body and thrust him into his partner, knocking them both to the ground. Blake took his chance with the one who was still conscious and lying on the ground. He jabbed him with his staff. The blue energy spread across him and onto the ground, cracking the pavement.

I pulled my staff back to my hand just in time to clash with my two attackers, who had quickly recovered from the push. Blake rushed over to help. One attacker broke off to go after Blake, leaving me with the leader. We were now much more evenly matched.

"ALI, Where's that armor?" I asked, trying to keep my focus on my opponent.

"Just coming across the highway, sir"

I looked over the attacker's shoulder and could see the armor reflecting the sun as it flew through the air. I landed a blow across the helmet of the soldier and he stumbled backward. The armor flew around him on both his left and right as it came to Blake and I.

76

I turned to Blake and used my power to push his opponent out of the way. He flew through the air sideways but was able to turn and secure his footing about twenty feet from Blake.

The armor attached to both of us. Now, feeling much safer, I walked toward my opponent who was backing up, trying to regroup. ALI used the lights of the heads up display to turn my attention to the two, initial attackers who were recovering from being hit with the car.

Knowing I had a moment before my attacker would begin his second assault, I drew my gun from its holster and shot the two soldiers. Before they could even get stood up, they fell back to the ground, out cold.

My attacker lunged forward. I raised my gun to shoot at him but he used the staff to knock it from my hand. I stumbled backward but caught my balance and continued to dodge his attacks. He was better than me. I wouldn't beat him like this. I would have to use my powers.

"ALI, He's wearing armor right?"

"Yes, sir. What are you thinking?"

"That's all I needed to know."

I caught his staff with my hand. It hit with great force, but I didn't focus on it. He did what I expected and pulled it away. That gave me the opening I needed. I held my hands in front of me and formed a beam of plasma, hitting him in the center of the chest. I could hear the clank of the energy meeting the metal armor.

He was thrust backward into the windshield of a car. His shiny chestplate was visible and red-hot. The armor disconnected itself, floated to the side of the car, and dropped to the ground.

I turned back to Blake. He was still fighting his opponent. I found my gun and drew it to my hand. I shot and hit the attacker in the neck, between his helmet and his jetpack, one of the few gaps in the armored suit. The attacker dropped to the ground and Blake looked to me.

He retracted his staff and helmet and placed the staff back on his waistband, "Now that... wasn't so bad..." he choked, out of breath.

I almost felt bad. The fight had barely affected my breathing. "So long as that was the last of them. Now, what do we do with them?"

"Might I suggest interrogation?" ALI chipped in.

"ALI, we're the good guys. We don't interrogate people." I said.

"Yes, but, A few of them seem to have sustained wounds that require medical attention, especially the one on the car who has third degree burns. We could simply strap them down, treat their wounds, and ask them some questions."

It wasn't actually a bad idea. "And where do you suggest we do that?" I asked.

He replied, "I hear this church has a wonderful Sunday school department... lots of different classrooms."

Chapter 8

I told Blake to keep an eye on the defeated soldiers and to stun them if they so much as breathe too heavily. Then, I walked back into the church. The doors to the sanctuary were closed. A group of men stood in front of them. I knew that many men of the church carried handguns. These men were guarding the people in the sanctuary.

Pastor stood in the middle of them, "Son, I think you'd better tell me what's going on."

I knew I didn't have much time before the soldiers woke up, so I told him a condensed version of all that had happened over the past week. He stood in silence, allowing me to tell the story and taking it all in. I finished, "And now, we need the Sunday school classes. Some of them out there are injured. We need a place where we can separate them, tie them down, treat them, and ask them some questions. The Sunday school classes are the best place."

"Uh huh," Pastor paused, as if replaying everything I had told him back to himself, "I don't know that it's the best place, but it's the only place you've got. I will help you."

Pastor and the group of men followed me outside. They helped pick up the soldiers and carry them inside and to their own Sunday School room. The rooms were brightly painted, each telling its own story from the bible. We laid each soldier on a table then got some ratchet straps and rope to tie them down.

I came to the room which held the leader. He was in the "David" classroom. Goliath towered over the soldier's table. I looked down at the soldier who lay almost lifeless. "ALI, can you override this suit and get all of this armor and stuff off so that we can treat him?"

"I believe so. Hold up your vanguard," I did as he instructed and a small chip stuck out of the top, "Now put that on his neck at the base of his helmet."

When I did, it spread out and seemed to dissolve. "What was that?" I asked.

"It's a form of nanotechnology. It will find its way into the major circuit boards and give me access to the suit." As he spoke, All of the soldiers' armor fell off and the helmet detached from his neck, though it did not retract, so it still sat on his head

A white circle of light appeared in the middle of his chest and spread out across his body. The black tactical suit disappeared as the light moved over it. All that was left was a skin tight, black t-shirt and three-quarter length pants. They both appeared to be made from a spandex-like material.

The shirt had a hole in it where the blast had hit. It looked as though the material had moved out of the way in order to keep from melting to his skin. The burn was severe.

Pastor walked in behind me, "I'm going to get everyone to leave except for a few men who have agreed to help. I have a first aid kit in my office. I will get it for you."

"Thank you," I replied, "While you're at it, tell the person whose car I threw that I'm sorry. I'm sure when this is all over I can find a way to pay for it."

"It's already been taken care of."

I knew it was him who had taken care of it, but Pastor walked out of the room before I could thank him. I looked back to the soldier and began to examine the burn. It was fiery red and was already beginning to ooze. Around the edges there were blisters but in the center, it was just too raw. All that was there was red flesh. The burn was an area about the size of a softball. It sat right over his sternum, directly in the center of his chest.

"Well, let's see who the unlucky attacker is," I said. I reached and lifted his helmet off of his head, and what I saw overtook me with shock. I stepped back. It couldn't be. Under the helmet was a kid, no older, perhaps younger, than me. His face was young, but I assumed he had to be older than he looked. His blond hair was cut short, longer on the top than the sides. A bit of blood sat dried under his nose.

"ALI, did you know they were this young?"

"Not until I took control of the suit. The log says that he's 16."

"Why... How... How do they get these kids?"

"I am unsure. It is not recorded here or in the data files that I have access to, and this is something your father and I never uncovered. Shall I rouse him?"

"No, not yet, let's get him strapped down first." As I spoke, a man walked in carrying the ratchet straps and rope. He looked at me, then down at the table, then back at me.

80

"You're all a little young for this aren't you?" he said.

"I guess you work with what you're dealt." I said, a bit aggravated at the question. It wasn't like I wanted to be doing this. The kid probably didn't either.

We took the straps securing them tightly across his body at both his ankles, thighs, stomach, and neck (though we left the one over his neck a bit looser, only tightening it enough so that he couldn't sit up). We then took the ropes and tied one end around his wrists and the other around one of the supports under the plastic table.

"Go help Blake do this to every other soldier, exactly the same way, only on the rest be sure to also put one across their chest." I instructed the man, "And close the door on your way out, please."

"You got it," he said as he walked through the doorway.

As soon as the door was shut, I called ALI, "I want all of my armor and weapons off and on that wall over there. Then change my suit to something casual. I don't want to look like a soldier, I want to look like a boy."

"Certainly, sir" He did as I said and the suit changed into a long-sleeve T-shirt and jogging pants.

"You mean you could make it this comfortable the... never mind. Wake him up"

A blue spark of energy appeared on the boy's neck. His eyes opened. They were wild. His muscles tensed. He gritted his teeth then screamed, "Guaa!" He jerked his arms and legs trying to free himself from the table.

I held out my hand. Streams of energy flowed over the table as I held it steady. I didn't want him to flip it over and hurt himself any worse. "Calm down! I'm not trying to hurt you!" I said, "Relax and it won't hurt as much."

The boy continued to scream and struggle with the restraints. ALI's emblem appeared on the other side of the table, "Shall we put him back under, sir?"

"No, no, just give him a second." I looked the boy in the eyes, "It's ok. I'm going to help you. I promise."

81

He must have either believed me or just given up because he stopped shaking the table and relaxed.

"Now that's better," I said. The door opened. It was Pastor carrying the first aid kit. He looked at the boy on the table. I could tell he was surprised at his age, but he didn't mention it. "I've got the first aid kit. Is there anything I can help with?" he asked softly.

"Yes, I'll need your help treating him."

"Of course" He walked over and sat the kit at the Boy's feet. He opened it and pulled out some gaus, a can of burn cream, and a burn spray. He walked to the side of the table opposite of me. "Now, this is going to sting a little, but once that's over, it won't hurt near as bad," said Pastor, "Dylan, hold these gaus and put them on there as soon as I'm done."

I took the gaus from him as he began his work. The boy only lay there, eyes closed, gritting his teeth. A couple times he winced from the pain, but over all he hid it well. When Pastor was done he looked up to me, my signal to put the gauze on. I did and held slight pressure on the wound. Pastor reached over the boy and grabbed a sort of bandage tape which he used to hold the gauze to the wound.

"Now then, you let me know if you two need anything else," Pastor said.

"Yes, sir," I replied and he walked out of the room.

I looked at the boy, "I wouldn't have blast you if I had known you were so young. How did you even get mixed up in all this?"

The boy opened his eyes and looked at me, "First, don't look at me like I'm just some kid, like you're better than me. You're probably the same age as I am. Second, I'm not telling you anything. There is nothing you can do to me that isn't worse than what The Organization would do if they found out I talked."

"The Organization can't hear you here. ALI is making sure of that. All communications, including cell phones, are being blocked," I assured him, "Can you at least tell me your name?"

"Alex"

"Good, we're getting somewhere. How did you come to work for The Organization?"

He closed his eyes and turned his head back to the ceiling.

I continued, "Ok, well if you won't tell me how you came to be here, then I'll just tell you how I came to be here. My life was normal until last Sunday. Well, actually, not normal, but more normal than this, and then I found this crystal." I summoned it from the armor on the opposite wall. It came to rest in the palm of my hand, "It electrocuted me and gave me my powers."

Alex opened his eyes and looked at me, "I know that. I brought you in. It was my directive. I had to comply."

That was interesting. He "had to comply." That didn't sound like someone who served the Organization willingly. I remembered my ability to sense emotion. I quieted my mind and looked into his. I could see fear, pain, loss. He was suffering, but not from the burn.

I leaned in. I had an idea but I wasn't sure, "When did they take you?"

Alex's eyes grew wide. He looked at me in shock. "How did you know that?"

I smiled. I had gotten it right. I chose to keep my elusiveness, "That doesn't matter. I know a lot of things. Did you have a family, or were you orphaned?"

"I have a family," he corrected, "I make sure of that."

"How so?"

Alex looked around nervously. I could feel his fear, even over the little bit that he had said. I needed his full trust. I held out my hand with the crystal and from it projected a shield around us. ALI had taught me this trick earlier in the week. It was different from my normal shield. It looked like the one at the base, a column of energy coming from the crystal and arcs of energy leaping from it near the surface of the light purple shield.

"This shield creates interference. No technology can work in it and sound cannot pass through it," I informed him, "You're safe. Let me help you."

Alex looked back at me. I could still feel his fear, but it was not toward me. There was something else. Something deeper. He finally began to talk, "The Organization took me six years ago. They put me through rigorous training. My only incentive to follow their commands was that they knew where my family was and that if I ever failed or betrayed them, they would kill my family, then imprison me." His face grew cold, "So I did as they said. I killed for them… to keep my family safe." He began to plead, "Look, you won, but if I don't show back up they will kill my family, and the families of the others with me. Please, let us go!" A tear slipped down his cheek.

He was telling the truth, "Don't worry," I said, "I'll let all of you go. But you don't have to live like this. You can spread the word, rally people against the Organization and when the time is right, you can fight against them instead of for them. Just tell me where your family is and I will go to protect them. All of your families. I'll bring them here, where they can be safe. We can tear down the Organization. You can choose to be better."

Alex stared at me coldly, "And if you fail my family will die."

It had been a while since he had hope. He was reluctant to it. But this was a chance. A chance for me to get help from within The Organization. I decided to show him how hopeless denying my offer was. "You already know it's just a matter of time before that happens anyway." I was stern, "The Organization is evil. Everyone messes up. It's only a matter of time before you mess up and they pay the price."

It was a harsh statement but he knew it was true. He sat for a moment, thinking, "Deal, what do we do?"

I did it. I got someone on my side! Though it was only one person, to me, this was starting to look more like a rebellion. It was hard to contain my excitement, but I kept my cool, "I will have all of you write down the names and last known locations of your family members. Write down anyone who could be in danger. Once they are safe, I will find a way to contact you."

I really didn't know how I would find them, or when, really any of the details. I was honestly just making this up as I went. But it was enough for him, because it was hope.

"How long do you think it will take?" Alex asked

"I can ask ALI. He will be the one finding them and coordinating the mission," I told him, "Are you okay with me lowering the shield now?"

He nodded. I lowered the shield, closing my hand around the crystal, and turned to ALI, "How long would it take to find Alex's family if you had names and addresses?"

"Well, with that information, it would not take long at all. I would likely be able to have surveillance of them within just a few minutes."

"840 Montana Drive Westland, Indiana! Hillary, Jake, and Matthew Bridger." Alex blurted.

"I'll see what I can do." ALI's bubble faded.

"As soon as we find them, I'll send someone to pick them up." I waved my hand horizontally and used a small slash of plasma to sever all of the straps that held Alex to the table.

He sat up, "Thank you... "

"It would be wrong of me not to. I do have a few more questions before you go and we talk to the rest of your team. How many more soldiers are there like you?"

"You mean the taken? Not many. From what we can tell, it's a new program. They are testing to see how effective soldiers like us can be since it only takes about two years to have us in the field."

"Why would they send potentially disloyal troops to deal with something as important as the crystal?" I asked.

"The Organization works on levels and districts. The base that you broke into is over a small district dedicated to research. They don't send their best troops to areas of low importance. The reason they sent us is because we are the best troops that base had. Districts don't send aid or even contact one another unless a problem is too big for them to handle. After today, you will have likely caused another district to become involved."

This was information ALI had not shared. I was curious if he had withheld it, or if he didn't know. That question would have to wait.

"Well, we were about to involve another district anyway. Blake and I have family being held captive on another base."

"I know. They are already expecting you to go there. They're using them as bait. We were only sent because they tracked the crystal here."

"We know they will be expecting us."

"And you're still going? That base is a hundred times more fortified than the one you escaped from."

"What do you know of it?"

85

"Only rumors. The base they are being kept in is the most secret of all the North American bases. They say it holds one of the crystals."

"Really?" I asked. This was new information. If it were true we could save the Vales and steal a crystal all at the same time, "Are you certain?"

"I can never be certain of anything," Alex said, "But if I had to bet, I would say it was true."

ALI's bubble appeared back in the center of the room, "I have located your family. They are alive and well. I have them on surveillance. Would you like to see them?"

"Yes!" Alex exclaimed as he jumped up from the table.

A button lit up on my vanguard. I pressed it and a small hologram was projected up from it. Alex rushed over and peered into the tiny image. It looked to be the security footage of a supermarket. Three people, a young couple and a boy about ten years old were shown in the center of a produce aisle. I was going to ask Alex if it was them, but his tears answered that question for me.

I put my hand on his shoulder. He attempted to hug me but was forced to pull away because of his wound. He winced through his sobbing. I countered with a side hug. Through his sobbing he whispered, "Thank you... thank you so much."

Chapter 9

I spent the rest of the day going through the same routine with all of the other soldiers. They all reacted similar to Alex. All seemed to be good kids, stolen, and set on a dark path. None seemed to be sinister at heart. Though some were colder than Alex. Some had been through worse, seen more, killed more. But all broke down at the sight of their family and friends safe and sound. After that, their hearts softened. They remembered who they were.

After everyone was on our side, we gave them back their armor and sent them on their way. I gave Alex a small, one way communicator and told him I would be in contact as soon as their families were all safe.

I talked with Pastor and the group of men. There were twelve men not including Pastor. They agreed to go in teams of two to collect the Taken soldiers' families, bringing them back to the church. In order to convince the families of our pure intentions, a video was taken of each boy before they left explaining, in short, what had befallen them and how urgent it was that they listen to the men. Pastor would stay behind and coordinate the mission in the absence of Blake and I. Each family would be put up in a local hotel (courtesy of the church) until we could get everything sorted out.

Once all of this was set in motion, Blake and I took a seat in the foyer across from one another. He had been keeping watch outside while I talked to each of the taken soldiers. "Do you really think it will make a difference? I mean, do you think they'll help us?"

"I think so." I replied, "Once they know that everyone they care for is safe, there will be nothing tying them down,"

"It just seems strange though. How fast they turned to our side."

That I did find strange. How could The Organization have such disloyal soldiers? While I distrusted The Organization for this fact, I believed in the change of the soldiers. I decided to stay positive, "Well, they did say they were experimental. I guess if they turned, The Organization just assumed they could still track the crystal and send someone else for it."

"Maybe so. I just hope they come through when the time is right."

"I believe in them," I said. And I did. I only hoped it wasn't some elaborate trap set for all of us.

We sat for a moment. Everyone except for Pastor had gone home. The men were preparing to head out to the families of the Taken the next day. Pastor, however, was not preparing, at least not physically. He was in the sanctuary. I wasn't exactly sure what he was doing. Probably praying. The foyer was empty. Everything was finally still.

I broke the peaceful silence, "ALI," I called. His emblem appeared between Blake and I.

"Yes sir."

"Tell me everything you know about the Montana base. I want to know what we are going to be walking into."

"Well, as the boy, Alex, was telling you, the different parts of the Organization are very secretive. One branch knows very little about the next. All I know is what the boy told us and what your father and I discovered."

"So you did know there was a crystal there!" Blake said as he sat forward.

"I knew that one used to be there. I assumed that when they figured out he knew of it they would have changed its location."

"We're gonna need more information than that," I commanded, "Whole story - top to bottom,"

"As you wish." ALI's emblem turned into a flat plane, then began to depict his story, "There were two crystals in the lab that Daniel and Alfred worked in. The power crystal, which you have, and the red crystal, which we called the parasite and is now at the Montana base." The depiction showed two crystals, indistinguishable from one another in the black fog of the mist.

"They were unique in composition, but connected to one another. Their energy was similar in frequency. They probed them and found out that they were connected to stars in a binary solar system." The crystals on the depiction morphed into two stars, one orbiting the other. A rippling current flowed from the larger star to the smaller, which was about one third the size of the host. "The star of the red crystal orbits the star of your crystal, stealing its energy from the star."

"Your father lost track of this crystal after the lab accident that killed Alfred and gave your father his powers. But because of their special connection, he was able to track it. He looked for an energy signature similar to that of his crystal and tracked it to the Montana base. He was going to steal it, but then he learned of the yellow crystal being stolen from Russia. Since he could catch that one in the open, he abandoned his plans to raid the Montana base. The rest of the story goes just as I have told you before."

The star system faded back to ALI's emblem.

"What made you think that they discovered his plan and moved it?" Blake asked.

"Well, his lab was locked up, but his house was not. They found a computer holding a part of his plan. I was able to take over the device and kill it before they could take too much from it. I knew that they had seen at least some of his plan, schematics of the base and such. I assumed that with the location exposed they would move it. Apparently not."

ALI paused. I was angry at him for not telling us, but how was I supposed to react? He was just a computer. I wanted to scold him, but that didn't seem right. I felt like ALI was holding back information. He knew more than he was telling us, but I knew he was just a program. If I wanted information I had to ask. But he was so human-like. I guess I held him to a higher standard than this.

ALI broke our stunned silence, "I do have some of the schematics and old data in my back-up memory. I think you two might be able to use them."

"And when were you going to tell us this," I asked agitatedly.

"When it became important."

I rolled my eyes. I almost wanted to laugh. He was so serious though. I decided to move on, "Well that time is now. Wacha got?"

"A plan" ALI said. My vanguard flew from behind me and situated under ALI's emblem. It projected a hologram of what had to be the base. It was situated between two giant mountains. A river ran through the middle of it, separating it into two halves.

On one side was a large landing strip. Hundreds of strange warmachines, seemingly built for flying, sat parked around it. The hologram was too small to see details. Some looked like jets with large guns and missiles hanging under them. Others were U-shaped, with a cockpit situated in the middle of the "U". These had two guns directly

89

under the cockpit. Aside from these were other strange craft; they were nearly rectangular and seemed to be unarmed.

On the other side of the river were buildings, no more than ten stories tall. Each one had a turret on top. The turret was very boxy and had one long barrel protruding from the center, facing the sky. All together there were about twenty five buildings. All around the base, up the mountains and down the center of the valley, were more turrets of various sizes, hundreds of them.

Up from the base was a dam. It was bigger than any dam I had ever seen or heard of. It towered above the base and went almost half way up the side of the mountain. Above the dam was a narrow lake, confined by the mountain range. The river originated from the bottom of the dam.

"This is Montana Base. It lies in the Madison Range of the Rocky Mountains." The map zoomed in on the side of the river with the buildings, then revealed a massive underground portion of the base.

"The base is mostly underground, running a mile under the surface. The prisoners are housed here." A red dot appeared on a portion of the map not far from the surface. There was a long hallway with cells on each side.

"Getting your family will be the easy part. The crystal is stored half a mile under in a secure vault."

The map scrolled up. In view was a large room with a vault door. "It is stored in a specialized container that extracts the energy of the crystal and sends it to power, what they call, a legion of their army. Specifically, the legion tasked with capturing North America in their imminent takeover."

"So does that mean once we steal it their weapons won't work anymore? " Blake asked.

"Temporary. They do have fail safes. They will have to change out their quantum batteries for ones that are connected to one of their remaining crystals. It will take them about fifteen minutes to get up and running again. If we do this part of the job first, it will be much easier to escape"

Two green dots appeared at the front door of the base. Three more appeared in the cell block, each representing a member of our family.

"To pull this off, we must break in stealthily. You two look like Organization soldiers so that shouldn't be a problem so long as you try to blend in" The dots moved through the corridors of the base, "Once we reach the crystals holding facility, Dylan can use his power to blow a hole in the door. It should be relatively easy to open. Since it is so far down, they don't care to re-enforce it. Once this is done, the alarm will sound. We must steal the crystal and then fight our way back to the surface, grabbing your family along the way."

The map scrolled, plotting the best route joining all of the dots together on the way up, "Once to the surface, we will need to secure a jet and a transport." A "U" shaped ship and a box ship turned green. "We can use a nano chip to override their systems, allowing everyone to get on and escape." The map zoomed out to its original position.

"I like the plan," I congratulated, "But I have one problem, one problem with any plan that ends in success, what about when we win? What about when the full might of the Organization comes after us? We could barely hold off six disloyal kids."

"A valid point," ALI conceded, "One for which I can offer no valid counteraction."

Blake stood up, the look of determination filled his eyes, "We can worry about that when we get there. We have a family to protect. We may not be able to take on their full might, but we've done pretty good so far."

"You have seen only a small part of perhaps the weakest branch of The Organization." ALI said.

"It doesn't matter," Blake was not backing down, "Right now, we have one thing that we may never have again: an advantage. They don't know what we can do. They don't know what we know. They just know that we're coming."

"That means security will be increased, especially in the cell block." I said.

"So then we need a distraction." He said, looking at the map. "We split up. You go for the crystal loudly, draw them away. I'll go for the family quietly and then make a run for it."

"This is acceptable," ALI said.

"I agree." I said reluctantly. I didn't like the idea of leaving Blake, but I knew the plan made sense. Plus, ALI could watch his back, be his super sense. Honestly, I couldn't believe it. We had a plan, and

91

one that sounded like it could work. It sounded like we had a real chance of winning.

I stood up, "Just one thing. If anything goes wrong, our number one priority is saving our family. If I can't make it back up, you leave."

Blake looked up from the map. His face was scrunched, deep in thought. "I mean it." I said, "I don't want to split up, but it's the best we've got. So is this. You leave as soon as you are done with your part."

"I can't agree to that," Blake said squarely, "I can agree to get them on their way, but I leave when you do."

It was a touching gesture but I had to disagree, "If I do get stuck, and you come back, they'll just catch us both."

"Then we'll have to break out together," Blake said.

I didn't like it. I would rather him just be safe, but I knew I would do the same thing. I had no choice but to concede, "Fine, but only after our family is home free. ALI, If that happens, you must place them in the protection of The Taken or else The Organization will just take them back."

"With that I agree." ALI said, "I will add it to my base programming."

As we headed for the door, mine and Blakes armor flew in from the direction of the Sunday school classes and attached to our bodies. Pastor must have heard the commotion because he walked out of the sanctuary.

"Where are you guys off to?" he asked.

"We are going to save our family," I answered.

He looked at us. I wasn't sure what he was doing. I tried to look into his mind but I could see nothing, I was blocked. "I'm not going to ask you to stay," he said, "I don't think you would, or could, obey if I did. I only ask that you are careful, as well as mindful of your thoughts and actions. War is a tricky thing. I believe you are being pulled into one, and that fact is one beyond your choice. If you must be a part of it, make sure you don't lose yourself, or your God in the middle of it. I'll be praying for each of you."

His words sat heavy. He was wise, and I wished I had more time to speak with him, but our window was closing. If we stayed, The Organization would send more soldiers to this place. That was the last thing I wanted. I looked back at him and as truly as I could I said, "We will. Thank you, for everything."

"Blake?" Pastor said, wanting a promise from him as well.

"Yes, sir. We'll be careful. Thank you,"

And with that we walked through the front doors, activated our jetpacks, dawned our helmets, and flew off toward the setting sun.

Part Two: The Exodus
"Let my people go"

Chapter 10

We flew, passing state after state. We had to take frequent breaks, every hour or so. The suit provided support so that our legs didn't have to work to stay stretched out behind us, but it was uncomfortable. The jetpacks weren't made for such long flights, but they were all we had. Our determination to complete the mission at hand was stronger than the pain the flight caused.

Our conversation during the fight consisted solely of going over the plan and reviewing the various functions of the suit. There were so many that memorizing them would be impossible, but we wanted to try and be ready for any situation. ALI warned that there may come a time when we cannot use him. We needed to be well versed with the suit controles if this were ever the case.

I had never left Tennessee before. It wasn't that I didn't want to travel, I just didn't have a need to. I loved my town, and the Smoky Mountains was the only getaway I ever needed.

The geography of the west was strange compared to the mountains and valleys of Tennessee. Most of the land was just so flat out here. I was glad when we were finally nearing the Rockies. It was dark by then, but the change to a more familiar landscape was welcomed. It wasn't completely familiar though. The mountains were different here, more jagged.

We flew over mountain after mountain, traveling deep into the wilderness. At first we could see the lights of various settlements, but once we got so deep, there was no trace of civilization.

Eventually, we stopped and hovered in mid air. "What's up, ALI?" I asked.

"We're here," he said, "Just over that ridgeline is the base. We need to head down and make camp. We attack at first light."

We floated down beside a patch of trees. The foliage here was opposite of Tennessee. Back home, there would be woods with grassy clearings. Here it was grass with patches of trees.

Blake pressed a button on his vanguard. The black mist flowed from his puck and made his pad under the trees. He then tapped his puck. His armor came off, the suit retreaded inside the puck, and he pressed it to a tree. His armor floated up and rested on the tree.

I did the same to the tree beside it. I took my vanguard from it and pressed the button to form my pad in the open. I threw the vanguard back to the tree where it formed up with the rest of the armor. I laid down and looked up at the stars.

There was less light pollution here than back home. I could see the milky way with impressive definition. I thought it only existed like this in pictures. It was breathtaking. I stared at it for a while, thinking.

I had no idea what the next day would bring. I didn't even know if I was ready for it. How could I be? One wrong move and everything I cared about could be lost. And worst of all, they needed me. They wouldn't kill me because I could use the crystal. I would be stuck in a life of mental and likely physical torture.

Though I had been praying between conversations all day long, this line of thought brought me to prayer once more. I finally shook the anxiety (or more like temporarily suppressed it). Once this was out of the way, there was nothing holding back my overwhelming fatigue. I gave in, and drifted off into darkness.

***

I woke up to my bed vibrating violently. That was ALI's wake up call. I rolled off the bed and onto the grass in order to get some relief.

"Ok ALI! I get it! I'm up!" Blake scolded from the other pad.

It was still dark. I could just make out the first notes of the sunrise coming over the mountains in the distance. "We must get going!" ALI's voice called from our gear, "They are changing the guard now. That means there will be more on the surface than down in the base."

"Making them easier to deal with," Blake said, "We know!"

I sat up from the soft grass and looked over to Blake. He was putting on his armor. I could tell from his sharp remarks he was nervous. I walked over, "We're gonna do it," I said putting my arm on his shoulder, "Just stay in the moment."

Blake took a deep breath and exhaled, "I know. There's just a lot of pressure to get this right."

To say the fate of the entire world was at hand would not be an understatement. If we got that crystal, it would be a major blow to The Organization. But more than *the World* being at stake, *our world* was at stake.

"There is a lot of pressure," I said, "We just have to make sure it doesn't affect our judgment."

We each dawned our armor and said a final prayer before our mission. Then, we flew up to the top of the mountain. We made sure to stay close to the ground. They wouldn't be looking for people on jetpacks at a distance, but this close, they would detect us. We reached the peak and the base came into view.

It was mostly like the map, there were a few subtle differences, such as a bridge that now crossed the river and a red paint job that now dawned all of the aircraft. Two nano chips projected themselves from my vanguard. I lifted them with my powers.

I moved one forward, toward the airfield. The craft we needed was about a mile from us still. There was no way to see the nano chip after just a few feet. I had to feel where it was. I aimed for the fighter jet first. As soon as I thought I had made it ALI spoke up, "We have a successful connection with the U Jet. Now for the transport."

I did the same thing and once again, we had success. "Blake, don't forget to change out the quantum batteries. The craft won't work if I steal the crystal."

"Got it." Blake said, "Batteries are in my pocket."

"Then let's go show 'em what for." I ignited my jetpack and began to fly toward the front door. I was to break in loudly, and Blake would slip in behind me. They would only be expecting me, since Blake had no powers and was not to be mentioned in the mission report of the Taken.

I decided to blatantly fly into the airspace directly over the base. I wanted a dramatic entrance in order to draw as many troops as possible away from Blake. It worked. A spotlight sliced through the dim, morning light, shining from one of the buildings across the river. My visor darkened to compensate. As I began to fly toward the ground, I shot a blast of energy at the tower housing the spotlight.

It was a direct hit. The spotlight burst into flames and the soldier operating it jumped from the tower and glided to the ground using his jetpack. I was answered with a barrage of red plasma fire that came from every side. I weaved back and forth, now trying to make it to the ground as quickly as I could. There were so many blasts, it was hard to find a clear path, but I did. As soon as I dipped below the tallest building, the fire from the turrets stopped.

I landed right in front of the green target that ALI had set for me. The targeting display deactivated and I could now clearly see what I was looking at in its true colors. I was staring at two, reinforced doors that lead to the underground portion of the base. There wasn't really a building, just a bunker-like structure. I looked around. All was quiet. I could see no one, "ALI, Where are all the troops?"

"They are coming. Just give them a moment."

I looked around. I didn't see anyone. Then, I thought to quiet my mind. I could sense them. This wasn't good. They were coming up the elevator from the base below, and from the buildings. I would be surrounded.

I looked for a better vantage point. I used my jetpack to jump on top of the bunker. "There he is!" A voice yelled. I looked to see about twenty soldiers coming from behind the bunker. Running to meet them were about thirty more coming from one of the buildings off to the right. This was a lot, but I could make it less.

I drew my staff. It extended and the signature blue blast shot from each end. I twisted it, causing the rutters to stick out. I held it out in front of me, pointing it at the group of thirty. A small flame appeared on the end facing me as it thrust itself forward. It moved so fast that the group of soldiers didn't have time to react. It hit the ground just in front of them and knocked every one of them to the ground.

I wasn't sure how many had been incapacitated and how many were just knocked off their feet, but at the very least, it would slow them down. The smaller group responded with a rain of plasma fire. My staff returned to my hand a fraction of a second before the blasts reached me.

I spun the staff around, almost eloquently, intercepting blast after blast. I could sense the trajectory of each blast and made sure my staff was in the precise location. I had to hold them off. Wait for them to get closer, then I could begin picking them off.

That chance never came. The elevator below me reached its destination. The doors crept open, and a flood of troops poured from them.

I jumped off the roof and landed in front of them, "Mornin' boys." I said as I thrust my staff into the nearest soldier's chest. He was thrust backwards. Everyone moved out of the way and he smashed against the back of the elevator. The doors closed. The rest of the soldiers turned from the doors, looked at me, and drew their atom swords and guns. I backed up.

I had to rely on my powers rather than my skill. I reached out to my powers and blue energy spread from the crystal on my chest, to my arms. They lunged forward, hoping to secure a fatal blow, but I thrust both arms forward. A concussive blast radiated in front of me and knocked them all against the doors.

I think I knocked the soldiers in the back out, but the ones in the front were merely thrown off balance as their blow was cushioned by the troops behind them. This group consisted of five soldiers with their atom swords at the ready. They began to fight.

I took the one on the far right first. His sword clashed with my staff at eye level. I spun my staff around, hitting his sword from the top, and knocking it from his hand.

It made a sharp hiss as it cut into the pavement below us, but upon realizing it was not in his hand, it turned off and the blade retracted.

Before I could deal with him, I was forced to move my staff to block the advances of another troop. This continued, blow after blow. I couldn't make any advances because it was all I could do to block their swings. I was being pushed back, but was holding my own. I saw an opening and jabbed my staff at the attacker on the left. He was blown backward, but the soldier beside him grabbed my staff and swung his sword at me.

I was forced to let go in order to dodge the attack. The soldier beside him followed up with a jab, but I raised a shield and stopped the sword. I pushed the shield forward, pushing the troop back. Another soldier swung his sword at me. I countered by shooting a blast of energy at the sword.

The force of the blast ripped it from his hand and sent it flying into the air. I immediately called it back to my hand. I swung at him, purposely hitting his armor. Sparks flew and an unnatural zing filled the air. He was pushed back. The soldier that had taken my staff tossed a sword over to him.

They were regrouping and I was overwhelmed. The reinforcements would be reaching us soon.

"Rethinking the non-lethal strategy yet?" ALI asked.

"Shut up and help me!" I exclaimed as I shot a blast of energy at one of the troops from my free hand. He blocked it with his sword, and the energy radiated down to the handle where it was absorbed. This reignited the fighting.

Suddenly, my jetpack detached and flew at the attacker on the right. He was caught off guard, and it hit him in the head, knocking him down. I reached out and summoned his sword to my other hand before it hit the ground. I now began to advance on the remaining three soldiers with both swords in hand.

As I fought, I had a couple of times where I could have dealt a fatal blow, but I refused to take them. The soldiers in back were now catching up, and the soldiers that were knocked out against the doors were waking up.

"Dylan, have you forgotten your training so soon? Trust your power," ALI commanded, "In you is the ability to access the entire power of the star."

I pushed a soldier's sword from me and did as he said. I used my power to lift one soldier off the ground. I held him in mid air and restrained him. The blue waves spread across his body in rope-like bands. He couldn't move.

It took a lot of focus to hold him there, but it took more to fight them all at once. I was quickly able to defeat the remaining two. I saw an opening. I turned to the soldier on my left who was fighting with my staff. He was clearly untrained with a staff. I swung one sword at him, which he blocked, but this opened up a gap. Before he could react I used the other sword to cut into his side, just below his chestplate.

It wouldn't kill him, but it would hurt. He let out a wail in pain, muffled and distorted by his helmet. I yanked the sword out of the wound. He dropped the staff and grabbed his side. I knew once he was over the shock he could still fight, so I finished him off by giving him a gash on his upper thigh and arm. He fell to the ground in anguish.

Now there was just one. I retracted the swords and clipped one on each side of my waste. I then called my staff to my hand. The soldier was running back to meet up with the others. Everyone came together just as a new wave emerged from the bunker.

Now there were too many to count. "Surrender" said one of the soldiers stepping to the front of the group, "Turn yourself over to the Organization and we will release the prisoners you came after."

"What is your call, sir?" asked ALI.

"I'm not done yet." I said, then I spoke where the group could hear me, "Unfortunately, you are in no position to bargain, and I need both."

I pulled the soldier to me that was still suspended in the air. I lifted my staff and jabbed him in the gut at the same moment as I released him. He flew backward through the air about thirty feet.

"You will never succeed at getting the crystal," he called back.

"We'll see." I said.

I ran at the group. His remarks filled me with determination to prove him wrong. Blue energy radiated over my entire body now. They began to fire, but I ignored their blasts. They were absorbed in my energy field before they could hit me.

A group of melee troops ran to meet me. Just before they reached me, I leapt into the air and as I came down I thrust my arm to the ground. When my hand made contact with the pavement, a blue shockwave radiated forward.

The pavement cracked and buckled from the blast. Energy bolts lept in every direction, hitting a few of the troops. All of them were thrust backward and landed in front of the firing squad.

I didn't know I could do that. It was almost instinctual, like fight or flight. The act drained me, but I had to press on. The energy returned to being concentrated at my arms and chest. I assumed that I wouldn't be able to do that again for a while.

I didn't have much time to think about it. I was still being shot at. I held my left arm out and raised a shield.

I held my right hand with the staff in front of me. I ran at the mob. Some of them were drawing their short range weapons, which included both swords and staffs. Before they could get in position to counter, I reached the soldiers and began to take them out one by one.

Troop after troop, I plunged my staff into their chest. I had taken out about half of the firing squad before they had changed over to close combat weapons. This left me with about twenty opponents left.

As I fought, I changed from dealing attacks to blocking them. Because of their numbers, they quickly overwhelmed me. I was surrounded. I couldn't block blows from every direction. Another wave of troops arrived as the bunker doors opened. Just as quickly as the odds had turned in my favor, they turned right back against me. I blew it.

They all pointed their weapons at me. "You're beaten. Surrender, Crystal bearer."

I stopped the power from radiating down my arms. My staff fell to the ground. The clanging haunted me as the consequences of my defeat began to manifest in my mind. Hope was lost. I raised my hands over my head. "Now retract your helmet," A soldier commanded.

I did as he said. A hot tear slipped down my cheek. "Weak!" A soldier yelled. He slapped me across the face and I fell to the ground. I should have been mad, but I was just in shock. I had run through the plan so many times in my mind and not once did I see this outcome. How could I lose? Was God not with me?

"Get up you pathetic..."

"He's not weak." A voice interrupted him.

Another voice spoke up from a different part of the crowd, "Or pathetic."

Another voice, "He is strong."

Another, "Compassionate."

Now all of the soldiers, and myself, were looking around for the people speaking. Their voices were modified by the helmets so they were hard to pinpoint.

An explosion erupted over my head. All of the soldiers ducked down. I looked up to see one go flying over my head as a blue wave of energy spread over his body. Gun fire erupted. I noticed some of the soldiers fighting each other. What was happening?

A soldier walked over. He reached down and grabbed my staff, then lifted me to my feet. He handed it to me, "I think this belongs to you." He retracted his helmet. It was Alex!

My frustration turned to joy! A second chance!

101

"Perfect timing!" I said taking the staff from him. I wrapped him in a hug. I saw a soldier coming at us over his shoulder. I twisted the staff, pointed it at him, and let go. The staff flew at him and he was sent flying backward. "How did you get here?" I asked, pulling away from the hug and catching the staff from the air.

"We got transferred." Alex said, "They knew you were coming so they were rallying all available troops. We knew you would need help, so we made ourselves available."

"Well, you were right! Thanks for coming." I said, "Are all of you here?"

"Well…" we ducked as a soldier was tossed over our heads and hit the door of the bunker, "There's more than that. We got more people on our side. There are about thirty of us here."

"Thirty!" This shocked me, "How did you manage that?"

"It's nearly all of The Taken." Alex said, "They even came without a guarantee for their families. We all decided that there may not be another chance as good as this to stand up to the Organization, and if we didn't take it, we may not have families left anyway."

More soldiers were running from across the river, and coming from the various buildings. I didn't know who was on my side and who wasn't. It was chaos. Plasma blasts were now erupting all across the base. "Did they revolt across the entire thing?" I asked, deflecting a blast with my staff.

"Yes!" Alex answered, shooting a troop to my left, "Should be enough chaos for you to do everything you need to do!"

"Blake?" I called over the coms, "Are you seeing this? Get down here!"

As I spoke, Blake flew down from overhead. "Alex? Long time, no see," Blake said, retracting his helmet.

"Ok, new plan," I said, "Alex, get two of your guys to go with Blake to the cell block. Then, you go with me to the vault to steal the crystal. With all of the chaos going on, it should be quick and easy."

"Sounds like a plan," Alex said. He pressed a button on his vanguard, "Taken 8 and 12, get over here!"

Two soldiers flew over and landed on either side of Alex, "You two go with commander Blake here."

"Oh, I'm not a…"

"You are now!" Alex cut Blake off.

"ALI, get that bunker open," I said.

Chapter 11

The door to the bunker opened revealing a poorly lit elevator. It was very large, the entire length of the bunker. This is how they were able to supply wave after wave of troops.

The elevator began its descent. I could hear explosions as they radiated down from the surface. When this battle was over, I was going to have a serious talk with the Taken about how to preserve lives.

A map appeared in the bottom right of my Heads Up Display. "You two do know where we're going, right?" asked Taken 8.

"We do now." I answered. "ALI just uploaded the schematics to my HUD."

"Who are you in an alliance with?" asked Taken 12.

"No, not *allie*, ALI, 'A', 'L', 'I'. He is an artificial intelligence that helps Blake and I," I explained.

"Oh, interesting." Taken 12 said.

"And now I can help you too." I heard ALI speak over the com channel.

The three Taken began to look around for the source of the noise. "That's ALI," I said, "He talks over the same com channel Blake and I use. I guess he just put you three on here."

"Indeed I did," said ALI, "Now we can all stay in touch."

"Next time, ask me first." I scolded.

"Yes sir."

We finished our conversation just in time for the door to open. In front of us was a long corridor, with hallways and doors branching off on either side. "This place is a labyrinth," Alex said, shaking his head.

"Not for us," I said. A green line appeared on the floor through my HUD and turned right, just up the hall. A blue line was beside it and turned left.

ALI spoke up, "Blue is Blake, green is Dylan."

"Got it," said Blake, "You two, with me."

Blake and the two Taken ran off ahead of us. "We go this way," I said.

We followed the green line (or I followed the line and Alex followed me). We didn't pass any soldiers. I assumed that they were all dealing with the chaos on the surface. After going down a seemingly never ending flight of stairs, we reached a hallway that, at the end, had a red elevator door.

"That will lead directly to the vault," said ALI.

"Perfect," said Alex.

We ran over to the door. Just before I hit the button to call for it, I stopped. Something wasn't right.

"What is it?" asked Alex.

"This. It's too easy," I said, "You messed them up a little, but they knew I was coming. There should be security down here."

"I can scan nothing below this point," said ALI, "I am either being jammed or we are too deep."

"It's a trap." I backed away from the door.

"If you're sure, then what do we do?" asked Alex.

"We spring the trap," I said with a smile, "But on our terms. I'll pry open the doors and we can go down the shaft. We'll surprise them."

I grabbed the doors and forced them apart. I looked down the shaft. It was dark, seemingly bottomless. Rather than cables, there was a track on the back wall for the elevator to run on.

I jumped in and ignited my jetpack. Alex jumped in above me and matched my speed. As we floated down the shaft, I looked at the map. It showed that the shaft was about 300 feet long and led to a very large room. It didn't take us long to reach the bottom.

We landed gently on top of the elevator car. I closed my eyes, quieted my mind, and attempted to sense the room. "What are you doing?" Alex asked quietly.

I broke my concentration to answer him, "I can sense things through a sort of sixth sense. I can sense emotions, thoughts, movement, stuff like that. I am trying to sense what is in the room."

"Oh, Well, what do you see?"

"Give me a second."

I returned to my concentrated state. I couldn't sense anything. Or, more accurately, I sensed nothing, an absence of thought and emotion. "There's no one inside," I concluded, "ALI, would they protect it with some kind of security system instead of using soldiers?"

"As easily as we got down here, not likely." He replied

"I agree," said Alex, "This is not like them. We may have caught them off guard, but they are not sloppy."

"Well, I guess we're going in blind." I said.

I drew one of the atom swords from my waistband. I pressed the button to turn it on. The blade ejected from the hilt, just as fast as my staff could. Once it was fully extended, white energy moved up the shaft. I twisted a small knob to adjust it to my height, and the blade slightly retracted. The energy of these swords was not fluid like other weapons. It was volatile. It leapt up and down the blade, eager for a victim.

I used the light from the blade to find the door on top of the elevator car. It was located right in the middle and had a latch. I used the sword to cut through it. The signature, sharp zinging noise was produced from the cut. The high pitch shrill echoed through the shaft. The cut metal glowed red hot.

I stretched out my hand and used my power to lift the door. "After you," said Alex.

I jumped down into the car. The doors were closed. Alex jumped down and landed beside me. He drew two guns, one from each hip and held them out in front of him.

"Ready when you are."

I grabbed the doors with my power, ready to fling them open.

"Three"

"Two"

"Now" I said, ripping the doors open. We ran out of the elevator into the room. To our surprise, there was no one, not even a security alarm. The room was large. Everything was black: the floor, the walls. Lights hung from the tall ceiling, but did little to light the room. There were multiple stations throughout the gymnasium sized room. They had large monitors and control panels that cast a glow through the dim room.

In the center of the room was a cylindrical column that stretched from the floor to the ceiling. Large cables stretched the entire length of the column. The ceiling, walls, and floor were cut straight from the bedrock. At the base was a large steel door that matched the curvature of the column.

"Well, maybe they really are all on the surface," said Alex.

"I find that very unlikely," said ALI.

"Doesn't matter where they are," I said, "Let's just get the crystal and get out."

"Agreed," said ALI.

We walked over to the door that was on the column. It was made of steel and seemed very thick. Beside it was a control panel that had a retinal scanner.

"How do we get in?" I asked, "I don't think I can blast a hole through that."

"You could if you believed you could," said ALI, "However, your swords should cut through it."

"Why wouldn't they make it out of what the armor is made out of?" I asked as I pierced the blade through the door. There was lots of resistance because it was so thick, but I made slow progress. It made a shrill noise, but ALI caused my helmet to block it out.

"They only just discovered how to make such a metal a few years ago. The one they use is weaker than ours and very hard to form. We use Unitum, who only your father knew how to make. They haven't figured out the formula." ALI answered.

"Interesting," I said, "So we can cut through their weaker version?"

"If you were to swing that sword hard enough, you might," ALI consented, "Their failure to find the proper formula is why Alex's heated up so much when you blasted him."

107

"Yea, I have heard of people's armor being cut through before," Alex added, "but only when the armor was too thin."

I was about halfway through cutting a circle in the door. Then, I sensed something behind me. I yanked the sword out of the door and spun around just in time to catch the sword of some sort of robot.

I knocked it away from hitting Alex and drew my other sword from off my hip. I stabbed it in the mid section. I pulled the sword out but the creature seemed unphased. It began to attack.

It was very strong. I was forced to tap into my power for strength to counter it. It dealt a few smashing blows, but I quickly got the upper hand and sliced it in half. It fell apart and crashed to the ground

Alex and I stood over the robot to examine it. It was a tall, metallic, humanoid figure. Its torso was almost triangular, wide at the top and narrow at the bottom. It had two legs, two arms, and a, rather small, head like structure from which protruded many sensors. The robot had been about seven feet tall when it was standing and was complete with a black paint job.

"ALI, are these the robots you told us about?" I asked.

"Well, I have never seen one, but I would assume so."

Alex spoke up, "I've heard rumors about these. But from what I've heard, there is never just one."

Just then we heard sounds, like heavy footsteps, coming from the other side of the pillar. They were loud, metallic. More robots!

"Wanna weapon other than those guns?" I asked, willing to offer either of my swords or my staff."

"No," Alex declined, "I'll stay ranged, you get close."

"And these are robots, so feel free not to pull your punches." ALI coached.

This was true. I had never been able to fully fight. I was always holding back, trying to preserve life. In a way, this fight might actually be fun, I thought.

We stepped to the side of the pillar to see a multitude of the same robots marching toward us from a large hangar that had opened across the room. None of them seemed to be carrying guns, only staves. They must have been planning to capture us alive.

Alex held up his guns and began to shoot. The robots were quick. Some were able to block the shots with their staff. The entire front row responded by holding their staves out in front of them and activating a shield. This created a wall.

"Wanna take care of that for me?" Alex asked.

"Gladly," I said, retracting my swords and placing them on my hips. I called on the crystal's power. It radiated across my arms and chest. I stretched out my arms. Blue energy surrounded them as I lifted the front row of robots and threw them backward. This removed their shielding and knocked them into the ones behind them.

I fired a powerful blast into the exposed crowd, completely destroying a few robots. I kept firing and so did Alex. We took out quite a few, but then they regained their battle array and raised the shields once again. I charged at the group and drew one sword, so that I would have one hand free to use my power.

When I reached the group, I jerked one robot forward. It deactivated its shield and began to attack. I blocked its initial blow, simultaneously blasting it in the midsection. This left a gaping hole and affected its function. I pushed the robot's staff down and sliced it in half.

I knew that even if they were easy to take out, I could quickly become surrounded. I needed to take out the front row so that Alex could cover me. I used my free hand to deliver a concussive blow to the robots on my left. They stumbled and the two closest to me fell. All together, about five shields went down. Alex shot each one in the head. They were done.

Alex began taking more shots at the rows further back, but they quickly regrouped and raised their shields. I began to slice my way through the front rows. I drew my other sword, needing it to better protect myself, and made quick work of the droids. They never made more than three attacks before I dismantled them. Eventually I found myself in the middle, fighting and defending on every side.

I couldn't keep this up. I needed a concussive blow in every direction to knock them back. I followed ALI's training, envision what I want the power to do. I pulled my arms in, pulling as much power as I could from the crystal. The energy swarmed around me as if it were a cyclone. Then, I thrust my arms outward.

The blue shockwave expanded outward, and tossed the attackers back. This was the most powerful blast I had conjured yet. The robots that had been close to me were scorched and smoking from the energy.

I spun around and sliced through all of the robots closest to me. I was making good progress. Then, they stopped, forming a circle, all of them about ten feet away from me.

Their staffs retracted into their arms and were replaced with swords. On their free arm, a red shield radiated in a flat circle.

"I guess they're done with the non-lethal strategy," I said to myself.

They pulled their arm with the shield in front of them and raised the sword over it, pointing it at me. I spun the sword in my left hand around to a reverse grip, as to cover every side.

There was now a group, no longer focused on me, and headed toward Alex. I need to fall back to help him. All at once, the robots surrounding me lunged forward. I had just enough time to activate my jetpack. It ignited and I burst into the air, just escaping the attack.

I flew back and landed beside Alex, who was walking backward as he shot at the approaching robots. Their shield covered their head and midsection, so he was unable to get a good shot.

"Here," I handed him one of the shields, "keep working on getting the crystal and I'll take care of them."

"On it!" He said.

We were now standing just in front of the vault. Alex ran around to the back and began to work. I moved forward and began my attack. With every second, they seemed to get better, almost as if they could predict my moves.

"We have a problem," said ALI.

"What is it?" I asked, as I sliced through a robot's leg, then, when he fell, his head.

"They are analyzing your strategy, using your own moves against you," ALI explained, "The longer you fight them, the better they get."

"Oh, great!" I said sarcastically.

I continued to fight. I could see now that only about half of the group was left from what there had originally been. The ones I had left behind were now catching up to the group that I was fighting. I drew my staff from my side, twisted it, and sent it flying into the robots further back. They were quite heavy, so the blast only made them stumble.

I caught my staff upon its return, but spun with its momentum and threw it back at them. I continued to fight the robots closest to me, I was being pushed back.

As I was forced closer to the column, I saw one try to slip around back to Alex. I noticed my staff returning to me. Instead of catching it, I used my power to push it toward the robot. It hit it in the center of the back. The blue energy erupted from the tip and sparks flew from the robot as it was thrown forward.

I let the staff fall to the ground in order to focus on the robots closest to me. I used a blast to push the robots back again. I noticed that the robots in the back were running toward me, but passing under a large rock in the cave-like ceiling. I grabbed hold of it with my power and dislodged it from the rock ceiling. It crashed down on top of them, crushing them and the control stations nearby.

At this point, I was merely able to block their advances. There were too many of them and they were getting too skilled. Just as my back was almost against the column, I heard Blake over the coms, "Need some help?"

Before I could process this, I saw a sword go flying past me, slicing the head off of the robot that was closest to me. I turned in the direction that it came from to see Blake, sword in hand, running at the group. He joined the fight.

"Why are you here?" I asked almost angrily, "You were supposed to be getting your family out."

"I did," he replied, "They're already headed back to Tullahoma."

"Alone?"

"No. They are on a transport with the two Taken that helped me, and I had two other pilots escort them in fighters," Blake looked over at me, "I told you I wasn't leaving until you did."

"Thank God!" I breathed. A wave of relief washed over me. No matter what happened from here, the mission was a success. Everything we did now was just a bonus.

111

"Are there gonna be any jets left for us?" I asked.

"The Taken are holding the airfield," Blake said, as he sliced through a robot, "We're not just taking a jet, we're taking the whole fleet."

"Sounds like you've been busy," Alex said over the coms.

"Yea, well, now I'm ready to call it a day," Blake said, "They can't hold it for much longer."

There was a loud crash behind us.

"Well, you're in luck. I just got into the vault," Alex said as I sliced through the final robot.

"Let's hope that was the last of them." I sighed.

Blake and I walked around to the vault. In the door was a large circular hole that Alex had cut out. The metal was still red hot. I ducked down to look inside. The room was filled with a red glow coming from a part of a smaller column in the center of the room.

I backed up and took a running dive into the room, clearing the hot metal of the hole and the piece of the door on the other side. I stood up. Around the center column were massive cables that spanned to the ceiling, which was very low, and disappeared to the other side. I assumed it was part of the cables that we saw on the outside.

Rather than look for the off switch, I charged up my power and blasted the column where the glow was coming from. Red energy erupted out and threw me against a control board behind me on the wall.

"You good?" Blake called.

"Yea," I groaned, getting back down, "I'm fine."

I noticed that the glow was much less intense now. The room was almost dark. Still, there was a small red light, coming from the new hole in the column. I walked closer and looked in. Floating in the middle of the housing unit was a small red crystal.

112

Chapter 12

The crystal was surrounded by a dim red energy field, much like the blue one that would surround my crystal. I reached through the opening to grab it. "Stop!" ALI called, but it was too late. I had already taken hold of it.

Blue energy from my crystal ran across my chest, down my arm, and to the red crystal. The energy surrounded it and turned purple then, red as it was absorbed into the crystal. The energy was being ripped from me. The pain was unexplainably excruciating.

I wailed. The crystal was drawing me in. It was difficult to let go, but finally I yanked my hand away. "Dylan! What happened?" Blake called.

"The crystal was draining his power," ALI answered for me, "There is a reason we call it the parasite."

"Are you okay?" Alex asked.

"Yea, I'm fine." I answered, rubbing my hand, "One of you, come in here and get it."

Blake answered by diving through the hole. I used my power to keep him from hitting the ground and lifted him to his feet. He walked over to the opening and reached in.

"Are we sure this is safe?" he asked before grabbing hold of the crystal.

"For you, yes." ALI answered.

He reluctantly gripped the crystal and pulled it out. He let out a sigh of relief. "What do I do with it?" Blake asked.

An opening formed on the chest of his suit, just like the one that held my crystal. "You can keep it there for now," ALI said.

Blake placed the crystal in the opening and we exited the vault. "Let's get outta here!" Alex said.

Blake and I seconded the motion. We ran over to the elevator shaft. The doors were still open as was the hatch. We flew, one by one, through the top and up the shaft. Then we ran up the various hallways and stairs on our way back to the surface until we made it to the bunker elevator that led to the top.

The base seemed deserted. It seemed strange at first, but then I realized that The Taken were brought in as back-up. The base was short staffed because their soldiers turned against them.

Blake pressed the button on the elevator to call for it, and the doors opened. We got in and began our ride up. The closer we got to the surface, the more violently explosions shook the elevator.

"Sounds like they're still putting up a fight," I said.

"Well, they won't be for long," Alex sighed, "The Organization's reinforcements will be arriving soon. We need to get out of here."

The doors opened. The base was in ruins. The buildings were crumbling. Smoke could be seen coming from many of the anti-aircraft cannons. To our right, across the river, the Taken and the other soldiers were in a brawl for control of the airfield. It was hard to tell who had control because everyone wore the same uniform, but Alex confirmed that The Taken were currently on top.

"We need a jet." I said.

"I was able to gain access to the network once the first chip was placed. We can steal whatever we can get our hands on and they won't be able to track us." ALI informed us.

"ALI," I said, "Open up a secure channel to The Taken." The coms turned on in response. I addressed them, "All Taken soldiers, the aircraft are under our control, steal as many as you can and make for Tullahoma."

Alex, Blake, and I ran to the airfield. ALI aided me by identifying the soldiers who were on our side through the HUD. I noticed that everyone on the bridge was against us. I shot a blast of energy to the center support of the bridge. It collapsed and sent about five soldiers into the rapids of the river below.

The three of us jetted over the water and began to fight our way to an aircraft. Many were beginning to lift off. There was a steady exodus from the airfield.

"That one!" I said, pointing to a unique, mid size aircraft. It was smaller than the troop transports, but larger than a fighter jet. It was solid black. Its wings were folded to point straight up and hinged near the top of the ship. They were adorned with missiles and guns. The ship had a dual cockpit and room in the back for passengers. It was heavily armored and heavily armed.

"The drop ship? Perfect!" Exclaimed Alex as he fought a soldier.

There were hundreds of soldiers in the airfield, but because they were spread so thin, only five were blocking my path. I drew my staff, summoned my power, and charged at them.

When I was close, I used my power to create a concussive blast toward the legs of two soldiers, knocking them down. The remaining three started their attack. I caught one's sword with my staff, pushed it away, and jabbed one of the soldiers on the ground, who was trying to get back up. A blast came from behind me. I sensed that it was headed for the other troop on the ground.

I moved my staff to block it, then blocked the advance of another soldier. He pushed down on my staff, but I redirected the force onto the soldier who I had saved, knocking him out completely. I then pointed the staff to the ground, causing the sword to slide off. I quickly swung my staff, trying to catch him while he was off balance, but another soldier blocked the blow while he jabbed his sword at me.

I dodged and countered by removing one hand from my staff and blasting one in the chest. He was thrust backward. The two remaining soldiers quickly continued to attack. I blocked one's blow with a shield just above my hand. As he pulled back for another swing, I saw my opening. I jabbed him in the abdomen and he was blown backward, as a blue wave of energy spread across his body.

There was just one left standing. He stepped back and waited for me to attack first. I was able to use both ends of the staff to deliver lots of hits, one after the other. Since he only had one sword, it was hard for him to keep up. Finally, I got him off balance. I gripped one end of the staff, swung it over my head, and struck him across the face. This caused a few pieces of his helmet to fly off, and he collapsed on the ground.

I jabbed my staff down on his chest plate. The blue energy dispersed across the ground and cracked the pavement. Then, I threw the staff to hit the soldier who I had blasted earlier. He was trying to run from me, but the staff hit him in the back, knocking him into one of the jets. I called the staff to my hand, retracted it, and ran over to the drop ship.

ALI directed my attention to a button on the side of the ship. A panel opened in front of me to the interior of the plane. Seats lined the walls, and in front, there was an opening to the cockpit. Blake ran up behind me and jumped into the ship.

"Where's Alex?" I asked.

"He's over there," Blake answered, pointing across the airfield.

Alex was climbing into the cockpit of one of the "U" shaped craft.

"What are you doing?" I asked over the coms.

"You said to steal as many ships as we could," Alex answered, "I'll meet you in Tullahoma."

Alex lifted off, then Blake and I got in the Dropship. We rushed to the cockpit. There were two chairs. We each took one. There was a control board in front of us, but rather than physical buttons and switches, it was a large screen with system stats, dials, and buttons. It might as well have been in another language. I didn't know how to read it.

In front of each chair, there was a joystick, with a button on the top and front. "ALI, how do we fly this thing?" I asked.

"I will teach you later," he huffed. A chip protruded from my vanguard, "Just let me take care of this."

I took the chip and stuck it to the control panel. The ship's engines started, and a blue shimmer rushed across the windshield as the shields were brought online. Symbols and lights flickered across the screen, and a holographic targeting system projected in front of us.

We began to take off. As we did, the ship turned toward the steady stream of ships lifting off. Once above the mountains, they quickly darted off toward the rising sun on the horizon.

As we were flying up to get above the mountains and speed off, I saw an orange flash out of the corner of my eye. The ship in front of us then burst into flames and fell to the ground.

I looked out of the drop ship to see the soldiers of the base, lined up, with rocket launchers. The ship Alex was in turned around and dove toward the attackers, firing at them from the gun under the cockpit.

They fired back, but he was able to dodge the shots. Still, they managed to hit a few more jets off in the distance. About five had turned back to help cover for the others to escape. ALI began to circle the airfield, firing down on them as well, but still following my instructions not to kill anyone. He always hit just to the side of them- close enough to knock them down or knock them out.

I noticed, on the ground, a shadow began to stretch across the base. At first, I thought it was a cloud passing by, but I noticed geometric shapes.

I looked to the horizon. Coming over the mountain, passing in front of the sun, was a massive, flying ship. The hull was curved and ovular, but mostly flat on top. Protruding from the hull were two triangular wings that dwindled down and ended about three quarters of the way up the hull, making the ship broad in the back and narrow in the front. On the back of the ship were four massive engines, two on each wing.

Covering the entire ship were small cannons like the ones that had populated the base before our attack. On the belly of the ship were small yellow flames: small engines, keeping the ship steady. On the nose of the ship was a large glass panel, from where I assumed they controlled the ship.

"Get out of here!" Alex commanded over the coms.

"No," said Blake, "We need to stay and help. We still have people down there."

"I'll wait on them. You two have to go," Alex commanded, "You are the spark that started this. If you die, they won't have anyone to rally behind. You have to live! You have to go!"

"I agree," said ALI.

The ship rose above the mountain and began to pick up speed.

"We can't just leave Alex to die," I said, not realizing the com channel was still open.

"I'll be fine," Alex assured me, "I'll meet you in Tullahoma with everyone else."

We were now flying above the massive ship. I could see that on the top of the ship were bays, from which fighters were launching. There were the more advanced, "U" shaped fighters that we had seen on the base. They were fast, but they weren't chasing us.

They swarmed on the base like bees from a disturbed hive. They opened fire. Orange blasts came from the front under the cockpit, firing on both the Taken still on the ground, and the ones in stolen ships.

118

They were after Alex. He was a good pilot, but they were overwhelming him.

"ALI, do something!" Blake said.

"One second, I've almost got it." ALI answered vaguely.

Orange blasts began to rain down on us from the massive ship. Our, tiny in comparison ship, rocked violently as the shields tried to hold off the shots. We dipped and wove, but ALI kept us in the general area.

"ALI, now or never!" I said.

"Now," he replied.

Instantly, all of the plasma fire ceased. I looked back to the base and saw that there were no more blasts coming from the enemy, only the friendlies still had weapons.

"Alex," ALI spoke over the coms, "I suggest you leave. All enemy systems are offline, but it won't last long. There is nothing you can do now but flee."

"Yes, Alex, get back now!" I said.

"Fine," he said, pulling away from the base.

"Thank you," I said. I don't want to leave anyone either, but its either their lives, or their lives and our lives. We can't fight that ship."

"If we can't fight it, then there's no sense in fleeing," Alex growled, "They have plenty more of those, and that one is small in comparison."

"We can't fight it alone," I said. There was a part of the plan, my plan, that I had not revealed yet. I wanted to focus on saving the Vales first, "ALI, I need you to plot a new course."

"Where to sir?" ALI asked, compliantly.

"No, hold on," Blake said, "What are you talking about? You have friends I don't know about?"

"No, but I was hoping I could make some," I said, "I want to go to D.C. If I warn the president about The Organization, we may be able to prepare America, or even the world, to fight them."

"You've seen their technology," Alex doubted, "Nobody has anything even close to that."

"Not that we know of," I pointed out, "and, if we have enough time, we could equip them with what we have, show them how to make it."

"There's not enough time," Alex said, "That massive ship back there is proof. They have never used a cruiser openly before. They're already taking over and America has to know that thing is in their airspace."

"No, The Organization is deeply rooted in the government," ALI chimed in, "I doubt anyone in D.C. knows."

"I think it's worth a shot." Blake said.

"I agree." said ALI

"If that's true, then I do too," Alex conceded, "A slim chance is better than no chance, and we can't take them on alone."

"Then I suggest Blake and I go to Washington while you rally The Taken at Tullahoma. You may be able to convince more to join you."

"Yes, I only was able to reach out to the Taken in North America, and the only ones you saw today are the ones who transferred to the Montana base," Blake said, sounding more hopeful, "There may be hundreds more that revolted today that we don't know about. The day is just getting started."

I only just now realized that the attack, though it felt like an eternity, had really only taken about thirty minutes. If Alex really had been able to call more Taken to our cause, the reports would likely not be in yet.

"Then it's settled. ALI, take us to Washington, D.C." I said, "Alex, we'll see you in Tullahoma."

"Yes, Sir," Alex said as we veered from his course.

"ALI, What keeps the Organization from following us?" Blake asked. It was a valid question. Could they not just over run Tullahoma and take us all out?

"They have not yet taken control of the world, or even the country for that matter," ALI answered, "Though they must do so quickly, in order to prevent anarchy and chaos, they must do so strategically.

They can't just fly over the country. It would raise suspicion. It could start the war prematurely. One wrong move and all of the countries of the world are firing nukes at them. What good is taking over the world, if there is no world left."

Blake said, "If that's the case, what keeps us from being detected by the U.S and them declaring war on the wrong people?"

"Well, we are flying over only rural areas until we reach Washington," ALI replied, "Also, this ship is equipped with stealth technology. We are high enough that most people won't see us, the ship flies silently, and we are invisible to radar. We won't be seen until we are landing on the Whitehouse lawn."

"And when will that be?" I asked, ready to get some help.

"Three hours. Now is a good time to get some sleep." ALI suggested.

Blake and I both liked that idea. We left the cockpit and made our pads in the back, where the seats were. I laid back, wanting to drift off to sleep, but I found myself replaying the events of the morning in my head.

I knew that there was still a lot of fighting ahead of us, but I couldn't help but feel anything other than relieved. Blake was safe. We stole the red crystal. The Vales were safe, though I hadn't got to see them. I wanted to ask more about their condition, but it looked as though Blake had already drifted off. I didn't want to wake him.

The reality of other Taken being on our side was only now setting in. Alex had said back at the base that nearly all of the taken had responded. I assumed that meant the thirty or so that were there. He must have meant more. Could other bases be going through what we did this morning? If they all stole equipment like we did, and if they all followed Alex, Tullahoma may be a fortress by the time we get back. That was what I imagined anyway.

I was just beginning to feel my eyes grow heavy when ALI called, "Dylan, get up here. You to Blake."

I sat up, but Blake jolted awake, ready for a fight. He quickly composed himself, realizing there was no danger.

"What is it ALI?" I asked, slightly aggravated that I didn't get to sleep.

"The organization just broke through the encryption that I used on their systems, but when they did, it gave me access to all of their active missions. There are about ten going on to clean up bases that The Taken ransacked."

"Ten bases?" Blake jumped in.

"That was more than I imagined," I said.

"Yes, but that is not what I called you for," ALI continued, "They are conducting a mission in Missouri to capture another Crystal bearer."

"What? There's another one?" I asked.

"Yes, She just got her powers. This is a crystal nobody knew about. It's white. It seems they got a tip about the whereabouts of a new crystal, but when they got there, they found her. It says she engaged their first operatives and they are sending in another group."

"She killed them?" I asked, wanting to see how much of a threat she could be.

"No, more like, chased them off," ALI said, "I have the body cam video here.

The dials and stats of the dashboard went away and a video began to play. It was quite low quality. I couldn't tell much about the background because it was dark. In the center of the screen was a table, maybe in a basement. On it were vials of chemicals, a laptop, and an odd looking cube. It was golden and looked ancient. Maybe an artifact of some sort.

There was a noise in the background: a door opening. The camera turned revealing a figure. A girl, seemingly mine and Blake's age, with long blond hair. She wore a light blue, silky, long sleeve shirt, and an athletic skirt. The soldier's gun was drawn. He fired. An orange bold lit up the screen, but the girl was holding up a pulsating, white shield.

He fired a few more times, but realized that wasn't working. He holstered his gun and drew an atom sword. The girl lowered her shield. The white energy flowed elegantly across her arms. The energy condensed at her hands. She shot a few blasts at him. He dodged, while running at her.

The camera was now shaking violently. It was hard to tell what was going on, especially since her powers and the sword were both white. She must have hit him out of the room because the next clear shot was of a ceiling fan in a living room.

It wasn't long before he scrambled to his feet. He turned back to the room he had come from. The girl was standing in the doorway. Her entire body was now surrounded with a white glow and the energy radiated all around her. She held her hand out in front of her and a white crystal flew from somewhere off screen, to her hand. The glow intensified around the hand holding the crystal.

The soldier turned and fled. Then, the video ended. "They are sending a group of special forces. Their objective is to kill the girl and take the crystal."

"They aren't worried about learning, because we stole the red crystal." I said somberly.

"That would be my guess." ALI agreed.

"Then we have to help her," I said, "Not only is it the right thing to do, but it's also our fault that they want to kill her. Plus, we could use another crystal bearer on our side."

"Do we know when the next soldiers are arriving?" Blake asked in agreement.

"If we change our course right now, we will get there two minutes behind them." ALI said.

"Then change course immediately," I commanded.

Chapter 13

We didn't fly for long before we came to a small subdivision. ALI told us we were about an hour south of St Louis. We considered landing outside the town, but it was too late to be discreet.

Three Organization drop ships, identical to ours, flew in while we were still a ways off from the town. They flew and hovered over one house, surrounding it. They were becoming more bold, they weren't trying to hide. Perhaps we had made them desperate. Or... maybe we just made them angry.

It was just me and Blake this time. There would be no Taken to assist us in this fight. We were now very close to the other ships, but ALI used some sort of forged code to tell them that we were reinforcements for the mission. Blake and I moved to the back of the ship, opened the door, and prepared to exit.

"ALI, You keep the ship in the air," I commanded, "See if you can take down those drop ships."

"Yes, Sir"

As we spoke, a white blast of energy shot from the yard of the two story, brick house they had surrounded. There was a tall, wooden fence blocking my view of the source. The energy hit one of the drop ships on the wing, pushing it back, but their shields held up.

A missile lowered from the same wing, aiming at the house from where the shot came. "No you don't!" I cried, leaping through the open door of our drop ship. Just as the missile released, I blasted it with a bolt of my blue energy. It exploded right next to the ship, damaging the wing and one of the engines, which sat below the wing and behind the door.

Smoke poured from the engine and the ship spun to the ground, landing in the middle of the road. The road quickly gave way to the weight of the ship, crumbling as the ship slid across it.

My jetpack ignited, my helmet formed around my head, and I flew over to where I saw the energy come from. There were now about ten soldiers flying to the ground from each drop ship still in the sky. Both ships turned and started firing at ALI, who flew off. The ships followed.

I sensed Blake flying behind me. "I'm going for the girl," I said, "You go for the downed ship and keep them from getting to us."

"Got it"

Blake changed his flight path, going toward the crash site. I continued on. More blasts of energy came from behind the fence, taking out soldiers on their way down. They opened fire. I could see the white glow of her shield over the fence.

I cleared the fence. I finally laid eyes on the girl from the video. She lowered her shield and began to fight the soldiers. She was quite skilled in using her powers, but not coordinated in her fighting. There were too many of them for her. I drew my staff and flew down beside her.

I jabbed one soldier, who was coming at her from behind with an atom sword, which sent him flying into the wall of the house. Soldiers were coming from every direction so we stood back to back. "I'm here to help you," I said.

She said nothing, and continued to fight. I had landed just as the soldiers were nearing her, so I conjured a powerful concussive blast. I thrust both of my fists forward. The blast rippled through the air and knocked all of the soldiers back.

I sensed the soldiers drawing close to the girl, so I spun around to help her. I threw my staff, hitting one soldier in the back of the group. I used my power to blast the soldier closest to the girl in the chest. Then, I drew my staff back to my hand. As soon as it returned, I used it to catch the sword of another attacker.

As I held his sword up, I fired behind him, hitting a soldier who was firing orange blasts at us. I continued to fight the soldier who was attacking. The girl shot a blast of energy behind me and at another soldier using a gun. The white energy arced across his body, much like electricity, then he fell to the ground.

I was able to get the upper hand on the soldier that I was fighting, and jabbed him in the upper thigh. This blew his feet out from under him, and his head was smashed into the ground. It was a good thing he had on a helmet.

I continued to fight and was able to take down two more soldiers. The girl also took out two more. I sensed the soldiers behind us getting up and re-grouping. Before they could finish helping one another to their feet, one of the jets came crashing down toward them. I knew when they got up that there would be too many of them, but I couldn't just let them die.

I summoned another concussive blow, knocking the soldiers closest to me back. I left the rest to the girl. Then, I turned and grabbed hold of the falling ship with my powers. It usually would not have been too heavy for me, but it was moving very fast.

The radiating blue energy around my arms and chest intensified until it covered my torso and legs also. The blue energy surrounded the ship as I tried to slow it down. The two soldiers who were left behind me were still attacking, but the girl held them off well. They blocked her shots with shields that radiated from their staff, but they were pinned down.

It took all of my focus, but finally, the ship stopped just a few feet above the ground, forcing all of the soldiers who were standing to dive back to the ground, most of them scrambling to get away from it.

I summoned more strength, then tossed it over to the side. It crashed through the picket fence and into the neighbor's yard. As I did this, the girl had finally built up the courage to charge the cowering soldiers, and took them out in the same manner as she had the rest.

Her powers seemed more electrical than mine. My powers moved in fluid, plasmatic patterns. Her powers moved in elegant, yet geometric patterns: bolts and arcs. She seemed to stun those who she hit with her bolts of energy, rather than cause any real damage.

She turned around and walked up beside me. We both prepared to fight the remaining soldiers. They all stood with their weapons drawn, but didn't attack. Some looked at each other through their helmets. I assumed they were talking over their coms.

The girl charged up her powers and began to step forward, but I held my hand out in front of her. She stopped and looked at me, "What are you doing?"

"Trying to see what they're doing," I replied, "There's no need to fight if they aren't."

An explosion rang out. Everyone looked in that direction. ALI had shot down the other ship. He must have hit it broadside, because it fell in two pieces, both landing in an open field outside the subdivision. Two parachutes opened near the explosion as the pilots floated to safety.

One of the troops lowered his helmet, "We surrender." He threw his sword to the ground, then unclipped his utility belt, and threw it in front of him as well.

126

The rest followed suit, throwing their weapons down and retracting their helmets. Blake walked up behind them having dealt with the other soldiers at the downed ship. He held his weapon ready, skeptical of their surrender.

"Just let us take the girl and anyone she feels should come with her, then you are free to go," I said.

The girl turned and scowled at me. I could sense her unease at what I had said. I needed her to be patient until I could explain myself, "I'm not taking you," I assured her. I didn't want her to think that I was just there to abduct her or something, "I'll explain myself after we deal with them."

I looked back to the soldiers, "You're not taking us hostage?" the speaker asked, confused.

"I have no need for you in a cell," I said, "You can take off all of your gear, walk outside of town, and wait for The Organization to pick you up."

They did as I said. They stripped themselves of all of their tactical gear until they were down to their tight fitting pants and T-shirt. As they did, ALI flew over to us and hovered the ship at a safe distance, in case anyone decided to turn and fight. No one did.

Once their armor was off, I could tell that they were all young men. They weren't quite as young as the Taken, but still likely in their early twenties. I had questions I wanted to ask them, but I feared that I didn't have time to hear the answers.

As they walked off, one soldier began to walk over to the girl and I. I didn't let him get too close before calling, "That's far enough."

I pointed my staff at him with my right hand, and summoned my power to my left.

He held up his hands in surrender, "I just wanted to thank you...for saving us, all of us." He looked at the unconscious soldiers. He wasn't just talking about saving them from the jet; he was talking about saving the others by not killing them.

I was put a bit off guard by their humanity. This Organization may have been run by evil people, but these soldiers were just...regular people. "I don't wish death on anyone"

He nodded his head in thanks and walked back to the rest. Once they were a little ways off, Blake joined the girl and I, and ALI landed the drop ship in the road. The town had seemed deserted when we first arrived, but I could see some people looking out their windows to see if it was over.

"I guess I should introduce myself," I said, retracting my helmet and looking at the girl, "I'm Dylan, this is Blake. We came to save you from The Organization, and give you and your family a safer place to stay."

In all honesty, home wasn't even that safe of a place. But it was safer than her being here alone. At least with The Taken back home, there would be more people to help protect her.

"I'm Bailey," she said reluctantly, "how do I know that you're not just here to take me like they were."

"Well, for one, we just saved your life," Blake said, irritated that our heroic gesture didn't win her over.

"And also because they weren't here to take you," I said, "They were here to kill you and take your crystal."

"And you don't want the same?" she asked.

"No," I said, "If we wanted that we would have let them do it. If you care about your life and your family, you'll come with us. Those people that just attacked you are a part of an organization that is about to declare war on the world, and if they get your crystal, they'll most definitely win."

I didn't get to finish convincing her. A woman ran out of the house, hysterical. "Bailey! Oh! Bailey!" She ran up to her, crying, and attacked her with a hug.

Bailey hugged her back, clearly not nearly as distraught as the woman. The woman wore a long jean skirt and a red shirt with flowy sleeves. "Oh, Oh! I thought they were going to kill you! And you fought them… and Oh!" she paused for a moment, composing herself, "Who are these people?"

Bailey pushed her away, "These people saved me," she said, "They say they came to take us somewhere safe. Dylan, Blake, this is my Mom."

"It's nice to meet you," I really wanted to be more polite, but there was no time, "Now, you have to come with us. You can bring whoever you want, but we have to go right now, or their reinforcements will be here."

128

Bailey looked at her mom, then at me. I saw a bit of energy flow across her arm. Her eyes squinted looking deep into mine. I stood in anxious silence. Bailey's expression changed after a moment. Her mistrusting glare softened. Then, she looked back at her mom, "I think we should go with them."

My convincing must have worked after all.

"I'm not so sure that I just want to go with some strange teenagers," she replied.

"It's either go with the strange teenagers or go with the evil organization where you'll die," Blake said bluntly. I cut my eyes at him. He just shrugged his shoulders to say, "What? It's the truth."

"I think we should listen to them," Bailey said, "At least they aren't trying to kill us."

"Well… I guess you're right." She conceded.

"Great!" I said, "Who else needs to go? You need to bring anyone who you are close to."

"Just me and my Mom," Bailey said, not somberly, but in a way that was so blunt it commanded that the subject change.

"They will even go after your close friends," Blake said, not picking up on it, "anyone they can use as leverage."

"Well, lucky for us, I don't have any," Bailey said sharply, "Now, if you're taking us somewhere, then let's get there."

I wanted to press, to make sure there really was no one, but I didn't want to upset either of them further. I just had to take her word.

"Okay, then let's go."

The two went into the house to fill a sack with personal effects and clothes, and returned in less than two minutes. I had told them to hurry. ALI was tracking five incoming dropships, eleven minutes out.

We all ran over to our drop ship and got on board. ALI took off, getting us as far as possible from the new troops.

"Plot a new course for D.C." I commanded ALI as I sat down in one of the pilot chairs next to Blake.

"Yes sir."

Bailey and her mom were sitting in the seats in the body of the plane. They each sat on opposite sides.

"You work for the government?" Bailey asked.

"No" I replied

"Then why are we going to Washington?"

"We are going to warn the president about the plans of The Organization."

"How does the government not know about them if they are big enough to wage war on the world?" Bailey's mom asked.

"The Organization works its way into the foundations of world powers," I explained, "They pull funding and other resources, but go undetected because of a few people they have on the inside."

"And how do we know that the president isn't one of those people?" Bailey asked

"We don't," Blake answered.

"We can only pray that he isn't," I said, "If we can't get the military on our side, then the war is all but lost before it even starts."

"You don't have a back-up plan?" Bailey asked.

"No," I said, hanging my head, "Warning the world is our only hope."

We flew for a while. The ride was mostly silent. It was probably a breach of privacy, but I took the time to look into Bailey's mind. I sensed fear, confusion, hostility and pain. I wandered to the origins of her power, how she got the crystal. She looked quite resolved on the outside, but after looking in I saw that it was just a front. She was in turmoil. Something terrible must have happened. What I sensed could not possibly be caused by what I witnessed today, but I didn't have the ability to see thoughts, only emotions.

She was quite skilled, though not as potent as Blake and I. She had to either be trained or have had her powers for a while. I decided that wasn't a very invasive question, so I walked over and sat beside her., "So, Bailey, how long have you had your powers."

"About a month," she answered.

I hoped she would offer more information, but she didn't. I decided to compliment her, rather than pry for information, "You're pretty good with your powers. I'm sure ALI could help you hone in on your skills. He's the one who taught me. He's a pretty good teacher."

"He is, is he?"

"Yea, He taught me everything I know about them in about a week."

"Really?" She seemed more interested now.

"Well, I did do martial arts for, well, all my life really, but everything I know about my crystal, my powers, and the Organization I learned in one week."

"There must not be much to know," She said with a smirk.

"Well, it's definitely not that," I smiled, "I just had to know."

"And why is that?"

"I had to save my family from an Organization base. Did that this morning actually. That's how we found you."

The ship jerked. Everyone was jolted. "ALI, What's going on?" I said.

There was no response, "ALI!"

I dashed to the cockpit. Blake was pounding the dashboard, "It just turned off!" He said.

The nose of the plane was tilting more and more toward the ground. I pulled up on the joystick, but it was loose.

"I'm really wishing I had taken that flying lesson from ALI right about now," I said, scrambling to find anything that could save us.

I looked under the dashboard and found a lever that was labeled "manual flight". I pulled it. The plane jerked like something hit us from behind. I looked out of the cockpit window and tried to see the back of the ship. I noticed that the wings were now wider and longer. I tried pulling the joystick upward again. There was quite a bit of resistance now, and the nose of the plane turned up.

131

We were now flying with a ridgeline on each side of us and were still gaining speed. "Everyone get harnessed in!" I yelled.

There were large buckles on the back of each chair in the cockpit and large pull bars sat above each seat in the hull. Everyone buckled in and prepared for a rough landing.

"I found a button!" Blake called.

"What kind?" I was answered with a sharp jolt forward.

"A parachute." he said.

It was actually a drag chute. It was slowing us down, but it was still going to be a hard landing.

"Bailey, help me make a shield around the ship!" I called behind me.

I tried to summon my powers. The crystal on my chest glowed in response to the command, but nothing else happened. "They aren't working!" She said, I could tell she was crying.

We were now cutting through the trees. "Jesus help us" I prayed. We broke through to a clearing, then made contact with the ground. I was jared forward, then everything went dark.

Chapter 14

My eyes opened. Light poured in, but everything was just one big blur. I took a second, blinking and rubbing my eyes. White light gave way to color, then blurred images, then, finally, my vision returned.

The windshield had been busted, but not shattered. The nose of the ship was facing the ground. The fancy dashboard was shattered. Electronics hung from just about everywhere, having been jared from their proper places.

As soon as I had my senses about me, I looked over to Blake. He was still strapped into his chair, just as I was. Between He and I, a large section of tree had penetrated the hull of the ship. It looked to be more on his side.

I unclipped myself from my seat and stumbled over to him. I could immediately see that a fragment of the tree had pierced his thigh, on the back side of his leg, above his knee and protruding on the top of his upper thigh.

"Oh, God!" Panic almost got the better of me, but I managed to keep myself calm by reminding myself that it had missed everything vital. I used my strength to snap the branch from the tree, freeing his leg. Then, I unclipped him from the seat and carried him to the back where Bailey and her mom were.

They appeared to have both fared well. Bailey's mom was still out, but Bailey was coming too. I laid Blake down on his back. I was more worried about him than them at the moment. It looked like the tree had a lot of the bleeding stopped up. I knew it would have to be removed, but right now it was doing him a favor by being in there.

"Is he okay?" Bailey asked while removing her straps.

"Could be better," I said. I was trying to think of what to do. I had no idea how to doctor him. Bailey was walking over to her mom. I guess she could see Blake over my shoulder.

"That looks bad," she said, "It's close to his Femoral Artery. Don't touch it. My Mom's a nurse. She can help."

Bailey gently patted her mom's cheek, trying to rouse her. Eventually, she came around. "Are you okay Mom?" Bailey asked.

"Yes... what happened."

"I don't know, but one of these boys needs your help. He's got some debris stuck through his leg."

Bailey undid the straps and helped her mom over to me. I knew to hold pressure on a wound, but I didn't know about one with something still in it. I was just awkwardly, half holding the wound, as if it would make a difference.

Bailey's mom politely pushed me aside and went straight to work examining the wound. She pressed his leg in a few spots then said, "We are lucky it was a thinner branch. I think it missed his main arteries and may have slipped past the bone without breaking it. We are looking at only slight nerve damage, so long as we can get him some help."

I rushed back to the cockpit. There weren't any lights on. Everything looked dead. I tried nodding my head to call for my helmet. When that didn't work, I pressed the button on my collar that was supposed to do the same thing. Still no response. I was beginning to get suspicious.

I drew my staff from my side and jolted it down. It extended, but no blue energy came from the tips. I attempted to retract it. Nothing. I pressed the button on my sword. Nothing. I called for ALI. Nothing. I called for my powers. Nothing.

I walked back to the others. "Everything's dead," I said, "I mean everything. Even my powers aren't working. I think something is messing with them."

Bailey held up her hand and tried to call her powers. They didn't come, but I noticed her Crystal began to glow brighter as if the energy was still being drawn from it. Seeing this, I attempted to draw my powers again. I noticed the same thing with mine. The energy was still coming from the crystal, but where was it going?

"I can't get my powers to work either," Bailey sighed.

"I'm going to take a look around outside," I said.

I walked to the door of the ship. Since the power was out, I had to force it open. I walked outside. The ship had come to rest in a clearing in front of a small natural lake. Behind it, there was a clear path of destruction and debris from our crash. The tops of trees were missing, bits of the ship were left behind, and the top layer of soil was stripped from the ground where the ship had skidded to a stop.

134

I walked to the front of the ship. The nose was crunched in, but likely saved both Blake and I. I looked out over the lake. We had landed in a winding valley. Mountains seemed to be on every side. The closest mountain was to our left.

As my gaze looked up the mountain, I noticed paths in the trees. It looked like other older crash sites. This piqued my interest. I climbed up on top of the ship and began to scan the surrounding area. There were no other mountains with the same pattern. Only to one closest to us.

I peered further down the valley. It turned, and in the bend was what looked like a small hill. But as I peered through the smokey mountain haze, I noticed that it wasn't covered in trees. Before my mind could run through options, the sun peeked out from behind the clouds. The rays of light reflected off the surface of the small hill, revealing a black, metallic sheen.

This was no hill at all. It was an airship, just like the one we had just fled from. At first I was worried that it was one that was parked. Maybe the interference was from an Organization base and that was one of their ships. But I soon noticed the dirt pushed up around the the ship, then the broken wing which sat off from it, then the path of bare ground that led to it.

The ship wasn't parked; it had crashed just like us. That didn't rule out that this was a base of some sort, it just meant that if it was a base, it wasn't The Organization's.

I hopped off the roof of our ship and walked back inside with the others. Blake was still unconscious, and Bailey's mom had cut off one of the seatbelts to make a tourniquet for his leg. Bailey was holding his leg still, while her mom secured the strap around his leg. I noticed a pool of blood under Blake now, coming from the wound.

"Is he still doing okay?" I asked.

"He is stable, but he needs a doctor," Bailey's mom said, "He shifted while you were out there and must have knocked something loose because he started bleeding again. The tunicate will only help him for so long"

My face turned red as tears filled my eyes. I tried to be strong, but the more I tried, the more I realized how helpless I truly was. I was just a 17 year old kid, and at this moment, I didn't even have my powers. I was inexperienced. I wasn't a soldier. What was I thinking? Trying to save the world? I couldn't even keep four people safe.

"I'll be right back," I choked out, "I... need to check something." That was a lie. I didn't want to cry in front of them. I hastily walked out of the plane, managing to keep it together just until I walked out. Then the tears began to flow.

I ran over to the bank of the lake and kicked a stump. It was still rooted in the ground, but my strength yanked it up like a weed pulled from a garden. Its roots broke and it flew out into the lake. I picked up a stick and screamed in anger, throwing it out in the direction of the stump that was now floating in the water.

My anger was more at myself than anything: my helplessness, my arrogance. After the anger faded, I was left only with sadness and disappointment. I collapsed on the stony bank. "Why God?" I asked, "Why allow it? Was I not just trying to protect people? Was I not doing what was right?"

I sat for a while, thinking and praying, as I looked out across the lake, the Organization ship towering in the distance. I heard footsteps behind me. I couldn't sense anything, so I was forced to turn around and look. It was Bailey.

"We got the bleeding to stop again," she said softly.

"Does it do him any good if we're stuck out here?" I said, turning back to the lake. I wiped the tears from my cheeks.

"Well, It does give us longer to find help." she replied.

"I don't know if we can," I looked at the ground, "That Organization ship had to be caught in whatever we got caught in. That means even if people knew where we were, they couldn't even come after us."

"I only met you today, but I didn't take you for the type to lose hope." Bailey sat down beside me, "Was I wrong?"

"No. Yes? I don't know... I never used to...but." It was true, when my dad died, I never lost hope that things could be better. When I had to go live with my mom, I always looked for the bright side. When the Vales got captured, I knew that we could help them.

"What changed?" Bailey asked.

"What didn't change?" I stood up and turned away from her, feeling tears begging to start flowing again.

Bailey stood up and put her hand on my shoulder, pulling me to face her, "A situation is never hopeless, unless you lose hope." She moved her hand down to my arm, teared up, then smiled. She took her hand back to wipe her eyes, then walked back toward the ship.

She was right. If we believed that we still had a chance, then we did. I sat at the lake, watching the sun set. As I did, I thought back to all of the times I had done the same thing back home.

Whenever I needed to feel God, I could always look to the sunset and be comforted. To know that he cared enough to paint a masterpiece for me to see every evening, was enough to give me hope. It seemed that even when I couldn't feel him, I could still see that he cared for me.

Tonight's sunset was spectacular. The reds and yellows reflected off of the clouds, outlining them and making them radiating beams of color in the sky. The tall mountains funneled the sunlight, making a frame around the majestic scene.

When the last notes of the sunset were beginning to disappear, I noticed a purple tint on the last rays. This would have just been a normal sight, but I had seen that specific color somewhere. But where?

I studied it for a while, but then dismissed it and walked back to the ship. Bailey's mom sat in the seat she had sat in for the flight here. Bailey sat on the floor next to Blake. I walked over and sat on the floor across from Bailey and next to Blake.

"He was just starting to wake up." Bailey said.

I looked and saw Blakes eyes beginning to flutter open. "Blake? Blake!" I called, putting my hand on his chest.

He slowly came to consciousness. "Dylan? What happened?" He asked, trying to sit up. I pressed my hand down on his chest, holding him to the floor.

"We hit some kind of... something. We crashed. You're hurt. Bad. You need to stay laid down for now."

Blake winced and raised his head. I could tell he was looking at his leg. He was waking up and beginning to feel the pain. "I think we did more than just crash. There's a tree in my leg." He was trying to keep his humor, but his face bent as the pain hit him. "Is anyone coming to help us?"

"Whatever happened made all of our technology useless and our powers too." I explained, " We can't call for help."

"Did it affect the crystals?" he asked.

I looked down at mine. "No. I guess not. We just can't use our powers."

"No more questions." Bailey's mom said. I hadn't even noticed that she was standing over me, "He needs to save his strength."

"But." Blake was cut off.

"You need to rest!" She said sternly, "You may be the soldiers, but I am the nurse. When it comes to nursing, I am your authority. Now lay there and rest!"

I looked up to retaliate, but I didn't really know how to argue with that. It did me a lot of good just to hear his voice, and when I looked back to Blake, he was asleep again (or unconscious from the pain).

I stood up and looked at Bailey's mom, "Thank you for taking care of him. He wouldn't have made it this long without you."

"It's my job," she said, "And the least I could do for you two saving myself and my daughter."

I smiled at her. I knew he was still in just as bad of shape as he was before. I was still worried sick, but I at least had hope. I looked at Bailey, trying to think of something to say to her too. Looked back and said in almost a whisper, "It's never hopeless."

I walked out of the ship. I really just needed to be alone and breathe for a second, but I thought I may also try to look for the reflection of city lights on the night sky. I walked out to the lake once again. The moon reflected off the surface of the water. Even if there was a small town nearby, the moon was so brought I never would have seen it by looking at the sky.

It was strange. I was in no better a situation now than I was when we crashed, but my mind was so clear now. I guess seeing Blake show signs of life and my talk with Bailey was enough to give me a boost.

I began to think about my powers. ALI said that I was entangled with the stone, which was entangled with the star. The stone still worked, and I could clearly still draw energy from it. Clearly there wasn't a problem between the star and the crystal, and since I could get the crystal to glow, there wasn't a problem between the crystal and me. That meant it had to be something externally affecting it.

I called for my powers. The crystal began to glow, but nothing else happened. I began to pull more energy from the crystal. Still, I saw nothing, but I could feel the energy moving through my body. I strained and pulled even more power from the crystal. Finally, I saw something. A wisp of energy came from the crystal on my chest and traveled to my elbow before dissipating.

I was right! I just had to pull a lot of power for small results. I began to draw from the crystal again. This time, I focused on trying to make a ball of energy above my right hand. I summoned the power. I could feel it flowing through me. I called it to my hand. My arm began to shake. It took a lot of physical energy to use the power, only I never noticed it in a fight. I did now.

As the power began to flow down my arm and the blue energy began to form a small orb above my hand, I noticed that the energy was not dissipating, but rather being pulled away. It looked like a strong wind when it blows through a fire. The energy was being pulled upward, and slightly toward the mountain.

Still focusing on calling the energy, I looked up. I could see a soft purple glow darkening against the white glow of the moon. It was the same color I had seen at sunset. Then, I remembered where I had seen the color. It was the color of the shield at Arnold Base!

I had seen what I needed to see. I let go of the energy and ran back to the ship. "Bailey! Bailey!" I called

She ran to the door, "What!"

"There's a shield here! We're on a base!" I exclaimed.

"Are we under attack?" As I neared I could see the alarm on her face.

"What? No. No," I realized my excitement had been mistaken for panic, "I could see a shield in the sky. That means we are sitting on a base. That means there are people here and they may be able to help Blake!"

"You had me thinking they had come for us," Bailey said angrily.

I guess I had been a bit hysterical. "I'm sorry," I apologized, "But just look up. You'll see what I mean."

I called on the power of the crystal just as vigorously as I had before. The purple hue became visible against the moon once again. "I think that this shield is drawing all of the plasmatic energy from everything, making our technology useless. The only thing strong enough to give it a struggle is the crystal. It must radiate from the top of the mountain because that is where the energy is drawn to."

I stopped using the energy and waited for Bailey's response. She looked deep in thought. Finally, she spoke up, "Well, it probably isn't Organization because of the crashed ship, but I didn't think anyone else had that kind of advanced technology according to you."

"Well, no one that I knew of, but I've only known about the organization for a week." I made my tone softer and more serious, "Whether they are friend or foe, Blake has to have help. Another day with that tourniquet on and he loses his leg."

"If they are foes, how would we get their help?"

"We bargain with the crystals. We take all three. When we're there, we should be able to use our powers if they can use weapons. We stay at a good vantage point, bargain with the red crystal, and then leave with the two we still have."

"It might work, but what if we can't use our powers there and they have some sort of weapons that still work within the shield?"

"It's either risk it all now, or live in the mountains until we die."

Bailey looked in the ship, then back at me, "Might as well risk it while we've still got something to lose."

Bailey and I walked back in the ship together. Blake was awake again and Bailey's mom was tending to his wound. "We found what we think is a military base at the top of the mountain" I said, "Bailey and I are going to hike up and try to get some help."

"What kind of base?" Blake asked.

"We don't know," I replied.

"But we hope that it doesn't belong to any of our current enemies." Bailey added.

Bailey's mom stood up, " I don't guess I get a say in this. Do I?"

"No," Bailey said softly, yet still stern.

Bailey went to hug her mom and I knelt down next to Blake, "I'm going to use the red crystal to bargain for a ship. I think our powers will work when we reach the top. I'm going to do my best. You have to stay alive until I get back."

"Well, I'll see what I can do about that." Blake said, "Just make sure you come back alive too."

Blake sat up just enough so that we could give each other a hug. He laid back, "Good luck."

"It's never luck," I said.

"I know"

Bailey finished her parting remarks with her mom and I told her to take the red crystal from Blake's chestpiece. "I can't touch it. It's like a parasite to my crystal, but you should be okay."

"Should?"

"Yea, but like 99.9% should. It's good odds," I reassured her, "Just let go if it hurts when you touch it."

She reluctantly plucked it from Blake's chestpiece. Nothing happened. She put it in her pocket and walked out the door. "See you in the morning." I said as we walked away.

"Are you ready to climb a mountain in the middle of the night?" I asked Bailey.

"It was never on my bucket list, but under the circumstances... You sure you can't just carry this red one in your pocket or something and let me know how it went when you get back?" she joked.

"Positive" I said.

We headed out and hiked nonstop. The power we drew from our crystals kept our strength up and our determination to complete our quest kept us wide awake. We talked as we went. At first it was about general things like school or church. We actually found out we had been at the same conference for our churches not long ago. But soon, the moon moved away from us and with it, our filters. The conversation began to get more personal.

"So, you say you've only been in this for a week? How did you get involved a week ago?" Bailey asked.

"Oh, where do I start?" I said. So much had happened, it was hard to remember it all. I thought for a moment.

As I did, Bailey spoke up, "We've got a long night ahead of us. Just start at the beginning."

"Well, two Saturdays ago, I came across an old case that was my dad's. When I opened it, it had the crystal inside. I took it out and when I did, it began to spin and some strange rings appeared around it. Then, it shot me with its energy. I didn't know I had powers at first, but that night, a soldier from the organization broke into Blake's house where I was staying. He took me and Blake's whole family into some facility.

They wanted to know information about the crystal and my dad but he died in February. I didn't know anything about the crystal. They would have killed us if I hadn't discovered my powers. I saved Blake and came across my dad's old lab. He worked for them without me knowing it, experimenting on the crystal and ultimately keeping them out of the hands of The Organization."

"So your dad was a spy?" Bailey asked.

"I don't really know anymore," I said, "He had powers and worked to take down The Organization from within, and somehow, he kept it a secret. He stole this crystal from them and died soon after. I think they killed him, but the records say it was a car crash."

"I would say I'm sorry for your loss, but I know it gets old. I lost my dad in a car crash as well. Not that long ago actually."

"He would be proud of you." I said.

"Wandering up a mountain in the middle of nowhere? Somehow I don't think that's how he imagined my life turning out." Bailey tried to laugh, but I recognized the underlying hurt.

"I mean how strong you are." I consoled, "You brought me back to earth when I was losing it earlier. Not to mention you are probably the literal strongest female alive after you got your powers."

"I guess you got super strength too?" She asked.

"I kicked a rooted stump about a quarter of a mile while I was mad today."

142

"Oh, that's nothing. You've clearly never seen what an angry woman can do." Bailey said.

"Hell hath no fury like a woman scorned." I joked.

"It is true." Bailey said, "So, what about after you broke out?"

I continued the story, "Well, I found ALI in my dad's lab. We escaped from the base and hid in the woods near my old house. ALI knew where Blake's parents were being held. He helped Blake and I learn to use the technology and helped me learn to use my powers, so that we could perform a rescue mission. Blake and I both took years of competitive martial arts so we were already good fighters.

After a week, ALI said we were ready. We attacked the Montana base and took the red crystal.

Then, I heard that another Crystal bearer was in danger of being taken by The Organization. So rather than go home, I came to save you. Some rescue mission, huh?"

"Well, I'm not with The Organization am I?" Bailey said.

"I guess not."

"Then, I would say your mission was a success."

"We can call it a success when Blake is safe." I said, "Now, what about you? I keep saying 'a week ago' you keep saying 'a month ago'. What happened a month ago?"

"You'll think I'm crazy."

"Did you not just hear my story? I don't think anything is crazy anymore."

"Well, remember that when you hear my story." Bailey said.

"I'll keep it in mind."

"My dad was a historian, but he was obsessed with ancient technology. He thought that man was more advanced in the past than in the present, especially the ancient Mayans. He believed that they onced ruled both Americas with their advanced technology.

His hobby of archeology turned into his passion alongside his day job as an engineer. He wanted to find ancient technologies and use them to improve his own. One day, a month ago, I came across an old

143

journal of his. I was reading through it and found that he was close to finding an ancient Mayan temple in North America, and it wasn't far from my house.

He died before he could find it. I convinced my friend Kensie to go with me. We found the temple. In it, we found the technologies that my dad talked about. They were old and most of them didn't work, but inside one column was a floating, glowing box."

"The box that your crystal was in?" I asked.

"Yes," Bailey answered. She continued, "Well, I'm leaving out a few details, but I went to grab the box and when I got colse it exploded. I woke up in some sort of cell next to my friend. I did discover my powers, but not..." Bailey choked up. We stopped our ascent, "Not before... I couldn't save everyone." She began to cry, "I wasn't strong enough then."

"Bailey...I" I didn't really know what to say. I could tell who she couldn't save was her friend. I couldn't imagine if I lost Blake. Now I was faced with it, but to truly deal with it is something I would never want to imagine. But Bailey had lived through it. She sat down on the hill and I sat next to her.

"You know, it's not even that they killed her, that's the hardest part. It's knowing that I had the power to take them all down. It's knowing that if I had been better, she would still be alive."

"Bailey, you can't blame yourself." I said.

"Oh, I've told myself that 1,000 times." Bailey looked up through the trees, "Every time, I just think of 1,000 more ways I could have saved her."

"I know if I lost Blake now, I would do the same thing as you. And people would tell me the same thing I told you. And I would respond the same way you did to me. Bailey, I wish I had never found that crystal. I wish I didn't have these powers. I wish I could undo the whole last week, but I can't. And somehow I try to comfort myself by saying it's all a part of God's plan.

I can't see it, and I sure don't understand it, but we have a power that can save the world. We have a chance to kill an evil Organization. Why did God give the means to us? The only thing I can think of is because for some reason he chose to trust us.

Why did he see in his sovereignty to take Kelsey or crash us here, injuring Blake to the point of death? I don't know. I can't always

144

see him, but I have to trust that it was for a reason. Maybe we're just on one side of the mountain, and we cant see the full picture yet."

After my little speech, Bailey laid her head over on my shoulder. I knew she was tired and the tears had made our eyes heavy. "You know, for the first time in a month, I actually feel safe." She whispered.

In the midst of all that was happening, the mystery that waited for us on top of the hill, the injury of Blake, somehow, I felt safe too. It wasn't because of my powers or her's. I knew that because they weren't working right now.

I thought about the words I had said and I realized I needed to hear them just as much as I needed to say them. I couldn't see the plan now, but one day, I would. One day, it would all make sense. That made me feel safe.

We were about three quarters of the way up the mountain. I knew we needed sleep before we found whatever was up there. I felt Bailey relax, and I knew she was asleep. I decided to give into my heavy eyelids as well. I leaned my head up against the tree behind me and fell asleep.

Chapter 15

I slowly came to consciousness as the golden rays of the morning sun warmed my face. I looked over to see Bailey still asleep on my shoulder. It must have been mid morning because I could see no hints of the sunrise left. I felt refreshed and rested against the tree, thanking God for another day.

As my prayer continued, my mind thought of Blake. We overslept! There was no time to relax. He needed help now. I nudged Bailey until she awoke, her eyes fluttering open, and the look of serenity on her face. Her night must have been restful as well.

"We slept too long," I said as I stood up, "We need to get moving."

"Yea," Bailey stretched, "Yea, you're right. Let's go."

She stood up and we continued the last leg of our journey. "How'd you sleep?" I asked, trying to keep today's conversation light.

"Honestly, that's the best I've slept in about a month," She said, "How about you."

"The best I've slept in about a week." I replied, smiling.

We both chuckled, not because it was anything very funny, but because we finally felt light enough to. Something was changing. I couldn't help but feel it, even without my senses working. Things may not have been looking up, but we were. Maybe that was enough to make a difference.

We trudged on, up the side of the mountain. Finally, we neared the top. As we came to a clearing, we stopped. I could hear the low hum of something mechanical coming from just over a small rise in the landscape. Bailey and I looked at one another, silent, not wanting to alarm any soldiers who might be nearby.

Bailey pointed, directing my attention to a soft purple glow coming from the edge of the rise. Where it met the ground, there was a dark red line. It was the edge of the shield. I looked around on the ground and eventually found a slender stick, about the same length of my staff.

I picked it up and slowly walked to the edge of the shield. From there, I could peek over the rise and see the entrance to a bunker, much like the one at the Montana base. There were no structures around it, but the area nearby was cleared of trees and was covered with well kept grass. Coming from the top of the bunker was a beam of yellow energy that transitioned to purple, then dissipated the closer it got to the sky.

I held the stick out and tested the shield. The stick passed through with no problem. Next, I tested it with my finger. I felt nothing, so I stepped through. The instant I was on the other side, I felt my senses return. I could feel everything around me once again. I tested the crystal, calling the power to my hand. One flicker of blue, and I knew I was back to normal.

There was no one around, so I gently called Bailey's name and she joined me. She tested her powers when she came through as well. I gestured for her to stand there, while I walked around the bunker. There really was nothing, no one. I walked all the way around and back to Bailey. "Looks clear to me," I said.

"Shouldn't there be guards or something?" Bailey asked.

As if to answer her, the bunker doors flung open and a group of soldiers poured out. There were about ten of them and they all carried guns in their hands and swords on their waist.

Bailey and I called for our powers, blue energy flowing down my arms and white energy down Bailey's. "We don't want a fight," I said, "We just want to talk."

The soldiers said nothing, only pointed their guns at us, so I continued, "We have the red crystal." I poked Bailey, telling her to show it to them. She pulled it out of her pocket and held it up, "We wish to trade it for medical supplies, a ship, and safe passage."

The soldiers said nothing still. I studied the soldiers. They didn't seem to be Organization. Their uniforms were light gray, with an almost blue tint, not black. They wore a signet on their chest and right shoulder. It looked like a bird of some fort, surrounded by a ring. But also their guns and helmets were different. The guns were more slender and their helmets were smooth.

"Hello?" Bailey said, waving her hand, "What are they doing?"

"I don't know," I replied, "I would almost rather them be shooting at us."

I began to walk toward them, hoping to get some response. It worked. They all holstered their guns and drew their swords with one quick motion. I stepped back. "You will be patient." Said a soldier in the middle. He must have been an officer because his uniform was more

147

decorated than the others: Pins on his chest under the signet and bands under the signet on his arm.

"Okay," I said, holding up my hands, "I'll wait. If you don't mind me asking, what are we waiting on? Because if it's reinforcements, I would rather fight you now."

"Dylan!" Bailey scolded, "Don't make them angry."

"No, he is justified," said the soldier, "We are waiting for our leader. He wishes to speak with you"

"See, asking questions is helpful," I said to Bailey.

She shook her head. We waited for about three minutes, but the silence and suspense made it feel like an eternity. It was hard to stay strong, but I didn't want to show them my fear. Honestly it was very strange more than anything, and that was unsettling.

Finally, an elevator reached the bunker. The doors slid open revealing a figure. As he stepped into the light, I could see that his uniform was decorated much more than the leading soldier. The uniform was also a bright white rather than a gray. He clearly was very high in the ranks. He must have been the leader we were waiting on.

The soldiers in front of the elevator moved aside with one motion, falling between the other soldiers and keeping their weapons ready. The new soldier walked in front of the rest and over to me.

He was taller than me. He wore the signet just as the rest, but he also had one on each side of his smooth helmet. He was close enough now that I could just make out his eyes through his visor.

"It's been a while since I've seen a crystal bearer, let alone two." He said. His voice was familiar. The helmet didn't really distort it, but I still had a hard time placing it with a face.

"I'm sure it's been even longer since you've had a chance to possess a crystal." I said ready to plead our case, "We need medical supplies for our injured crew mate, and a ship to leave on, in exchange you can take the red crystal."

He turned his face away, then looked back at me, "Son, I'll give you so much more."

At first I was taken aback. There was a quiver in his voice. For a moment, I thought of who the voice sounded like, but it couldn't be. Then his helmet retracted, revealing the face of my father.

148

I stepped back. It was as if I had been kicked in the chest. I couldn't breathe. I couldn't think. "Dad?" I whispered in unbelief.

Tears rolled down his face, "It's me, Dylan."

All of my unbelief fell with the tears that flooded my eyes. It was him. Somehow, it was him. I threw myself into his arms and we embraced one another. My mind raced through all the time I had been without him. His presence began to fill the holes of his recent absence. I was flooded with relief and joy. "How?" I asked, still refusing to let go.

"There are so many answers to that question, but now we must help Blake." He commanded, grabbing my shoulders and pushing me from the embrace, "There will be plenty of time to talk later, and I am sure you would like him to be there for it." He turned to the soldier who was leading the others, "Lower the static shield, raise the plasma shield, and get a medical crew down to the crash site."

"Yes sir," He said, turning and entering back into the elevator.

A black mist poured from the puck on my chest and formed ALI's emblem, "It's good to see you again sir," ALI's voice called.

"Good to see you too, old friend," Dad told him, "Looks like you've done a pretty good job of taking care of them... for the most part."

"How was I supposed to know there was a static shield here," ALI barked back, "Even I thought you were dead."

"You still don't know everything my friend," Dad remarked, "Secondary Sub-radio scanners can detect them if you are looking for them. They aren't completely invisible."

"I suppose you are right. "ALI conceded.

The sealed generator over the bunker turned off and all around us I could see yellow beams of energy shoot into the air. They reached their desired altitude and then spread out, filtering the sunlight and surrounding the mountain with a golden glow.

As soon as the shield was raised, a ship flew by and hovered overhead. Its engines were quiet. The only sound was the intense wind created by them. The engines appeared to be golden disks that changed direction based on where the ship needed to go. It was unlike anything I had ever seen. There were three on each side of the ship, positioned toward the back, the one in the front to stabilize the ship. The

149

ship itself was streamlined with an ovular body, allowing for seating. A ladder dropped down from the ship.

"You two grab on and go help your friend." Dad said, "I'll meet you in the med bay."

Bailey grabbed onto one side of the ladder and I grabbed onto the other. I didn't want to leave my dad, but my desire to help Blake superseded that one.

The ship lifted up above the canopy and flew us down to the crash site. It gently placed us down at the door of the dropship, retracted the ladder, then landed beside the lake, on a flat grassy spot, about thirty yards from the ship.

When it landed, the engines retracted up under the ship and four leg-like landing gears folded out of the belly. Four soldiers in white uniforms (much like the others but with no helmets) rushed over. Following behind them was a levitation gurney.

Bailey and I entered the downed ship to find Bailey's mom looking up at the commotion, but still holding pressure on Blakes wound. "We brought help!" Bailey said.

"Good, I wasn't sure how much longer he could go and still keep the leg." She replied, "Did this help come at a price?"

"No, at least it shouldn't." I said, "The people here are alleys."

The medics rushed in and pushed all of us out of the way. They loaded Blake up on the gurney and rushed him back to the ship. "You guys better come on if you want a ride!" one of them said as the other spouted off medical terms to one another."

Bailey and her mom rushed out of the ship. I looked over to my staff that now sat retracted on the floor of the cockpit. I called my power and summoned the staff to my hand. For a moment, it was as if time stopped. I looked at the staff, seeing a bright future. For once, I couldn't wait to see what happened next!

"Dylan! Come on!" Bailey called, waking me from my daydream.

"Coming!" I called, latching the staff to my waistband.

I rushed to the ship and jumped onboard. The medical team was quick to start I.V.s and began assessing the wound. The inside of

150

the ship was white and steril. Medical instruments were tucked neatly into the walls. Some I could recognize but others were foreign to me. Blake was slightly conscious and groaning.

I grabbed his hand that wasn't being used. He squeezed my hand, trying to get his mind off the pain. "Hang in there." I said, "You're gonna be fine now."

The ship flew around to the back side of the mountain. As we flew around, I could see trees falling as they were pushed over by cannons and radars. Entire pieces of the mountain gave way exposing hangar bays and other entrances. I couldn't make out much within the bays, but I could see that the ships were different from ones I had seen in the past. They were more advanced.

We came to one bay filled with other ships that looked like the one we were currently in. Our ship landed in the middle of the bay and Blake was rushed out. Bailey, her mom, and myself followed out after them, but were stopped by a medic that was already in the bay waiting for us.

"He's going into surgery," she said, "You can't go with him."

Bailey's mom spoke up, "I am a nurse. Let me go with him. I have kept him alive this long."

"You're a nurse out there" said the medic, "Not here. Our technology is far more advanced. You will have to be trained on it first."

"Then let me go back and watch so that I can learn," She demanded.

"That may be acceptable." The medic replied, "You can come with me. The other two must stay here and wait for Director Daniel."

We couldn't argue. We were out ranked and out of our league here. They walked off leaving Bailey and I in the hangar. We found some crates and sat on them, waiting for my dad. I had time to examine the hangar. The floor and walls were a dingy white color, making the solid white uniforms of the medics stand out, and the black ships even more so.
Everything was sterile and futuristic. I had never seen anything like it outside of a science fiction movie. Clearly our presence had caused the base to suddenly spring to life. Ships were now buzzing around the outside of the base, seemingly going from platform to platform with deliveries. I could see ships flying in formation outside the dome of the yellow shield. It was hard to determine whether they were performing drills or patrols.

151

"This place is amazing," Bailey said in awe.

"It's more than I ever dreamed we would find when we reached the top," I replied.

"I can guess you never dreamed that you would find your dad at the top either." She chuckled.

"Are you kidding? I went to his funeral! I still can't believe it, but it was him. I can't believe it, but I can't deny it."

While we spoke, I saw Dad walking across the hangar. I stood up and Bailey behind me. "Let's find out what's going on." I said, walking to him.

I gave him another hug, then loaded the cannon, ready to fire all my questions at him. I started with the most obvious, "How are you alive? I went to your funeral. You died in a car crash."

"I should have." He said, "ALI likely filled you in on what he knows. You know that I was in possession of two crystals, the yellow and the blue."

"Yea"

"Well, I left the one I was tied to with James, hoping that The Organization wouldn't find it before you did. The other one I took with me to this place. I've been building it for years, it's been a secret from The Organization and from anyone on the outside - even ALI. Before I came here, I had to cover my tracks, so I faked my death.

I knew the pain it would cause, it pained me, but I knew if The Organization thought I was dead, I could go off the grid and build a true resistance."

"So you started all of this?" I asked, "You rounded up all of these people?"

"I've been rounding them up for years," He answered, "It's made up of Organization Defectors, soldiers from the US military, and normal citizens whose lives were endangered by The Organization. They all helped build this place."

His answer only gave me more questions, but I stuck with the big ones, "Why did you leave us down there? Why didn't you come get us when we first crashed?"

"This base was created to sit in a dormant state either until you found it or until the Organization attacked the world. The field protected it, but it also kept us from being able to see. The only information we got was from a single wire that runs to a town about eighty miles from here. We didn't know you were here until you came through the shield."

"Well, I guess I can forgive you for that then..." I thought for a moment, trying to find my next biggest question, then I remembered hearing his voice when I was shot by the crystal, "Did you have something to do with me getting my powers?"

He smiled, "Yes, I used my connection with the crystal to feel when you touched it. As soon as you did, I reached out and connected with the crystal for the first time since I had left. I knew you had the mutation that would allow you to connect to the crystal. I knew it would be safer with you than with me."

"Safer with me? How? You're the one who knows what you're doing!" I rebutted.

"You're young. You have longer to learn from it, plus, your mutation is more refined than mine. You can connect to the crystal on a deeper level than me."

I had more questions, but he spoke to Bailey before I could get the next one out, "Now you, I see you have a connection to your crystal as well. Your energy is unique. I've never come across this crystal before in my studies. Where did it come from?"

"You won't believe me." Bailey said.

"I have a very open mind," He replied.

"It was in an ancient Mayan temple in Missouri." She informed him.

"Interesting," Dad got a look on his face. I knew it; it was his thinking look. He knew something about it, but he moved on.

"I ran a scan on your energy as soon as you summoned it. The energy is both similar and different from that of Blake's crystal. Each crystal has a sort of frequency at which its energy vibrates, determined by the contents of the star that sits on the sending end of the power. In musical terms, Bailey, your crystal's energy sits at the same note, exactly one octave higher than Blakes. Hold hands."

Bailey and I looked at one another shyly. Though we were forging a connection, we had only met the day before.

"Don't be that way. You both want to, now falter me and do it," Dad commanded.

We did as he said and awkwardly took each other's hand in the "friendship" kind of way.

Dad continued, "The connection to one another that you feel is in part due to the frequency of your powers. They complement each other. Call out to your powers, you'll see what I'm talking about."

I did feel attracted to her. I was almost disappointed that he had said it might have to do with our powers. I just thought she was a good person. I liked who she was.

We did as he said. Her power flowed down her arm to meet mine. Once our powers met, I felt a surge of energy travel through my veins. Rather than just being on our arms, the energy flew across our entire bodies, the white energy mixed with mine and my blue energy mixed with her's.

It didn't stop there though. It hit the floor and burst into the air around us. Blue and white dots of light filled the hangar. A beautiful pattern formed around our feet, the white and blue energy swirling in flowing patterns, within a fog at our feet. My senses could detect every detail of the room: every ship, every person, every crate. I could even sense the emotions of individuals, most of which were in awe of the spectacle in front of them.

Bailey and I looked at eachother, smiling in amazement. "See what happens when you listen to me!" Dad laughed, "As long as you are together, your powers will be exponentially stronger! It's flying all over the room because you don't know how to direct it. I think we can fix that."

"Do we have to?" Bailey asked, intrigued by the fog around the three of us.

"Not right now," Dad said, "Enjoy it. You both deserve it."

Chapter 16

I sat in Blake's recovery room waiting for him to wake up. Dad had given me some jeans and a T-Shirt to change into. They were a little bit big since they were my dad's, but they were better than the dirty uniform that I had been wearing.

Bailey and her mom were getting settled into their new living quarters and Dad was arranging to have a division sent to Tullahoma to evacuate all of our allies. I still wanted to talk to Dad more, about my mother, about the crystal, about all this technology, but there was too much to be done right now and I wanted to be with Blake when he woke up.

The doctors had saved his leg by nothing short of a miracle. One more hour and he would have lost it due to lack of blood flow. Thanks to their medicines here, they expected him to make a full recovery in about two weeks. He should be walking in a couple days.

I wasn't there for very long before he woke up. I noticed his beeping heart monitor begin to speed up, then his eyes eased open. He turned his head and looked at me.

"Next time you want to scare me, pop a balloon or something." I said smiling.

"Wouldn't work, you can see everything." Blake whispered. His throat was dry from the surgery.

I grabbed him a glass of water from the night stand next to me and handed it to him. He tried to hold it but his hands were too shaky, so I held it to his lips for him.

"So…" He swallowed and cleared his throat, then spoke in a raspy version of his normal voice, "Who helped us? Don't tell me you made a deal with The Organization."

He was only half joking. He knew I would do it to save him, "Believe it or not, it was my Dad."

Blake shook his head, "No, actually."

"I'm being for real!" I said, "It was my dad. Apparently he had the same powers I do. He faked his death, built this base, and then he gave them to me a week ago."

"But we went to his funeral!" Blake said in disbelief.

"I said the same thing! But it really is him. He said he's been building this place for years."

"Well, now I have even more questions" Blake said.

"Believe me, I do too!"

"But they're going to have to wait," said a nurse as she walked in the door, "Dylan, your father needs you and it's time for Blake to take his medicine."

"I told my dad I would be a while," I said, "I really need to be here."

"I understand," said the nurse, "but Blake is doing just fine and you father said that it's urgent."

Urgent? What now? Things were just starting to look up!

I shook my head and cut my eyes to Blake. "Duty calls." he said, giving me a solute.

"I guess," I said, reluctantly standing up from the chair. I only now noticed a soldier with the same badges as the one that had met us at the bunker, was standing in the hallway. It had to be him, but he wasn't wearing his helmet. He looked to be in his thirties and had short-cut black hair.

"Commander Dixon will take you from here," said the nurse, stepping out of the doorway to let me past.

"Good to see you again sir," he said stoutly, "This way." He walked off down the hallway in a very fast paced walk. I jogged to catch up.

"I'm not a soldier or anything," I explained, "You don't have to call me sir."

"You're a crystal bearer. One that's on our side. You outrank everyone here except the boss."

"Flattering, but I'm sure that's not necessary," I said, "I'm not a fighter."

"You are now."

I wanted to protest the point, but I thought it was better to let it go. I moved on, "What's going on that's so urgent?"

"You'll find out in the war room."

"Aren't you just as vague as ever," I complained, "Since I outrank you, I order you to tell me what is going on."

I thought I was clever but clearly not. Commander vague was not having it, "Telling sensitive information in the hallways is against regulation."

"Okay" I shrugged.

We marched on, eventually stopping at a door labeled *WAR ROOM*. The Commander scanned his vanguard on a panel beside the door and it slid open. Inside was a long wooden table surrounded by several decorated soldiers. At the end closest to the door, Bailey sat in a chair. My father was at the head and behind him was a holographic screen with what looked like a satellite map of Tullahoma.

"Thank you for joining us," Dad said, "For those of you who are unaware, this is my son Dylan. He is now the bearer of the blue crystal."

Everyone took their seats. I chose the one next to Bailey. Everyone was silent and Dad began to speak, "This map shows my hometown of Tullahoma. [the map zoomed out. And a red dot appeared over a portion of it. Dad pointed to the dot.] This is Arnold Base. It is where my first lab was located and one of the first crystal research facilities. It is significantly under armed. The band of Taken soldiers who helped my son take on Montana Base also took over this base and are using it as a makeshift headquarters.

[The map zoomed out revealing the entire U.S. Three red triangles appeared over Montana and tracked across the map, moving toward Tennessee, but stopping about halfway there.] There are three Organization cruisers headed for Tullahoma to wipe out the rebels, their families, and my personal friends.

They will arrive in exactly four hours and twenty four minutes. That means we have exactly that long to contact the rebels, send in a squadron, and evacuate them.

This is our highest profile mission and it will depart soon, but that is not, however, why this meeting was called. My Dad's face turned cold and somber, "The takeover has started sooner than we anticipated."

Tension filled the room. The distinguished soldiers took deep breaths. They began to shift in their chairs and rub their foreheads. I

157

looked at Bailey, Bailey looked at me, then we both looked at my dad. He made eye contact with us, then continued his speech, "In the last thirty minutes, we have confirmed at least eighty battle cruisers, forty carriers, and five dreadnoughts world wide.

Since Dylan was able to steal the red crystal, they were only able to spare three ships from Asia to attack Tullahoma first, then DC. Once the rest of the world has fallen, half of their fleet will fly to America, while the rest work to hold the rest of the world's superpowers hostage."

"Do we know how many countries have fallen so far?" Asked a soldier about halfway up the table.

"No," Dad said, "World communications were all but shut down overnight. We won't get an official count unless we get word from other pockets of resistance"

"Is the US fighting back?" asked another man.

"Not yet." Dad replied, "The corruption runs so deep that every effort to try and mobilize the army has failed. It will take military bases standing up for themselves if the U.S. is to fight back," Dad continued with a plan, "I suggest we send a large force to quickly evacuate all friendlies from Tullahoma then immediately send that same fleet, ahead of the battle cruisers to evacuate DC. If we put enough resources into it, we should be able to stay ahead of them. Our base here is virtually impenetrable to The Organization when all of our resources are here. As long as we get back here before they find out about us, we'll be safe."

"I second his plan," said a soldier.

From there, going clockwise around the table, each soldier responded with "Aye". Bailey and I each said our part. The vote was unanimous. "It's settled then," Dad said, "Prepare the fleet and set a course for Tullahoma."

All of the soldiers stood up from the table and soluted Dad. Then, they turned and exited the room. Bailey and I walked up to my Dad. "Looks like you scared them," Dad said somberly (but still trying to be congratulatory).

"Does this mean the war has started?" I asked.

"War?" Dad looked at the hologram map which was now displaying a revolving image of earth with little red dots over many of the countries. "This isn't a war. A war suggests both sides have a chance of winning. We are one base against the rest of the world. We can protect what is ours, but for now, there will be no war."

I was taken aback. I thought all of this was to fight back, not just run mercy missions.

"So we're just going let them take over?" Bailey asked.

"Absolutely not!" Dad said. I could tell he was aggravated. Not at the question, just at the situation, "There just aren't enough of us to save the whole world right now. That shield is impenetrable as far as we know, but outside of it, we would quickly be picked off. There are just too many of them."

He stopped talking for a moment and we all stood there, deep in thought. I couldn't think of one thing specifically because there was so much to think about. My mind raced through all of the changes that were happening.

After a moment, Dad began to speak again, "I was hoping that by saving the US leadership, they may be able to rally enough troops, give us access to some European troops. At least something. I have some connections who I know aren't a part of the Organization.

I do want to fight, but I would have to call in a lot of favors to a lot of people who wouldn't want to do favors for me."

I didn't really understand what he was talking about. Why wouldn't people want to help him? I opened my mouth to ask more questions, but I couldn't get myself to ask them. I concluded that I trusted him and I didn't want to annoy him.

Dad walked Bailey and I back into another room adjoining the war room. It was brightly lit and white. It took a moment for my eyes to adjust, but when they did, I saw that the room was lined with weapons of all kinds. There were staves made of a white metal hanging on a gray display panel. Under the staves were guns, also white, and very slender. They were shorter than a rifle, but longer than a pistol.

Across the room were three full sets of armor like what ALI had given us back at the lab, but the metal was a pure white and much thinner. It was also segmented for easier mobility. Beside the armor were three other pieces of the metal. They were about half the size of the chest plate and had a slight bulge built into them. It took a moment of examination because of how different they were, but I realized they were jetpacks.

In the middle of the room there was a gray work table, cleared of everything but three pucks. Behind the table, on the back wall, were two doors, each with a keypad beside them.

"This is my private collection," Dad said, holding up his arms, "I've been keeping it just for you and any friends you might bring with you."

"Wow!" I said, "Running up to the staves and taking one from the wall. I thrust it down and the two ends shot out, creating the signature blue burst of energy from each. It startled Bailey. I realized that she probably didn't have a clue what she was looking at.

"Now try your powers with it." He said.

"Huh?" I didn't understand what he was asking me to do. Use my powers with the staff?

"Just summon your power like you did while you were waiting for me at the bunker." Dad instructed.

I did as he instructed. The blue energy flowed from my chest and down to my hands. When it reached the staff, it spread across it, giving it the same blue, flowing patterns as my arms. I waved the staff in front of me, examining it.

"Now your weapon is an extension of you." Dad said, proud of his work, "I always found that it was easier to focus my power if I had an object to focus it though."

"I still have a lot to learn," Bailey said, shaking her head.

"You both do," Dad said cheerfully, "And I can't wait to teach you both everything I know."

I retracted the staff and placed it back on the rack. "How long have you been working on this?" I asked.

"Mostly since I had to leave," Dad said, "I've been preparing it for when you got your powers and we could see eachother again."

I reached up and took one of the guns, "Those are stun phasers: the best we ever made," Dad boasted, "When I heard chatter over the line about the soldier who wouldn't kill a few days ago, I moved out the lethal weapons and made sure you would have all non lethals. A reputation can be a powerful thing. I wanted to make sure you kept yours."

160

"They're calling me that?" I asked, "I've only fought them twice."

"And no casualties came at your hands," Dad said, "Word like that travel fast in an organization where they think everyone wants to kill them. Those two fights have gained you sympathy in some places."

This was exciting news. In two days I had not only caused an effective uprising in the Organization, but I had also made a name for myself doing it. Maybe I was making a difference after all.

Dad looked at a monitor on his vanguard. "Time to suit up," He said, "Both of you grab a puck."

We did as he said, though, Bailey was reluctant. She didn't know what it was. I looked at her and then demonstrated what it was by pressing it to the middle of my chest, just under my collar bone.

A white mist spread across my body then solidified into fabric as it replaced the clothes I was wearing with a uniform. It was complete with gray boots and the signet on my chest and shoulder. The armor on the wall floated over and attached itself in the appropriate spots and was absorbed under the fabric.

It was much closer to the surface of the material than the last armor and so thin that I could barely feel it. Each crevice and plate of the armor was visible. The crystal that was in my pocket was somehow repositioned over my heart in a gray holder in the shape of the scare.

Standing out from the white material was the signet of the bird I had seen earlier. It was positioned in the very center of my chest and made from a gray leather like material. It was about the size of a saucer - much bigger than the ones I had seen on the other soldiers.
With it this close, I realized that it was a dove whose wings appeared to be flaming, surrounded by a ring. I had on my right arm as well, set above two thin blue bands.

Bailey watched the process in amazement, seemingly at a loss for words. "Pretty cool isn't it?" Dad asked her, "Are you ready for your own?"

"Yes!" She exclaimed, looking around me to the other pucks on the table. Dad took one and handed it to her. She followed the same process I did. The uniform spread across her body. Her's was slightly different from mine. Her arm had two white bands instead of blue. She wore a skirt that came just above her knee and under it, white, tight fitting pants. Her boots were a light gray like mine, a bit more feminine, having a slightly taller heel and coming up closer to her knee.

The white light moved up the back of her head, but left nothing besides a neat braid that wrapped her long hair close to her head. Her armor floated over but distorted itself to fit the couture of her body. The vanguards were more narrow and sat more in line with her arms.

She looked down to examine her outfit and then up at me. She was excited and the movement was sudden causing her helmet to appear over her head. "Oh!" she yelled, and jumped backward. She soon realized that she was in no danger and began to laugh, and us with her.

"Nod your head and it will go away." I said as I chuckled.

She did as I said and the helmet retracted. "Very good then!" Dad said, "Let's go pick up our allies." We walked out through the War Room and headed down the hallway, following my dad. Soldiers passed us, some walking and some running.

As we went, ALI's voice sounded over the PA system, "Attention all personnel. We need all hands on deck. All soldiers report to your stations and see your commanding officers for details. This is not a drill!"

"ALI runs the base now?" I asked.

"He's my assistant again," Dad replied, "He just goes where I need him."

"So that AI has access to the whole base?" Bailey asked.

"Oh, no!" Dad said, "He could be hacked just like anything. He has soft access. He knows protocol, but I don't let him into any weapons systems or base functions."

"Smart." she said.

"One of my many gifts!" He replied, "ALI does have access to your suit however. He will teach you how to use it, just as he is teaching Dylan."

"You can talk to him when your helmet is on or if you call his name." I said.

"ALI!" She called louder than necessary.

"Yes, ma'am." he said from a speaker near her neck.

162

"Oh, that's cool!" she said looking at Dad.

"I am not a toy, ma'am!" ALI barked, "I have emotions and critical thinking skills just like you. I am an Artificially Living Intelligence, as per the name, and I would like you to treat me as such."

Bailey looked almost remorseful, "Oh, I'm so sorry. I didn't mean to... I didn't know."

"ALI, be nice!" I said, "Don't let him fool you, he has thick skin."

We came to a hangar where a large ship was being loaded with troops and weapons. It looked just like a bigger version of the Medic's ship, just without the medical instruments. There was a door on each side and a ramp came down from each of them. We walked around to the side and I looked in. The middle had two rows of seats that faced the walls, each one had a rod that bolted it to both the ceiling and the floor. The doors to the cockpit were closed.

"Are we taking that?" I asked. I turned around from the ship, but Dad and Bailey weren't even close by. They were walking to some smaller ships that were heavily armed with guns and missiles. I ran over to them.

"This is your ship," dad said pointing to one that had two seats, one elevated on the back of the ship and one more sunk in on the nose. It was streamlined with wide, but short wings and two jets for engines on the back instead of the disks like the other ships.

"It 's fast and agile. ALI will teach you how to fly it as you go," Dad took a chip from his vanguard and placed it on the ship to give ALI access, "Dylan, you take the pilot's chair and Bailey can take the gunner seat."

We both climbed into the ship. Once we sat down, the windshield slipped over top of us. There were no buttons, but a screen like the dropship had. There was a joystick with a button that I assumed controlled the forward gun.

"You've got this!" Dad yelled from outside the ship, "I'm going to my fighter! I'll see you there!

I waved as he walked off. The dashboard lit up and ALI spoke up, "Welcome back to the good fight sir!"

"Thanks ALI." I said, "When do we take off?"

"Momentarily. That transport is the last one that has to be loaded. Once it's done, we're off!"

"I'm not so sure this is the best idea," Bailey said nervously, "I don't know the first thing about this."

"Neither does anyone else when they start!" ALI encouraged her, "I am going to teach you as we fly. If something goes bad, I can fly this thing by myself."

"He's good at it too!" I said.

"Good at crashing!" Bailey retorted.

"I had no control over that!" ALI said offended, "And remember, I was the one who took down those ships at your home the other day!"

"Well, I guess that's true." Bailey said.

I looked out the window and noticed that there were no longer people in the hangar and the doors to the ship were closed. "Dylan," ALI said, "You see that green light flashing in the upper right hand corner of the dash?"

"Yea"

"That means this hangar has been cleared for take off. Protocol is that you follow the largest ship out, then you can form up."

The large ship started its engines with a low hum. The landing gears pulled up, and it hovered in place.

"Okay, how do I take off?"

"There is a slider that controls your hover engines"

I looked on the dash and found a slider labeled 'Hover'. I pointed, this one.

"Yes, slide it up to 10%. It will stay there until we land."

I did as he said and we lifted off the ground. As we did, the larger ship began to pull out of the hangar.

"Now use the joystick to move the ship. It will go the direction you push it.

164

I pulled up on it to lift us up over the tops of the other ships in the hangar and moved forward at the same speed as the ship until we were outside the hangar.

"Very good! Now move to be in front of the larger ship, we are going to escort it."

"Got it!" I did as he said.

"How's it going up there Bailey," I said, pressing the button labeled coms.

"Good!" she said, cheerful, but still not convinced of the safety of this plan, "ALI's teaching me what all the buttons do."

"Can you be in two places at once?" I asked ALI.

"With sufficient energy, yes," ALI informed me, "Right now I am connected to the yellow crystals power core, so I can be in about three or four places at once."

"Good to know!" I said.

I looked out in front of us. A large convoy of fighters, medic ships, transports and ships that I didn't even have a name for, was forming, coming from all sides of the mountain. In front of us was a large group of about eighty other fighters of all shapes and sizes.

A small sliver of the shield opened for us to pass through and a voice came over the main coms, "Shield is open, increase to cruising altitude and speed."

The convoy made its way out from under the yellow hue of the shield and then turned upward. I followed. "When we reach 50,000 feet, we will speed up to 600 miles per hour. That should get us there in just about one hour."

I did as he said and reached cruising speed. As we flew, ALI rambled on about all of the various functions of this jet and how to use them. I paid attention for the most part, but I couldn't help looking down at the Earth below. Everything looked so small from here. We passed over cities, towns, homes. None of them even knew we were here. None of them knew what was coming. They were just living life as normal as possible, but change was coming to the world.

Soon, all of those people would long for normalcy, that is, if they survived. And I could do nothing to help them. What a paradox. To have so much power, and yet still feel so powerless.

Chapter 17

We began our descent over Tullahoma. I had lost my communicator in the crash, but Dad said that he had a way to get word to Alex and the others. He never said what, but I trusted that it would work.

Part of the squadron turned and went toward town, but most of us went toward the base. I saw the shield, but not long after I saw it, it turned off, allowing us to land in the base.

ALI instructed me on how to land and I sat the ship down next to the transport we had escorted there. The windshield retracted into the ship and Bailey and I climbed out. I could see Taken Soldiers exiting from the many buildings to greet us and board the ships.

None of them wore their helmets and many of their uniforms were ripped or burned from all the fights they had been in. It didn't take me long to spot Alex. We made eye contact and both smiled uncontrollably. I ran up to him and we gave each other a hug.

"Good to see you in one piece, Dylan!" Alex said.

"You too," I said. With that out of the way, only one thing was left on my mind, "How is my family?"

"All of the Vales are doing just fine and getting packed up." Alex consoled, "Looks like we're missing one, though." Alex looked around through all of the bustling troops running around, "Where's Blake?"

"Alive thankfully!" I said proudly, "He was injured when our ship crashed on my Dad's doorstep. He's back at the base."

"Oh, well, I'm glad he's okay," Alex consoled.

"So how much did they tell you?" I asked, adopting a more serious tone and skipping over any further pleasantries.

"Well, not too much other than they confirmed that they were the ones that wore the flaming dove. The Organization had caught a few of them in the past, so I knew they could be allies. We already knew about what's happening everywhere else right now and about the three ships headed this way. They never said anything about you being there though. We figured it was a long shot that they would actually send help," He looked around, "I think it paid off!"

Bailey walked up behind me. I sensed her presence and turned to her, "Alex, this is Bailey, Bailey, Alex."

"Nice to meet you"

"You too"

They shook hands and I continued, "She is the crystal bearer we went to save."

"Looks like that gamble paid off too," said Alex.

"More than I could have imagined," I said, "She's an amazing person and great with her powers."

Bailey blushed, "I don't know about all that..."

"If Dylan says you're good, you're good."

A white, "U" shaped fighter flew over us, so low that it captured all of our attention. Leaves and dust blew up around us. The ship landed nearby. "That crazy pilot almost took our heads off!" Alex complained.

The cockpit opened and my Dad got out. "Well, apparently, that homicidal pilot is my Dad," I laughed.

"Skilled! Skilled pilot," Dad corrected as he walked to us. He came near and stretched out his hand, "Nice to finally meet you Alex."

Alex shook it, "Pleasure is mine. How can my men help?"

"By getting every single person here on those transports as soon as possible," Dad suggested.

"That is the plan, sir." Alex assured him.

"There is one other thing I require of your soldiers," Dad added, "The civilians will be sent straight back to our base, but I need the rest of you to help me evacuate the leadership from Washington. I'm hoping that their loyalty might be able to win us some troops to aid in the fight."

"I'll relay it to the men," Alex said.

"Thank you Commander," Dad said.

Alex looked at me, "I've got work to do, I'll see you in Washington. Bailey, it was nice to meet you. If he likes you, you must be alright."

167

"See ya there, Alex"

"It was nice meeting you!" Bailey agreed.

Alex waved and walked off. When he was a ways away he called back, "The Vales are in this building here!" pointing to the structure to his right.

"Thank you!" I called back

"Don't mention it!"

Dad turned from Alex to us, "Bailey, I want you to ride with me into town. We are going to try and get the weapons system that I installed there online to cover our tracks. Dylan, you meet us there. Send Kinsie and Cassie back on a transport. Bring James. We have a lot to catch up on."

"Yes, sir!" I said, grinning from ear to ear. I never even got to see them after we rescued them. I couldn't wait!

I ran to the building and grabbed the handle. It was locked, but with the mix of excitement and super strength, I ripped the handle right from the door by accident. I wasn't expecting it and looked down at the handle trying to see the problem, not noticing the door swinging open.

"Dylan!" a small voice cried. It was Kinsie.

"What's up meanness!" I called, dropping the door knob and running into her little open arms.

I looked up from the hug and saw Mr. James and Mrs. Cassie, having just looked up from their packed bags. Mrs. Cassie put her hand over her mouth and began to cry while Mr. James came up to me and pulled Kinsie aside to give me a hug. Mrs. Cassie came over and joined in, then Kinsie joined back in the group.

After a few tears were shed by all parties, we pulled away from the group hug. "Looks like we have a lot to talk about," said Mr. James.

"You don't even know!" I said. I wanted to tell him everything right then but we had to stay on schedule, so I got straight to business, "Do you know who sent all of this to evacuate you."

"No," he shook his head, "All Alex told us was that it was a man who he knew was against The Organization."

"That man is my dad," I said smiling.

"What? Daniel?" he asked. Mrs. Cassie leaned in.

"Yea. Dad's alive. He faked his death in order to drop off of The Organization's radar," I explained, "It was his only choice to protect me and give us a chance to do what we are doing right now."

"Which is?" asked Mr. James.

"There's a base that Dad built. It has a very strong shield, 1,000 times stronger than the one here," I said. I wasn't sure if that was the exact statistic, but I knew impenetrable also wasn't, though it was the one my dad used.

"Once we're inside, they can't get to us. Dad sent me to get Mrs. Cassie and Kinsie on a transport headed back to the base. Blake is there waiting for you. Mr James, Dad wanted me to bring you into town. He wanted to get to see you before you went back."

Mr. James looked more surprised than anything now. He smiled, "Well, I guess we can do that."

I helped them finish packing and got the girls on the big transport nearby. It and a group of fighters were about to take off and head back to base. We wanted to get as many out as possible in case the Organization showed up before we were finished.

We all waved to each other as the door to the transport closed. Kinsie looked terrified, but I was surprised at just how strong she had been in the little time that I had seen her. She had been through so much for a kid that age.

The transport engines turned on and it began to hover above the ground, kicking up leaves and dust. The fighters around it did the same, then they all pulled off with one motion.

Mr. James and I watched as they faded into the clouds. Then, we went and found a small transport, about the size of the ship I crashed. I commanded the pilot to fly us into town to find my dad and Bailey.

"Any idea where he might have been headed?" The pilot asked.

"Uh," I didn't actually know where I was going. I assumed the pilot would know.

"306 Lake Circle Drive" Mr. James spoke up.

I gave him a confused look, "My old house?" I questioned.

Mr. James smiled, "There's a lot you don't know."

It wasn't long before the lakeside subdivision came into view. There were about twenty transports and fighters parked along the road near my house, my dad's ship among them. The pilot sat the ship down on the outside of the pack. I thanked him for flying us and then Mr. James and I got out.

There were a lot of people going in and out of my house, but every other resident of the neighborhood was shut up tight in their houses. We came to the front door. Many of the soldiers stopped what they were doing to look at me. My white uniform made me stand out against their gray ones. The glowing crystal on my chest only made me stand out more.

We walked inside. I was so caught up in everything that was happening, I almost didn't realize that this was the first time I had been there since my mother sold it. I recognized the floor plan, but all of the furniture had been changed as well as the paint color. It didn't even feel like my house anymore.

Mr. James saw someone walk through the kitchen in front of us so he went to go talk to them and find my dad. I stood in the living room. To the right there was a staircase leading to the basement. All of the furniture was made from a fancy brown leather. The coffee table was long and skinny. It was made of oak and matched the T.V. stand. The rug was a white, shag material. The floors had been redone to some sort of light gray planks. The walls were white and finished with a high gloss.

Dad walked up from the basement. "Love what you've done with the place," He said with a wince.

"It wasn't me," I said, "My mother sold it after you died."

"You're mother?" Dad looked puzzled.

"Yea… She claimed you never actually divorced her and had the paperwork to prove it. She took over your estate."

Dad's face turned red. He gritted his teeth and clenched his fist. "Those dogs," he growled, "Your mother helped me fight in the very beginning, but she was killed. I had to tell everyone we divorced in order to keep my fight against The Organization a secret."

"What?" I said, or well, sort of yelled, "You never told me this?"

"It was to protect you!" Dad snapped back, "And it worked. They never went after you until you found the crystal, just as I planned."

"Then who have I been staying with?" I asked.

Dad forced his anger away and calmly replied, "I would have to assume somebody the Organization sent to keep you from finding out the truth."

So that lady, drinking, partying, keeping the house a wreck was just to keep me busy? Everything I had to endure here was set up by The Organization? Now I was angry too. I clenched my jaw thinking of every sleepless night and every wrong that had been put on me by her, by them.

I turned to walk out, but Dad called after me, "What's done is done, son. You are where you belong now. Don't let them take another second from you."

I stopped and his words sunk in. I couldn't undo the things they had done, but I could stop them from doing it to anyone else.

I turned back to him, "What do we do?" I asked.

"Did you bring James?" he asked.

As he spoke, James walked around the corner with the soldier he saw in the kitchen. The two made eye contact. "I almost didn't believe him when he told me," he smiled.

Dad walked up the rest of the stairs, "After all we've been through you think a car could kill me?"

The two gave each other a hug. "I get the feeling there's something you're not telling me," I said.

"We weren't much older than you are now when we found out about The Organization." Mr. James said, "You're dad got his powers when one of their ships carrying the crystal exploded over his house."

"I learned how to use the powers and we fought against them for years," Dad added "We called ourselves 'The Guardians'."

171

"So you knew that she wasn't actually my mom?" I asked Mr James.

"Yes, and I'm sorry," he hung his head, "I tried to fight the legal system since the day it happened, but I couldn't expose her without exposing all of us. I had hoped her mistreatment of you would give us a case for DCS, but that was interrupted by all of this."

There was a moment of reflection on the situation and Dad took his chance to put us back on task. "Well, there is much to discuss, but at a different time," he said, "We have to get the weapons systems online."

He led us down the stairs. The basement, like at the Vales house, was mostly for storage, but there was something here I had never noticed before. In the back corner, boxes had been moved out of the way to reveal a trap door that led to more stairs. We followed them down into a large open space.

There were many control boards and work stations scattered all around. They were simple and looked almost patched together, with dangling wires and small screens. There were hallways that branched off of the central room and ran as far as I could see. "What is this place?" I asked.

"It's our old command center." Mr. James said.

"Why did you stop using it?" I asked.

"After your mother died, we decided we needed to fight another way," Dad said.

"Infiltration?"

"Exactly," he replied, "I started focusing on my work at Arnold base. While that gave me cover, I used ALI to gather intel."

"And since my mind was never as scientific as his was, I agreed to stay close to you and protect you," Mr. James added.

"Why did I need protection?" I aksed.

"If they found out your dad had powers, they would assume you had the mutation as well," he said.

We walked over to one of the control panels where one soldier was working. "Are the defenses almost online?" Dad asked him.

"They will be popping up any second, sir," he replied.

I looked over his shoulder at the screen. It was a map of Tullahoma and all over it there were red dots. I couldn't find a pattern so I asked, "What's the map showing?"

"They are cannons that are hidden just below the surface of the ground," the soldier answered without looking up.

If every dot was one cannon, then there were hundreds. I wanted to inquire how they got there but Dad and Mr. James had walked off. Each was managing a different station, so I asked the soldier if he knew. He replied, "This was the first base ever established. The cannons were put in, not to fight the Organization, but to cover an escape if they ever found the base. They are a bit dated, but I assume that is what they will use them for today."

"Interesting," I said, "Thank you soldier."

"You're welcome, sir."

It didn't sound like he had much hope that these would do much defending, more, drawing fire. I looked around, trying to find something to help do. I walked over by one of the hallways and saw a white uniform. It was Bailey.

She was carrying a box of guns. They were smaller guns, but the box was big and there were lots of them. She wouldn't have been able to carry it if not for her crystal-aided strength. I called for my powers. Blue energy flowed over the box and I lifted it from her arms.

"I had it." she said.

"Now I have it," I said, "Shivery doesn't have to die just because there's a war going on."

She smiled and shook her head. "Now... Where was this going?" I asked.

"Upstairs." She said, We began walking in that direction. "Have they evacuated the base yet?"

"The first shuttles were taking off when I left," I replied, "We probably need another thirty minutes to get all the people out, an hour to get the equipment."

"Did Dad just bring you along to carry guns?" I asked. I was curious about his reason for splitting us up.

173

"Well, he didn't ask me to do this. He just said he wanted a bearer with him at all times. I guess he feels safer that way."

"Or he doesn't want us both captured if something goes wrong," I replied. I thought that since our powers amplified each other, he didn't want there to be any chance that The Organization could get a hold of both crystals.

We were just heading up the first set of stairs to go to the basement when an alarm went off, coming from the coms on our shoulders. It startled me and I lost focus, dropping the box of guns that was floating along behind us. The alarm paused and ALI spoke up, "We have a squadron of enemy fighters closing in. They are approximately five minutes out. Everyone to their defensive positions."

Soldiers in the control room began to scramble around to different computers. Dad spoke over my coms, "Dylan, you and Bailey get to ground level. I'll meet you there. We are going to have to fight them off."

"Yes, sir." I said

I looked to Bailey who had clearly got the same message. I nodded my head and my helmet formed around my head. She did the same. We rushed up the stairs, leaving behind the box of guns, through the house and out to the front yard. A group of soldiers poured out behind us.

Tornado sirens were going off as makeshift air raid sirens. Ships along the road were taking off and fighters were beginning to buzz around in the sky. Suddenly, I felt the ground shake. I looked around for the source. Was it the incoming fighters?

I looked out over the lake, trying to get a view clear of trees. Then, two massive turrets emerged from the lake. Another burst through the ground in a roundabout just up the road, another on the grassy hill behind us. The roar of the fighter engines was consumed with crumbling earth and small explosions as the cannons emerged all around us.

I turned to say something to Bailey about getting ready for a fight, but her arms glowed with her radiant white energy. She looked from the sky to me. I nodded my head in agreement and summoned my powers. I could see specks in the sky off in the distance. The Organization was here.

Chapter 18

Dad emerged from the house and called to us, "The cruisers are still a ways out. They sent in the faster ships to try and keep us here. You two ready to have some on the job training?"

"Define ready," Bailey said.

"I'm ready," I said, ready to hurt them back for what they had done to me.

Dad walked over. Draw your staff. I did as he said and the blue energy ran down it. "Let your power flow through the staff, let it be an extension of you. The Unitum metal is a perfect conductor of your powers. Place your hand on one end and use the other to aim it like a rifle."

Once again, I did as he said. I placed one side of the staff in the palm of my right hand and the other I used to steady the staff about half way up the shaft.

"Now send a blast of energy through the staff."

I focused as much power as I could conjure through the shaft and a focused beam of blinding blue energy shot from the staff across the lake, and exploded in the woods on shore of the other side. Three trees toppled into the lake.

"Good, just next time shoot a ship instead of nature," Dad now focused on Bailey, "Your powers are almost electrical. If you feed into your powers, the same field that gives you super senses will also interfere with the electronic equipment around you. Be mindful of that. It may help or hurt you. Draw your staff."

She pulled it from her waistband, "I don't know how to use it. I can't fight with it."

"You can focus on your fighting later, right now, we are shooting." He gave her the same instructions as he had given me. Bailey fired across the lake, but when her's hit the ground, it spread out over a large area and made a white glow for about thirty seconds.

She looked disappointed. Dad spoke up, "You're blast won't be concussive like Dylan's. Your's can disable ships and disrupt even the strongest of shields for a short period. You two can work together. Bailey will disrupt the shields, and Dylan will bring them down. Make sense?"

"Yes, sir" We both said.

"Good, 'cause here they come."

The roar of engines filled the air. I could see a fleet of hundreds of fighters, now only about three miles away. Another roar came from behind us. I hoped it was our ships, but I couldn't see over the hill.

"Hold your fire until my command." Dad said over the coms. Bailey and I stood with our staves ready. He looked at us, "You two ready for your first battle?"

"Oh, I've already battled them once and won," I said with false arrogance.

"That was a fight, this is a battle," Dad said.

"Was that supposed to make us feel better?" Bailey asked.

"You've got this," He said, dawning his helmet. He jogged over to his ship.

"Where are you going?" I asked.

"To fight," he said bluntly. He opened the com channel again, "Open fire!"

The canopy on his ship closed and a swarm of fighters raced over our heads toward the Organization fleet. A rain of blasts erupted from the cannons and filled the sky with yellow blasts of energy. The Organization retaliated with their fiery orange blasts and seeking missiles.

The two swarms met over an open field, just on the other side of the woods across the lake. From there the fight began to spread out. The turrets in the lake fired shot after shot. An Organization ship dove at the two cannons and flew between them. I lifted my staff and fired a shot at it, hitting it in the wing.

The blast erupted on the fighter and tossed it to the side. Smoke poured from the wound, but the pilot managed to pull up and keep flying. He flew over our heads, just missing the top of my house.

"You have to shoot too, or that's gonna happen every time." I called to Bailey.

"I know, I'm sorry."

"We'll get the next one."

It wasn't long before we had another chance. I sensed a fighter coming over the hill behind us. Bailey must have sensed it too, because we turned at the same time. It cleared the hill and we both fired. Her blast hit the cockpit, and mine hit just below. The blast detached the entire front end.

I dropped the staff and held out both hands in an attempt to save the pilot. I grabbed hold of the cockpit with my power and stopped him from plunging into the lake. The back half of the ship crashed into the opposite shore, but I sat him down gently in the place where my practice shot had taken out the trees.

"Yes!"

"We got one!"

Bailey and I celebrated, but ALI decided to kill the moment, "The power of two stars between the both of you and all you take down is one ship? No! I won't stand for it. Dylan, I expect this from her, but not you. Fly up there and be useful."

I looked at Bailey, "I'm sorry, I don't know what has gotten into him."

"You will not apologize for me! I trained you better."

"ALI, you saw how strong the shield was!" I retorted, "It just took both of us to take one down."

"No, all I saw was how weak your faith was! Your powers will protect you. Believe in yourselves. Think of everything they have taken from you; are you just going to let them take more?"

Dad spoke up over the coms, "It's not exactly how I would have put it, but he's right. I didn't teach you how to shoot for you to forget about the rest of your power. Get out there and follow your powers. Let them take the lead."

I suddenly had a new sense of determination, though it was crippled by my uncertainty of my ability. I wanted them to pay. I wanted to protect the base. I had to. I broke through the wall of uncertain emotion and ignited my jetpack. I looked at Bailey, "He's right, we can do more. I can do more."

I hated to just fly off and leave her, but I was sure ALI would guide her just as he did me. I had something to prove. More to myself, but also to The Organization. I didn't want to kill any of them, but I wanted them to fear me and what I could do. I wanted to show them that everything they had tried to do to stop me was in vain. I wanted them to have the humiliation of having to respect me after treating me like trash.

I flew at full speed toward the dog fight. Now that I was in the air, I could see troop transports coming in in the distance. They would be heading for the base. Dad called over the headset, "Dylan, these are drones. The real pilots are flying in with the transports. You can have fun with these."

I felt good not to have to pull my punches. I summoned my power and reinforced it with my resolve. The energy radiated across my entire body and down the staff. An enemy ship flew past me and I thrust the staff into it as it went. It tore through the shield and the metal of the jet sending it crashing to the ground. I shot a blast of energy through the staff at another ship. It was powerful, but was distributed by the shield. The ship was pushed, but regained control..

"Now, that's more like it," ALI said.

"I would have to agree," Dad said.

A fighter behind me opened fire, but I sensed it and put up my shield. The blasts were powerful, but I stood my ground. I focused the shield down into an orb of energy, containing all of the shots from the ship, and I thrust it back. The blue energy encased the orange. It hit the fighter right on the nose. The blue energy dissipated, but the orange cut through the shield. The ship exploded.

I fired shot after shot taking down ships. They tried to converge on me, but they never became too much for me because of the other pilots helping me out. I soon noticed my Dad's ship. He was a good pilot, swerving and diving. He maneuvered between two enemy ships and they crashed into one another. One ship fired a missile at him, but I shot a blast from the staff and intercepted it.

"Thanks!" He said over the coms.

"Anytime!"

Suddenly, with one motion, every enemy fighter dove down. It caught me and every other pilot off guard. Then, like a school of fish, they turned back up again and opened fire. It was a sneaky maneuver

178

and an effective one. The shots coming from the organization's ships caught many of our pilots broadside. They began to fall from the sky.

I retracted my staff and placed it back on my waistband. Then I pulled as much power as I could from the crystal. The air filled with blue energy and the flowing streams raced after each crashing ship. I managed to catch every single one (about thirty), but the enemy fighter began to pick off the floating targets one by one.

"Guah!" I yelled desperately trying to set the ships down easily, "I need some help over here!"

"I'm coming!" Dad said.

His fighter came over, but there were too many for him to take on alone. It took too much focus for me to hold every ship that I couldn't fight. The enemy was still picking them off. A ship flew toward me. It fired a few shots, but missed. It pulled up and circled around for another attack. I couldn't let go, and I couldn't fight.

"You have to let go, Dylan!" ALI said, "Save yourself, they did their job."

I gritted my teeth and choked out, "If I let go, I am no better than they are."

Then, without warning, a white glow filled the air. A bolt of white energy raced through the enemy ships, one by one they began to fall. The energy would leap from one to the next, killing the engines.

I looked around for the source of this new weapon until I saw that it was not a weapon at all. It was Bailey. She was flying up from across the lake, a heavenly glow of white energy around her. Her gauze guided the energy from ship to ship. Her helmet was retracted and her long blond hair was flowing behind her as if it was weightless. She had one leg pulled up slightly and the other held down straight. Her hands were down at her sides, each radiating with a bright white light.

I almost lost my focus on the fighters looking at her. They slipped a bit, but I gained control again. As Bailey and the remaining fighters continued their defensive maneuvers, I sat the disabled ships down in the open field below. Now that I was free, I looked back at Bailey. I couldn't see a flame coming from her jetpack. "ALI," I called, "Is she flying on her own?"

"Somehow… yes." He replied.

"I thought you said that was impossible."

179

"It is for you."

The remaining enemy fighters fled her attack and flew toward the approaching troop transports. I flew over to Bailey, "Looks like you found your confidence too." I congratulated.

"Well, like ALI said, they've taken enough from us. I couldn't let them take anymore," she said.

"Where'd you learn to do all that?" I asked.

"Everyone regroup at the base," Dad interrupted over the coms.

We obeyed and started our flight back. I wanted to know more about her story with her powers, but incoming gunfire made a conversation impossible. It seemed like there was so much that had happened to her. I knew she had only told me so little of the story, but I suppose that's a story for another day. We were too busy for a heart to heart.

We neared the base in only a few minutes. All of the fighters hovered at the perimeter ready to defend the base. Bailey and I followed my dad's ship which landed in the same spot where the transport Mrs. Cassie and Kinsie got on had been. Alex was there waiting for him.

The canopy of his fighter opened and Bailey and I landed beside it. Dad hopped down. "How is the evacuation going, Alex?" he asked.

"It's going quickly," Alex said with urgency in his voice, "The last of the civilians, prisoners, and wounded just left, but we still have a lot of equipment to load up."

"Forget the equipment. We need to get the base's data core then we need to leave."

"What's the data core?" I asked.

"It has everything this base has ever done on it. Every order and every piece of intel it has ever received," Dad said, "If we have it, we may be able to piece together what is going on in the rest of the world and how to take them down."

"I'll send some of my people to get the core," Alex said.

180

"Take Dylan and Bailey with you." Dad suggested, "If those transports land and the troops make it here, you will need their help."

"Yes, sir," Alex said.

Bailey, Alex, and I ran off toward the main buildings of the base and Alex called for backup over the coms. We reached one small building, about the size and shape of a silo, where ten of the Taken soldiers were waiting on us. "This is it." Alex said.

"Awful small," I pointed out, "Why does it take so many people?"

"You'll see," Alex said, opening the door.

The room was brightly lit. In the center, extending from the floor to the ceiling, was a column glowing with different colored buttons and sensors. All around it were what looked like bookcases, ascending up the column.

"The data core is the round column in the middle," Alex explained, "We have to get all of the individual file disks off of it."

The Taken came in the door behind us and jetted up to different levels. They began removing the books one by one, flying down, placing them in a stack and flying back up again. Bailey and I joined in the effort but it was like we weren't even putting a dent in it. I could hear explosions begin to ring out again.

"This is going to take too long," I said, flying down to the ground. I looked around for an idea.

"What do you suggest?" Alex asked, "They are too fragile just to throw down."

I thought for a moment more. Then I had it, "Not if I catch them!" I said, "You all throw them down and I'll use my powers to slow their fall."

"Can you do that with so many at once?" Bailey asked me. I was sure she was thinking about my struggle with the jets.

An explosion shook the ground and I heard a fighter crash very close to the silo. "We're just going to have to find out." I said.

They began to throw the books down. I closed my eyes and used only my senses to catch them. I didn't stack them up, but gently

181

placed them on the ground. They started out slow, but when they saw that I could handle it, they threw them down in handfuls.

More explosions shook the ground. They were getting closer and becoming more frequent. The troops must have landed. I tried not to think too much about it. I had to stay in the moment. Finally, I stopped sensing more falling books. I opened my eyes.

I was surprised to see all of them floating around the center column, slowly revolving around it about two feet off the floor. The blue energy flowed around them in its elegant streams. I lowered them down gently, piling them on one side of the silo.

"Think you can carry them out like you were just catching them?" Alex asked me.

"Yea, I…"

There was a loud crash as the top of the silo was ripped off by a falling ship. Bailey and I both raised our shields, pushing the debris away. The fighter exploded behind us. "Time to go!" Bailey said. I picked up all of the books with my powers and herded them over the wall since the top had been taken off the building. Everyone filed out the door, and I came out last.

I could see, near the landing site, phaser blasts. The troops were here. I looked to the sky and out of the swarm of fighters, a transport flew down and landed beside us. The doors opened and the pilot yelled over the ambient roar of engines and explosions, "Load it up!"

I pushed all of the books in and to the back of the ship. "We cleaned out the data core," Alex said over the coms channel.

He was answered with my dad giving the evacuation order, "All troops to the nearest transport. We're headed to Washington!"

Then the Taken climbed on the transport. Alex, Bailey, and I stayed behind. Alex waved the pilot to take off. The door closed and he looked at the firefight happening across the base. "I'm not a mind reader like you, but I have a feeling we're all wanting to go be a part of that fight, right?"

"I'm not leaving until every person is off this base," Bailey said.

"Yea, what she said," I added.

Bailey and I summoned our powers and we all flew off toward the fight. I drew my staff. Alex drew his pistols. From the air, I could see both sides of the fight. There were about two hundred Organization soldiers coming through the treeline and about fifty of our guys, pinned down behind the building where I had met the Vales earlier. They were without a ship to escape on.

A transport tried to land but it was run off by three manned enemy fighters. There was chatter on the coms about not being able to land. I spoke up, "You're about to get a chance. Just keep an eye on those troops and watch for an opening." I turned to Bailey, "You stay back and keep the fighters off of us, We'll fight back the troops."

She nodded in agreement and pulled back. The Organization troops were making their move. They dashed across the open ground between the building and the woodline. I sped up and landed right in front of them. When I hit the ground, a blue shockwave spread out and blew the first few rows backward.

A white bolt of energy raced through them, stunning them before they hit the ground. It came from Bailey, but she had to turn her attention to the skies. I threw my staff into the mob, then called it back to my hand. Alex landed beside me and began to fire into the group. They were wearing armor, but every shot was placed in the gaps, either in the thigh, or in the neck.

"Alex, fight with mercy!" I commanded, blowing back another large group with a concussive blow. I generally felt that the decision to kill or not to kill should be left up to the individual, but I felt Alex and I would likely be fighting along side quite a bit. I wanted our tactics to align. "Use my guns, they stun."

"But!... Ugh, Fine!" He conceded, getting in one last kill shot. He holstered his guns and pulled mine from my waistband as I used my powers to hold them off.

He resumed firing. The soldiers pivoted and began to draw their melee weapons. I used my power to yank the weapons from the front row and Alex took them all down. They were now too close for ranged attacks, so I took my staff and charged into the group. They were skilled, but my strength was enough to give me an edge. I could see the white energy leaping through the crowd again. Bailey was keeping them thinned out enough to make fighting them manageable.

We had been fighting long enough now for the soldiers we were protecting to catch onto what was happening. All of them poured out from behind the building and opened fire on the Organization troops.

183

With another wave of soldiers now coming through the tree line, we would have soon been overwhelmed without their help.

After a few minutes of fighting, we overpowered the Organization troops and they retreated back to the woods just as three transports were descending on us. They landed in the opening between the woods and the building, and all of the troops loaded up.

Alex and I flew up to Bailey, who was on the roof of the building. "Are there any others?" Bailey asked.

"I don't know," Alex admitted, "I can ask." He turned on his com, "Are there any other soldiers in need of assistance? This is the last call before all forces are called to retreat."

There was silence over the coms. We waited for a moment, firing into the swarm of fighters above us.

After a moment Dad contacted us, "Sounds like everyone's out. Let's go. We need to stay ahead of the cruisers."

"Agreed." Alex said, He turned on the coms again, "Retreat! All forces pull out and head to the rendezvous outside of D.C"

We all three dawned our helmets and flew up to a transport. The pilot opened the door and we landed in the hold. We were the only passengers. It was carrying crates of food.

As we pulled off, I could see smoke rising from Tullahoma. The remaining turrets were still firing their yellow blasts into the air. The glow of fire and explosion lifted over the trees. It had felt like such a victory until now, looking at my home, the only home I had ever known, being burned to the ground.

Somehow, even though we accomplished our mission, The Organization still found a way to take more for me.

The transport was packed full with crates. All of the seats had boxes in them. The only room left was a small aisle down the center of the cargo hold. Bailey and I found a big box, and sat down next to one another. Alex walked up to the front to talk to the pilots.

I wanted to say something, but nothing came to mind. Now that we were safe, my mind began to catch up with the events that were unfolding so quickly. This had been my first time in a battle of that scale. I couldn't help but think of all of those, on both sides, who had given their lives.

I realized another truth of this war, much like the one I had thought of on the way here. If we won, then every person who fought for the Organization died in vain. If The Organization won, everyone who died on our side, died in vain. And no matter who won, everyone who was not on a side, every civilian, died in vain. How could one justify such death and destruction?

Those on our side had deemed the loss of life worth defeating The Organization. Perhaps rightly so. But those allied with The Organization had clearly done the same toward us. Was any cause really worth all of this? Would the rule of The Organization be so bad as to justify the means of overthrowing them?

Bailey broke the reflective silence, "Do you think it's possible?"

"What?" I asked.

"Do you think we can win?"

I sat for a moment, trying to come up with an answer. If I was honest, it didn't feel like it. I really didn't know. So I was honest.

"You know, I really have no idea," I leaned back in my chair, "All I have done so far is run. I went to save Blake's parents, but what I didn't tell you is that I lost. I would have, if Alex didn't show up with the taken. After that, we ran. Then I saved you, and ran. Then we evacuated Tullahoma and ran. Now we're going to D.C to pick up the president and run some more. We have to run out of places to run to eventually. Then, I don't know what will happen."

Bailey stared at the boxes in front of us, thinking about what I had said. I knew it wasn't encouraging, but I was pretty down myself. Bailey spoke up, "I thought when I finally figured out how to use my powers, I would be able to take on the whole Organization myself. Back there, when we were fighting, I realized something."

"What's that?"

"I can't. I can't take them on myself. Neither can you, or even just us. There aren't enough of us. If there really is no one else out there who can help us, it's only a matter of time before The Organization traps us in that mountain." Bailey started to cry, "I thought... I thought..."

She never finished what she was trying to say. It didn't matter. I put my arm around her and she leaned her head over on my shoulder. Usually I was very empathetic. Seeing someone cry would usually bring tears to my eyes, but not this time. This time, I was so confused about my own emotions, I couldn't feel anyone else's. I just sat there, holding her with a cold expression on my face.

She stopped crying after a couple of minutes, but her head stayed on my shoulder and my arm stayed around her. I thought of something I had heard before; I didn't know where, but I thought it was appropriate for the time.

"I heard once that 'if we let the enemy take our hope, then they have already won.' After all they have taken from me, I know that if I do lose, it will not be because I handed them the victory."

"What if they take everything?"

"Then I'll fight like I have nothing left to lose," I held out my free hand and sent some energy to my palm, "But it won't come to that."

"How do you know?" Bailey questioned, not yet taking my hand.

"There are some things they can't take: my morals, my beliefs, my faith. Then, there are some things that I refuse to let them take without killing me first."

It was then that Bailey sent her white energy to her palm and took my hand. I respond by sending my energy down that arm to my hand. The two colors expanded around us and swirled over the surfaces of the boxes in an eloquent dance. A white and blue mist formed in a ring around us.

Bailey lifted her head from my shoulder and looked me in the eyes. There was a white rim of energy around her pupils. Then I saw my blue energy flicker through the white ring.

Up to that point, I hadn't thought of her as someone I would fall in love with. Mostly because that was about the furthest thing from my mind with all that was happening. Sure, I had felt protective of her, I was the one who promised to keep her safe. But when I looked into her eyes, all I felt was love and security. It was deep and comforting.

Bailey smiled and I smiled back. She was feeling the same thing. I didn't need to read her thoughts to see it. I could see it in her eyes. She laid her head back on my shoulder and I leaned my head over on her's. I guess, in all the explosions and fights, it just felt good for the both of us to find a bit of peace.

I looked across at the boxes in front of us and the swirling patterns on them. They formed spirals, the white following the blue, the blue following the white. They would move across the boxes in currents and waves. It was soothing. So soothing in fact, I fell asleep.

Chapter 19

I was shaken to consciousness by the landing of the transport. I raised up and Bailey quickly followed. We were still holding hands, but the patterns on the boxes and around us had vanished. Alex was sitting at the front of the row of boxes. "Nice of you two love birds to join us," Bailey and I subtly let go of each other's hand, "We're here; your dad needs to see us all."

Bailey and I stood up. I stretched my arms and back, then followed Bailey and Alex off of the transport. I was surprised to see that we had landed in a deserted shopping center parking lot. There were not just our troops walking between the fighters and other ships, but there were also U.S. military troops mingled in with them.

"Why are they here?" Bailey asked, pointing to one of the military men.

"Beats me," Alex said, "Maybe Daniel can fill us in."

I didn't know how I felt about the two of them being on a first name basis now. It felt weird, but I let it slide.

"So..." Alex continued, "What were all the fancy patterns you two were making in the back?"

I didn't really like that he was insinuating we were in a relationship. Not because I didn't want to be, but because I wasn't sure she wanted to be or if that was appropriate, considering we had only known each other for a few days. Still, I answered his question, "Well, we don't exactly make them, they make themselves."

"When we combine our powers." Bailey added.

"Interesting," Alex said, "So, you can stack your powers?"

"We aren't sure how it works in combat." I said, knowing that was where his mind was going.

"Well, as good as the two of you are, I would be scared to see what would happen if you could amplify what you already have," Alex complemented.

"The Organization would be scared." Bailey corrected.

"Oh, yea," Alex laughed, "I was just speaking for them."

We walked until we found Dad standing by his ship. He was talking to two highly decorated officers from the U.S. military. They looked like generals but I didn't know how to read the pendants to figure out their exact rank.

When Dad saw us, he waved us over and introduced us to them, "Hey soldiers! These gentlemen are from the U.S. government. They will be overseeing our meeting with the president. General Pale, General Housen, these are our two crystal bearers, my son, Dylan and his friend Bailey. And this is Alex, the leader of the Organization defectors."

General Pale was a tall man, about fifty years old if I had to guess. His hair was close cut and hard to see, but what I could see was silver. He wore the uniform of the army, a green color suit with a tan tie. On his chest were his insignias and medals, none of which I recognized outside of maybe movies.

General Housen was a shorter man, but very muscular. I guessed he was closer to being in his early forties and he wore a navy uniform, also decorated with many pins and medals that I didn't recognize. Both men wore a traditional pistol on their hip.

We shook their hands. "They're younger than I expected," General Pale said.

"Fate would have it that way," Dad said, "But I assure you they're all very skilled."

"I'm sure," General Housen rolled his eyes, "And you claim they have superpowers too! If it were not for your potential to equip us to fight this Organization, you and your outlandish claims would not have been awarded this meeting."

All of us were a bit taken aback by this statement. I couldn't believe they would talk to Dad this way after what he was offering to do for them. I called my powers down my arms to prove they were real. The Generals' eyes grew large but they said nothing of it and quickly regained their stoic composure.

"If it were not for these soldiers, America would have already fallen," Dad defended, "They stole the one thing powering the fleet that was supposed to take over America just like the rest of the world has been."

"We were sent here to find proof of your legitimacy. If you can prove to President Jaxson that you do in fact have the crystal, this would help your case," General Pale said.

189

"Does the technology and manpower I brought with me not help my case?" Dad said frustrated, but keeping his composure.

"I'm not questioning the legitimacy of your people or weapons, that we can see," General pale gestured to the fighters surrounding him, "I am referring to the legitimacy of its effectiveness."

Dad said nothing. He simply reached down to his waistband and pulled from his belt a small box. He pressed a button and the lid opened revealing the red glow of the crystal. The two generals observed it.

"Now, have you any further questions of our legitimacy?" Dad smirked.

"No, sir" The generals said, defeated.

"Good!" Dad said, a bit too animated, "Now, we are running out of time. The Organization cruisers are hot on our tail. I can order reinforcements to join us at the capitol once I have assurance they will not be shot at. With the combined power of the United States and my forces, we may be able to stave them off for the time being."

"You may bring one of your transport shuttles, escorted by two fighters," General Housen commanded, "Once you speak with the president, he can direct you on what will be allowed."

"Very well," Dad said. He called for a transport over the coms and it wasn't long before one landed on the opposite side of Dad's fighter. Alex, Bailey, Dad, the generals, and I all got inside and took a seat in the cargo hold. I sat with Bailey on my right and Alex on my left. Dad sat across from us next to the generals. Everyone fastened their seatbelts. Dad instructed the pilot to leave the doors open so we could see out.

The transport lifted up and was flanked by two fighters. We lifted over the supermarket and started forward. I could see that we were just outside of D.C. and would be flying in. The aerial view allowed us to see the hundred or so fighters we had brought with us. Most of the transports and many of the fighters had gone back to base, but I hadn't realized how many had stuck with us.

The fight was mostly void of conversation. I couldn't think about anything but how Dad's tone had changed. He seemed so determined just to get the president back to the base earlier. Had his plan truly changed? Did he want to make a stand in Washington, or was he just trying to say anything to land a meeting with the President?

As we flew over the landmarks of D.C, I could see a massive military presence in the area. They were clearly preparing for what was coming. There were tanks and military vehicles down every street. No civilian car could be seen. It seemed like they had evacuated the entire district. Some longer streets had seemingly been turned into runways, with fighter jets lining highways.

We flew right up to the White House and landed on the lawn. We all unclipped our seatbelts and climbed out. Dad thanked the pilot for the ride and instructed him to wait until we came back.

Still not saying anything, we followed the generals in the front door. I had never been to D.C. I had seen the White house in documentaries, but never in person. It was so much bigger than I imagined.

"I bet you never thought you'd meet the president like this!" I said, leaning over to Bailey.

"I never thought I would meet the president at all," She retorted.

"I always thought if I ever entered the White House, it would be because The Organization wanted me to assassinate someone," Alex added.

He was sort of joking, but not really. I hadn't thought about how strange this must be for him, considering his past. It's hard for me and Bailey, but it had to be so much harder for him. The Organization really had taken everything from him.

"Well, man, be glad you're walking in this way." I said, patting him on the shoulder.

The Generals walked us in through the front door and down various hallways until we came to a room, which on the outside was labeled "Oval Office". The Generals opened the door and walked in, followed by Dad, Alex, then Bailey. I was the last one to go in.

On the far side of the room, there was a wooden desk, flanked by two flags. Behind it were towering windows with cascading, golden drapery. The navy blue carpet was stamped with the presidential seal. In the center of the room were two white couches which faced one another and a wooden table between them.

On the couch to the right sat the president. He was young as far as presidents go, probably in his forties. His hair, which was thick

191

and perfectly combed to the side, still had its black color. He wore a navy suit with a white shirt and red tie.

He stood up, "Ahh, the people I've heard so much about! Please, have a seat." He gestured to the couch in front of him. We all sat there while the generals sat with the president, one on each side.

"It's an honor to meet you, Mr. President." Dad said solemnly, "I wish we could be here under better circumstances."

"As do I," He said. Bailey, Alex, and I watched in silence. I wasn't sure why, of all people, Dad chose to bring us. Why not his generals. "I hope these Generals weren't too harsh on you, we just needed to be sure you weren't with The Organization."

"It was nothing we couldn't handle," Dad replied.

"Very good," The President replied, "Now, My generals tell me you propose a way to defeat our enemy."

"Yes, sir, but the way I will propose may not be favorable to you," Dad said.

"And why is that?" The President asked.

"Because it would mean breaking age old treaties, every national barrier, and goes against everything you were likely planning on doing," Dad said bluntly.

"Well, I am a reasonable man," The president said, "This Organization, as you call them, has already broken the order of the world, so if we do it as well, I see no harm."

"It has been a plan of mine for years," Dad continued, "But tensions between the various Organization resistances had always been too high. We disagreed on how to fight, so we disconnected ourselves from each other. Now that we have no other alternative, I think my plan for an Ekklesia is a viable one."

"There are other resistances like yours?" The president asked. I was glad he did, because I had no idea either.

"Yes," Dad answered, "The one here is the largest, but there are many across the globe with stolen Organization technologies as well as technologies I have given them. They have all worked in secret for a very long time, but I have been in contact with many of them in the past few hours. "

"And what is an Ekklesia?" the President asked.

"My ultimate plan. An assembly, from every nation, that comes together to fight The Organization!" Dad said, "I have tried to petition presidents before about the existence of the Organization and was ignored. I have done the same across the world. I don't blame you for your unbelief, but now you have no choice but to believe. It is the same with every nation. In every one of those nation's there is already at least one cell standing in opposition to The Organization. I can contact them all eventhough world communications are down. I can send word through those cells, to other governments, and we can call them here to make a final stand. If we win, we can slowly take back the world."

The President looked to his generals. He nodded. They nodded. "Well, we have no other choice. You will have the full might of whatever is left of the United States Army. It will be commanded in conjunction with your troops and the ones that you rally. Understand that it is the U.S. Army and not yours. We will be partners."

"That's what the Ekklesia is." Dad said.

"It's settled then." General Pale said, "Make your calls to these other cells."

"That I can do," Dad leaned in, "But you must move all of the troops you have to my base. The Organization cruisers will crush you here."

"We can't move even a quarter of our troops out before they get here, even if you slow them down," General Housen said.

"Guh.. I didn't want to do this yet..." Dad grumbled under his breath. He sighed, then said, "I have three battle cruisers I can bring here. I didn't want to reveal them yet, but it seems I have no choice. It'll still be close."

We have cruisers? I thought. I didn't know about this "ultimate plan". I didn't know about our cruisers. What else has he been keeping from me? I was led to believe this fight was hopeless.

Maybe he just didn't want to get my hopes up. We still had so much to talk about. I tried to hide my surprise in front of the important people but it was difficult.

Dad continued, "I can't get them here quicker than The Organization can get here. We'll have to hold out for about thirty minutes."

"Our men can handle it." General Pale said.

"You've never fought The Organization before," Alex spoke up, "If you had, you wouldn't be so confident. They won't send human troops to invade. They will send mindless, ruthless androids. You won't be able to kill them with guns. If they do send in humans, they will be wearing bullet proof armor. Or they may not send anyone and just rain fire down on you. Either way, we are bugs and they're a boot."

"Then how do you suggest we fight them?" General Housen asked.

"Nothing that won't require heavy casualties," Alex's face became cold.

"If it can get some of our troops out of here, it's worth it," The president said.

"They will send in fighters first. You send your jets to meet them. They will be target practice, but will buy us time. Meanwhile, all of your tanks and missiles are firing as fast as you can reload. If you make us look like a scary bug, you can buy us about twenty minutes.

"And the last ten?" General Housen inquired.

"That's when our fighters move in. When they see them, they'll send in their troop transports because they'll think we're out of moves. No one stands in their way. Let them march here where soldiers equipped with phasers will be waiting along with the two Crystal Bearers. That should keep them busy long enough to buy you the time you need. Once our cruisers show up, we call in the calvary and focus our attacks on their cruisers."

"I like it, what about you two?" The president looked at the generals.

"It sounds good, but we don't know what we're dealing with."

"We do." I said, "I say go with his plan."

"I second the plan." Dad said.

"I like the plan." Bailey added.

"I agree with his plan," Said General Housen.

"Then it's settled. Daniel, Call in your cruisers. Generals, Bearers, Taken, Prepare your soldiers.

194

Part 3: Rise of the Ekklesia
Ekklesia - ec·cle·si·ae - Noun - Greek - a gathering or assembly
"The called out ones"

Chapter 20

We marched out of the White House and back to our ship. The president got on with us and we flew back to the supermarket parking lot. The temporary base was static, awaiting the orders coming with our transport.

The ship landed and we all exited. The President was quickly escorted to a new ship where he would be transported to our mountain base. As he left us, he wished us "Good luck and GodSpeed".

The generals briskly walked to their communications station and Dad pulled a communicator from his waistband. He looked at the three of us, "You all know the plan. Stick to it. I've got a lot of calls to make. I'll be back soon."

"You're not staying with us?" Alex asked.

"No, I'm going with the president, but I'm coming back," He assured us, "I have to go get the Cruisers."

"You really think we can do this?" I asked. I wasn't talking about the army. "You think I can do this? I'm not even trained."

My dad walked closer and put his arm on my shoulder, "Why do you think you and Blake were always in martial arts classes? Why do you think I taught you to shoot when you were six? I've been training you for this your whole life. You are more capable and smarter than any soldier. I know you can do this."

I smiled a nostalgic smile. I hadn't seen until now that he had been preparing me for so long. "I love you Dad." I said, wrapping him in a tight hug.

"I love you too, son," He said, hugging me back, "See you soon."

And with that, he let go and jogged over to the transport that was talking off with the president. I turned to Alex and Bailey, "Well, here we go." I said. Coming behind them was one of our generals.

"Here we go is right," He said, "The US generals just briefed us on the plan. You guys ready to head back to the White House?"

"Ready as we'll ever be," Bailey said.

"I'll go gather the Taken that we have with us and ride in with them." Alex said.

"Very well," The General agreed, "Dylan, Bailey, You two can ride in with us. Follow me."

We followed him over to a transport with gold-tipped wings and a gold stripe down the side. On the stripe were black letters that read "LEADERSHIP". It felt strange to be considered a leader when I had only been here for a few days. I guess that's what happens when your dad runs the show.

I climbed up into the cargo hold and helped Bailey in behind me. We found the two remaining seats in the back of the ship, conveniently side by side. We took a seat just as the ship lifted off the ground and we began our journey back the way we came.

Again we rode with the doors open. I could barely see out since I was in the back though. From what I could see, the tanks were repositioning closer to the White House. I also noticed that many of the jets were starting to take off. Trucks with missiles pointed their payloads to the sky, ready to fire.

No one spoke on the ride over. The roar of the wind coming through the doors would have made it too loud to hear anyway.

Bailey and I only exchanged nervous glances. We had been in a battle, I had been in two, but we had never seen the full might of the Organization like we were about to experience. Every fight seemed to grow in intensity: from that first one back at Arnold base, to fighting the Taken, to the Montana base, to Tullahoma, to now.

The thought of this battle scarred those of us in the resistance. I could sense the fear even now in this transport. I felt that those in the U.S. military didn't fully appreciate what was about to happen.

We landed back on the lawn. I hadn't noticed, but behind us was a massive procession of every fighter and transport that we had. They all flew over the White House, opting to park about a mile away.

This way they wouldn't be an easy target, but we could still make a quick get away. Once everyone was out of our transport, it took off and joined the rest.

The coms on my shoulder turned on. The general we had flown over with began to speak, "Alright troops, remember, our goal is to draw out their troops in order to keep the cruisers away. They think that the president is still here so they won't blow up the district yet. They want him alive. We've got to hold them off until our help gets here. We do that, we'll be able to get most of these American troops out of here alive."

Just as he finished talking, a siren sounded. I looked around, trying to see what had set off the alarm. Then I saw them, in the distance three cruisers, all larger than the one we had fled from at the Montana base, were closing in. Out in front of them were hundreds of tiny dots- fighters.

Almost on que with my realization, hundreds of American jets flew over our heads. The roar of their engines was deafening. I, along with everyone else, activated my helmet. The heads up display loaded, and the helmet dulled the sound to a bearable level.

A group of soldiers ran up behind us. Their uniforms were that of The Taken. One of them ran up to us. It was Alex. "You guys ready for some real action?" He asked, drawing his atom sword.

"Not exactly," I said, "Drawing my staff and calling my powers.

Bailey held her arms slightly out to her sides, called her power and lifted a few feet off the ground, "I'm ready," she said. Her voice was cold.

"That's what I like to hear!" ALI said.

"Been a while since we talked to you." I pointed out.

"Well, we've all been busy," ALI said, "Bailey, I'm not sure how much training you've had, but just be sure not to do anything rash."

"Got it ALI." She said. Her tone was a bit better now. I hoped that whatever anger she held toward The Organization wouldn't get the best of her. I knew I would need to keep an eye on her.

Explosions rang out in the distance. I could see debris falling from the sky, I assumed mostly the U.S. jets, since they had no shields. Missiles flew up from the ground along with the cannon fire coming from the tanks. Bombs fell from the Organization fighters as our front lines were quickly overwhelmed.

The coms lit up on the helmet's display. A frantic voice cried out, "We've done all we can do up here! They're coming back to line two!"

"That was a little too quick," I said.

"That was expected," Alex replied, "They'll start sending in the androids next."

The explosions began to move closer and I started to notice a new wave of ships coming from the cruisers. They flew closer to the ground and landed below where the fighting in the air was happening. They must have been the transports with the robots.

The explosions moved closer, but with every bit of ground they gained, they moved slower. The fighting was now only about five miles away. It had been only about ten minutes and we were already running out of jets. The organization cruisers were just pouring ships back into the fighting as quickly as they were losing them.

Another frantic voice called over the coms channel, "That's all we can do! You guys better start sending everything you've go..."

The transmission was cut short but was quickly followed by the voice of General Housin, "You heard the man! Give 'em everything we've got!"

Right on que, all of our fighters flew overhead and entered the battle along with a barrage of missiles. The fighting was now about two miles away. The missiles thinned out the enemy fighters, but another large wave could be seen coming from the cruisers.

"We've got incoming androids," an unfamiliar voice said over the coms.

"Here we go!" Called Alex, "Taken, ready your weapons!"

Alex held up his sword, and all of the Taken behind him ignited their blades and assumed a ready position. I drew more power from the crystal and allowed it to radiate down the staff.

Coming through the park across the road were the same style of robots we had fought at the montana base. They were in a full sprint with their weapons drawn. All of them were sporting atom swords as well.

They tore through the fence and our troops ran to meet them. I was one of the first there. It was hard to tell just how many robots there were, but it was clear that they vastly outnumbered us.

I put both hands on the staff and released a powerful beam of energy. It ripped into the crowd of robots, breaking them into pieces and sending many of them crashing into one another.

I grabbed one that had fallen to the ground with my powers and thrust him further back into the crowd. I then summoned another large blast, to keep them at bay. There were so many that even these blasts couldn't keep them all away. There was no way to keep them from getting around me, but the soldiers behind me were doing a good job fending them off. I just had to keep them thinned out.

Bailey was further down the yard, doing a good job keeping them back as well. Her electrical powers were a bit better than mine at incapacitating the robots, but mine could cover a larger area.

I kept them pushed back, but seeing all of their fallen swords on the ground gave me an idea. I used my power to pick up about a dozen of them, ignited them and began to spin them. Then I thrust them back into the crowd of robots. They sliced through a few, but many used their swords to block them.

They were begining to get smart, and less were coming in front of me. "Dylan, They're flanking us!" Alex said over the coms.

A large amount of the robots were coming in the far left side of the yard. I sent a blast that way, blowing many of them back out into the road. As I did that, I sensed something coming at us. I instinctively raised my shield, stopping a small rocket that was shot at me. I saw that across the road, the robots had set up rocket launchers. There were about twenty of them and they all began to fire.

I raised my shield again, making it as large as I could out in front of me. A few made it through and exploded near the back rows of the taken, sending some of our troops flying into the air.

Bailey flew up over the top of the shield and fired down on the launchers. She took out about five with her white blasts of electricity, but they turned and began firing at her. She dodged and ducked behind the shield.

Now the robots could only come in on the edges of the yard, but there were too many and they were begging to adapt. They were taking out our soldiers and moving toward me.

199

Bailey couldn't get above the shield anymore without them firing at her and I couldn't shoot without lowering the shield. If I did something to take them out it would have to be quick.

"Bailey!" I called, "I need you to shoot me with as much energy as you can!"

"What?"

"Our powers combined on the plain. Let's do it again."

"Yea, but I didn't shoot you!"

"It'll work. I can feel it."

I didn't think she was actually going to do it until I felt the white energy hit my back. It raced across my whole body, combining with my blue energy. I lowered the shield, held my hands out in front of me and shot a massive, blue and white beam of energy out in front of me. I started at the furthest left launcher and moved to the furthest right, and in a matter of a couple seconds, they were all destroyed.

Cheering came from our side of the battlefield.

Bailey stopped shooting me with energy and flew down, landing beside me, "Yea! Take that!" Alex yelled!

"So that's what happens." I said to Bailey.

"Good to know." I could tell in her voice it brought her great joy to see them all blow up. It did me too.

"Wanna do it again?" I said.

"Of course!" she said, grabbing my hand.

We once again combined our powers and with our free hands blasted plasma into the remainder of the swarm of robots. Between my half of the energy pushing them back and her half disabling them, it didn't take us long to finish them off.

Once they were, everyone stood there for a moment. Half assessing the situation, while the other half started at Bailey and I who were high fiving and congratulating each other. "Looks like we got 'em all," I said to Alex.

The fighting in the sky was still about two miles away. The tank fire rang out as did the explosions of falling planes, but for now, we had held them off.

"Don't celebrate too soon," he said walking back over to us.

"That was just the first wave." Alex said," They soften you up with the robots, then they send in their troops."

I looked around. The battle had given us many wounded. About a fourth of those who started with us were injured or worse.

"If they don't get here soon, there won't have been any purpose in staying to save the U.S. Troops," Bailey said.

"I don't think that was the point" I said, receiving a revelation about what my father was up to.

"Then what was the point?" Bailey asked.

"I think he just wanted to show off his cruisers," I proposed, "I think he wanted to end it here instead of them just wiping everything out here and following us back to the base, keeping the battle all in one spot."

"That sounds like Daniel," ALI said, "Either way, help is almost here."

"We'd better hope so, look." Alex said, pointing over the trees across the road.

I looked and saw Organization transports landing somewhere on the other side of the park where robots came from. After the ships were behind the trees, their escort of about five fighters came flying right at us. Bailey and I called our powers and as they passed overhead, each of us sent a blast at the ships. We both made a direct hit. The fighters were so close to the ground, we could see the soft orange glow of the shields as the blasts of plasma broke through them. They crashed behind the White House.

"We need an airstrike at 38.54.02 and 77.02 11" ALI said over the coms.

"Yes, sir, look out!" A voice said. For a moment, the words he said didn't register with me. Just as they did, I heard a whistling noise, followed by a blast of yellow plasma falling from the sky. It erupted in the same area as where the transports had landed. Then another followed it, and then another.

I didn't fully catch what was going on so the explosions made me jump. "What was that?" I asked.

"Our Cruisers are within firing range now" ALI replied, "We've almost done it. They just have to launch the transports to come pick everyone up."

"Everyone, fall back to the White House," My Dad's voice said over the coms, "We'll pick you up from there."

"Sounds like we did it!" Bailey said.

"Don't let your guard down yet," Alex warned.

"We've got incoming through the park," ALI said.

"See," Alex said. He turned off his atom sword. It retracted into the hilt and he clipped it back to his waste. He then drew his pistols off each hip. All of the soldiers in the yard spread out, took cover, and drew their weapons. I noticed that this time they all opted for guns.

"You gonna call for another air strike?" I asked ALI.

"It's too late, they are too close to us," He informed.

"Alright then," I said and I drew my staff.

After what felt like a lifetime of waiting, an orange blast from a phaser came through the trees. It was shot at me. I lifted my staff and the Unitum metal absorbed the plasma. As though it were the command to open fire, both sides sent a barrage of phaser blasts at each other.

Even though they were outnumbered by our forces (because of the airstrike), The Organization troops had heavy repeating weapons and were overwhelming us with their firepower. Both sides had trees for cover so little progress was being made. However, the trees were being turned to splinters.

I spent a bit of time blocking the blasts with my staff, but then resorted to cowering behind my shield. Alex ran over from the tree he was hiding behind and dove behind me as the tree fell. Bailey was just a few feet away, holding up her shield as well.

"Any ideas?" I asked Alex.

"Yes actually," He said then turned on his coms using his vanguard, "I need about twenty soldiers up here with me, melee weapons ready," he turned off his coms, "Make the shield bigger and get ready to charge," Alex commanded.

"On it!" I called more power to the shield and expanded it. As it grew larger, Bailey lowered her shield and got behind mine, quickly followed by twenty soldiers running and jumping in behind the cover of the shield. Once recovered from their hasty maneuvering, they gathered around Alex, awaiting his next command.

"Alright, here's the plan," Alex said, "Dylan is going to hold up this shield until we get across the road, through the robot graveyard, and to Lafayette Square," He gestured to the park across the road, "We'll run them out of the trees and hopefully the rest of our people back there can clean up after us."

I listened but I had to keep a lot of my attention on the shield. They had noticed us grouping there and were focusing quite a bit of fire on us.

"Why don't the two crystal bearers just do what they did last time?" One of the taken soldiers asked.

"It doesn't work that way," Alex said, quick to come to our defense, "We'll be doing it this way. Be thankful they are here to help or we would already have fallen."

I was kind of shocked at his answer since he definitely didn't have a problem with killing, but I was thankful that I wasn't going to have to defend myself, in the middle of this battle, against my own people.

"Ready Dylan?" Alex asked.

"Let's do this." I said.

The soldiers spread out slightly, still staying behind my shield, and drew their Atom swords. I held the shield with one outstretched arm, and held my staff with the other. Seeing that they were waiting for me to move, I took one last second to leave common sense behind and ran toward the source of the orange blasts. The soldiers followed me.

I hadn't done anything quite like this with my powers before. It took quite a bit of focus because the shield didn't move with me, I had to keep pushing it forward as we charged.

We all stumbled through the large pieces of still smoldering robots and finally made it to the other side of the road. We entered the park. There were trees on either side of the main entrance. Our pack split up. Alex led a charge to the left with mostly Taken soldiers and Bailey. I followed the group to the right.

Nearly all of The Organization soldiers' attention had turned from our people across the road, to us. Some Organization soldiers drew their swords while others kept shooting. I shot blasts of energy at the soldiers further back that were shooting, while the other soldiers fought with their swords.

I could sense behind me that Bailey was following a similar strategy. Both teams quickly advanced. It didn't take long for the Organization troops to order a retreat. They all began to sprint back toward where their ships had landed. We pursued them.

Once we got to the other side of the park, I could see where the blasts from the airstrike had landed. There were three large craters within a few feet of one another in the middle of the road. Debris from the destroyed ships lay scattered about as well as lodged in the sides of the buildings that sat on either side of the road. Behind all of this was a single transport, the sole survivor of the attack.

The troops ran in front of us. Our soldiers fired as we chased after them. Most of the shots hit their armor, but Alex took down two by shooting in the gaps. As we neared the ship, Four U-Jets came into view. They were coming straight at us. Each dawned two orange stripes right down the center, signifying that they were linked to the Organization's orange crystal.

All of our troops came to a stop. "Everyone get close to me!" I yelled. Yanked the crystal from its place on my chest. I held it out in my hand and raised a shield, from it, around all of our remaining soldiers. "Bailey, Get in!" Alex yelled, looking behind us. I looked to see Bailey radiating with the white energy of her crystal. She lifted off the ground.

The U-Jets each released two missiles, but Bailey intercepted them with a lightning bolt, which split, taking four down at the same time. The remaining four crashed into my shield. Thankfully it stopped them.

I could see through the dust of the explosion that Bailey had turned her attention to the Jets. They opened fire, not at us, but at her.

I let go of the shield, forgetting that everyone was under it. I placed the crystal back on my chest and held up both hands. I released a powerful beam of blue energy from each.

The blasts each hit a different fighter. I hit one in its left engine (the left leg of the "U"). The engine exploded, sending the jet into a barrel roll. The other I hit in the underbelly. The blast penetrated the shield but not the armor. The ship was thrown to the side but recovered.

The crashing ship, however, was coming right for us. I used my powers to grab hold of the ship. The blue energy radiated around it. It was heavy and moving quickly. I couldn't completely stop it, so I lifted it up over us and allowed it to crash into the park behind us.

During this, Bailey had taken out one of the ships, but there was still one left, which flew over as I let go of the jet I shot down. It began to pursue Bailey, but before they had even made it back over the White House, one of our fighters came out of seemingly nowhere, unleashing a furry of plasma fire. It intercepted the U-jet and flew off. Bailey turned around and came back.

All of this happened in a matter of seconds, but it was enough time for The Organization soldiers to make it to their ship. The doors of the transport slid shut and the shield formed around the ship.

It began to lift off. Before it had even made it ten feet off the ground, the same fighter that had helped Bailey, came flying from behind us. It released a missile that struck the transport in the back. A fiery explosion engulfed the ship.

As the fighter flew off, the soldiers around me cheered. Bailey landed back beside me and retracted her helmet. "Is it too early to celebrate now?" She asked, looking past me at Alex.

"Probably," He said. He retracted his helmet, "But it looks like we won this round."

I followed suit and retracted my helmet as well, "Now we just have to bring down those cruisers," I said, Looking off in the distance where they should have been. My view was blocked by the building though.

"Well, that looks like it's about to happen," ALI said from the retracted helmets, "Fly up and have a look."

We looked at each other with hopeful, yet nervous expressions, then did as he said. Bailey summoned her power again, and Alex and I used our vanguards to activate the jetpacks. We all flew up to the top of the building on our right. When we made it over the top, I was filled with fear at what I saw.

205

About a mile away, were the three Organization cruisers. They were massive. These weren't like the one we had seen at the Montana base. They didn't have wings. They were black with two orange stripes down the sides and of an ovular shape, completely rounded on the bottom, but on top they had a flat platform.

Starting about halfway back on top of the ship, protruding from the platform and flush with the curved sides of the ship, five stair stepping notches lead back to the rounded dome of the top of the ship. Each stair step had gargantuan turret cannons. The top stair step, before going back to being an ovular dome, had a protrusion that stuck up just a bit higher than the top of the ship with a glassed-in platform. From the largest platform at the front of the ship, fighters were launching to join the battle. At the back of each ship, there were three large engines in a straight line, one on top of the other.

About a mile past them were our cruisers. They were smaller and of a completely different design than the Organization cruisers. The ships were white and reflected the vibrant oranges and yellows of the sun, which was setting behind them.

Their shape would be difficult to describe. From front to back they were generally triangular, but still rounded. Their sides came up to make them taller in the back and narrower in the front, this was more subtle on the top of the ship, but most of the ships' mass sat on the bottom, so its angle was more pronounced.

On each side of each of the ships, there was a large triangular protrusion turned on its side compared to the rest of the ship. The base of the triangle faced the back of the ship and it came to a point about a third of the way down the side of the ship. The point of the triangle never came together, rather there was an opening that led to the middle of the triangle. Lining either side of this opening was a bright yellow plasma that had tendrils crossing back and forth across the gap. The engines themselves were not visible from where we were, but the yellow plasma blazing from them told us that each ship had two.

The three of us landed on top of the building in awe. "Have you ever seen these things face off?" I asked Alex.

"I never even knew there were others for them to face off against," He said, not taking his eyes off of the ships.

The dogfight that had been happening over where the last line of tanks were, was now taking place between the two sets of cruisers as each side tried to bomb the other. I noticed a few blocks over, a precession of U.S. tanks, Army vehicles, and soldiers were headed toward the White House.

Back at our cruisers, I saw a fleet of smaller ships, heading not toward the fight, but toward us. They were coming to get everyone.

I noticed the cruiser leading the charge on our side had risen a bit in altitude. The channel of yellow light on the protrusion on the side of the ship began to glow brighter. Rather than a trench, it became a solid beam of light. From it shot a yellow blast of energy like the one from the airstrike. It was long and moved quickly across the sky. It zipped over the dogfight and crashed into the shield of one of the Organization cruisers. The blast radiated over the shield, sending Orange ripples, mingled with yellow, across the front of the shield. It would take a lot more of those to take down the ship.

The Organization ships fired back, using the large guns across the front of their ships. The much smaller blasts of plasma flew through the dog fight, forcing the pilots on both sides to dodge and weave. This split up the swarm and spread out the fighting. The blast hit the shields of our cruisers, but no damage was done. Now that the dogfight was broken up and our people weren't in the way, all three of our cruisers opened fire.

It was our six big guns, versus their many little guns. The sky erupted with the yellow and orange blasts, nearly invisible against the sunset of the same colors.

The transports made it through the slurry of plasmatic blasts and began to land all along the streets near the White House, including the one we had just come from. Cables fell from some as soldiers attached them to tanks.

As a group of ships flew overhead, one smaller transport, like the one we had flown in on, stopped and landed on the roof. The door slid open revealing the cargo hold. There were only two soldiers inside. They donned the clean gray uniform of the soldiers from my fathers base. One came to the edge, walking with a pronounced limp, "Need a lift?" he asked.

I instantly knew who it was, "Blake!" I yelled, running over to him. He retracted his helmet just as I reached him. We wrapped each other in a hug. I pulled away, "What are you doing here?" I questioned.

"The doctors at the base are pretty good," He smiled, "Your dad said it would do you good to see me."

"Well, yea! But I could have waited till we weren't getting shot at!" I said, shaking my head, "You're hurt."

"It's just a limp now," He smiled, "And… It was my idea to come, your dad just agreed."

"The truth comes out," I said, in a jokingly dismissive voice.

Alex walked up behind us, "Good to see you not kicking my butt this time," He extended his hand for a handshake.

Blake shook his hand, "That was all Dylan," He laughed, "I nicked your friends butts."

Bailey walked up next, "Good to see you in one piece," she hugged Blake.

Before he could talk, the other soldier interrupted, "So are we just going to stand here and talk, or are you guys gonna get in?"

We all just looked at him in a way that let him know he killed the moment. Then, knowing he made a good point, we got in the transport. We all grabbed onto the handles that hung from the ceiling, and with the doors open, flew off.

"Where are we going, exactly?" Alex asked Blake.

"We're going back to the cruiser," He yelled. The wind roaring made it hard to hear since our helmets were off, "Daniel wants us back."

We met up with an escort and subverted the dogfight with little difficulty. As we neared our cruisers, their size and detail came into full view. All over the surface there were small turrets to fend off enemy fighters. There was also a host of missiles sticking out of the surface, ready to be launched at the first command. Like the guns, some were smaller than others, I assumed for different tasks.

We flew past the massive triangular gun on the side of the ship, careful not to be caught in one of its blasts. Then, we dipped down under the ship, to get to the other side without being singed by the engines. On the bottom of the ship, I could see six downward facing guns that held almost the exact shape of a cannon. They looked like they were deactivated for the moment.

We flew up on the other side of the ship, lifted up to the top, and found a landing platform near the back. The Transport landed and let Blake, Alex, Bailey, and I out. Then, it took off, meeting back up with its escort and heading to get more people.

The landing platform was a notch cut out of the side of the ship. Next to us there was a metal door. Blake quickly led us over to it, and it opened as he neared. Inside was clearly the bridge. It was full of highly decorated officers and complex dashboards.

In the front of the room was a large window overlooking the entire ship, the city, and the Organization cruisers. Noticeably, it had a hole busted into the middle of it. Damage I assumed came from the battle somehow. In the middle of the room was a chair in which my dad sat.

No one but him even looked at us. He stood up and told a man standing next to him to take the chair. Dad walked over, "You guys did good holding them off," he said, clearly very proud, but he looked worried.

"What did you need to see us for?" Alex asked, "I left all of my men back there."

"The Taken are being evacuated as we speak," Dad reassured him, "I wanted you here because there is something I never told you and you all need to know - Now."

Dad's face was solemn and serious. We listened, "The red crystal is one that I and a man you know as Alfred Henry experimented on. That man's name was not Alfred Henry, but it was Darren Flyhe. His name along with everything about him was erased because he was recruited for a top secret position by The Organization."

This was an interesting variation of ALI's story back at the base a while back, but I was having trouble understanding why it was important right now. Still we listened.

"He was recruited because the explosion that I and the world thought killed him actually gave him powers. These powers allowed him to rise through their ranks and become the leader of the Organization. I fought him many years ago, tried to kill him, and thought I did. Except, half an hour ago he summoned the crystal back, right out of my hands."

"Dad... Why are you telling us this," I asked, matching his somber tone.

"Because he is on his way here and I need your crystal to face him. Follow me," He commanded.

I was very confused, "I thought that you gave me your powers. Are you taking them back?"

209

There was no answer. "Dad?" I said befuddled and frustrated.

Dad walked us out of the bridge and to a room labeled "CAPTAINS QUARTERS". All that was in the room was a twin bed and a recliner. To the right was a door that I assumed went to the bathroom.

"Dad, what are we doing?" I asked, refusing to go any further until I knew what was going on.

"When I gave you your connection to the crystal," Dad answered, "I kept a small part of that connection for myself. I can draw its power if I am touching it, but it is impossible for more than one person to draw power from the crystal at a time. I am going to have to temporarily merge our consciousnesses to face Flyhe."

"What does that mean?" Blake asked for me.

"It means that Dylan will be unconscious, but seeing what I see as well as feeling my thoughts while I draw power from the crystal," Dad said, "We must act quickly. He's almost here. Dylan, lay down!"

His voice had become urgent, as close to frantic as I had ever heard him. I backed up a bit, fearful. Not of Dad, but of what was happening. He calmed himself and put his hand on my cheek, "Everything's going to be fine, son. But if he gets here and I am not wielding that crystal, he will kill us all."

I wasn't calm, and that didn't make me feel any better. I wasn't onboard with this plan at all. I would have to give up all my control. That was something I had a hard time doing.

Still, I obeyed. I pressed the button on my vanguard that made the jetpack detach and it floated over to the side. I climbed up on the bed and laid down. I looked at the crowd in front of me, Blake, Alex, and Bailey, all held the same worried and confused look. Dad looked worried, though he tried to hide it with resolve. He wasn't worried about me, he was worried about what was coming. That made me all the more unsettled.

I laid down and rested my head on the pillow. The armor made laying down uncomfortable, but it didn't feel like there was time to take it off.

"Now Dylan, I need you to relax," Dad said, reaching out his hand. He put his index finger on the crystal. "I am going to take control of the crystal. All you need to do is allow it."

210

I saw the blue swirling energy begin to radiate up his arm. "Relax," he commanded in a gentle way. I did my best. I felt the energy moving from my feet, up my legs, from my arms, and finally to my chest. As it moved up, my eyes grew heavy. I felt the crystal be pulled out of its holding spot, just as I lost consciousness.

Chapter 21

The energy pulsed through his body. It had only been about two weeks since he had last felt the connection to the crystal, but it had been nine months since he had felt the warmth and might of its power. He looked at the glowing blue crystal in his hand, remembering the past times he had wielded it.

Then, he looked over at his son laying on the bed. He placed his hand on his neck to check his pulse. It was strong as was his breathing. It worked. He had successfully regained the power of the crystal. He looked at his son's friends who were all staring in wonder and disbelief.

"Dylan will be fine," he said, "Once I'm done with the crystal, he'll wake up. Blake, Bailey, why don't you two stay here with him. Alex, I would like you on the bridge.

They all followed his instruction without a word. He could tell they were in a bit of shock over the whole deal. It wasn't, after all, what they expected to happen when they got on the cruiser.

Alex followed him back to the bridge. He looked out through the panoramic front glass of the command center. The Organization cruisers' shields were still holding strong, but they were running a bit low on fighters. "How is the evacuation going?" he asked the officer sitting in his captain's chair.

"Slow, sir," the officer replied, "We need more time."

"More time than we have," He said. He turned to Alex, "No matter what happens, you make sure that when those cruisers come crashing down, all of our people are back here and that my son does not leave this ship."

"What's the plan, sir?" Alex asked, his voice edged with concern.

"I'm planning on keeping the parasite busy while the rest of you win this battle," he said.

He pressed a button on his vanguard calling for his fighter to arrive at the platform outside the bridge. As he waited he continued looking out the window. His thoughts lingered on Dylan. Pride welled up in him, tainted with regret. If only they had had more time together—time stolen by this relentless war. Their reunion had been so quickly covered up by the Organization's takeover. He swore to himself that when he came back he would make sure to spend as much time with Dylan as possible.

As he looked and thought, something caught his attention. A red explosion came from the evacuation site at the White House. Following it came a frantic voice over the bridge's intercoms, "We need immediate assistance at the White House! A crystal bearer is on the field!"

Daniel looked down at his vanguard to see a small light changing from red to green, signaling that his fighter had arrived. He nodded his head to activate his helmet and marched toward the door, "Send no support. I will take care of this alone," He said to the bridge crew and he walked out onto the platform.

Waiting on him was his customized fighter jet. He climbed up the ladder into the cockpit. The jet lifted off, and he flew full speed toward the red explosions.

"ALI" Daniel called.

"Yes sir," ALI replied.

"If anything happens," He paused, thinking of how much he didn't want anything to happen, "I need you to make sure Dylan is told all of my secrets and that he sees the video I left for him. Make sure it is clear that he will be my sole heir to power, possessions, and secrets. There will be no election or following of the chain of command in this matter."

"I will do my best, sir," ALI said solemnly, "They will want an explanation."

"I recorded that one a long time ago," Daniel said, reminiscing, "You can play it."

It wasn't a specific sounding answer, but he knew ALI would know exactly what he was referring to.

Daniel flew down until he was on the street level, flying between two rows of buildings. A few blocks up and to the right was the White House, but he didn't want Flyhe to see him coming.

"Here we go," He said, slowing the plane to a stop just one block over.

The cabin opened and there was a swoosh of air as its seal was broken. Daniel hopped from the cockpit, down to the pavement. He could see the red plasma, along with fiery explosions coming over the top of the building that separated him from the battle.

He called the power from the stone. It raced from the crystal, across his chest, and then over the rest of his body. "I wish I had taught Dylan this

213

trick" he thought as he secured his hands firmly at his sides and then conjured two concussive blasts, one from each hand. He was propelled upward and the pavement below him was crushed. The force from the blasts pushed him the all the way up to the top of the building, where he landed gently. "I still got it," He said to himself.

He walked to the edge of the building and looked down on the battle. In front of the White House, hundreds of soldiers who had been awaiting their evacuation were running in terror. Coming behind them was Flyhe. His body radiated with the energy of the red crystal. He shot blasts of red plasma into the crowd of fleeing soldiers. Some tried to fire back but their bullets were ineffective as they were deflected by the energy that surrounded the parasite.

Daniel built up the courage. It was time to face his past. He leapt from his resting spot at the ledge. As he fell, he held his hands toward the ground and just before he landed, he used dual concussive blasts to cushion his fall. He landed about twenty feet away from Flyhe in a crater of broken pavement he created.

Not wasting a single second, Daniel used his powers to grab hold of half of a tank that lay destroyed behind him. He hurled it over his head. The blue energy radiating across the tank turned to red as Flyhe took hold of it and pushed it to the side. The momentum stayed with the tank as it screeched across the pavement.

As soon as the tank was deflected, Daniel quickly followed up with a powerful blast of plasma, but as it reached Flyhe, it turned red. The red consumed the blue all the way back to Daniel's hand. Then, the red energy began to travel up his arm, headed for the crystal. The pain this red energy caused was excruciating. Daniel couldn't help but yell in pain.

Thinking quickly, Daniel drew his atom sword with his free hand, and lifted the blade to sever the connection between the two. Once the beam of energy was cut, the red energy dissipated from Daniel's arm and the pain left.

He took a moment to refocus, then leapt to his feet and charged toward Flyhe. Flyhe conjured red blasts of energy and directed them at Daniel. He knew that using his powers to deflect them would allow the parasite to take hold again, so he intercepted the blasts with his sword.

He quickly reached Flyhe and swung the blade toward his unprotected abdomen. Flyhe lifted his hands in a cupping motion and caught the blade with a small, focused shield. Daniel lifted the blade and again swung, this time coming from the other side and aiming for Flyhe's neck. Again the blade was stopped. Then, Daniel pulled the blade back to

214

himself, and jabbed it toward Flyhe's gut. Flyhe caught the blade again, but the point of the sword began to slowly slip through the shield.

The two men made eye contact and held it for a brief second as they attempted to assess the other's next move. Flyhe moved first, moving his right hand away from the blade and using the other to blast the sword away. With that same motion he drew his sword.

Daniel used the force of the blast to spin around and take another swing at Flyhe, but his blade was drawn and intercepted Daniel's sword. The two continued to fight. With the swords, they were an even match.

As they fought, Flyhe retracted his helmet and began to speak, "Do you remember the night that you tried to kill me?" His voice was cold and his face showed no emotion. He pushed Daniel's sword away and stepped back for him to answer.

"I remember the night you took everything from me," Daniel said, his eyebrows narrowed behind his helmet. He lifted his sword and attacked with rage. Their blades clashed. Flyhe was quickly being pushed back until he got an opening. Their sword met and Flyhe lifted his left hand, conjuring a concussive blast that sent Danile flying backwards through the air.

He landed on his feet in a crouched position and thrust his sword into the ground to slow his backward movement. He slid for a few feet and then stopped. The two were again about twenty feet apart.

"I don't remember many people that I've killed," the parasite said as he walked toward Daniel, "I've killed so many that they all run together now. I assume you know the feeling. But I do remember your wife. Riley, right?"

Daniel was filled with rage. His face contorted with hatred. His teeth showed as he scowled. Losing control, the blue energy began to spread across his body. "You keep her name out of your mouth!" He yelled.

Daniel charged at Flyhe. Flyhe thrust another ball of energy at Daniel. Knowing that the red energy was attracted to his own, Daniel allowed his energy to flow down the atom sword.

He moved to the side and held out his blade just as the energy reached him. He spun around, keeping the energy just behind the blade. Once he had made a full circle, he flung the blade forward, sending the red energy back to the parasite. It caught Flyhe off guard and crashed into his chest. The force of the blow caused him to stumble backward.

215

This time, Daniel gained the upper hand. He swung his blade at Flyhe, and being off balance, caught the blow but fell to one knee. He rolled out of the way of Daniels next swing, which sliced into the pavement, then stood up.

Daniel redirected his attention and once again their blades met. After a few strikes, Daniel directed a concussive blast at Flyhe's feet. Both of his legs were knocked out from under him and his face smashed into ground. Daniel lifted his sword to finish him, but before he could, a red blast of energy knocked him backward.

Daniel landed on his back this time and his sword was knocked from his hand. Now Flyhe was standing up, blood pouring from his nose. He launched another ball of red energy at Daniel and instinctively he lifted his hands and raised a shield.

The blast spread across the shield. As it did, it formed tendrils stretching across the surface. They sunk into the shield. And ran through the blue energy field and to Daniel's hands.The red energy began to pull at his energy. The Parasite had once again latched onto his powers.

Daniel winced in pain as energy was pulled from his body, but he would not give Flyhe the satisfaction of a single sound. He tried to use his powers to call the blade back to his hand, but when he did, the pain only intensified. The red energy now engulfed his entire body and surrounded the blue crystal on his chest.

Flyhe walked over. His hand was stretched out in front of him as he absorbed Daniel's power.

"I remember the look on her face when she realized you weren't coming to save her that night," Flyhe proclaimed.

Daniel's body shook, not with pain, but hatred. "I remember the look she had when she realized that you had finally lost for the first time; that light had lost; that evil had won…" he paused, "Ah, yes, it was that look right there."

Flyhe leaned over Daniel. He clinched his open hand that was drawing the energy and with that motion pulled Daniel's breastplate off. Then, without breaking eye contact, he plunged his blade into the center of Daniel's chest.

Daniel could feel nothing but pain. His body burned from head to toe, the blade had pierced his lungs but nothing hurt worse than his heart. He had lost his wife, abandoned his son, and had grown so full of hate and pride that he had lost to this same foe again. Losing all of his hope and strength, he dropped to the ground. "I'm so, so sorry," he mumbled

216

to both God and his son. His eyes closed and he slipped from consciousness.

Chapter 22

"Dad, No!"
"Ah, yes, it was that look right there"
"Guah"
"Dad, Please! No!"
"I'm so, so sorry"

"DAD!" I screamed, flinging myself out of bed. Bailey, who was sitting on the end of the bed, jumped to her feet. Blake scrambled to his feet from sitting on the floor next to me.

"Dylan?"

"What's wrong?"

I gave no response. I sprinted out of the room, into the hall, then busted through the door of the bridge. I ran, vaulting over the dashboards. I activated my helmet, balled my fist, summoned my power, and punched through the window of the bridge shattering the entire thing, and jumped out as my jetpack latched to my back.

My head was throbbing and my entire body ached as I flew across the front of the ship. Gunfire rang out and an explosion erupted from one of the Organization cruisers. Its shields were down and all three were turning to flee.

My mind could not celebrate though. I could see nothing but the fear, hatred, and pain that I had just felt my Dad experience. I could hardly separate my reality from the one I had just experienced through my father. All I could really focus on was that I had to get there to save him.

I soared, propelling myself faster using the concussive blast trick I had seen Dad use. I reached the site of the battle and saw the Parasite still standing over him. I reached out my hand and summoned my crystal to me.

It flew past the Parasite and into my open hand. The blue energy radiated across my body. I concentrated the power at the fist gripping the crystal. Just as the parasite turned to see where the crystal went, my fist slammed into his face. An aurora of blue energy erupted from the blow as he was knocked to the ground.

With one motion, I spun around and stopped myself with two concussive blasts before I hit the ground. The Parasite was on all fours, next to my dad and I was now on the other side of the parasite. I called the energy to my right leg, and before he could recover, I kicked him in the midsection and sent him flying through the air. As he was in the air, I held out both fists and shot him with the most powerful blast of energy I could conjure.

The blast cut through the air and made contact with him, sending him even further back down the road. Before he could hit the ground, a white bolt of lightning fell from the sky, stomping him into the pavement. Bailey flew down to his right. She must have followed me. She lifted up his limp body with her white energy and then blasted him into the row of buildings on the left.

Seeing that she had it under control, I deactivated my helmet and put the crystal in its place on my chest. I knelt beside my father, cradling his head. Tears blurred my vision, but I couldn't accept what I knew was true. "Dad... come on, Dad," I pleaded, my voice breaking. I was sobbing now.

I was filled with anger and confusion. How could we be reunited just to be torn apart again? This wasn't supposed to happen, we were supposed to win. We were supposed to be unstoppable.

I looked up from my dad to see that The Parasite was fighting Bailey. He couldn't latch on to her powers like he could my father's. He shot blasts of energy at her, but she could block them, and fire back.

I gritted my teeth as I lay my father's head down on the cracked pavement. I stood up, balled my fists and summoned my powers. I looked over to Dad's sword which lay on the ground. I called it to my left hand and drew the blade that was on my belt with my right.

I started walking toward Bailey and The Parasite, but the walk turned into a sprint as my anger welled up within me. They were about fifty yards away, but I closed the distance quickly. Just as the Parasite gained the upper hand on Bailey and blasted her backward through the window of a store front, I lifted my right blade and swung at him. He dodged, but I had another waiting for him.

As he moved backward, he intercepted my swings with the same shields he had used on my dad, but since I had two swords it was much harder for him. I advanced until he thrust himself backward. This bought himself enough time to draw his sword.

As I stood, waiting for him to make the first move, he tilted his head and, with his left hand, rubbed his cheek where I had hit him, "Now, I thought I heard my soldiers calling you the Soldier who *wouldn't* kill. Amazing how quickly we can abandon our beliefs for the right reason."

219

I gritted my teeth and scowled, but said nothing. He moved toward me, but before he could do anything, Bailey came at him from the side. She shot a bolt of energy at him, but he intercepted it with his blade and blasted Bailey backward once again. While he did that, I lunged at him and attacked with both swords. He was pushed back, but still managed to fend off both of us.

As we fought, I was close enough to hear his coms on his shoulder, "Sir, you must come back. Two of our ships have no shields. We must pull out."

Immediately after that transmission, a massive explosion filled the air. All of the windows of the row of buildings on either side of the road shattered. With that, The Parasite conjured a concussive blow that moved in every direction. I had not seen this before and it caught both me and Bailey off guard. The blast was large and sent us both flying through the air. I landed about thirty feet from the parasite, dropping both blades and Bailey landed to my right.

"Looks like we'll have to continue this another day" he called out as he used his jetpack to fly away.

I stood up and was about to pursue him, but Bailey grabbed my arm. Not thinking and filled with rage I yanked my arm away and spun around at her, calling for my powers. I held up my right fist and the blue energy circled around it.

We both stood there for a moment. Tears ran down my face. She took hold of my fist and retracted her helmet. She allowed her powers to travel down her arm and to my hand where they merged. She spoke firmly, "Let's not lose another fight today," she said firmly yet filled with empathy.

I closed my eyes for a moment, trying to gain control of myself again, but failing. I was being ripped apart. My hatred wanted to fly off after The Parasite. My sorrow wanted to go stand over my dad. My confusion wanted me to crumple down where I stood and weep on the cracked pavement. This led me to simply do nothing as nothing pushed me more in one direction than another.

As I stood there crying, I heard two jetpacks flying in. I opened my eyes as they landed. They retracted their helmets. It was Blake and Alex.

"We've gotta go," Alex said, urgently. He opened his mouth to say more, but a terrible roar surrounded us. I looked in the direction of the sound and saw that one of the Organization cruisers was heavily damaged, falling from the sky, and coming straight for us.

Feeling so many emotions that I couldn't feel terror, I broke away from Bailey and ran over toward my father, finally having a push in one direction.

As I ran, a massive piece of debris fell from the sky and landed between me and my dad. It narrowly missed crushing me. It was so massive that when it landed, a wave of air and dust came from it. I instinctively raised my shield as I was thrown backward.

The hunk of metal was so large that it took up the entire road and destroyed the buildings on both sides.

My friends raced over, "Dylan," Blake cried, taking hold of my arm, "Come on!"

"No!" I screamed, scrambling to my feet and pulling away, "We can't leave him!"

"Hold your fire!" I heard Alex yell over the coms.

"Dylan! There's nothing we can do now!" Alex pleaded, also grabbing hold of me.

"No! No!" I screamed hysterically. The energy of the crystal engulfed my body. They both became fearful and let go.

I started toward the piece of debris, intending to go over it, but Bailey stepped in my way, her power surrounding her body. Blake came around to my front and looked in my eyes. Tears were still running down my face. "We have done all we can do," he said somberly, "look around."

His words reached me through the wall of emotions. I looked around.

Debris was raining down all around. Explosions and crashing could be heard as they reached the ground. Behind us, the massive ship was still falling from the sky. Its engines were slowing it down, but were failing.

"We would all die trying to save you, just like your father did," Blake said as tears flowed down his cheeks, "Don't make us."

This pierced my heart. I bowed my head in shame, sorrow, regret, and many other emotions I could never hope to describe. I pressed the button on my vanguard to start my jetpack, then looked up at Blake, saying nothing.

With that, we all lifted off of the ground and headed back to the command ship. The flight was easy. All of the ships were out of the air. The gunfire had stopped. We had won even though we had lost.

We reached the landing platform next to the bridge and all of us turned to watch the Organization ship crash to the ground. It landed right where we had been, destroying everything in it's path. We couldn't see it happen for the dust and smoke, but it certainly destroyed the White House and many other timeless monuments.

The four of us shared a somber glance and then turned to enter the bridge. We were greeted with clapping, cheers, and shouting, "We did it!" "Yah!" "Well done!"

It only took a moment for the room to grow silent and curious. "Where's Daniel?" the man in the captain's chair asked.

I looked away and began to walk off the bridge toward the captain's quarters. I didn't look, but I sensed the man standing up, "I asked you a question, soldiers."

I spun around furiously, my rage breaking through the surface of the front I had attempted to raise. I thrust out my hand and used my power to take hold of him by the neck. The blue energy gripped him and lifted him off the floor. "Dylan!" Bailey cried in shock.

"My father..." I looked at the captain, clawing at his neck, unable to take hold of the energy that was strangling him. I lost it. I started sobbing and in shame I let go of the captain. He fell to the floor gagging and gasping for air.

I momentarily composed myself enough to speak as the crew looked on in bewilderment. "I'll be in the captain's quarters. Ask them if you have questions." I gestured to my friends and briskly walked off the bridge as tears began to flow again.

Not a word was said as I left the room. I guess my point had been well made. I couldn't stop the complete loss of my composure that was building within me. I held it back just long enough to make it into the captain's quarters and close the door.

I fell to my knees at the foot of the bed and screamed as loud as I could. A fountain of tears sprung from my eyes. Needing some way to let out my anger, I took hold of the bed and threw it across the small room. It smashed through the white end table that sat beside it and crashed into the opposite wall. Blue energy leaked from my body as it slipped out with my emotions. Unable to even form words, I screamed again as I formed a ball of energy and thrust it at the bed, slamming it into the wall again.

I leaned over in emotional agony and thrust my fist into the floor as hard as I could. I did it again and again and again. "Why?" I screamed, "Why give him back and then take him away?" I stood up and punched the wall where the bed once sat. Screaming one last time, my rage plummeted into defeat. I opened my fist and put both hands on the wall. As I cried, I slid down the wall, back onto my knees.

I don't know how long I was there until eventually I heard the door open. I sensed Blake. "Please go away" I said. I was no longer sobbing quite as hard, but tears still stained my cheeks.

He knelt down beside me and put his hand on my shoulder. Without a word, he pulled me off the wall and into his arms. I began to sob again. No words were said. His hug didn't make me feel any better. Instead it just seemed to be stirring everything back up again. Still, I couldn't let go. In a way, I guess it was helping me get it out.

"I felt it..." I cried, "I felt him die..." I couldn't keep it in any longer, "We were connected... and he..." I couldn't continue. Not right now. I sobbed a bit longer.

I never noticed the ship landing, but it did. I only knew because eventually Blake spoke up, "We're back at the base," He informed solemnly, pulling away from the embrace enough to look me in the eyes, "You wanna go in?"

I looked around the room. The bed was broken in half across the room. Pieces of the nightstand littered the floor. In the center of the room, there was a massive indention in the floor and on the wall above where we were was a gaping hole. I hadn't realized that I had done as much damage as I did. "I guess we can't really stay here."

We stood up, "Where's Bailey?" I asked, thinking of how I had just left them in the bridge earlier.

"She's back in the barracks," He said, "Waiting for you I'd imagine."

"Alex?"

"Back with The Taken for now"

There was more I should have probably asked about like 'Where is the Organization?' 'Are we preparing for an attack?' 'Who is commanding the base?', but everything I was worried about was safe for the moment. I just wanted to be with them and the Vales, and grieve…again.

Blake walked me down the halls of the Cruiser and we eventually boarded a transport at the hangar bay. It shuttled us from a couple ridge lines away, back to the base. I looked down and noticed that aside from the three cruisers we had taken into battle, there were at least four more parked in different places on the flight back, all under the safety of our base's shield.

The shuttle flew us into one of the hangars of the mountain base. We exited as the captain saluted us and headed across the bay. I noticed that there were both U.S. troops and our troops in the hangar. It looked like our people were giving them jobs to do. It was the same across the entire base as we walked back to my quarters.

As we walked up, I saw Bailey standing outside the door of my assigned room. When she saw, or sensed, it was us she ran over and gave me a hug. We stood in the embrace for a moment. I felt no emotion. I had spent it all earlier. It didn't feel good, but at least I could controls myself.

"Dylan, I…" Bailey tried to find words to comfort me but they failed her. Though, it was okay. The hug was doing more than words could.

I felt tears trying to form, but there was nothing to move them to action. After a while, she pulled away, "Let's get you inside," she said softly, "I'm sure you're ready to get that armor off."

I nodded, following her into my room. Blake trailed behind us. I walked over to the cabinet that stood on the right wall of the room, opposite of the bed. I pressed a button on my vanguard and the armor and jetpack detached and floated to its assigned spots in the cabinet. I slid the vanguards off and hung them up as well.

I was now just in my black, one piece, suit. The material morphed from its more rigid form into a more comfortable texture. I turned back to my friends. Bailey sat on the edge of the bed and Blake sat in the chair of a desk which sat beside the bed.

"Dylan, there's something we need to tell you," Blake said.

A black mist came from the puck on my chest and formed ALI's emblem in the middle of us as he spoke. "He already knows." ALI said.

224

"I already know what?" I asked.

"Your father made you our leader," Blake said, finishing his thought.

I thought back to the conversation I had seen Dad having with ALI while we were connected. "Effective when?" I asked reluctantly.

"Technically, now," ALI informed, "But they want you to be in the right state of mind. They have elected to work as a council until you take the job."

"And I'm supposed to lead?" I was becoming overwhelmed with the responsibility, "How? I don't know anything about this base. I don't really know much about The Organization. I don't know how to lead an army. I don't even want to lead an army."

I put my hand on my forehead and looked away. "When you're ready," ALI started; I looked back at him, "Your father left you a recording. Many in fact, but one in particular that will hopefully explain his actions."

"I want to see it now," I said.

"After the day you've had, maybe some rest," I cut ALI off

"Now," I said, desperate for closure and guidance, "Please."

"As you wish," ALI said. One of my vanguards came from the cabinet holding my armor and floated to where ALI's emblem was. The emblem disappeared as a hologram projected from the vanguard. My father's face appeared in the light and tears came to my eyes just seeing him again. The recording started.

"Hello, son. If you're seeing this, I'm guessing things didn't go quite as I planned them. Or maybe I didn't plan at all and that was the problem. Either way, I'm sorry that I had to leave you early.

I'm recording this video on my way back to Washington. I had the red crystal in my possession when it was summoned away from me. That means The Parasite will be joining us. I assume that's why you're watching this. I don't have much time, so I need you to listen.

In my absence, you will be the sole heir to everything that is mine. That includes the pocket of resistance that I lead, but also the weight my name carries. Remember that. Use my authority and respect as you lead until you build your own. I know you don't want to lead, but it

225

must be you. I don't trust anyone else to do it besides you and the team you choose.

Also, I haven'th been able to call the Eklesia. That is now also left up to you. I need you to go to my office, behind the war room, and use my communicator to reach them. I'm sure you will think of something to say.

ALI knows all my secrets. The ones he doesn't know are documented in a vault beneath our house. You inherit those as well. Read them, know them, and carry them to your grave.

[He changed his glance from looking directly at the camera, to looking at something past it. There was some indistinct chatter, but I could make out the word "airstrike". He nodded his head and then turned back to the camera. He moved a bit closer and stared intensely into the lens, making eye contact with me from the other side.]

Son, I believe in you. You feel unqualified, but you aren't. You don't want to lead, the best leaders never do. I have been preparing you your whole life. I wish we had more time, but this is just the hand we have been dealt. I hope you never have to see this. But if you do... I love you son. God go with you."

The recording ended and I stumbled over to the bed. I was now crying again. Seeing my father again reawakened my emotions. I hardly had any tears left to give. My eyes burned from running out of fluids. My face tingled and felt swollen, as if it were about to explode.

Bailey put her arm around me as I sat down. "You don't have to do it," She said, "We can leave, hide, find a place to ride this out. This war isn't yours."

"You're wrong," I sobbed, gritting my teeth, "It wasn't mine until I just inherited it."

I was so angry all over again. Angry at The Parasite. Angry at my Father. Angry at God. Blue energy began to flow over my body as I struggled to gain control of myself. I clenched my fists. The blue aura surrounding me intensified. Then a soothing sensation covered my whole body. I began to feel warm, like the sun shining on my skin. My mind went almost blank. My muscles relaxed. My anger slowly began to fade, revealing the underlying hurt. Then that hurt began to fade away into a white abyss.

I was catching my breath and my vision became less blurred. It was then that I noticed Bailey's white energy mingled with my blue energy spreading over my body and through the air around us.

I looked over at Bailey. Her eyes were closed, but opened when I looked at her. I only now noticed her index finger was placed on my temple. "What did you do?" I asked.

"You're not the only one with training," she eluded.

I noticed that, though the hurt of losing my father was still extremely present, the hurt the video had stirred up was gone, and I was back to just feeling sad. Still, I could think clearly now.

"What are you talking about?" I asked. I was confused. What did she even just do? Invade my mind?

"A story for another day," she smiled, "Let's deal with our problems first."

I didn't like the answer she gave me, but there were just too many things happening right now for that to even slightly concern me.

Blake looked over. He wore a puzzled look. I guess these powers must feel even more foreign to him than they do to me. Realizing that I had calmed down again, his look became a bit more focused.

"We need a plan," Blake said, standing up from his chair and walking in front of Bailey and I. ALI's emblem appeared beside him.

"Seems simple," I sniffled, "I take command, call the Eklesia, defeat the Organization, well, at least drive them out of this part of the world."

"Lets focus on the first part," ALI suggested, "You need to have at least part of your leadership picked out. You need to take charge and show no weakness, even in light of what's happened."

"Obviously Blake, Alex, and Bailey," I said, "Bailey bears the white crystal, Alex leads The Taken, Blake is my second in command."

"That's a good start," ALI said, "Until you get your feet under you, you still need more."

"Who was on Dad's team?" I inquired, wiping away tears with my sleeve.

227

"Your father and I did everything on our own, simply giving orders to our commanders," ALI answered, "But I can recommend specialists that we used as advisors."

"I trust your judgment ALI," I said, "But rather than making them a part of my team, let's make them that, advisors. That way I don't have to keep them in my circle."

"So, tomorrow," Blake started, "The four of us march into the war room."

"Is tomorrow too soon," Bailey interrupted.

"No," I affirmed, "I want to get this going as soon as possible. We march in, I demand a briefing from whatever council is running this place right now, and go from there."

"There will be those who will oppose your father's wishes and seek leadership for themselves," ALI said.

"Then they are instantly silenced," I said quickly, "My father's wishes will be respected, which means mine will be or they will be asked to leave."

"Good!" ALI congratulated, "That's the Iron-fisted leader we need."

"Never thought I would hear Dylan described as Iron Fisted," Blake chuckled. I was actually refreshing to hear a bit of comedy.

"Well, I have punched through a few walls lately," I smiled, but the joy soon escaped me as I thought back to using that same power to punch The Parasite only hours ago.

I immediately focused back on the topic, "After we are briefed, I think we need to make a call out to anyone ALI can contact," I said bluntly, "The quicker help gets here, the quicker we can get organized."

"I agree," ALI said

"Me too," Blake confirmed

"Yea... Me too," Bailey was a bit reluctant, but I chose to look over it.

"Alright then," I said standing up, "Let's get some rest. We'll meet outside the War Room at 7:00."

ALI's emblem faded. Bailey stood up and gave me one last hug for the night, "Don't stress yourself too much," She said in my ear.

"I won't," I assured her.

"I mean it," she reaffirmed, "You can only do as much as you can do."

We let go of one another and she walked toward the door. Blake gave me another hug and then turned to leave. As I watched them walk to the door, fear began to grip me. I didn't know why. The further away they got, the worse it got. I looked around the room trying to shake it, but that only made it worse. Then I realized: I was scared to be alone.

"Blake!" I called out. It came across a bit more frantic than I intended. He and Bailey both turned to look, "Can I talk to you for a second?"

"Yea... sure," He said, caught off guard but ready to help. He and Bailey told each other good night. Bailey looked disappointed I didn't call for her, but I could explain later. Blake walked over.

"What is it?" he asked.

"Do you think you could stay here tonight?" I asked, "I can have someone bring you a cot. I just..." I looked for the words to explain why I needed him to stay but he didn't need them.

"Of course," He said, patting my shoulder.

"Thank you," I sighed with relief even though I knew he would stay before I asked.

I called ALI to have a bed brought up for Blake. I walked and sat in the Bed, and Blake sat in his chair. I leaned against the wall, trying to relax. I couldn't keep my mind off of the events of the day. I couldn't close my eyes without seeing through my Dad's again.

Tears would well up, then subside as I pulled myself back together, then well up again. I frantically searched for peace, but only uncovered more hurt. I slid down in the bed, rolled up in the covers, and attempted to relax my body.

My mind refused to relax, but somehow, even with tears streaming down my cheeks, I fell asleep before the bed arrived.

Chapter 23

An explosion rang through the air. I jumped from my bed. My armor and jetpack flew from the cabinet across the room and attached themselves in their proper places; I summoned my powers all before reaching the floor.

I saw Blake also jared from his sleep standing up, looking for the source of the sound. Another explosion rang out. It came from the hallway. The glow of red fire could be seen reflecting off the white walls. "We gotta go!" Blake exclaimed.

We ran out of the room, joining a stampede of soldiers fleeing the fire. "ALI," I called, "Where do we go?"

There was no response. "ALI"

The power went out. The white lights flickered off and red emergency lights kicked on. An alarm rang out followed by a voice, "We are under attack. Evacuate the base."

Blake and I ran as fast as we could for the hangar bay as the walls shook with explosion after explosion. My ears rang. I noticed on the walls, cracks beginning to out run us. The fire spread fast and was burning brighter and brighter behind us. It always stayed just out of sight, but close enough I could see its reflection on the wall.

Just as we reached the hangar, the ceiling gave way and collapsed. I stopped and used my powers to hold the tunnel up. I held my hands over my head. The weight of the rock was crushing, and I was losing my grip. Once all of the soldiers behind me made it to safety, I let go and jumped out of the hall into the hangar.

Blake was waiting and gave me a hand standing up. The transports and fighters were just beginning to lift off from the dim room. The only light came from the lights of the ships. I saw across the bay Bailey, her mom, and the Vales emerging from a red lit hallway. "Look!" I said to Blake, pointing to the group.

We ran toward them. As we reached about half way across the hangar, gunfire rang out. The first shot I saw hit Mrs. Cassy in the chest. "No!" Blake and I screamed at the same time.

Blake ran to her and I looked for the source of the shot. An army of robots was climbing in at the mouth of the hangar. They were black and hard to see, but still I charged at them. I summoned a beam of energy. I held out both hands in front of me as I blasted them off the ledge.

The hangar was empty now except for one transport and my family. Where are all the soldiers? I thought. Did they abandon us?

I looked back for a moment. Everyone but Bailey was huddled around Mrs. Cassy. Bailey and I made eye contact and knew what the other was thinking. She summoned her power, held her arms at her sides and flew up. She rained a furry of bolts on the robots. Though we were doing good, they were still coming over the sides. They were far enough into the hanger now that I couldn't knock them over the edge. I drew my sword from my side and charged into the group.

Bailey covered me as I sliced them limb from limb. They were so unskilled. It was almost too easy. Then, one caught me off guard and thrust a staff into my chest. I was blown backwards. My head throbbed, but I was still conscious.

I stood up and looked around for my next target, but there were no more figures coming into the hangar. As I looked at the mass of robots we had defeated, I noticed their forms were more human than normal. A different model? No. They were human. Hundreds of organization soldiers lay dead on the floor of the hangar. Their limbs severed, or worse.

"No..." I stumbled backward. How could I have mistook them for robots? I was filled with remorse. I had no time to dwell on it. I saw a red glow coming from beneath the edge of the hangar. A figure leaped over the side and landed in front of the mass of dead soldiers. Red energy flowed over his body. It was The Parasite.

"And they told me you were the soldier who didn't kill," he said, his voice masked by his helmet, "Guess they were wrong about you."

I clenched my sword in my hand. I gritted my teeth in hatred. I screamed as I ran at him, but before I reached him I was knocked to the ground by something that came flying from behind me. My sword fell from my grip. I looked up from the floor. He had Bailey by the neck, her feet lifted from the ground. The Parasite drew his sword.

"NO!" I scrambled to my feet but the red energy surrounded my body. I wailed in pain as I watched helplessly.

"So weak," he demented. He thrust his sword through Bailey's chest. He withdrew the blade and tossed her lifeless body to the side.

"Guah!" I wailed. Hatred consumed me. Through the pain of the red energy I stood up and used my power to draw my sword back to my hand. With one motion I grabbed hold of the parasite's armor and ripped it from his chest, and I plunged my blade into his heart.

The moment the blade was through, his helmet retracted revealing the face of my father. The blood rushed from my face. In shock I pulled out my blade and jumped back. Tears fell down my face. I had no words.

My dad fell to his knees. He looked into my eyes with shame and confusion. The red energy that had once surrounded his body faded to nothing. He fell forward. When he hit the ground, the crystal that had been on his chest came loose and rolled to my feet.

"Dylan, Help!" Blake's voice cried out across the hangar. I looked in the direction of the voice. Blake was ushering everyone onto the last transport. Emerging from the hall where they had once been standing was a wave of Organization soldiers. I ran toward the transport, but before I could take very many steps in that direction, a missile flew from the enemy soldiers.

I shot a blast of energy at it and intercepted it between the transport and its point of origin. "Nice sh..." Blake was cut off by the explosion of the transport.

"No!" I screeched. The rocket had come from over my shoulder at the mouth of the hangar. Blake, who was standing at the door of the transport, was thrown from the explosion.

I summoned the largest ray of energy I could and blasted the hall just above the soldiers. It collapsed on them, sealing off the Hangar. I ran to Blake.

The hangar was silent as I knelt beside Blake in the flaming wreckage. I lifted his head into my arms. He was still alive. Blood ran from his forehead, near his eyebrow. He started to speak, "If you just wouldn't have picked up the case and found the crystal. We'd all still be alive."

"I didn't know," I said through sobs.

"You got us killed," Blake breathed, losing his ability to speak, "You... brought me... here."

Life left his eyes and his muscles loosened. "No! Blake, please." I leaned over his lifeless body, sobbing relentlessly.

Then, a white glow illuminated the room. I looked up, confused and ready to die. The wreckage around me began to dissolve. It turned into white energy then faded away. Blakes body dissolved from my hands. I stood up and looked around. I was now standing in a white landscape. No texture, just endless white.

Then, a red streak broke through the white, and another. It revealed I was in a white box. The box was crumbling. The red was breaking cracks in the white box. Feeling no fear, I walked over to the cracks and looked through. I could see again the hangar I had just been in. In the middle was me, leaning over Blake's body. I stepped back. I couldn't process it anymore.

Voices began to fill the box.

"Well, run him out!" Blake cried.
"Your crystal will be mine," The Parasite claimed.
"I'm trying," Bailey's voice called frantically.
"You can't hide behind your father's legacy forever," The Parasite said.
"Dylan! You gotta help me!" Bailey pleaded.

I couldn't think. There was so much chaos and confusion. I could hardly feel anything. I could hardly move. I closed my eyes and called my power. I tried to raise a shield, but it was difficult - like something was blocking it. I tried harder. As I did, I noticed it repairing the red cracks. I tried harder. The white walls began to flow with blue energy. The cracks retreated and the box enclosed again. There was peace and calm. I began to grow tired. I couldn't fight it. My eyes closed, I lost my balance, and began to fall.

***

My eyes opened and I gasped for air. I jolted up into a seated position from being laid down in my bed. I gasped for air. I darted my head around wildly attempting to get a grip on my surroundings. I saw Blake and Bailey standing at my right side. Bailey had her hands on her knees and was out of breath. "Got you," she breathed, her white energy dissipating from around her body.

As soon as I somewhat had my senses back, I sprang out of bed and wrapped them both in a hug. I began to cry… again. "Is this real?" I asked.

"I think you asking that, proved it is." Blake said.

"I'm so sorry," I sobbed, "I never should have made you come here. We should have just gone and hid."

"You didn't make us come here," Blake assured me, a bit of offense in his voice, "If I remember right, we crashed here."

"We choose to be at your side," Bailey said, "You don't keep us there."

I didn't say anything else. I only soaked up their loving embraces and soaked their shoulders with tears. After a few moments I regained a bit of a grip on reality, and we all pulled away.

I sat back down on the edge of the bed and put my hand over my face. My mind raced. I quickly lost my grip again. I began to hyperventilate. I gagged. I rocked back and forth.
"Dylan!" Blake said, trying to call me back. I couldn't come back. I was spirling down into my twisted emotions. Hatred, fear, anger, sorrow, hurt. I tried to come up for air, but I was suffocating.

Suddenly, there was nothing. It was just gone. I opened my eyes to see Bailey's face only a few inches away from mine. Her hands were on either side of my head. Her eyes were closed.

I took a deep breath. Then, I lost consciousness.

***

My eyes fluttered open. I was a bit confused about what had just happened, but I felt my emotional pain was suppressed for the time being. I sat up slowly.

I looked at Bailey who was still in a robe that she had clearly frantically thrown on over her nightwear and Blake who was fully shod in his battle stained armor. Bailey looked at me with a hopeful expression, but Blake looked utterly confused.

"What did you do?" I asked Bailey.

"You were losing control," she replied, "I used my powers to repair your neuron pathways."

I looked at her in thought for a moment, "You hacked my brain?"

"I repaired it," she corrected, and for the time being, it felt corrected.

Sure all of those emotions were still there, but I could see through them. It was like the bleeding of a massive wound had been stopped. It still hurt, but I wasn't losing blood.

234

I looked at them both, "Well, since we aren't getting any more sleep tonight, why don't e get ready, and head on to the war room," I suggested.

"Sounds like a plan to me," Bailey said, putting her hand on my shoulder one last time, "let me go get dressed."

She turned and walked out of the room.

Blake waited for her to leave then asked, "So what just happened?"

I took a moment to think about my answer. I didn't fully know. I knew the parasite had infiltrated my mind. I assumed it had something to do with our crystals being so closely connected, only I had no idea how he was able to do it or how Bailey was able to save me. I told him what I did know, "The parasite got in my head somehow. I saw..." I paused. I knew if I described the dream exactly I would be at risk of losing control again, "He made me live terrible things. Then, Bailey got in my head and kicked him out... somehow. What did it look like for you?"

"Well, I started hearing you move around," Blake explained, "enough that it woke me up. There was this bright red energy coming out of your crystal swirling around you and, like, little red lightning bolts coming off of it. Then, you started flailing your arms and the red energy picked you up out of the bed. Then Bailey burst through the door and shot you with her energy stuff, and eventually you floated back down and your energy turned blue again. Then, you woke up."

"I was floating?" I asked. Mostly all I got out of that was that I could fly when I was asleep, but not when I was awake.

"Yea, right over the bed," Blake confirmed.

I walked over to the bathroom while Blake replaced my armor with his in the cabinet so that it could be cleaned. It was a feature I wasn't aware of until tonight. I'm not sure how I thought the armor was cleaned before then.

I cleaned my face and looked into the mirror. The man looking back was one I almost didn't recognize. This man looked strong, and confident, and brave. He looked like he had it together. How could this be the same man who was broken and falling apart? The same man who could hardly keep himself from crying at any given moment?

235

I took a deep breath. I knew the man in the mirror was the man I was going to have to be or else this resistance would fall apart.

I pressed my hand to the puck containing my crystal and my armor flew from the bedroom to its proper places on my body. I summoned my power. I looked in the mirror at the blue energy flowing across the armor on my chest, around my arms. I allowed the flowing patterns to mesmerize me for a moment. 'That's who you have to be' I told myself.

"You ready?" Blake asked, peeking his head through the open door way.

"Let's do this," I said.

We marched out of the room and met up with Bailey at her pod. Once the three of us were together, I told ALI to have Alex meet us at the war room. We made our way there ourselves and found Alex outside the door.

"Hey," He greeted, "What's up with the early morning call/"

"You'll see," I eluded, "I just need you at my side."

I took one last look at the three of them. Somehow, though we hadn't known each other long, I trusted and loved each of them greatly. I knew they would have my back no matter what. Thus, I knew I had better make sure whatever I did was worth their loyalty. With that on my mind, I turned, opened the door, and walked into the room.

It was now only about 3:30 and still the room was full. It looked as though we had walked in on a meeting. The entire room stopped their conversation and looked down the long table at the four of us standing at the door. I wondered why ALI hadn't felt the need to inform me that there was a meeting going on. I expected only to find a few officers here, not the whole team. Still, I had to show no weakness or surprise.

"Good morning, gentlemen," I said formally, "It would appear I was left out of this meeting." It wasn't probably the most "leader" thing of me to say, but every scenario I had run through in my head walking up here was not this.

"We wanted to give you some time," A decorated officer at the head of the table said. I recognized him, but I had met so many people I didn't know from where, "With everything that's happened, we thought some rest might do you good."

"Some rest would do us all some good I'm sure, but unfortunately there is no time for rest," I said with the most authoritative voice I had, "I was left a message by my father. I'm sure he left you all one as well. I don't know what he said in yours, but I was instructed to take leadership over this operation as well as make a call to his allies."

"Son, I don't know what your father said, but if we had any Allies we would have called them long ago," the same man said, "We once had a united resistance and it fell apart years ago."

"Maybe so," I consented, "But I know my father. Now, if you could pause your meeting for a moment, I need to make a call. Then, I will join you all and you can bring me up to seed."

I looked at the door behind the man, and took a step toward it, but the man walked over and stood in my way. The rest of the room simply looked on in silence.

"It is the opinion of this council that an untrained child is not fit to make decisions on which the fate of the world depends," the man commanded.

I stood there for a moment, speechless. How had my father put people in charge who wouldn't obey his dying wish? I didn't want the position for any other reason than to kill the parasite and put an end to this. If my father said I was the only one who could do it, that was the way it was going to be.

I summoned my powers. The blue aura radiated across my body. I sensed the entire room shift. Everyone in the room looked at us. "Sense the room," ALI coaxed in my ear.

I thought back to that week of training in the woods. I closed my eyes and sensed what emotions I felt in the room. From the men at the table, I sensed unease, uncertainty, and doubt. It was as if they were unsure of something they were doing. From the man in front of me, I sensed ambition and haughtiness. From my friends I sensed a bit of unease, but mostly loyalty and determination.

I opened my eyes and looked away from the man in front of me, whose hand was on his sword's hilt. I looked at the men left sitting at the table. "I sense uncertainty from you gentleman. Perhaps it is about your decision? Maybe you worry that my father, who always did what was in your best interest, did in fact make the right decision?"

The men looked to one another, but before they could speak, the man in front of me spoke up, "We made this decision together and it was not taken lightly. Now stand down bearer!"

237

"And now you let this man speak for you?" I continued, "What makes him so qualified?"

"Stand down bearer," the man said sternly.

Still the men said nothing. There wasn't much room between the table and the wall. It wasn't a place I wanted to fight. Thus, I resumed diplomacy.

"Then give me a chance to speak for myself," I suggested, "Then the council can vote on whether or not I should be in power."

"I see no problem with that," One of the officers at the table said.

"Neither do I," said another.

The men nodded at each other in agreement. I looked at the man in front of me. He was glaring and his hand was still on his sword. I allowed the glow of my powers to subside, then said to the man, "Stand down soldier," and walked toward him, politely pushing past him to the front of the room. I didn't need to be able to sense emotion to tell that he was boiling mad.

My friends stayed standing at the door and I walked to the front of the room to address the men at the table. "So what do you have to say for yourself young soldier?" a man at the table asked.

I thought for a moment. I hated being put on the spot, but that seemed to happen a lot lately. I thought about the message my dad left me. I thought about the evils the Organization had done to me and countless others. I thought about how my life had been turned upside down over and over again over the past nine months. Without knowing what I was going to say, I began to speak, "My father was the smartest man I've ever known. Everything he did, he did with purpose.

I stand before you, not wanting the title of leader, yet still seeking it, because like you, I trust my father. And I want the same thing he did," I gritted my teeth and narrowed my eyebrows, "to see The Organization burn. They have lurked in the shadows for centuries and destroyed the lives of nearly every citizen of the world in one day. They have sought to take everything that I hold dear, and seek to take it from you as well.

My father was a fighter, and a unifier. I hear stories of how he once united the world together against the Organization when they were in the shadows, yet now we can't seem to agree to unite against them?

238

Disunity has no place in this effort. And if you can't unite behind me because you don't know me, then I understand, but you should at least be able to unite behind me because you knew my father."

I took a pause to catch a breath and gather my thoughts further. As I did, ALI spoke in my ear again, "You're live."

I was confused for a moment, but looking to my left, I realized the door to my father's office was open and Blake was standing inside holding a recorder linked to Dad's communicator. He must have snuck in while I was talking.

I turned from the men at the table and looked into the camera lens, "So with that I make a plea to all those who knew my father, and every nation plagued by these attacks, and all those who want to see every Organization ship fall out of the sky, and to all those who want to be free, come to this base and join us. Together, we will make them pay for what they have stolen and we will take it all back as one Ekklesia. We will make their world rule the shortest in history.

And to The Organization who is no doubt seeing this and trying to turn it off, I invite you here as well in the entirety of your might. Come see what happens when you tick me off. And better yet, see what happens when you tick *US* off."

I took a few steps toward the camera and stared into the lens, hopefully into the eyes of the Parasite, "And to the one who killed my father, the Parasite, stop your cowardly mind games and come face me."

I nodded my head for Blake to stop recording and looked back to the men at the table. They looked on with wide eyes. The man who had caused such a problem stood up, thrusting his chair out from under him, "He just challenged them to a battle we can't win."

"One we can't win without help," I corrected.

"You gamble our lives on your unfounded hope!" he yelled.

"If the world won't stand with us, there is no use in standing at all," I defended, "We can't help those who wont help themselves."

"He's right," said an officer at the table.

I continued, "They were coming here anyway. Inviting them only makes us more favorable to the people."

239

"I elect to keep Daniel's son in charge," said another officer.

"Aye," said another
"Aye"
"Aye"

And so it went around the table until the vote was unanimous with the exception of the man. All eyes looked at him.

"Nay!" he said, flustered.

"The vote is settled," said the man who started the vote.

Everyone no looked at me. "What are your orders?" he asked.

"My first order is to remove this man from this council," I said pointing.

The man glared at me but said not a word. The shoved his chair out of the way and walked to the door. As he walked out, he turned, "You'll regret putting a child in charge of a war," he said, then walked out.

"Now," I said, changing the subject and ignoring him, "I am going to establish Blake, Alex, and Bailey as members of this council. Have a seat," I gestured to them and they each found an empty seat at the table. There were just enough for the three of them to sit down.

"Welcome soldiers," one officer said.

"Now, I'll admit, I don't know many of your protocols and secrets," I acknowledged, "That is why ALI, my father's assistant, is advising me. But I also need your help to update me and keep this base running as smoothly as it always has."

"That won't be a problem," one officer said, "This base can basically run itself. It's not even a problem that you challenged the Organization. You're right, they were coming anyway. Our biggest problem is, even if your people show up, The Organization will still be bigger."

"And now they have the red crystal, so their American division can deploy," another said.

"They'll bomb our American cities to a pulp and try to draw us out," said another.

240

"Wait," Blake spoke up, "Don't they need both the crystal and their reactor to deploy the American division?"

"Yes but no one knows exactly where it is," said the officer who had spoken up for me earlier.

"But we do," Alex replied, "We stole the crystal out of it."

Seeing where this was going, I commanded ALI to put the schematic of the base on the three holo-projectors that ran down the middle of the table

"There is a massive dam that supplies backup power to the base," Blake continued his plan, "If we send a team in to destroy the dam, it would flood the base and destroy the reactor."

"How can we be sure it would flood it?" an officer asked.

"There aren't any blast doors," I said, remembering running through the halls of the base, "There is so much fortification surrounding the base, not much was done to protect the tunnels."

"If we deploy immediately, and get there before the crystal does, we could still take the base while they are on backup power," another officer added.

The room was becoming tense with anticipation. This was the beginning of a good plan and they knew it.

"Our cruisers will be too slow," An officer said, "They'll send ships to intercept us before we make it."

"But our smaller craft could make it," I said, "We don't have to lead a full scale assault on the base, we just have to get close enough to bomb the dam."

"According to the schematic, there is only emergency electricity run from the dam to the defenses closest to the base," ALI informed

"Without the cruisers for cover, there will still be heavy casualties," an officer consented.

"But if they deploy the North American division, there will be even more casualties," another rebutted.

"Let's vote then," I suggested, "All in favor of sending a strike team of fighters and bombers say aye,"

241

The vote went around the table and was unanimous.

"It's settled then," said the officer who stood up for me, "Admiral King, ready your team."

I assumed this admiral must have been over the fleet. "Until we receive word on the strike, this council is adjourned," I said.

Everyone stood up, soluted, and headed for their respective divisions. "Can I get the one who is over communications to stay here?" I called into the crowd. A man turned to me and walked over.

"Yes sir?"

"I need you and all those under you to be looking for any distress calls," I commanded, "Any ally who is trying to get here but can't. Also, be looking out for anyone answering the call. We don't want to lose anyone because they can't find us."

"Yes sir," he replied, "I will get my men to work on it."

As he walked off, the officer who had stood up for me came over, "That was quite the compelling speech," he congratulated.

"Thank you, sir," I replied.

"I'm General Raddick. I worked closely with your father. I specialize in ground operations and weaponry."

"It's very nice to meet you," I said politely.

"You know, before you walked in here, we were about to let that man convince us to go back underground," he said, "He fed off of our fear. Fear of losing. I apologize if I lost sight of your father's legacy."

I stood there in shock for a moment. My throat went dry and I felt the blood drain from my face. I was taken back to the dream the Parasite had sent me - to when he said I could not hide behind my father's legacy.

"Are you alright, sir?" he asked, looking at my stoned face.

I thought for a moment. Was I? The weight of this position hadn't fully set in. What if my father's legacy was all that was keeping me here. What was past that? I didn't know. But I did know turning them back to my side was me and not my father. I looked up at the man, "All is forgiven sir, I have to make my own legacy now."

242

"You're already off to a good start," he congratulated.

Chapter 24

Blake, Alex, and Bailey walked up as General Raddick walked off. "Gotta say, when ALI told me to sneak into that office and start broadcasting, I was a little worried I was going to capture you getting shot on camera," Blake said.

I laughed.

"You did good," Bailey said, "I knew you had it in there somewhere."

"I'm already getting tired of it," I admitted.

"Oh, don't lie," Alex said, "You've gotta like knowing what's going on."

"The job does have some perks I guess," I conceded.

"You're Dad knew what he was doing," Blake said sentimentally.

I smiled, but changed the subject, "I guess I should probably prove my loyalty by going on this mission. Blake, they ever teach you how to fly?"

"No, but they taught me how to shoot," he said.

"Good enough," I allowed, "You wanna be my gunner."

"It would be my honor, your lordship," he poked.

"Stop," I said.

"Yes, sir," he saluted.

I rolled my eyes. "Alex, keep the Taken out of this mission," I requested.

"Are you sure?" he asked, "I have some really good pilots."

"I know," I replied, "But I want to make sure when people start to show up, they see that there are defectors from The Organization. It might make them view The Organization's soldiers as people rather than animals. The only animals are the ones giving the orders."

"The rest are just indoctrinated to act like animals," Alex scowled.

"Yes, but aren't you glad I had mercy on you?"

"I was already having a crisis of faith," he rebutted.

"Well, others clearly were too," I reminded him, "We wouldn't be here if not for that fact."

He shook his head in agreement and we all walked out of the room. I could tell, as we walked toward the hangar, that Bailey was a bit disappointed. I fell back to talk to her.

"What's wrong?" I asked.

"Nothing, really… it's nothing," she assured me.

"You just said nothing twice, which clearly means it's something," I pried.

She looked down, then reluctantly spoke up, "I just want to be a part of things," she admitted, "Everyone has a job, but my only job is to stay safe."

I took a moment. I really did want her off the battlefield, for today at least. "I just need someone here to look out for things," I lied.

"You have a whole team for that," she said.

"I don't know them though," I replied.

"You know Alex," she rebutted, "longer than me."

"That's by like two days," I said

"That might as well be two years around here," she rebutted.

That much was true. We stopped walking and faced each other. Realizing that this argument was going nowhere, I confessed the truth, "I just can't lose anyone else," I admitted, "I can only protect one person in battle at a time."

"I can take care of myself you know," Bailey said, "I did for a long time before you came along."

"When I came along, I remember you not being able to fight off the Organization," I reminded her.

"Maybe you saw what you wanted to see," she pointed out.

"Please Bailey," I pleaded, "I can't win this argument, and you're right, just please stay here this time."

She looked away, then back, and forced a small smile, "Okay," she conceded, "But only until we get some time to talk about this."

"It's a deal," I agreed. We shared a hug, made awkward by our stiff armor, then continued on.

We entered the Hanger where Blake was already in a U-Winged fighter and others were already taking off. "Come back safe," Bailey said, staying at the opening of the hallway.

"I will," I said, waving.

I ran up to the fighter Blake was in and climbed up the ladder, which was hanging over the side of the ship, and into the cockpit. Blake was positioned behind me. "You ready?" I asked over my shoulder.

"That depends," he said, "Are you a good pilot?"

"I've flown once," I said.

"What!?" Blake questioned.

"Don't worry," I assured him, "ALI's gonna fly mostly. We're just going for moral support."

"Oh, I feel so much better," Blake said sarcastically.

"I'll have you know I am the best piloting program ever crafted," ALI chipped in. The canopy over the cockpit closed and the engines started.

"Yes, and the last time I rode with you, you crashed and I almost died," Blake insulted.

"I technically was not flying when you crashed," ALI corrected, "I was taken offline."

"Alright, that's enough," I said, grabbing hold of the controles. I followed ALI's teaching and lifted us up gently. I turned us around toward the door. We were the last fighters in the hangar. I engaged the engines, and we flew out.

246

"Oh, God help me," Blake breathed as the g-force pushed his head back in his seat.

"It's better than jetpacking the whole way there," I said

"We'll see," He countered.

We followed the convoy and exited through the opening created for us in the shield. It looked like they had deployed about 100 fighters and 25 bombers. We would likely be outnumbered, but that wasn't new. I prayed we would make up for it in skill and speed.

We reached cruising altitude and I gave ALI the controles. The ride would be dark most of the way. The sun would just be beginning to rise when I arrived. For now I enjoyed the view.

We flew over a few cities, their lights shining below us, untouched by the war. They were blessed, but I worried that blessing wouldn't continue much longer. No matter what happened today, we still had a lot of fighting ahead of us. Much of that fighting would no doubt be fought here, in these cities.

I wondered what was happening down there. Was life going on as normal? If communications with the outside world were down, other than the message I broadcasted, did they even really know what was going on?

"10 minutes from engaging the enemy," a voice said over the radio.

It roused Blake and I from our thoughts. "Alright ALI, keep us in the sky," I said.

"Yes, sir," he replied, "If I may sir, why did we come? There are others who would have easily taken your place."

"I just want to be here if something goes wrong," I admitted, "They may need a crystal bearer."

"And his best friend," Blake added.

The first notes of the sunrise began to softly illuminate the mountain range in front of us. Though we had flown in while it was dark the last time, I recognized the landscape.

Suddenly a red alarm started flashing on the dash in front of me, indicating a threat. The windshield of the cockpit lit up with a heads

247

up display, showing the targeting system and highlighting multiple fighters incoming.

I expected there to be a barrage of fire coming from the cannons I had seen the last time but I realized they were offline without the crystal in its place.

The front of the convoy met them first and the dogfight began. Orange and yellow blasts lit up the sky.

"Fighters, protect the bombers," a voice commanded, "Bombers, don't get caught up in the fight, press on to the dam."

The bombers were larger and easier to hit, but because they were larger they had better shields. It took three people to plot a bomber, a pilot, a gunner, and a bombardier. They were "T" shaped with large wings on top and a tall, narrow body holding the artillery. I spotted two flying together and piloted our ship that way.

We passed up the dog fight, but the dash highlighted more ships incoming. The protective, anti-aircraft guns on the bombers opened fire on them, as did we. Their shields held strong, but they were forced to break off their attack and circle around. I kept my eye on them, but stayed with the bombers.

We were now coming over the mountain that concealed the base. The dam was visible, just a few miles away. The mountain cast a shadow on it, prolonging the night in the base's valley a bit longer.

"There it is," Blake exclaimed.

As he did, a barrage of cannon fire erupted from the base. Our fighter shook as the blasts exploded on our shields. I watched the shield integrity meter on the dash go from 100, to 80, to 60.

"We can't take much of this," I said to the bombers over the coms, "It's now or never."

"It's now," said the female voice of the pilot.

A bunch of slots opened on the bomber and it began to launch basketball sized orbs at the dam. We watched on as they fell toward the base of the dam and waited for the collapse. There was a massive explosion as they made contact, but to our horror, the explosion illuminated the purple glow of a shield. The blast revealed that the entire dam was protected.

"No good!" said the pilot, "I repeat, no good. The dam is shielded."

"Pull off your attack, soldier," the officer in charge commanded, "We need to regroup."

The bombers and the other three fighters with us began to turn, but we realized that we were the only ones to make it this far. All of Montana base's limited firepower was on us. We were all ducking and weaving, but our shields were dropping quickly.

It was risky, but I had an idea, "We can't make it back," I pointed out, "but the dam is much closer. It won't be smooth, but I think we can land on the mountain next to the dam and find a way to deactivate the shield."

"ALI, take us down," I commanded, hoping the rest would follow.

"I'm coming with you," said one pilot.

"Better than being shot out of the sky," said another, "get above our bomber, our shields will last longer than yours."

The fighters did as they suggested and the six ships headed toward the right side of the dam.

"Shields at 28 percent," said one of the bomber pilots.

"Hold on just a little bit longer!"

Our fighter was shaken by an explosion. It wasn't a cannon blast. One of the bombers had damage to their engine.

"Looks like this is gonna be more of a crash than a landing," said someone inside.

I looked down and saw their wings expand into their glider position, just as our crashing ship had done when we found my father's base.

Another explosion rang out. One of the U-Winged fighters with us had lost their shields and was destroyed. The flaming pieces fell down and erupted on the surface of the dam's shield.

As it went down, we finally flew over the dam. Instantly, we went from being high in the air to flying over the surface of the water. The bomber which was gliding, hit the surface and sank to a stop. To my surprise, airbags flew out from the wings and the plane became a boat. The other bomber and the remaining fighters all flew over to the edge of the water and landed on the shore.

Everyone exited their ships. We could see three on top of the bomber in the water, climbing out through a hatch on the top of the ship. Once out, they jetpacked over to the rest of us. I could see, in the distance, fighters from both sides falling from the sky.

As everyone gathered together to discuss what to do, I found that my plan didn't go much further than getting to the dam. "So, does anyone have any idea what to do from here?" I asked.

I was met with blank stares. "This was your plan to land here wasn't it?" asked the female pilot from the crashed bomber.

"That was my plan to stay alive," I corrected, "I don't know how we're gonna get inside the dam and turn off the shield."

"We don't have to turn off the shield," ALI said where the group could hear, "There isn't a shield on the water side."

"How would we detonate something deep enough to damage it?" asked a pilot.

"We don't" ALI said, "We drop one bomb down its throat, where the water goes in."

Everyone turned to look at the dam. In the center, there was a swirling whirlpool, where countless gallons of water were being sucked into the dam. It was protected from debris by metal poles sticking up out of the water. We wouldn't be able to float it over there, we would have to drop it in.

"I have an idea!" I said optimistically, "Someone get me a bomb!"

One person, I assumed a bombardier, volunteered and opened one compartment on the remaining bomber. "You'll have to lift it out of there superman," he said.

I used my powers to reach inside the compartment and float out a bomb. "We only have two left so be careful with it," he warned.

My power radiated across my chest and my right arm as I floated it to me, then, out over the water. Someone started to say, "What are you doing?" but stopped mid sentence when they realized my plan.

I floated the orb across the open water and above the protective metal teeth of the whirlpool. Just as I was getting close, I heard the sound of gunfire. The bomb exploded with great force. Though it was about 100 yards away, the heat was still tangible where we were standing. We all shielded our faces and looked on hopeful, but all that had been touched were some of the metal poles sticking out of the water.

Our disappointment was interrupted by orange blasts of plasma flying our way. We all found a ship to take cover behind and some of the pilots started firing back.

"We've gotta carry it over there and drop it in," Blake pointed out, "That's the only way to keep it safe."

"If you say so," I consented. I knew he was right, but the catwalk over the dam was beginning to fill up with troops.

Blake and I activated our helmets and hustled over to the bomber and I floated out the last bomb.

"What are you doing?" complained one of the bombardiers.

"We have one shot left," I said, "We're gonna walk it over there."

"I've got you covered," said the female pilot, activating her helmet and pulling a plasma rifle from its holster on her jetpack.

"I'm Blake," Blake introduced.

"Alita," said the pilot, and she pulled up the rifle and shot a soldier off the catwalk. The shot hit his armor, but the force of the blast pushed him over the dam. Just as he tipped over the rail, I latched onto him with my power and pulled him back up.

"What'd you do that for?" Alita hotly exclaimed, "That was a perfect shot!"

"I agree," I congratulated, "But everyone is going to get a chance to flee this base before we destroy it. I value life."

"Me too!" she argued angrily as gunfire erupted around us, "That's why I tried to kill a murderer."

"You can kill him when I'm not around to save him," I contended. She gave me an angry scowl, "Still, the cover fire will be helpful. Alita, stay here and give us cover. The rest of you, follow me."

251

"Oh, so now you want me to shoot them?" Alita jabbed.

"Do what your convictions lead you to do, and I will do the same," I said. It was not my job to change her mind. Agreeing to disagree would have to do for now.

"Their only conviction is to kill all of us without mercy," Alita said through gritted teeth.

"And I want to be different from them," I was done with this conversation, "Now drop it and that's an order. The rest of you, with me.

The remaining ten of us grouped up and charged the dam. I concentrated and held a shield up for cover at the same time as I carried the bomb behind us. I was doing fine at keeping the blasts off of us until they got out a grenade launcher. I sensed the projectile coming, but I had no time to react.

The blast overwhelmed the shield and knocked us all down. Thankfully I had absorbed most of the force and nobody was hurt. Being distracted, I dropped the bomb, and it rolled toward the water. I grabbed hold of it with my blue energy just before it rolled off into the deep. Orange blasts hit the ground all around us. Many took hits to the armor, but one soldier yelled out as one found a gap in the armor and hit his thigh.

I raised the shield. They fired another projectile, but this time Alita intercepted the rocket over the water with a well placed shot. "Can you walk?" someone asked him as Alita took out the person with the rocket launcher.

The wounded soldier tried to stand, but the pain was too much. "Stay here and play dead," another soldier suggested, "if we all keep going, they'll think you're dead, and we'll get you when the dam is busted."

"That should work!" said another person.

The wounded man reluctantly layed down and allowed his body to go limp, trying to keep from rubbing his wound. I personally didn't like the plan, but I wasn't really in a position to think of a better one. "Let's move!" Blake said.

Everyone stood up and began to run again. We finally made it to the catwalk. It was a long concrete walkway with rails that went across the top of the dam. From the edge you could see the lake to the

252

left, the mile long drop off to the right, and the target straight ahead, blocked by about twenty soldiers.

The enemy realized that they couldn't shoot through my shield. Upon this, they threw a grenade just as we reached the walkway. Not having enough concentration left to move it with my powers, it exploded, leaving a gaping hole. It blew out a section of wall about ten feet wide and deep. The hole in the wall was just big enough to reach the surface of the water, allowing a bit to spill over the top.

The fire stopped and the soldiers drew their atom swords. They knew we would have to jump if we wanted over and that if we jumped, they could cut us down. I lowered the shield and looked at them.

"Come on over, scum," One said through the eri distortion of their helmet.

"Alita," I called over the coms where the Organization troops couldn't hear, "do you still have a shot?"
"Negative," she replied, "They have me pinned with a sniper. I can't move."

"Understood," I said, realizing I only had one option.

I dropped the bomb, which was behind the group of pilots and held both hands out in front of me, conjuring a concussive blast. This knocked the soldiers in front back, and caused the group to topple like dominos. After this, I held both hands down and used a blast to vault over the gaping hole. As I flew through the air, I drew my staff and thrust it into the chest of one soldier on the ground, knocking him out.

By now the rest were scrambling to their feet. "Everyone, back to the fighters!" I ordered.

"What about the bomb?" Blake asked.

"I'll take care of it!" I promised.

"What about you?" He furthered

"Pick me up on your way out!"

I turned back to the troops in front of me. The catwalk was too narrow for them to face me more than one at a time. I knew I could take them.

I advanced. Clashing sword and staff. Taking them out one by one as I neared the throat of the dam. The otherworldly zinging of the blades striking the Unitum staff filled the air as I easily bested each of them and finally reached the final troop standing in my way. I stepped over the motionless body of my last opponent and readied to fight once more. He looked at me, then tilted over to look at the ones behind me whom I had defeated.

He then retracted his sword, slowly placed it on the ground, and deactivated his helmet, revealing a young man, probably in his twenties. "I yield," he said, raising his hands.

Just as I was ready to let him walk away, his face turned pale and his eyes wide with shock. I looked behind me, but saw nothing for him to be so upset about. I looked back. He began to claw at his throat. A faint coil of red energy flowed around his neck.

With that I felt the blood drain from *my* face. It was The Parasite. But where was he? Was he here or just messing with me from a distance again? Could he even do this over a long distance?

"There is no tolerance here for cowards," said the voice of Darren Flyhe.

"Show yourself!" I commanded.

The soldier in front of me began to lift off the ground, fear gripping him, his legs kicking frantically. He began to lift over the edge of the dam, over the throat. I latched onto him with my power trying to save him, but that allowed the parasite to take hold of me. The red energy flew through the air and up my arm. My energy was being ripped from me. I could no longer hold the soldier and the Parasite no longer had a use for him. He let go and dropped him down the throat of the dam.

He screamed as he fell, but was quickly drowned out by the water. "No!" I breathed, barely being able to make a sound.

I fell to the ground on all fours. The red energy surrounded me, feeding off my energy. I saw in front of me a man walking up. It was The Parasite. I was unsure of where he came from, but I felt my hatred boiling within me. I racked my brain, trying to find a way out.

"How'd you like that trick?" he taunted, "I learned it from you."

He was referring to my outrage on the bridge. How could he know about that? Maybe he had looked deep into my mind or maybe there was a spy, or maybe he was watching. Still, as disturbing as his comments were, my mind quickly forgot about it as the pain overwhelmed my body.

His fist was held up in front of him, absorbing the energy drained from me. He looked from me to the fighters taking off across the lake. I looked too. Rather than flying off, they were flying straight toward us. "What are they doing?" I thought through the pain, "They need to get out of here."

The Parasite's demeanor changed. He let go of me and I fell completely to the ground. I tried to regain my strength. There were flashes of red and yellow. One explosion, then another. The dam shook. I saw a piece of the catwalk on the other side of the parasite be destroyed as the last bomber crashed through it. A fighter crashed, taking out some of the poles protecting the whirlpool, then the remnants of the fighter were pulled down into the throat.

I rolled over and used what strength I had to grab hold of the bomb I had brought with me. I lifted it over the destroyed catwalk, and out over the throat. I knew it would explode and take me with it when the dam fell, but it would take the parasite and the dam. I knew I was about to die at his hands anyway. I would rather us both die at mine.

"God, give me strength," I prayed and let go. I gripped my chest, unable to stand, as I prepared myself for the collapse of the dam. Before it had a chance to fall, a red blast of energy intercepted it. Immediately my entire vision was blocked by a blinding white light. My hearing was deafened by the explosion of the bomb. For a moment, I thought I was dead, but the light subsided and my hearing returned.

I saw the parasite standing up from being knocked to the ground and I saw one last fighter steadying itself from the concussion of the blast. The ship turned to him and opened fire. The Paraste raised a shield, but was having a hard time protecting himself. The large blasts from the U-Jet were too much for him. I saw through the smoke and red energy, the parasite drawing his blade with one hand and holding the shield with the other. Using his telekinetic energy, he thrust the blade forward. It flew through the air and sliced through the belly of the U-Jet.

The Jet began to spin out of control. Somehow, I sensed Blake inside. "No!" I screamed. By now, I had enough strength to stand and I scrambled to my feet. I took hold of the fighter with my energy. The blue Aura surrounded me and the jet. I steadied it and stopped it just before it went over the edge, but again, the parasite reached out his red tendrils and latched onto my energy.

I could see Blake in the cockpit, looking down helplessly. I felt the energy of the parasite begin to take over mine. Filled with determination, I pulled one hand from the Jet and blasted the parasite with a beam of energy. He blocked it with one hand, and I felt the red energy begin to pull there too.

Somehow I was resisting it. Realizing we were connected, rather than pushing against his energy, I began to pull. A shocked look spread across his face. He didn't know how I was doing it either.

For a moment, our energy formed a triangle between us and the fighter. Where our energy met, was a purple glow. I focused as hard as I could, I pulled as hard as I could. The only thing keeping Blake alive was this phenomena, whatever it was, and I couldn't let it stop.

Still, after only a few seconds, my strength gave out. I realized he was still pulling my energy from me and I was only countering it by using all my strength. I could hold it no longer. Every muscle in my body began to burn. The red energy began to reach closer to me. I was losing my grip on Blake. I began to scream in anguish.

Finally, my grip on the jet gave out. I dropped it, but by slowing its momentum, it crashed into the dam and hung on the side. Relieved, I used both hands to hold off The Parasite. He walked close and his grip on me grew stronger. The red energy reached my hands, then flowed down my arms, and across my body once again. I wailed in pain as I let go.

The parasite was standing over me now. "So much like your father," He said, a bit out of breath, "About to be even more like him."

He drew his sword and prepared to strike me down. "You'll never win," I promised through labored breath and hatred, "Eventually, by man or God, you'll lose."

"We'll see," He smirked.

As he pulled the armor from my chest, there was a horrible screeching sound. It caused the parasite to pause and look to the source of the sound. It was the bomber that had crashed into the lake moments ago. It was screeching over the broken poles that protected the throat.

"No, no, no!" he exclaimed, letting go of me, dropping his sword, and grabbing hold of the ship with his red energy. The ship was now falling into the throat. With such limited time, he was only able to grab the top of the ship, but it was so badly damaged and heavy from being waterlogged, the bottom part of the ship broke loose. He attempted letting go of the top and grabbing the rest containing the bombs, but it was already engulfed by the rapidly moving water and he couldn't pull it up.

256

"No!" he exclaimed again. He called his sword back to his hand and lunged at me. By this time, I was trying to stand to my feet. I tried to dodge but I was weak and slow from having my energy drained. The blade stabbed through my lower left abdomen, searing flesh as it went. He pulled out the blade and I screamed, as I fell to the ground.

I felt the dam shake. The bomb finally detonated. There was a great rumbling and I felt the dam begin to give way. I used all the energy I had left to lift my hand and use a concussive blast to push the parasite away. He didn't go very far, but he was no longer concerned with me anyway.

Realizing the dam was failing, he put his hands on the concrete. His energy began to spread out through the cracks that were forming. He was trying to hold it together.

Judging by the sound of water rushing out of the other side, it was too late. I lay back, unable to move. I thought of how ironic it was. I wanted so badly to kill this man that it led me here to die with him. I had such high morals that I wouldn't kill a soldier who tried to kill me, yet when my father died, I was willing to kill this man without thought. Maybe I deserve this fate, I thought, the death of a true hypocrite, two sinners dying together for their sins against one another.

There was so much I wanted to know. How would the war end? What would life be like from here on for the ones I loved? What could I have done to keep from being here, now?

In moments like this, I suppose seconds feel like minutes, but of all the great many things I thought about in those moments, I thought about the words Pastor gave me when I set off on this adventure - instructing me not to lose myself in this war. Had I done just that?

I allowed myself to get caught up in emotion and politics and forgot why I was really doing this. Actually, did I ever really know why I was doing this, I thought, or was I just doing it for some far off reason? Maybe at first noble in saving my family, but now just foolish, bringing Blake here on my quest of vengeance.

The light faded from my vision, I felt the blood running down my side and the hand I had over the wound. I felt the dam begin to give way as I began to fall with it. I heard the faint scream of anger from the Parasite, mostly drowned out by the ringing in my ears and the dam crashing down.

As I slipped from consciousness, I heard a voice, familiar, but I couldn't place it. In the last moments as my brain went from foggy to utter darkness, my only thought was a prayer, "Lord, forgive me.

Chapter 25

I woke up to a bright white light. I was disoriented and blurry on how I got there. I tried to think back to the last thing I remembered, but I could remember nothing useful to place me here.

The sharp smell of antiseptic, contrasted by the soft smell of linens filled the air. A gentle and rhythmic beeping came from my right. As my eyes adjusted, I could tell I was looking at a light on a white ceiling.

I moved my head from side to side and realized it was a hospital room with monitors and other equipment stationed all around me.

I tried to sit up but a sharp pain ran through my gut. I lifted up the covers of the bed and pulled up my white hospital gown to look for the source. Wrapped round my abdomen were gauze and I could see a thicker bandage where the pain had originated.

My memory began to come back. I could see the parasite plunging his blade into my body. But… the dam… it collapsed. How did I get here? How did I survive?

As I finished inspecting my wound, I readjusted my gown and lowered the covers of the bed. When I moved, an IV came loose from my hand setting off an alarm on the monitor next to my bed.

This alarm prompted me to look around the room more closely. There was nothing here but a monitor, my IV, a chair by my bed, and a door. My armor was nowhere to be seen and neither was the crystal. And where was Blake? He would be here right now if he could. He would be right by my bed. As a matter of fact, so would Bailey or Alex.

Just as I began to panic, a nurse walked in dressed in a uniform from my Father's base. That eased my mind a bit, but not much.

"What happened?" I asked, the second she stepped foot in the door. My throat was dry and the sound that came out was hardly a whisper.

As soon as she looked up, I realized that it was Bailey's mom. "You were stabbed," she said, vaguely.

Now I see where Bailey gets it from, I thought to myself.

"Where is my crystal? And Blake? And Bailey?" I demanded worriedly in my raspy voice.

"Your Crystal is back in your cabin with your armor," she answered, handing me a glass of water which she had carried in with her, "Balke, Bailey, and Alex are in a meeting. They've been here almost the whole time you have. They'll be disappointed they missed you waking up."

"How long was I out?" I asked, still raspy, but better since I had a few sips of water.

"About a week." she answered.

"A week!" I exclaimed. An alarm went off on my heart monitor.

"Calm down," she said gently before she continued, "It has been a week, but your friends say everything is going very well and the council is eager for you to get back. It would seem your heroics have gained the total trust of the Ekklesia."

"Wait, we're calling ourselves the Ekklesia now?" I asked, surprised since she had never heard me say the word.

"Well after your message and everything that's happened since, that's really the only proper name for us now," Ms. Boone smiled as she pressed some buttons on the monitor.

My brain was spinning with questions. What has been happening here? What happened to the Montana base? Who was actually running this place since I was out of it?

I didn't get a chance to ask any of those before Ms. Boone offered, "Since the machine woke you up, that means you're healed enough to be up and about. How about you get out of that bed and try walking around. Then I'll send for your armor."

"Uh, yea, yea that sounds great!" I responded.

She removed the tape holding the loose IV to my wrist. I sat up, feeling pain in my abdomen, but nothing I couldn't handle. I pulled back the covers and sat on the edge of the bed. Then, careful to hold my gown together where it mattered, I stood up and took a few steps to prove that I could walk.

There was a bit of pain when I moved, but overall I was shocked at how little pain there was. "Very good," Ms. Boone congratulated, "I'll get your armor for you."

259

"Thank you, Ms. Boone," I said.

She walked out and I walked over to the window that was embedded in the door. In the hallway, I could see various doctors and nurses. But then, a woman with a turban on her head, carrying medical supplies walked by. The woman was wearing an Ekklesia nurses uniform. She was the first Arab I had seen here.

After her, a soldier, wearing an Ekklesia uniform walked by, but on his arm was the Australian flag. With him walked others. I counted an Egyptian flag, a South African flag, a Spanish flag, and a British flag.

I stepped back in shock. People had answered my call. I backed up to the hospital bed and sat down. As I rummaged through my thoughts, a man walked in holding my puck with the crystal in it.

"Here you go sir," he said.

I took it from him and thanked him.

"Your welcome sir. It's good to have you back up and about."

With that he turned and walked out. I held the puck up in front of me and looked at the crystal. It amazed me how much so many had done to try and acquire this thing. How had an 17 year old high schooler kept it from them? It was no doubt a miracle.

I took off the gown and pressed the puck to my chest. The white uniform spread across my body, clothing me. I examined it. It looked cooler with the armor, but was much more comfortable this way. It had formed over the bandage rather than removing it and nothing was rubbing the wrong way. I was ready to go.

"ALI?" I called, hoping he was in the suit.

"Good to hear your voice again, sir," he said from the shoulder.

"It's good to be back," I said sincerely. I walked out the door, headed for the war room, "So what exactly happened after I blacked out?"

"Well, sir, Blake used his jetpack to brave the falling dam and grab you before the flood swept you away."

"And the base?"

"Submerged, no hope of coming online again."

"The Parasite?"

"MIA"

"And what happened here while I was out?" I inquired.

"Well, the day after you got back, people from all over the world started answering your call. Those who couldn't get here, we deployed troops to go and get with almost 100% success. Warships now line the East coast from New York To South Carolina and engineers are working as we speak to equip them with our technology."

"How many soldiers?"

"Over 6,000,000!" ALI elated, "And that's not the best of it, we had over 100 cruisers show up. I didn't know it, but your father had these things being built all over the world. That's why The Organization could only spare three ships for the attack on Washington."

"And what's the report now that we have eyes from all around the world?"

"Officially the organization owns every country in every continent except North America. The count of sighted cruisers is 300 at this time and climbing."

"We're a bit outnumbered then?"

"In weaponry, yes, but your attack on the Montana Base threw The Organization into a fit."

"How so?"

"They started bombing cities as retaliation," I sat back mortified. I caused cities to be bombed, "I know what you're thinking," ALI continued, "But they would have done it anyways. Those bombings only further turned the world against them and it drove the Ekklesia members here."

I wasn't at all proud to hear that innocents had been lost, especially as a result of our attack. Still, rather than blame ourselves, I knew the only ones at blame were the ones ordering the bombing. It only determined me to defeat them even more. Seemingly, it had the same effect on the rest of the world.

I made my way down the halls, and up some stairs, and finally to the war room.

"Anything else important I need to know before I walk in here?" I asked ALI.

He said nothing. With optimistic anticipation, I opened the door and walked in. At the table I saw all the officers, Admirals, and generals, but most importantly I saw my friends.

Blake, Alex, and Bailey all stood up and ran over. To my suprise, the entire host of officers stood up behind them and gave me a round of applause, accompanied with cheers.

Bailey embraced me first. Her hug was gentle and I only winced a bit from the pain as she squeezed. "I'm so glad you're back," she said.

Blake came up next, and too eager to wait his turn, he joined in on the same hug, "I thought you were dead," he breathed, "They didn't think you would come out of it there for a minute."

"Come on, You can't get rid of me that easily," I repeated the cliche, "Plus, I had to get you back for almost dying."

I could tell tears were being shed. I couldn't help but not be as emotionally impacted as they were. For them I had almost died and been unconscious for a week. To me it was just moments... and well, quite a bit of pain.

I eventually pulled away, wanting to save the hugs for a more appropriate time. When they pulled away, I shared a brief hug with Alex, then addressed the group, "I've been out for a bit and it's good to hear everything is going well. ALI has brought me up to speed for the most part."

"Well sir, it's truly good to have you back," said General Raddick, "Have a seat and we'll resume the meeting."

I took my seat between Bailey and Blake, everyone sat down, and an officer began to speak, "Converting these cruisers from their primitive fuel cells to our crystal's energy is proving to take longer than we thought. It is likely that some will run out of fuel in the next few days."

Another spoke up when he finished, "There is no room left in the shield. We need to check them in and send them to park elsewhere. Once they land, their nuclear reactors can recharge the ships, and we can work on them as we finish others."

"There is a plane not far from here that I know of where they can land," suggested General Raddick, pulling up its location on the hologram projectors.

"Looks good to me," I agreed.

"I'll send them there now then," said the officer who began the conversation.

"Another order of business is today's arrival of this unknown civilization and their bearer," said General Raddick.

What? Another bearer? An unknown civilization? "ALI," I whispered, "why didn't you tell me this?"

"I was going to, but you opened the door before I could," he said, "Still, you basically know as much as the rest of them."

I shook my head in aggravation. I noticed Bailey shifting uneasily in her seat.

"What do we know about them?" I asked.

"Nothing other than they want to help," said a general, "They said that they have been a hidden city for hundreds of years harboring technology similar to ours the whole time. They have a bearer, a girl. Her power is a purple... pink color, but like yours."

I thought for a moment, but before I could think of another question, Bailey spoke up, "I know who they are," She admitted, "At least I know of them," the room was silent and all eyes looked to her.

"I was trained by protectors of an ancient Mayan temple. They claimed to have been given technology and my crystal from the future by a time traveler and were instructed to wait for me to pass the crystal on to."

So this was Bailey's training she had alluded to. It made sense, and I could understand why she wouldn't have told me this when we first met. Of course, I was shocked at the story, but I was mostly glad to know the truth.

"So they claim a... time traveler gave them this technology?" questioned an officer.

"I know it sounds absurd, but putting that part of the story aside, I can say they are good people," Bailey defended, "They took care of me and my mom."

"If they want to help us I see no reason why not to let them," I said, "It doesn't sound like they sport anything similar to Organization technology. They can'n really fake that," I pointed out, "I would like to meet them and their bearer," I said turning to Bailey.

"I would too," she agreed, "I can only vouch for them as a people. I never knew they had a bearer or where they were located," she explained, "I only knew the people at their Temple in Missouri.

"Then if there is nothing else pressing to attend to, I suggest we adjourn for now and I can take a few people to go and meet them," I proposed.

The council was in agreement and the meeting was adjourned. As we left the room, I spoke with Bailey, "So this is the training you were so illusive about?" I asked.

"Well it always seemed like it would take more time to explain than we had," she sighed, "And the story is crazy anyway."

"Crazier than a couple of teenagers with superpowers leading a resistance against an organization bent on taking over the world?" I pointed out.

"Well, when you put it that way," Bailey smiled and we continued on. I suggested that Blake, Alex, Bailey, General Raddick, and I be the ones to go meet the bearer and her people.

We reached the hangar and boarded a transport I had never seen until now, a simple floating platform with rails. There was a small control panel on the front and it was powered by smaller versions of the round engines that powered the transports and other vehicles here.

General Raddick took the controls and flew us out of the hangar. The sight I saw was absolutely stunning. "Steampunk" versions of cruisers waited in a seemingly never ending line going out of an opening in the shield. Ones that had been checked in flew here and there, some landing, others on their way to be upgraded.

Traditional fuel powered jets soared through the sky above the shield, practicing maneuvers. Some flying within the shield sported new engines and guns, linked to our yellow crystal. Painted on their wings was the symbol that was on all of our uniforms: the flaming dove, wings outstretched, enclosed in a ring. I looked over at the pendant on my shoulder, really for the first time, admiring it.

We flew down the line of cruisers. Steam billowed from exhaust vents on the gargantuan, ovular machines. Guns, missiles, cannons, and shield generators dotted their rusty surfaces. Some were painted, others were simply the color of the metal they were constructed with. They were all a different size and shape. Each one was unique.

Finally we reached some cruisers in line that were completely different. They were triangular, with large engines on the flat, back end of the triangle. A command bridge stuck up near the back- a notch cut out of the slanted surface. The entire thing was built with a bit of a slant, building up more toward the back.

The gray, metallic surface sported large cannons. The cannons were built like small versions of the big guns on our cruisers, having a split barrel and magenta energy radiating between the two halves. From our angle I could tell that there were just as many of these cannons on the top as were on the bottom.

The nose of the ships were split down the middle as well, creating their main weapon, a large gun much like the ones on the sides of our ships, but larger.

We flew around the ship until we came to the main hangar bay, an opening in the side of the ship toward the back. It was a large hangar that ran all the way from one side of the ship to the other, where there was another opening.

Their ships in the hangar were black and compact, smaller than ours, and perfectly oval shaped. There was one engine on the back and two guns protruding from under the cockpit. They were quite an odd sight.

We flew inside and found a spot to land. The hangar was the same gray metal as the outside. Everything was simple and sleek. We exited our platform. Coming across the hangar was a group of soldiers, escorting two people, presumably leaders.

The soldiers wore Unitum armor. Rather than cloth concealing the armor however, the metal was visible, reflecting the lights that illuminated the hangar. Like our soldiers they sported a Jetpack on their backs, sleek and rounded like the rest of their technology I had seen so far. They didn't wear helmets, though I assumed that was likely because there was no active threat. The uniforms under their shining armor were a tan color.

One leader approaching us was a woman. She was clad in armor and a uniform similar to the soldiers following behind her. Rather than tactical shoes like the rest of us, she wore boots, the same color as

265

her uniform, that came up to her knees, their heels clicking across the floor. Starting near her knees was a skirt, much like Bailey's. Behind her flowed long, thick black hair. On her chest I saw the glow of a crystal, an almost pink color, but a bit darker than that - the same magenta glow that could be seen on the cannons outside the ship. I was curious as to, if it were the same energy, how the crystal was both on her chest and powering their fleet.

The other leader was a man, older, but in good shape. His hair was black, mingled with gray. His uniform was identical to that of the other soldiers, but what identified him as a leader, along with his position at the front of the group, were his golden lapels. They were metal, and I assumed simply gold plated with the Unitum metal underneath for protection against gunfire.

The race of the entire group was that of those from Central and South America: tan skin and black hair.

They reached us. The Soldiers stopped a few yards back and the two leaders approached us. I signaled for everyone but the general to stay back, then he and I walked forward to meet them.

"Good morning," I greeted, holding out my hand. I shook the man's, then the woman's while General Raddick did so in opposite order, "I'm Dylan Sons, the leader here, this is General Raddick. We are glad you could join our Ekklesia."

They looked at me and said nothing. After a moment of awkward silence, I continued, "We… came by to take a look at your fleet and get to know you. We are trying to get an inventory of the weaponry that is joining us. I must say, you've done a good job of staying a secret. We were quite surprised when we saw these advanced craft showing up."

"It has been our charge to stay hidden," the man said in plain English, "However, your father did find us."

I raised my eyebrows in surprise, "Really?"

"He left us no such account," confirmed the general in disbelief.

"Daniel came to us just over two years ago," the man assured us, "We still don't know how he located our hidden city. Many men have tried over the centuries, but only your father succeeded. We counted it as an act of God."

There was much mystery to uncover, but I chose the most pressing matter, "Why was he looking for you?"

"He was looking for help," the man said, "He spoke of this Organization trying to take over the world. We told him we could only act in self defense. He warned us of the danger of not becoming involved, but we didn't listen. Though our city remains untouched, we watched as the world fell and your father's words came to pass. When your cry for help reached us, we decided it was time to make ourselves known"

"Well for that we are grateful," said the general.

"I agree," I said, then turned to the woman, "I will admit, what intrigued our council the most was you."

The woman didn't blush and was overall unphased by the complement. Still I continued, "We only ever had knowledge of five crystals, then Bailey," I gestured behind me, "Showed up with a sixth. Now you have a seventh and not only that, you can wield it. May I ask how you came upon it?"

"It and its power have been passed down for generations," she said in a serious and demanding voice, "I was trained by my father from my youth and when I turned eighteen, he passed the connection on to me, just as his father did before him, and so on for many generations."

"Do you know of any others?" General Raddick asked.

"We know of a prophecy that there would be many stones in the future," said the man, "but we know the whereabouts of only the same seven you now know of."

"May I ask where you get these prophecies?" I requested.

"Some come from the same God you serve, others from the one who revealed that God to us about seven hundred years ago."

"There was a missionary that came to you before the colonists?" asked the general.

"In a way, yes," said the man, "This prophet crashed in the past, using the technology we have now recreated. He showed us secrets and in turn asked us to stay a secret until the time was right. When he had a way to return home, he did."

This story sounded a bit far-fetched, more like a legend than fact. But the fact was that they were helping us using technology, in some ways more advanced than ours. To me, nothing was impossible anymore.

267

"Well," General Raddick clasped his hands, "I have much enjoyed meeting you as well as hearing this history lesson, but we have much work to do. Allow me to show you where to land your ship for the time being."

The General pulled up a map using the Hologram on his vanguard and began giving instruction in case of an attack. While they talked, I spoke with the Bearer.

"So, I'm sure no one has told you, but as a Crystal Bearer you will have a seat on our council," I informed her, remembering my father's instruction regarding Bailey when we arrived.

"Should I be excited?" she asked, not rudely, more sarcastically. It seemed as though she didn't crave leadership.

"Well, you'll be in the know on everything, but I admit, it's no fun making decisions that have such weight." I said.

"And I gain this position simply because of my power?" she asked, "You don't even know if I'm a good leader."

"That's true," I admitted, "But I believe my dad's logic was that if you could wield a crystal, you would not only be a big target on the battlefield, you would also be our biggest asset. I guess he thought if the entire might of The Organization was coming after you, you should at least get a vote in how we fight them."

"I guess that makes sense," she shrugged.

Wanting to keep getting information while I had the chance I continued, "Can I ask how long you've been wielding the crystal?"

"Two years," she said, "But I have been trained, basically since birth. It's a really big deal in my culture to get to wield the stone."

"I can see why it would be," I said. Wanting to get to know my ally better, I made an offer, "How would you like to train with Bailey and I sometime? We are still trying to figure out all the secrets of our crystals,"

She thought for a moment, "Well, they say every crystal is different, but... I guess I could see if I could show you a thing or two."

"That would be great," I said, beginning to see her rigidness fade away into reluctant trust. I realized that she had likely never met people outside of her city. This was probably very strange for her. "How about we start today? You can ride back to the base with us."

"Yes, I think that would be fine," she consented.

The General finished the conversation with the man. Then, the woman talked with him for a moment about going back with us. Once he had agreed, we walked back and boarded our platform.

"I'm Mariana, by the way," she said as we stepped up onto the hovering platform.

I smiled and turned to the group, "Everyone, meet Mariana," I announced.

Everyone greeted her and introduced themselves on the way back to the base. I was worried my friends might bombard her with questions, but thankfully, they did not. I promised myself that I would try to explain what little I knew to them later.

We entered back through the opening in the shield and finally reached the mountain containing our base. We flew in the same hangar from which we had come earlier. On the way there I had explained to Bailey that we were going to train with Mariana for a while and Blake offered to join.

Having much to do, the General and Alex exited the ship and returned to their jobs. I knew the council would be wanting to hear from me, so the general offered to give the report as well as cover for me, saying that I was improving relations with the people. Which was true.

The rest of us stayed on the platform and ALI drove us down to the valley. I suggested that the best place to train would be the clearing where our ship had crashed a few weeks ago.

We floated down. The lake and the scare on the landscape (left by our crashing plane) was visible from quite a distance. ALI landed us close to the crash site and we all got off. As we did, Blake teased ALI, still not forgiving him for the crash, "See ALI, that's how you land. We actually all made it in one piece this time."

"The only reason there are any pieces of you left is because of me," ALI defended through our coms.

"Who are you talking to?" asked Mariana.

"That's ALI," I said.

"The most annoying and advanced Artificial intelligence ever created," Blake said.

269

"Occasionally annoying, but very helpful," I added.

"Thank you... I guess," ALI said.

"So, let's see what you got," Mariana said, taking a defensive stance.

"Oh, I don't want to fight you," I said, "ALI, pull up the training pro, ugh" I was blasted backward by a pink blast of energy. I rolled across the ground, coming to a slow stop, "Why'd you do that?" I said, raising up. Making eye contact with Mariana, she summoned two more blasts of energy.

I rolled out of the way of one, then summoned my powers to create a shield that blocked the other. That gave me time to jump to my feet. "I was testing your reflexes. Plus, I've trained with programs for years," she advised, "they're predictable and don't simulate a real, free thinking, opponent."

I shook my head, "If you say so," I said, tightening my fist and calling my power across my body. She did the same. Bailey and Blake looked shocked, but stepped out of the way.

She shot another blast of energy at me and she began to run toward me. I dodged and matched her pace. We fought hand to hand, aided by the strength of our powers.

"You're holding back," she said.

"Of course I am," I retorted, "I don't want to hurt you."

"You couldn't if you tried," she taunted.

"Okay then," I gave in.

I then started to fight with all my might. She either blocked or dodged each blow, but didn't hit back. Getting tired of missing, and getting a bit angry, I sneakily conjured a concussive blast and blew her backward.

As she flew through the air, she drew a staff that I didn't know she was carrying, and used it to dig into the ground and steady herself. I drew my staff to match her and we advanced at each other again.

 This time as she came close, she did something, I don't know what, to make her energy burst up from the ground under my feet. This caused me to fall. I winced when I hit the ground as it made my wound send tinges of pain across my abdomen.

270

Before I could recover, she came to me and began thrusting her staff at me. I was able to dodge and grab her staff as it hit the ground. I pulled her forward with the hand that was on the staff and used a concussive blast to take out her feet. Doing this, I threw her over my head and she landed on her back behind me. Both of us still held her staff.

Not letting go, we quickly rolled over and stood up. With one motion, she sent her energy radiating up the staff. As it reached my hand, I countered by sending my own back down. Her energy didn't mix with mine like Bailey's and didn't drain me like The Parasite's, but rather they simply grabbed hold of another.

Both realizing at the same moment that we could do this, we let go of the staff, still holding each other's energy, then connected our energy with our other hands. It was now a battle of strength. We pulled at one another, but got nowhere. Just as I began to pull her toward me, she let go.

I stumbled backward. As I did, she called the staff to her hand, then threw it at me. I tried to simply dodge it, but I didn't realize she was controlling it with her energy. It flew past me, but immediately changed its momentum and struck me in the back.

The energy of the staff radiated across my body and thrust me forward. I fell on my face, a bit dizzy, but unfortunately still conscious. The blast of the staff had caused the wound to start throbbing. I looked up to see Mariana standing over me, holding her staff over me. "Do you yield?" she asked, smirking.

"This time," I conceded.

She retracted her staff and held out her hand to help me up. I took it, and stood up. The pain was quickly subsiding. We walked over to Blake and Bailey who had raised the platform a few feet off the ground and were dangling their feet over the side. They both were chuckling a bit.

"Bro," Blake laughed, "She kicked your butt."

I rolled my eyes, offended, "I'd like to see you do better."

"Maybe I could if she didn't have powers," he gloated.

"I could refrain from using my abilities if you'd like," she offered.

271

Blake, knowing he couldn't back down now, sluggishly slid off the platform. "Haha, this will be good," I said to Bailey and I climbed up next to her.

"If he survives," she laughed.

"I give him ten seconds," I said.

The two walked out a bit and took their starting positions. I was wrong about the ten seconds part, but not by much. To his credit, he held his own for a moment, but once she decided he was going down, he went down. The fight ended with a staff pointed at his head.

"My! How entertaining!" ALI exclaimed, "Blake, try again! I think you've got a real chance!"

I don't think it was in ALI's ability to laugh, but if he could, I am sure he would have. He truly sounded joyful at Blakes defeat.

"Anything else to say?" I taunted.

"Yea, yea, get it all out guys," Blake sighed.

"Bailey," Mariana asked, "Do you want to try?"

"Oh, I'm not very good with hand to hand stuff," Bailey said.

"Then let me teach you," Mariana asked.

"Mariana, you don't have to do that," Bailey blushed. I don't think she was really interested in learning, but she tried to be polite.

"If we are going to be fighting a war, especially side by side, I'm going to teach you how to fight," She insisted.

"You have been telling me that you don't want me to worry about you," I coaxed.

"Well, okay then," Bailey gave in.

"And, please, call me Ana"

272

Chapter 26

To spare from droning on and on, our lives went, much like that day, for six weeks. We started and ended each day with a meeting of what we came to call the high council. Every day, the four of us trained and grew close. Alex even joined in some days, when he wasn't with the Taken.

Every day for about three weeks, more help showed up at the base until the number of soldiers neared 7 million. There was nearly no room for them all. Many lived in the cruisers and ships that they came in on. Others lived in the nearby abandoned suburbs of Washington D.C. Others constructed Barracks in the woods under the protection of the shield.

After a while, it became clear that we needed a second council composed of the leaders from all those organizations and countries represented here. That became known as the council of nations and it met once per week, mostly to create unity and brief everyone on what was going on.

When I wasn't training, I was leading. There were so many people wanting to give me information and ask me what to do. I typically pushed off the decisions to people who specialized in that field, and if possible, tried to bring the decisions before the High council.

Our only free time was after our final meeting of the day. When that was over, Blake, Alex, Bailey, Ana, and myself would join the Vale's for dinner. This was always the highlight of my day - a shred of normalcy. I noticed Blake and Ana sitting together more often. I interrogated him as to if there was a spark of romance catching between them, but he never gave me a straight answer. I assumed he had a crush at least.

Ana fit right in here. Her rigidly blount personality was a bit of a contrast from the rest of us, but as she loosened up and opened up to us, she found belonging in our makeshift family. Though she was the one from the secret city, it always seemed she was more curious about us and our world than we were about her's.

She had only ever experienced the outside world through a screen. It was enlightening for her to get to see it in this way. Really, it was a shame for her to see the world like this, so broken. Though, on the other hand, I suppose it was truly more united than ever before.

Of course, Blake and I remained unchanged, but as for Bailey and I, we grew closer. We finally had that time we had been wanting to talk about our lives before we came here. We had never addressed our romance out loud, but over these weeks, it became a topic of discussion. I only grew to admire her more. I fully intended to ask her to be my girlfriend soon.

Bailey also managed to make a lot of progress with her skills. Ana was a good teacher and had a lot of knowledge. She also helped me become more comfortable with my powers. By the time we reached October, Ana and I were an even match. Even Blake improved his skill. I did feel bad for him though. Even if Ana could turn off her powers, she couldn't turn off her heightened senses and superior strength. He always lost to her. Although, he was able to beat Alex, so that made him feel better.

We didn't get to see Alex much. He stayed busy, and to be fair, we weren't his only friends. He had a whole division of Taken soldiers who he had grown close with and needed to look after. We also weren't his only family. The original six taken that we encountered had been on a two week vacation back to what was left of Tullahoma to see their families. The men from the church had succeeded in their mission of bringing them there. I elected not to go on that vacation. My family was here, and I assumed Alex probably wanted some time alone with his family.

In this time, The Organization made no real move. They bombed the cities of America, sending small groups of bombers at random times. After them catching us off guard a few times, we instated constant patrols of fighters that would circle the country, or at least what was left of it.

Many of the major cities in the western U.S., Denver, Las Angeles, Dallas, Seattle, had been hit hard. They got the brunt of the first wave of bombings. We did our best to send relief. It turned out, one place The Organization wasn't was FEMA. They were able to deploy and get aid to the cities.

We were able to repair communications across the U.S. It wasn't much, but we could send out updates to the people. At least everyone knew what was going on now.

We were also able to establish a solid perimeter from New York to Florida using the War ships from across the world. Their old guns were replaced with plasma guns powered by our crystal. Their old missiles were swapped out for our superior ones.

Thanks to the massive amounts of weapons my father had created and stored up, we were able to upgrade almost every machine that was brought to us. It wasn't just the coast line that we were able to fortify; we were able to station troops as far west as The Mississippi River. But in an effort to stay compact and ready to quickly defend against the Organization, we didn't station troops any further. The most we did for the Western U.S. was send regular patrols of fighters. We wanted to protect the entire U.S. and Canada since it was not yet taken over, but both councils agreed that this was the best we could do for now.

After many High Council discussions on The Organization's relative inactivity, we decided that this must be strategic. They were allowing us to group together in one place, even bombing cities to push more here, so that they could crush us with one final battle. That would at least be their plan. It seemed as though it was only a matter of time before the largest battle to ever face the earth was to be fought.

***

It was now mid October. The trees of the mountains were turning their brilliant shades of red, yellow and orange. The sun was setting earlier. The crisp hints of fall filled the morning Autumn air.

It was 7:30 am and we had just finished our morning High Council meeting and we were headed to our, now routine, sparring session by the lake. Today Alex was coming.

The five of us boarded a floating platform and headed off. As soon as we landed, Bailey and Ana were ready to go. As the Platform neared the ground, they jumped off, Ana cushioning her landing with a magenta field reaching from the ground to her and Bailey flying around for a moment, then landing a few feet away from her.

The platform reached its landing spot and the three of us guys swung our feet over the edge of the platform and got ready for the show.

"You feeling lucky today," Ana asked, smiling.

"I don't need luck anymore," Bailey shot back.

"I like your confidence," Ana said.

"Ladies," ALI umpired, "You may begin."

Bailey led with a bolt of energy aimed at Ana's chest. Ana dodged by leaning back, her powers creating a pillar between her and the ground, propping her up. Using these pillars, she sprung up and conjured an orb of energy that she flung at Bailey.

275

Bailey raised her shield and braced herself. The pink orb erupted across the white shield. Then, unphased, Bailey lowered her shield and leaped forward, drawing her staff as she floated weightlessly through the air toward Ana.

Ana drew her staff at the last second and deflected Bailey's jab. Bailey's staff was now to the side and her body was unprotected. Ana used another orb of energy, thrusting it into Bailey's chest. This sent her flying backward, but she never hit the ground. She steadied herself a few feet off the ground.

Ana retracted her staff and used both hands to continue with a barrage of fast moving orbs of energy, but Bailey blocked them all with her staff. If there was one thing we had learned lately, it was that you couldn't really fight powers with powers. It would eventually result in a stalemate, forcing hand to hand combat. Still, the powers were a good tool.

Bailey flew around Ana in a circle and at a distance. All the while Ana continued her barrage of blasts. Both of them were looking for an opening. Then, as Bailey sensed the rhythm of the magenta blasts, she countered with her own white bolt. It flew between the oncoming energy blasts and struck Ana in her armor.

She fell backward and Bailey swooped down toward her. Just as Bailey went to jab her staff into Ana chest, Ana used her powers to pull her along the ground and under Bailey. Bailey landed, but Ana was already standing behind her with her staff drawn.

The way she had stood up, positioned them back to back. Ana jabbed her staff behind her back, but Bailey sensed it and moved out of the way. The two girls spun around to face each other and commenced in combat with their staves.

Bailey had grown a lot in being able to use this weapon, but she had never trained with one before she got here, making her no match for someone who had trained a lifetime.

After only about thirty seconds of this, Bailey had been pushed back to the edge of the lake. Realizing this, she took to the air again. Remembering a trick she had begun to master, Bailey conjured two orbs of energy, and from over the lake, sent them toward Ana.

The orbs dodged and weaved so quickly that they looked only like a streak moving through the air rather than a ball. They encircled Ana and began to try and make contact with her.

276

Proud, but now losing the match, Ana attempted to fight off the darting balls of white energy with her staff. They would get close, but somehow, she would knock them away at the last second.

Ana's powers were similar to mine, but in the opposite way from Bailey's. They were more solid and tangible. This fact seemed to inspire Ana. She surrounded herself with her purple/pink energy and sent out a wave of that energy in every direction. This pushed the orbs away from her and allowed her enough time to send one singular ball of energy toward Bailey.

It took a lot of concentration from Bailey to use this power, so she didn't sense it coming. I noticed her look up at the last second, but when she saw it, it was too late. The orb made contact with her torso and sent her flipping through the air and down into the water.

We had also learned in the past weeks that some of our abilities didn't work when we were wet. That wasn't something Bailey or I had encountered, but Ana had made sure to inform us of it. For Ana and I we can still do most attacks, it only takes more energy as it is absorbed by the water. However, Bailey, whose powers are more electrical in nature, can't use any of her powers once she gets wet.

Bailey waded up out of the water, "You almost got me that time," Ana congratulated, "You're getting better at controlling the orbs, you just need to leave yourself enough room to still sense other threats."

Ana and Bailey had achieved a unique relationship. You would expect Bailey to be frustrated with Ana beating her all the time, but that wasn't the case at all. She looked up to Ana as a coach, a master of the game, sharing her knowledge. Like a player playing against their coach, she didn't really expect to win.

I hopped off the platform and walked over to congratulate her on a good match. "That might be the best you've done!" I said.

"I actually feel like I'm making progress now," Bailey smiled.

It was true. In the beginning, their fights lasted only a few seconds. This one was about five minutes.

"Are you ready to test your luck?" Ana asked me.

"You think I stand a chance today?" I asked tauntingly. I had beaten her a few times. Our fights were pretty even.

"No," Ana gloated.

We took our ready positions like she and Bailey had just done. We waited on ALI to tell us to start. I couldn't tell if it was just the suspense of the moment, but it felt like it was taking him a while.

After waiting for a moment, it was clear something was up. "ALI," I called, "You gonna tell us to start or what."

There was a pause again, but just as I was about to get worried ALI spoke, "You all are going to want to see this," he said solemnly.

Now I was worried. A light was blinking on all of our vanguards signaling an incoming transmission. We all took it together.

To my horror, the face of Darren Flyhe, The Parasite, appeared on the hologram projecting out of my vanguard. My blood ran cold. We had all assumed he was dead. I had finally had time to grieve and move forward from my fathers death. Seeing him again was like ripping open a closing wound.

He began to deliver his message, "Six weeks ago, a transmission like this one went out to the world from a scared boy, angry over the loss of his father. It was allowed by us, the now governing body of the world, to consolidate all those who oppose the peace and order we are bringing to the world.

Dylan, you think you have turned the world against me, but in reality, the world is against you. The world around you has stabilized and we are now coming to crush your band of terrorists. The world is coming to crush you.

I just thought I would tell you. I know there are many there you hold dear. Of course, as treasonists, your sentence is death. Perhaps you should take these final hours with them."

He turned from the camera, then looked back, "I do hope you'll tell your father hello for me when you see him."

The message ended and the hologram went away. I gritted my teeth and closed my eyes as I tried to process what I just saw. It's sole purpose could be only to get in my head. He was messing with me as he so loved to do. It was working.

Though I had tried to get rid of it, it seemed the hatred I held for this man had never truly died. It was bursting up inside of me, out of every dark corner of my heart that I had tried to tuck it into. I tried to reason with myself every way that I could, but my mind only offered me one solution, that man had to die.

The five of us looked around at one another, not saying a word. After a moment, everyone looked to me, awaiting my command on how to respond. "ALI," I commanded, "Summon the Council of Nations."

"Yes sir," ALI complied.

"What are we going to do," Alex asked.

"What we prepared for," I said, "We're going to fight."

We all solemnly boarded our transport platform and rode back to the base. As we flew, I could see the ships and platforms flying in for miles carrying leaders from around the world.

We landed and walked to a hangar that had been emptied in order to house the meeting. There was a massive round table that took up almost the entire room. It had 208 seats. All 128 countries were represented along with various militant organizations from around the world.

We were some of the first to arrive. Walking in at the same time as us was the president of the United States and his escort. "Director!" He called to me.

"Yes, Mr. President?" I responded, not really wanting to talk.

"I just spoke with the surveillance advisor," said the president, "He says the entire Organization fleet is already coming across the Atlantic."

"I'm sure this will be discussed in the meeting," I assured him. This, if true, was not welcomed news. That would only give us a few hours to prepare. I tried not to let the rumor stir me.

We took our seats. The President sat on my right and Blake sat on my left. People were pouring in now. I announced that the meeting would start in five minutes and instructed ALI to start a timer. Time was of the essence.

As I sat, my mind swirled through my thoughts. The thing plaguing me the most was that if we lost today, we had nowhere to go. The war would be over. Still if we won, it would come at a high cost and today would not be the end, but more of an official beginning to the war.

"Sir, five minutes is up," ALI informed me.

I looked around the room and saw that every seat was filled. We were all here. I stood up and began the meeting, "As everyone I'm sure is aware, we have received a threat from The Organization." There was a stir among the crowd, "At this point, I know as much as the rest of you. High council members, what do you have for us?"

The communications officer stood up first, "The Transmission was universal. They lit up every device around the world."

"It's propaganda!" a leader from the crowd yelled out. There was a murmur of agreement and unease.

"They saw that the Ekklesia had a face," the communication officer continued as the room came to order, "It's likely they did this in an attempt to give their Organization a face as well."

Another member of the high council stood. It was the surveillance officer, "Our scans suggest that about 200 of The Organization's cruisers have assembled in Europe and set out across the Atlantic. They'll make landfall over Washington D.C. in seven hours."

A nervous chatter turned into a roar among the leaders at the round table. "We should have made a move already!" one yelled.

"We'll be destroyed!" yelled another.

"We must evacuate this base!"

"And go where?"

The roar of discourse filled my ears until I could no longer make out words. My anger boiled within me. Why had they come here if they didn't expect The Organization to attack us? We were running out of time.

"Hey!" I yelled, standing up, trying to take control of the group. No one listened, "Order! Please!" I yelled again. Still, there was no acknowledgement of my words.

I gritted my teeth. How had an insecure highschooler have more courage than these great leaders? My powers began to surge over my body in rigid patterns as I began to lose myself. When I realized this, I decided to use this to my advantage.

I thrust out my arms and allowed my blue energy to flow across the room. It released with such power that it made a loud bang, much like the sound of one of my concussive blasts.

The waves of blue energy spread out through the room, over the table and across the bodies of the men and women present. Stunned silence instantly fell over the room. Everyone looked at me.

"That's much better," I sighed, feeling a bit freer having let out my anger, "Now, you all came here a few short weeks ago to fight The Organization. Yes? It was a blessing that they didn't do this sooner. At least we have had some time to prepare ourselves. We are outnumbered, but they are coming to our base. That already gives us an advantage. Rather than bickering, we need to come up with a plan!"

The leaders all took their seats as I spoke. When I finished, silence still engulfed the room. That is, until General Raddick stood up, "I have worked on this base since it's creation nearly twenty years ago. We built it for this kind of attack. We have two choices."

He pressed a button on his vanguard and a massive projection of the base and the surrounding areas pulled up, "The base was built with the best shield ever constructed. We can leave it in the way that it is now, shorter range, but nearly impenetrable. This would force us to fight because they could eventually get troops inside the shield.

The other option is to expand the shield to a state where all technology becomes useless on the surface. This would give us a larger radius and would allow us to go back underground until they found a way to counter the energy field."

The room erupted into conversation again, but it was a bit more civilized.

"I would rather fight today than to put the same fight off to another."

"If we fight we will be crushed"

"There is another option," said a man through the chatter. The room gave him their attention. This man was a skilled engineer, responsible for the maintenance of the base. He sat on the high council.

"The shield can be stretched far beyond the perimeter you show here, but it would work at a lower capacity," he explained, "Shields are relatively low energy fields, condensed into a thin sheet. That makes it difficult for things to pass through. If you expand our energy dampening field, it will make all shields permeable. You'll be able to shoot right through them."

"That would disable our shields as well," said Admiral King.

"Yes," the mechanic continued, "but many of the nuclear cruisers' shields wouldn't stand very long anyway. They just aren't strong enough."

"We also have a large store of missiles," said General Raddick, "We can launch them once the shields are permeable and take out many of their cruisers. It might just make it an even fight."

"It'll be a quick one anyway," Admiral King said.

"Their goal will be to reach our crystal," General Raddick continued, "We need to staff the cruisers and then bring everyone who is not trained to staff a cruiser or fly a fighter to come here and defend the base."

"We send in the cruisers converted to crystal power first," Admiral King suggested, "Let everything else trail behind."

"What about the warships lining the coast?" the President asked, standing from his seat.

"We should send them away," I suggested, "They won't do any good in this fight."

"I agree," said the Admiral, "We'll split them down the middle. Half should amass in South Carolina and half in New York."

"So what exactly will be our plan of attack?" asked an obscure leader across the room from me.

"We wait just outside the shield," the General suggested, "Once they are in range of our weapons, we expand the shield into its energy dampening form. Missiles can target the ships toward the back and our Cruisers, the front."

"This won't be a two dimensional battle," the admiral pointed out, "We must expect them to attempt to board our cruisers."

"And we must remember," the General squinted his eyes, "We only get one chance to get another chance. We lose, we're finished. So fight with that in mind."

There was a moment of silence as everyone waited for someone to speak. I ran what I had heard back through my mind. We had a general plan and the specifics could be worked out as we prepared. Breaking the silence I suggested we vote, "All in favor of this plan, say aye." A simultaneous response came from the group.

"Opposed likewise," I said, giving any counter argument a chance to be made. No one was brave enough to speak.

"Then it's settled," I commanded, clasping my hands together, "You all know the plan. Now, prepare accordingly."

The group stood up with one motion and gave the customary solute, then they disbanded. I waited in the room until everyone had cleared out. Only the High council remained behind, assuming I had something to say. I didn't. I only wanted a moment to think. Still, since they were there, I thought I would ask the question pressing on everyone's mind, "So, do we really stand a chance?"

The group looked at one another. General Raddick spoke up, "It is a good plan, but they still have us out gunned. We will hurt them but I'm not sure if we can defeat them. It will be close."

"Still, I don't think we've given them false hope," Admiral King consoled.

"There is one part of the plan left unaddressed," I said. The group waited in anticipation, "The Parasite."

The General began to speak but I cut him off, "He must be killed today," I commanded. In my mind, I saw this as logic rather than hate. Maybe soldiers were just following orders. For that I had sympathy, but I had lost all compassion for this man. He was like the Devil, and didn't the Devil deserve to die?

"He will show himself in the battle," I pointed out, "He had tried to kill me twice and narrowly failed. It will be a thing of pride for him." I took a moment to think about what I said next. I knew there would be no going back, but everything had to be on the table. "I want Ana and Bailey to wait back with me. When we see him, we'll take him together."

The group nodded in agreement. Everyone but Blake, who only looked at me blankly. I knew he didn't approve. Not of Bailey and Ana going with me, but of me giving in and ordering his death.

After revealing this last bit of information, I sent the group on their way. There was a weight on my chest. It hadn't really hit until now. Every other battle I had been a part of was so rushed. It was like it just happened and there was no time to plan or consider other routes. No time to think about if the plan was the best plan or what the reprercussions of it would be. There was only time to react.

The past six weeks had gone by so fast compared to the long days that preceded it. It was amazing how much could happen in a day and yet still be able to waste one. Was that what we had done? Maybe we had gathered a great force here. Maybe we had fortified a bit of land, but what was it against the threat that was coming. Could we have done more?

I walked away from my friends and to the open hangar bay. I looked out across the mountains. We were on the side of the mountain facing west. Since everything was happening on the East side, it actually looked peaceful here. The rolling orange mountains casting shadows on the valleys and hollows, contrasted the brilliance of the blue sky and its white puffy clouds.

I rested my hands behind my back. The cool breeze coming up from the valley ran over my face and slightly tossed my hair. For a moment, I found a bit of peace. I always seemed to be able to find it in nature. But the realization of this peace only reminded me of how I had no reason to be peaceful.

My heart still carried wounds - deep wounds. I realized I still hadn't recovered from my father's death. Should I have? I didn't know. I knew I shouldn't hate Darren. It wasn't Biblical. But was it hateful if his righteous judgment was indeed death? The death of possibly billions were on his hands.

I was so lost in my thoughts, I almost didn't sense Blake walking up behind me. Still, just before he began to lift his hand to put it on my shoulder, I felt his familiar presence. It was strange how I was starting to identify people by the way their mind worked. It was like a low hum coming from their unique voice.

I turned to him and he patted me on the back. He joined me for a moment in looking out across the landscape then spoke, "If your father wasn't one of the people he killed, would you still want him dead?"

I shook my head in confusion, then gave Blake an annoyed look, "I thought Bailey was the mind reader?" I remarked, trying to keep the tone of our normal banter, but it came off a bit snarky.

"I've known you long enough to tell what you're thinking," he said softly, unphased by my rudeness, "I don't need superpowers for that." He looked me in the eyes intensely, "I just don't want you to lose yourself."

I thought I'd actually been doing a pretty good job of holding onto myself through all of this . "It's just a decision that had to be made," I told Blake and myself, "I just happen to be the only one able to carry it out."

"I'm not like you," Blake said, seemingly changing the subject. "My mind can't do what yours does. I couldn't hold myself to my values the way you do. But that's what makes you different. I just don't want you to lose yourself," he repeated.

His words fell deep into the cracks of my heart igniting emotions I thought had died. A love and a longing to go home. To go back to the way it used to be. To go back to my Pastor, my family, and my senior year. I just wanted to be able to be me again. This war, leading these people, it just isn't who I am. Maybe I hadn't lost myself, but I was lost.

Still, the calluses of my heart told me I was making the right decision. My mind said he had no choice but to die at my hand. "I'm trying not to," I told Blake, "How else do we win?"

"Like I said, your mind is different from mine," Blake said somberly, "If you determine that is the only way, then I trust you."

I looked down with a bit of shame. I wouldn't be here without him. I really would be dead if it were not for Blake. He was the only thing keeping me sane through all of this. I hadn't been near as appreciative as I should have been. Thinking this may be my last chance, without a word, I turned and gave him a hug.

Our armor got in the way, but it was still comforting. Finally, we were able to give each other a hug where we didn't shed tears. Though, it seemed like more than ever this moment deserved some. We faced death, not just of ourselves, but everyone and everything we had shed so many tears over. Maybe it was just the timing, or maybe we really were turning into soldiers.

After a moment, we ended our embrace and with a sense of grounding now about us. Then, the day went on and tension grew as the hour drew near. On every screen in the base a map of our Hemisphere marked with the current location of the Organization fleet was displayed. All day as one would pass a dining hall, a living quarters, or a hangar bay, they would be reminded of the urgency of their tasks.

Later in the day, I took an elevator to the top of the mountain with Blake and Alex to overlook the preparations being made. As soon as we got out, rather than the hustle of the base, I first noticed the place where Bailey and I first saw my father. I couldn't help but see the two of us, strangers at the time, ready to fight something we didn't understand.

It was strange actually, to be on this side of it - standing where my dad had stood. It was amazing how quickly we had traded places.

Though, I felt there was no way to fill his shoes. How could I learn all the secrets, make the connections he had, or even understand the world the way he did?

Moving on from my nostalgia, I walked over to Blake and Alex, who had walked past me and my thoughts, around to the edge of the mountaintop. There was a clearing there - a place where the trees weren't tall enough to block the view. From here, we could see the entire future battlefield.

A constant stream of transports came in and out of the shield, shuttling troops here from their stations across the east coast.

Just outside the shield, our best cruisers lined up on the front lines. Behind them were the rest of our steaming giants. There simply wasn't enough time to replace all of the nuclear power sources with ones connected to the crystal.

The nuclear ships ran off of batteries, not the reactors themselves. There would never be enough energy to run the whole ship if not. These ships would only have a few hours of run time once they powered up their weapons.

Buzzing around the entire base and the cruisers were fighters of all shapes and sizes. Each one reflected where it was made by its design, but all of them sported the flaming dove of the Ekklesia.

I noticed that on the side of some of the cruisers, there was a massive Ekklesia dove painted over their hull. I knew this sight would be much different soon, but I couldn't help feeling a sense of pride and awe at this spectacle. Whether we won or lost, this day could still be looked at as a victory. The whole world had finally put aside their differences. The history of the Earth's nations had climaxed at this moment. Though, if we lost, this day would likely be wiped from the history books.

A light started blinking on our vanguards. The three of us answered it and a message from the surveillance officer played, " As of 1600 hours, The Organization has made landfall. They will be within range in half an hour. All personnel, hold your fire until Director Dylan gives us the signal."

I hadn't been told that I was giving any signal. I guess it was just expected of me. I didn't know what that signal would be. I would have to think of something.

After the message was finished, I turned to Blake and Alex who were on my right. "Well, that was a short break." I sighed. I wasn't ready for this.

286

"Look," Blake said, ignoring my comment, "I know I don't have powers, but I am a good fighter. I took all the classes you ever did, and I've always been better than you at fighting," he paused a moment as I thought about whether or not to be offended, "I want to face The Parasite with you."

I turned my head to the side in a mix of admiration and frustration. Blake continued, "I know you and the girls are the only ones who can actually fight him, but somebody should at least keep a lookout and fight off other troops that may be around."

"Or two somebodies," Alex tagged on.

"What if he attacks you and uses you against me?" I argued, "I can't protect that many people at once."

"You're not protecting us, we're protecting you," Blake countered, "If he starts talking and messing with your head, I'll see it before you do."

I clenched my jaw and scrunched my eyes closed. I knew he was right. The Parasite would try to use his words to get under my skin. If there was one person who could talk me out of losing my cool, it was Blake. And I guess Alex would be good protection.

"Fine!" I conceded, "But stay on the coms and stay back." I put my hand on his shoulder and stared coldly into his eyes, "You are not to engage The Parasite at any time for any reason. If he kills me, your mission is over and you run."

"That's not gonna happen," Blake promised.

"But if it does, I want your word," I pushed, "You'll get our family and run."

"I promise." Blake shook his head and pulled me in for a hug. "We've got this," he said in my ear.

After our embrace, I gave Alex a hug as well. We wouldn't get another moment alone until the battle was over. Since we were all fully clad in our armor, including our jetpacks, rather than take the elevator again, we flew from the top of the mountain all the way to the command ship at the front of the battle field.

Our flag ship was one unlike any other at the base, and honestly, I had never seen it until today. Because Unitum was a hard metal to craft and highly expensive to obtain, it was seldom used for

287

anything but armoring people. It was also malleable which made it poor for anything structural. But this ship broke those rules.

A thick layer of Unitum had been cast over every piece of steel plating armoring the ship. The shape of the cruiser was the same as the rest of our base's cruisers (the ones who had staved off the attack on D.C.). Really, everything else was the same too: the large guns on either side, the cannons lining the hull. Most stunning was the Ekklesia's crest on the ship. Rather than being painted on, it had been meticulously crafted into the armor of the ship. Both the flaming dove and the ring around it were raised up from the surface of the ship, but still somehow curved with its contour.

The sun was preparing to set, but had not quite lit up the sky with its evening colors. With the sun at this angle, a shadow was cast over the reflective surface of the ship. This only made the dove more defined and stunning. I was glad this would be the first ship The Organization saw, since most of the rest were not very aesthetically pleasing or intimidating: patched together, falling apart, and billowing steam.

We flew around the ship and to the landing platform cut out next to the bridge. The doors opened for us and we walked in. Bailey and Ana were on the bridge waiting for us. The rest of the crew was at work keeping the battle arrayed cruisers from bumping into one another as well as charging the cannons and arming the missiles.

The Captain stood from his chair and gave command to his first mate, who was standing beside him,. He walked over. "Captain," I greeted, holding out my hand. He shook mine, then Blake's and Alex's.

"Director"

"Captain"

"Officer"

"Captain"

"Taken"

"What is our situation?" I asked after the customary greeting we had grown accustomed to.

"They are sitting just out of range," the captain informed, "They're performing initial scans, as are we, to detect firepower and decipher our plan."

288

"Can they?" I asked.

"Can they, what?"

"Decipher our plan?"

"They won't be able to detect the secondary capability of the shield, no" the captain answered, "But they can see how much firepower we have."

"Can they see the missile launching field that's out in front of us?" Blake asked, referring to the diagram back at our meeting. A few miles in front of us was where our missiles would launch from, hopefully catching the back of the convoy off guard.

"Only if they are looking for it," the captain replied, "They could, in theory, see the shafts, but the missiles are too deep. Since the shafts are concrete, they won't register as a threat. They should dismiss it."

"Let's hope so," I said, "Now we wait?"

"Now we wait," said the captain.

Chapter 27

The five of us watched out the window as the Organization cruisers hovered on the horizon. They were so far away now that they just looked like dots. I couldn't make out any details. We waited and waited for them to make the first move. I grew more anxious by the minute. Why were they waiting? Why postpone the battle any longer?

As the sun began to set, General Raddick landed on our platform and walked in. I walked over to him, eager to hear what message he must be carrying.

We soluted one another and he spoke, "Sir, I believe they have scanned and determined that some of our cruisers are running on battery power. I think they are forcing us to make the first move by waiting."

"Is there any other option?" I asked. I was worried that if we moved toward them, we would reach the edge of the force field.

"I don't see one," he conceded.

"Then order everything that flies to make for The Organization's fleet," I commanded.

"Yes, sir," he said.

He made the command over the coms and we made for the horizon. I walked over to my friends. "This is it," I said, feeling the worried expression on my face, "Stick to the plan.

I think I could have thrown up right there if I had allowed myself. My stomach twisted and contorted, my heart pounded in my ears and adrenaline pumped through my veins. The slow advance of our cruisers and gradual growth of the cruisers in the distance only made it worse.

I looked at the people around me and saw the same worried yet determined looks on their faces. Ana and Alex were handling it best. But even them, the true warriors among us, were fearful. Blake bit his lip and Bailey's eyes held back tears

We couldn't go out there like this. Just as I knew I had to say something, some words my father had told me came to mind. "ALI," I said, not knowing my voice would be as shaky as it was, "On my command, put me on the coms."

"Yes, sir,"

Without another word, I turned from the window of the bridge and walked out the door to the landing platform. I ignited my jetpack and flew to the nose of the flagship cruiser. I landed.

The wind was strong due to both our speed and altitude. I drew my staff and used it to stabilize myself on the surface. "Now ALI," I said, surprisingly more calmly.

A green light displayed on my vanguard, showing that I was live. As I went to speak, my words left me. I racked my brain in awkward silence trying to recover them. I looked ahead blankly. My mind was spinning. I closed my eyes.

I could see my father. I could see him looking up at The Parasite as his life was taken. I saw the dream I had had a few weeks ago as my friends and family died one by one. I saw the poor Organization soldier thrown over the rails of the dam at Montana Base. I saw the maps presented at every High Council meeting, displaying The Organization's reach with a red haze, turning redder and growing larger by the day.

I saw my home, the fighters falling from the sky, destroying my town at the Battle of Tullahoma. I saw Washington as it sat littered with debris, the White House as it was destroyed by the falling ship.

I could see the day we broke into Montana Base, the cruiser and fighter pursuing us as we escaped with our prize only to lose it a few days later. No matter how much we fought, or how much we won, we always seemed to lose. Our victories were short lived and came with consequences of destruction.

As my mind spiraled out of control, just before it reached the point of no return, I heard a familiar voice, "You can't wait for someone else to do what needs to be done. If you do, you will wait your entire life." It was Pastor! Pastor? That was his sermon the day we left home. I looked to my vanguard to see footage of him saying this from the platform at my church playing on the coms channel through a hologram.

The message cut to another clip of Pastor, "Sometimes we must lay down what we want, and take up the burden of others. It is the only way they will be saved."

Then I heard my own voice. The video changed to Bailey and I sitting against a tree on the side of the base, that is, before we knew it was a base, "We have a power that can save the world. We have a chance to kill an evil organization. Why did God give the means to you

291

and I? The only thing I can think of is because for some reason he trusts us."

Pastor's voice returned over a video of us fighting the Robots in D.C., "War is a tricky thing. I believe you are being pulled into one, and that fact is one beyond your choice. If you must be a part of it, make sure you don't lose yourself, or your God in the middle of it."

Then, my voice returned to the video replaying the piece of debris falling between me and my father's body, "I can't always see him, but I have to trust that it was for a reason. Maybe we're just on one side of the mountain, and we cant see the full picture yet."

My father's voice spoke up after me, "There aren't enough of us"

Then, the president's voice from our meeting in the Oval Office played over a map of the Organization's conquered territories, "This Organization, as they call themselves, has already broken the order of the world, so if we do it as well, I see no harm."

Then, my dad spoke again over footage of the, now Ekklesia, cruisers lining up at the base, "It has been a plan of mine for years, but tensions between the various Organization resistances had always been too high. We disagreed on how to fight, so we disconnected ourselves from each other. Now that we have no other alternative, I think my plan for an Ekklesia is a viable one."

Then, the message cut to a clip of my father speaking, "Hello, son. If you're seeing this, I'm guessing things didn't go quite as I planned them. I know you don't want to lead, but it must be you. I don't trust anyone else to do it but you. I haven't been able to call the Ekklesia"

Then a video of me, framed in the same way, "I stand before you, not wanting the title of leader, yet still seeking it, because like you, I trust my father. And I want the same thing he did"

The clip cut, but just to another part of the same speech, "Together, we will make them pay for what they have stolen and we will take it all back as one Ekklesia. We will make their world rule the shortest in history."

The hologram went blank but words continued to play.

"Good luck," said a weak voice I knew to be Blake after our crash.

"It's never luck," I said.

"God go with you" said my father

"We've got this," said a stronger Blake from only moments ago.

I sood in stunned silence and awe at what I had just seen. I knew I was likely on camera, but I couldn't stop a tear from slipping down my cheek. I had almost forgotten how I had gotten here. The events that lead to this moment. I realized now, they weren't just moments, they must have been orchestrated by God. How else would we have made it this far? How else would the story fit together so well?

I opened my mouth, knowing I had to speak, but I had no idea what was about to come out. Still, I managed to form words, "We were all brought here for a reason," I said a bit unsteady, but finding my words, "No matter where you came from, or what you did before today, it doesn't matter. You are a part of this Ekklesia."

I was hit with a rush of even more emotions as I spoke. I began to raise my voice, "Today we no longer fight against one another, but we unite against this organization. We unite for our loved ones and everything they [I pointed at The Organization cruisers] took from us. We unite for the nations!"

I didn't plan to, but I screamed my last line and because my emotions were so high, my powers shot across my body. Then, a gust of wind blew. It barely shook me, but it was enough I had to readjust my staff.

When it made contact with the Unitum plating that I was standing on, it spread across the ground around me. Remembering what my father said about Unitum and my powers, and also wanting a dramatic effect, I lifted my staff again, turned away from the bridge of the cruiser I was standing on, and faced the Organization's fleet. They were close, close enough everyone on both sides would be able to see what I was about to do. I pulled as much power from the crystal as I could, maybe the most I ever had.

A flood of energy rushed out of the crystal, across my body, and formed around the staff until it was engulfed in a blinding blue glow. As I thrust the staff down onto the surface of the ship with all my might, I yelled, "We fight for the Nations!"

The energy rushed off of the staff and across the entire cruiser, engulfing it in the same blue aura that surrounded my body. The raised

293

Ekklesia dove flamed with the blue hue. The sun was far enough down in the sky that the spectacle was quite brilliant. I believed even the coldest Organization troop would have been able to comment on the beauty of the cruiser at this moment.

The Glow lasted about thirty seconds, then faded. As if to applaud my actions, my eardrums were rattled as the cruiser on which I was standing fired the first shot of the battle. A blast of yellow came from both sides of the ship.

They soared through the air, about a mile, to the cruiser in the front of the Organization's fleet. The ship was small and looked very similar to the winged one we saw at the Montana base when we attacked it the first time.

They permeated through the shield and erupted in a violent explosion on the starboard wing. The shot didn't completely sever the wing, but thick black smoke poured from the wound.

As if to congratulate the first shot's contact, the entire Ekklesia fleet opened fire from behind me. Yellow and purple energy blasts from the smallest to the largest guns lit up the evening sky, striking their targets with precision.

The Organization was in chaos no doubt. The ships (of so many shapes, sizes and designs I could never hope to describe them all) broke formation, trying to escape the inescapable barrage. I watched in gitty awe as the front line of cruisers began to fall from the sky. Still, it only took them a few seconds to fire back.

Their Orange and green blasts were exchanged for our yellow and purple ones. I was happy to see that The Organization did not sport the same large guns that our flag ship (as well as the other nine original cruisers and the cruisers from Ana's people) had.

A few more seconds and missiles launched from the ground under us and headed to the back of the Organization fleet. There were thousands of them. They moved like a swarm of angry wasps, and like a swarm of wasps, The Organization couldn't hope to swat them all down. They futilely turned their fire from our ships to the missiles.

Our cruisers continued to fire. More Organization cruisers fell from the air, while ours had barely received a scratch. The missiles found their marks. All throughout the Organization's array of cruisers explosions rang through the air.

My fears, for a moment, were replaced with hope. So much hope, I didn't even feel the fear. That lasted only until I saw a new swarm forming. From every Organization cruiser, fighters and bombers were launching. Rushing to meet them, were our own fighters.

I was shocked to see just how many different kinds of fighters we had going into battle: sleek ovular ones from Ana's people, F-16s and B-52s from the U.S and European nations (decked with our crystal powered weapons), U-wings, jet fighters, and bombers from our base, and so many more.

The sky filled with color as the blasts powered by green, yellow, orange, and pink crystals filled the air. Stray shots and blasts from the Organization cruisers began to make it to the ship I was standing on. The Unitum armor absorbed the damage, but they were getting a little too close for me to want to stay outside.

I ignited my jetpack and quickly flew back to the bridge. Fighters of both teams swarmed the cruiser, but I stayed close to the surface, so they didn't hit me. I landed on the platform and walked inside.

All of the officers were busy at their stations, but my friends, who were still standing at the window, gave me a round of applause as I walked in. I walked over to them and was greeted with far shorter hugs than any of us wanted to give.

"You did great," Blake said.

"ALI did most of the work," I said, wanting to give him the credit he deserved. I knew I would have simply frozen without him doing what he did. The explosion of an Orange blast on the hull shook the ship.

"Kind of creepy everything we've done can be turned into a video," Alex said, hoping to keep the mood light while he could.

"Those are simply my memories," ALI said in his programed humanity.

"Well, it was very beautiful, ALI," Bailey congratulated.

I noticed Ana hadn't turned her eyes from the windows the whole time. Her face was serious and her arms were crossed. She felt me looking at her and made eye contact only to break it and point out the window.

I looked and everyone else with me. On one of the ships, a red dot hopped along the surface. Jumping, with a red blast of energy, toward the front. Just as it leaped from the ship, a magenta blast, clearly from the main weapon of one of Ana's ships, struck the cruiser.

295

This blast was so powerful, it blew a hole clean through the ship. Granted the ship was another one of the smaller ones like the first one we shot. The blast landed in the middle of the ship and the weight of the two wings broke the ship in half.

The red dot landed on a fighter that swooped by and began to fly toward our ship. My heart sank and my stomach leaped into my throat. I felt my face go pale. One way or another, I was certain this would be the last time I would face The Parasite. But with that thought came a bit of peace. This would be resolved today. In this moment. From that, I drew courage.

"Here we go," I said turning to the door, "We all know our jobs?"

Everyone nodded. In our afternoon of waiting, we'd rehearsed the plan over and over again. It was just a matter of executing it.

Bailey and I walked out the doors of the bridge together. "You sure you've got this?" I asked, not that there was time to turn back.

"No," she shook her head and pointed up, "But he does."

We flew down, me with my jetpack and Bailey with her powers, to the nose of the ship where I had just come from. Our eyes were on the rapidly nearing fighter carrying The Parasite on its back. As soon as we landed, about thirty feet from the nose of the ship, he jumped from the fighter and landed in front of us, about ten feet away.

The red energy surged over his body and little red bolts lept from his body onto the ground around him. "How's your wound?" he asked, deliberately reminding me of how our last meeting ended.

"Healed," I said cheerfully, "How's your pride?"

I knew losing the base and me, even in the face of his own victory, was not something he would think fondly of.

"About to be a lot better," he snarked.

A fighter was crashing behind him, but we all must have sensed that it would miss us because no one moved as it crashed into one of our ship's turrets, behind Bailey and I. The explosion shook the ship beneath us, but no one moved or broke eyecontact.

I nudged Bailey's hand, indicating that it was time to start our plan. She took hold of it.

"And is she your lit-"

"Well! As fun as this conversation has been," I deliberately cut him off with the most obnoxiously cheerful voice I could conjure at the time, "I'm sick of it."

Bailey and I combined our powers, held our free hands out in front of us, and shot a beam of white and blue energy at him. The two beams combined as they flew through the air.

The Parasite raised a shield, but the power from the blast was pushing him backward, and Bailey's electric energy made it hard for him to hold the shield stable enough to stop the energy.

He tried to latch onto my power, but the red would only travel a foot or two up the beam before failing to go any further. Our theory was true. He couldn't latch onto my power if it was combined with Bailey's.

We stood still as he neared the edge. I knew a fall wouldn't kill him. It was time to move onto the next part of the plan.

"Now!" I yelled to Bailey.

We let go of each other's hands. She continued blasting him while I drew my atom sword. I used my powers to thrust it, through the air, toward him. It flew with great speed and made perfect contact with his shield, piercing it with its sharp point.

Seeing it had hit its mark, I called it back to my hand. The parasite's shield dissolved and as it did, Bailey called off her attack.

Still standing there, was The Parasite, holding his ribs. "Close," he said, moving his hand and revealing a cut on his side, under his arm.

I'd missed. I gritted my teeth, knowing we had lost the element of surprise. Now that he knew what we could do, we wouldn't be successful in doing it again.

Following the back-up plan, I ran at him, sword still drawn. I knew we could fight if I didn't use my powers. As I attacked, he swerved and bobbed, and raised shields to block my attacks, just as he had done before.

Bailey took to the sky and began to fly around him, shooting bolts of her electrical energy at him. This forced him to draw his sword. He fought me with the sword in his right hand, and with his left, he

297

would absorb Bailey's attacks. We were at the same stalemate we had reached in Washington, but there was more to the plan.

Ana, riding a floating platform and rising up from the underside of the ship, jumped onto the nose of the ship. This finally caught The Parasite off guard. Ana used her powers to bind his feet.

In shock, he fell to the ground. Bailey unleashed a constant beam of energy as he fell. He used his left hand to absorb it. I swung my sword and pushed it down toward his body. Ana still held his feet together, and walked up, drawing her staff.

He grunted and he tried to hold us off and get free. I saw nothing he could do. The plan had worked flawlessly. Ana reached us, but no one said a word. She thrust her staff into the armored plate on his chest. A blue wave of energy spread over his body and he was thrust down into the Unitum plating.

He shook his head. We knew it would take a few strikes to knock him out. His will and his power were both very strong. She rared back to do it again. Another successful blow.

He shook his head violently and screamed in anger. As she positioned herself to strike again, The Parasite's crystal began to glow brightly on his chest. I didn't know what was happening, but I knew it wasn't good.

"Hurry!" I commanded.

Ana lunged forward again, but in the milliseconds before the tip of her staff made contact, a concussive blast came from his crystal. I was thrust backward. The blast was so strong, I was pushed all the way to the port edge of the cruiser.

I quickly got up, and tried to assess our new situation. I could see Bailey a few hundred yards away. She had been blown backward, through the air, and into the dogfight surrounding the cruiser. She was trying to make her way back through the fire and flying ships. My view of her was interrupted by a person, dawning a jetpack, darting across my field of vision and over the nose of the ship. Ana was nowhere to be seen.

I uttered, "Oh, God, help us," as a prayer for all of us, then charged back at The Parasite. The person on the jetpack was almost certainly Alex or Blake. I had to keep him distracted.

The Parasite was standing up and getting his bearings about him. His nervous system wouldn't quickly overcome two hits from a

298

staff. For the moment, though disadvantaged by the absence of my friends, I had a slight advantage in that fact.

I charged toward the parasite. As I ran, I realized my sword had been thrown over the side. Thankfully I always carried two, so I drew the second. I ran up to him and slashed, aiming for his head. My anger was beginning to rise again, and my determination to protect my friends only added to my hatred of him.

As I swung, he dodged and drew his sword, striking me in the back, on the Unitum jetpack. His swing was powerful and thrust me to the ground. Not losing my focus, I hit the ground, screeching my sword along the Unitum plating of the ship, and spun back to him.

He was already coming down at me with a crushing blow, but I rolled out of the way. I sprung up and swung again, but he used a shield to stop it before I sliced through the unguarded part of his abdomen.

He pushed the shield toward me, pushing my sword back and jabbed his sword at me. I moved out of the way. He pushed me back as he advanced and blocked my every move. I realized I couldn't beat him, not without being able to use my powers.

I prayed someone would recover and get back to help me. It was answered. Up from the nose of the ship, Blake popped over the side, carrying Ana. She jumped out of his arms and before she hit the ground, threw an orb of her energy at The Parasite.

He sensed the blast and raised his shield to meet it and his sword to meet my sword. At least the battle was about to be more even.

In her classic style, Ana unleashed a barrage of energy at The Parasite. He was using his shield to hold her off, but because of how solid her energy was, he was being knocked off balance.

In order to deal with her, he dropped his sword as I was swinging at it. This was a shock to me and I stumbled as I followed through. Before his sword could hit the ground, he summoned a concussive blast of energy that sent me flying to the starboard edge of the ship.

The curved surface of the cruiser separated me from the others – a ridge blocking them from view. Had I gone much further, I would have slid off of the ship. I steadied myself. I saw that Bailey had finally made it back as she swooped in overhead.

Being away from them filled me with anxiety. I ignited my jetpack and flew back up the side to the flat spot where the battle was taking place.

We were all three back at it again. Bailey and Ana were already attacking him from two sides with their staff. I was surprised at how well he was holding them off. If I didn't hate him so much, I might have been able to appreciate his elegant fighting style.

He now sported two blades and tracked each move of the girls, knowing exactly where their jabs and swings would land. I knew, even if they did land a blow, it wouldn't take him out completely. But all Ana had ever trained with was a staff, and since she trained Bailey, the same could be said for her.

Eager for this battle to end, I charged in with my sword. Just as I reached the group, The Parasite kicked Ana in her right leg. The blow came in at a downward angle and caused her knee to buckle. She shrieked in pain and fell to the ground.

I arrived just in time to keep his attention divided. We had quickly learned if it ever turned to any one of us on our own we would lose.

Blow after blow, he blocked our advances. We danced around the flat space at the nose of the cruiser, but no one, us or him, could make progress.

Ana couldn't stand. Blake had flown in again and was tending to her. He pronounced her leg as broken over the coms. It was now up to Bailey and I. Or that's what I thought.

As I fought, I noticed that Blake hadn't yet whisked Ana off. I then noticed a faint magenta glow begin to spread on the ground under our feet. I had an idea of what Ana was planning.

We wrestled on for a bit longer, then, one time as I went to strike The Parasite, rather than dodge or parry my swing, he was yanked down to the ground. Though his face hit hard on the metal beneath him, I still suspected that he saw this coming because when he hit the ground, maybe even before, he somehow managed to throw one of his blades.

It was so unexpected that it caught both mine and Bailey's senses off guard. The blade rushed past the arm Bailey was using to hold her staff. A few inches over and it would have cut off her arm. Rather, it sliced through her forearm.

300

As it did, still happening before The Parasite reached the ground, Baileys staff lit up with red energy and turned toward her. It thrust at her head and made contact with her brow. Her head was flung backward, then the rest of her body.

During this line of events, The Parasite's other blade was flung toward me, but never left his hand. It hit the armor on my thigh, but as it slid across, it fell off and cut about two inches into my leg.

Rather than jump back, which is what my body told me to do, I stood firm and thrust my blade down at his neck with a cry of determination and pain (mostly pain). Because he was still moving from Ana's energy, he was pulled just out of the way of the swing and the blade sliced through his shoulder.

Realizing I had missed, I flung the blade back up, hoping to get him on the return, but I missed again, this time because The Parasite rolled out of the way.

He quickly sat up and stretched out his arm that wasn't wounded. With that motion, a red coil of energy wrapped around Ana and Blake's necks. They were lifted up off the ground.

They clawed desperately at their necks and flailed their legs. The Parasite wasn't trying to make a point. He was angry. He was trying to kill them quickly.

"No!" I yelled. I stabbed my blade at him, but he dropped his sword and raised a shield with his injured arm. The point was slowly slipping through, but it was taking too long. I didn't have much time. Ana and Blake were already beginning to loose consciousness.

I could think of nothing else but to give him something he wanted more than their lives. I turned and looked at them. I saw their bodies beginning to lose life. It wasn't a good plan, but it was the only one I had.

I allowed the energy from my crystal to spread across my body. I let go of the sword I was shoving through the shield, but it still hung in the air, suspended by the shield. I pressed both hands against the energy field coming from the parasite and unleashed as much energy as I could conjure.

The energy spread across the shield, turning purple as it went. The Parasite looked at me, confused at first, but soon his evil grin spread across his face. He stood up, still holding me back with the shield.

301

Then, he balled the fist of his uninjured left arm and held it up vertically. The shield dissipated. He latched onto my energy and began draining it from me.

I resisted, like I had done on the dam. It took a great deal of effort, but I was holding up better than I thought I would. The Parasite began to talk.

"You would sacrifice yourself only to delay the inevitable?" he mocked, "You would forfeit your revenge for your love of them?"

He actually raised a good point. I thought as I fell to one knee. I hadn't thought of it that way. Revenge wasn't even on my mind when I allowed him to take hold of me, "I guess love makes you do crazy things," I said through labored breathing.

I turned my head from him for a split second to look behind me. Alex had flown down and was carrying Ana and Blake away. I had at least bought them some time.

"I'll never understand you and your father," The Parasite said as the red energy reached my body and began to surround me, "Hopelessly noble."

I gritted my teeth determined not to scream. It didn't want to give him the satisfaction. The plan had failed. Perhaps though, The Ekklesia could still win the battle without me. Maybe even the war. I would leave behind a good team. Then, his words registered with me.

I wasn't hopelessly noble. Even now, as I was about to die, I had hope. Hope that not only there could be a better Earth, but as I, in this moment, finally let go of my hatred, a hope of a better life after this Earth. I realized how sad it must have been for The Parasite to live life without hope.

"I…pity…you," I choked, falling down on all fours.

"What?" The Parasite laughed as he drew the energy from me with more fervency.

It's funny. This was the second time in my life when I had come close to death. Again, just as the first, time began to slow down for me. I thought of ALI's message and really everything else too. My life, mostly the past two months, flashing before me.

Though it had been such a time of loss, that's not the word I would have used for it. It was a time of love. A time when I learned to love, and the rest of the world with me. Maybe it took a threat like this to show everyone that love was the solution to our hopeless bickering.

My life flashed, my thoughts subsided, and there was an unexpected quietness. After six weeks I finally realized the storm that had been raging in my head. I only realized it by its absence. Forgiveness had quieted it.

In this quietness, I looked up at the parasite, no longer resisting the energy that was being drained from my body. I looked into his eyes which were made fiery red by his energy. He was so focused on taking my energy, he wasn't protecting his mind from me.

It was unusually easy to look into him, and I could see with greater detail than I had seen into a mind before. On the outside, he portrayed a strong, undefeatable foe, but on the inside, he was already defeated. He was drowning in depression and inner turmoil.

He was gripped with crippling fear. He was plagued by loneliness and separation. He had no love, not even for himself. His emotions raged like a destructive cyclone destroying his mind. His jabs, his evil comments, the words he used to break me down, even his determination for the world to bow before him, they all came from this place.

How do you forgive the man who murdered your father? By realizing your father was whole and that this man was broken, maybe beyond repair. For that I understood him. And for that, though I blamed him, I could forgive him, for I truly felt bad for him.

I realized that the only reason this man had power over me was because I thought he did. I allowed him to tell me that he did. But he didn't. It was I who had power over him.

With the storm in my mind quieted, I heard something. I looked at the crystal on Darren's chest. With a voice so still and small that I could only hear it in my heart, it called to me.

Feeling, not as though I would be escaping my fate, but as though I needed to follow this voice, I reached around to my back and drew my staff from my waistband. I extended it and wedged it in between the rivets of the armored plating under me.

I leaded on it and was able to raise up into one knee. The pain around my body was just as excruciating as it had been every other time, but my mind was untouched.

Darren looked at me with a surprise. Rather than try and make another jab, he pulled at my energy even more intensely. I gritted my teeth and winced, but continued following the call of the crystal.

Using all my strength, I held out an open hand. It longed to be reunited. With what, I didn't know.

I began to call it to my hand, just as I could do with my crystal. When I did, a bridge of blue energy began to reach through the swirling storm of red and purple energy between us. The Parasite was confused and even frightened.

He tried to stop the bridge from forming. Using his free hand, he crafted a beam of red energy to meet it. Slowed by the opposition, the bridge continued toward the crystal. Realizing there was no way to stop it, he let go of me, summoned his sword to the hand that wasn't fighting the bridge, and sliced through it.

The blade ripped through the blue energy and the connection was severed. He stood there for a moment, examining me. I put my weight on my staff and rose to my feet. I was weak, but I could feel my strength returning as the energy from my crystal ran through my veins.

"Looks like you learned a new trick," Darren said, trying to show strength, but his voice was nervous.

"No," I said, "I think I remembered an old one."

I, of course, wasn't referring to calling his crystal. I was referring to remembering my values.

Flyhe shook his head, out of tricks, and called his energy across his body once again. I did the same. He held up his sword and I held up my staff. It had been too long since I had used my weapon of choice. It felt calming just to hold it in my hands.

Flyhe charged at me with uncertainty and rage. I think he was nervous to use his powers after what I had done, so he attacked with the sword only. I stood in my spot and waited for him to reach me. When he did, our final fight began.

Our weapons clashed, me catching his blade, and him catching my staff. Neither one of us made much progress. Rather than fully attack him, I waited for his blade to swing at me before I countered.

After a while of this, Flyhe conjured an orb of red energy and flung it at me using his free hand while my staff was caught by his sword. I sensed it and jumped back, dodging it. He sent another and I intercepted it with my staff. He sent another, and perhaps in arrogance or maybe curiosity, I moved my staff down to my right side and with my left hand, I caught it.

The energy pulled at mine, but I fed it. I sent energy down my arm to it. The blue and red mixed to form purple. The orb sat in my hand, no longer pulling from me. I now had total control over it. I could feel it as if it were my own energy.

It was powerful and felt even stronger than when Bailey and I combined our powers. It felt complete.

After a second of me examining it and Darren watching on in astonishment, I hurled it back at him. He held his sword down and raised a shield. The orb hit the shield, but with such force that it pushed him backward a couple feet.

He lowered the shield and looked up at me with visible fear. A bit reluctantly, I made him an offer, "I won't kill you," I promised, "You can stop all of this!" I gestured to the battle that raged around us.

Cruisers on both sides were falling from the sky. Fighters crashed into one another and cruisers as they were shot down. Transports carrying troops burst into flames as they were intercepted on their way to board cruisers.

"All this death can stop! Just call your people off!" I suggested, yelling over the sounds of battle.

"This can never stop!" Flyhe said, "You have no idea what you've done today! No matter what happens, or how many battles you win, Earth will be owned by the people I serve. Whether it be through The Organization now, or something else later. You are on the losing side."

This came as a bit of a shock. I thought he was at the top of the hierarchy. Whoever these other people were, they were not today's problem.

"Everyone loses in war," I countered, "You only choose whether or not you lose yourself."

Flyhe stood there for a moment. It was almost as if he were examining his options, or maybe himself. Without another word, he raised his sword again and ran at me to attack.

Rather than fight this time, I simply called his crystal to me. My blue energy cut through the air toward him. When he saw it coming, he dropped his sword, held up both hands, and used all his might to keep the energy from reaching him.

The two colors met half way between us. They swirled around each and mixed once again to form the purple energy. The bridge moved closer and closer to his chest. I knew that when it neared, he would try and sever the line.

With this in mind, I walked closer to him. Just as I predicted, the moment before the purple reached his hands, he stopped fighting it and leaped to the side. I leaped with him.

When he called his sword back to his hand, I was there to stop it. Surrounding my staff with blue energy, I knocked it out of the way. As we landed, I swept my staff under his feet. They were knocked out from under him and he fell to the ground.

My landing was less than graceful, but I still recovered quicker than him. As Darren tried to scramble to his feet, I towered over him. I rolled him onto his back using my energy, and began to form the bridge once again.

My energy quickly reached his crystal. The moment it toughed it, the bridge turned purple. As a matter of fact, everything turned purple. The energy filled the air, and I felt my feet leave the ground.

A surge of power filled my body like the day I first received my connection to the blue crystal, but this time I was awake. A searing heat filled my body. It was only painful for a few seconds. It was quickly followed by a warm tingling sensation.

My body felt strong and my vision returned. I realized I was laying on my back. Surrounding me was a soft purple glow. I shook my head as I tried to regain my bearings.

I sat up. I was still on the cruiser, but back from Darren, who lay a few feet away, motionless. The battle still raged around me. I realized my right fist was clenched around something.

I pulled it up into my field of vision and opened it. Resting there was a purple crystal. It was larger than mine, and a bit of a different shape. It only took a few seconds for me to realize what had happened.

I looked down at my chest. My crystal was missing from its holding spot. The two crystals had combined. I finally understood. At some point, the two must have been one and something caused them to split. Somehow the energy split as well, the red longing to be reunited with the blue, and in a less volatile way, the blue longing for the red to return to it.

The Parasite was never really drawing energy from me, he was just trying to put the crystals back together. For some reason, the red must not have been able to unite the two, or at least, it had to try a lot harder.

I stood up and placed the purple crystal in the holding place on my chest. The holder morphed to the right shape to carry it, and it tightened around the crystal.

My entire body felt stronger. My power felt more powerful. For the first time in a long time, I felt complete. Though the biggest battle ever fought on Earth was raging around me, somehow, my mind had peace. Not only was this crystal back to its old self, so was I.

I walked over to Flyhe and leaned over him. He was alive and mostly conscious, but he was now powerless. I knelt down next to him. "Are you alright?" I asked.

"No," he opened his eyes and scowled at me, "Because of this I will die, and you with me. Everything we love will brun."

I never expected him to return my kindness, so his promise left me unphased. "We'll see," I said, avoiding conflict, "You will pay for what you've done, but not with your life." An explosion rocked the cruiser beneath our feet.

"ALI," I called.

"Yes, sir"

"Are all my friends inside?"

"Safe and sound and anxiously awaiting your return"

"Good," I breathed a sigh of relief. The Parasite hadn't hurt any of them too bad. I looked down at Darren Flye. He looked up at me with hatred. "Let's get a few troops up here to carry our friend to the brig."

"Yes, sir"

I waited with Darren for a few minutes while we were waiting on the transport team. He didn't say a word.

307

I allowed my powers to flow over my body. It was like that first day all over again. The power was fresh and new, no longer crippled by its division between two crystals.

A team of Ekklesia soldiers finally arrived on a transport. It never landed but hovered a foot or two off the surface of the cruiser. The team of soldiers hopped down, cuffed Darren and loaded him up.

Still, he didn't say a word, and I felt as though there was nothing else for me to say to him. We only watched each other and the ship flew out of sight over the edge of the cruiser.

ALI gave me confirmation when they had made it to the hanger. "Don't you want to go in?" ALI suggested.

"We only won a fight," I pointed to the fleet of ships in front of me, "We still have a battle to win."

"What are you suggesting?"

"Let's test out these new powers."

Chapter 28

Overfilled with confidence, I got a running start, headed for the edge of the cruiser. On my last step before running off, I nodded for my helmet to form and summoned two concussive blasts to propel me through the air.

I knew they would be powerful, but they were a bit more than I expected. I was launched out into the battle. After a moment of freefall, I ignited my jetpack and flew through the tangle of fighters battling it out between the cruisers.

I flew down and threaded my way through The Organization's fleet until I reached some ships in the middle that remained untouched. My senses were more keen than before which made the flying easy.

When I landed, I assessed my surroundings. I needed to take the cruisers down. The engines of the vessel next to the one I was standing on were even with me. Wanting to see what my newfound strength could do, I stretched both hands out in front of me and forced out as much energy as I could.

The beam erupted from my hands and effortlessly sliced through the ship. The engines lost their orange glow and the cruiser began to slip out of the sky.

By hitting the engines, the stabilizers would allow for a relatively soft descent to the mountains below. The soldiers inside would survive.

Boiling out from the hangar came transports and fighters and even floating platforms filled with people as they evacuated to another ship.

I jumped from ship to ship and quickly crippled over twenty cruisers. Some crashed into others on their way down, taking them down as well. Forming in the middle of The Organization's fleet was a gaping hole as the ships began to pile up on the ground below.

They sent their pilots after me, but over all, it was a pretty dull fight. My shield was impermeable to their attacks - the gunfire at least. After a while of this and a couple more downed cruisers, someone must have given the order to chase me off at any cost.

I stood on one of The Organization's largest cruisers, their command ship. It was massive, decked with every gun imaginable and about eight hangar bays (that's how many I was able to count).

When I was preparing to fly around behind them and take out their engines, a squadron of bombers flew up on me from under the ship.

With no regard for the vessel I was standing on, they unleashed a barrage of missiles and bombs. I saw them coming and began to run. The explosions started just behind me and neared until they were one my heels.

I knew that even if I managed to conjure a shield strong enough to absorb the blasts, the damage to the ship around me would pose the danger of me falling inside and being crushed by falling debris.

With this in mind, I ignited my jetpack. As I lifted off the ground, I boosted myself with a pair of concussive blasts. Seeking missiles followed me as I flew through the air, but another set of concussive blasts caused them to crash into eachother.

Setting my sights on returning to my own fleet, I flew as fast as I could. The ships pursued me, but were deterred when Ekklesia fighters intercepted them. They broke off from me, and I headed for the landing platform of our flagship.

The sun was almost completely below the horizon and what was left of its light dimly illuminated the mountainside.

From my view in the sky, I could see the damage of the battle. Not a single tree seemed to be left standing beneath the battle. I could see that some of our best cruisers lay in the debris field. Smoke poured from wounds in ships. Both sides had been devastated, but The Organization had received the most damage and humiliation.

The once intimidating fleet was now reduced to the same size as ours. I couldn't tell how many ships that was, but the sides were even. I determined that my day of fighting was over since the bombers would now be ready to chase me off if I returned to the other side. I landed back on our command ship, walked through the doors, and onto the bridge.

I was greeted by General Raddick who was waiting for me at the door, "Sir!" he said gleefully, "We have just received word from one of their generals. They will order a retreat if we promise not to pursue."

"That's Great!" I exclaimed, "Send word immediately, we accept their offer. It's time for this day of killing to end."

"I will tell them immediately," he said as he walked over to the captain. The transmission must have come in on his dashboard.

I walked to the window to observe the end of this dreadful day. Different shades of plasma still lit up the sky, dampened by the haze of smoke coming from below us. I longed for the second this was over. A blast rattled the ship.

"Ceasefire is to commence in five minutes," the General said over the coms, "Get in your best shots, then call in your fighters."

I hated that this would continue for even another millisecond, but I assumed this was standard procedure. Word needed to reach every ship on both sides to prevent misunderstanding.

I watched as the minutes creeped by. Ships still fell from the sky on both sides. We had victory, but that fact had not caught up with me or the battle just yet.

I looked over the surface of the ship. Even though the armor had kept it from having almost any damage, the Unitum plating was discolored and jared loose in many places. Still, the Ekklesia dove was visible, reflecting the Orange, yellow, purple, and green flashes from the battle. The grandeur and beauty of the ship was not stolen from it by the damage.

Finally, the five minutes were up. All at once, the fighting stopped. The constant rattling and banging ceased. The colors of plasma disappeared from the sky and, through the haze, stars became visible.

The light of the waxing moon softly illuminated the fighters as they flew to their appropriate sides. No one broke the truce. I felt everyone had a sense of relief now that the battle was over.

Organization transports flew from behind us. I didn't know it, but General Raddick explained that some had broken our line and were unsuccessfully trying to break into the base. They didn't make it very far.

When he finished explaining this and I saw that The Organization was turning around and making for the horizon, I had only one question nagging at my mind.

"Where are my friends?" I asked the General, knowing that they would have come through here.

Before he could answer my question, the doors from the rest of the ship opened up. Bandaged and filthy, the fearless people I called friends were standing in the doorway.

Unable to contain myself, I used a tiny concussive blast to launch myself over the consoles and officers to them. I landed in front of them and wrapped them into a group hug.

"We did it," I breathed, overcome with joy.

We embraced one another, not letting go. Every odd and statistic said we should have failed. Every standard of society said it shouldn't have been us. Every border and barrier said it wasn't possible. But we did it.

Not so surprisingly. We were the good guys. We stood up for the things of God. We were united. God was with us. How could we have failed?

The answer, of course, is that we couldn't fail, but I never believed or suspected it would be this kind of victory- one that we all got to walk away from.

After, well I don't know how long, we let go of eachother and admired our success. "Looks like you've got something new," Blake said, gesturing to my newly purple crystal.

"Not exactly"

***

That night went on in sorrow for some and celebration for others. We had lost many troops, but their sacrifice had prolonged our freedom. It was bitter sweet.

Darren Flyhe received a trial by the high council and, of course, was convicted of his crimes. The council voted for him to be put to death, but bargaining for his life, I suggested that we may need him for information. They agreed, and he was sentenced to life in prison.

The battlefield from that night was dedicated as a final resting spot for hundreds of thousands. It was the largest number of casualties to ever be claimed in a single battle. For those who died of their injuries after the battle had ended, we decided it was fitting, since they couldn't go home, for them to be buried with their fellow soldiers on that battlefield. We even started talks of constructing a monumental bridge there, between the mountains, so that future generations could look down on the rubble and remember that day.

I explained all the parts of the battle that my friends missed to them. I demonstrated my newfound power. I even became the new defending champion of our sparring matches.

The Organization didn't attack us, or even the areas that were once America. They left us alone. We worked on sending aid to the cities that had been bombed, and in doing so, we found many military bases that had not been able to make it to our base.

Rather than bring them here, we gave them new gear and charged them to protect the cities they were close to. Our cruisers began to patrol the fallen American territories, and we also opened up enlistment for citizens in those areas. They needed a government to prevent anarchy, so even though America had fallen, we used the structures of the state governments and put the president over them.

That government was trying to establish normalcy: sending kids to school, rebuilding cities, etc. The world was changing fast, so fast that, at times, they had trouble keeping up. Sometimes it was hard to get food, other times fuel, but overall, the former citizens of America were faring well. Better than any other place in the world.

My friends and I worked on running the base, and by the time Christmas arrived, we felt like we had it down to a science. We felt we could take a bit of a break for a day to celebrate.

***

"Alright guys," I said to those with me (The Vales, Mrs. Boone, Ana's parents - The Cantuns, and my friends) "Time for me to give you your present."

Everyone looked at the void under the tree, positioned in the corner of the Vales' living quarters. All the gifts that were once there had been opened. The group looked on in confused anticipation of what gift I would be giving.

"So I know we all miss home. We all miss normalcy," I paused for dramatic effect, "So I have worked with General Raddick and we are going to move our base of operations."

Their heads darted, looking at one another and searching for an answer to what I was getting at.

"We've fixed up my fathers old base in Tullahoma," I explained, "We're moving back home!"

"Actually!" Blake said with the most excitement of the group. He was the only one from Tullahoma that didn't already know. I had already discussed my plan with the Vales.

"Actually! Now, I know that doesn't sound like much to the rest of you, but there's more. Alex, I have a brand new house waiting for you. And waiting inside of it, your family!"

"No way," he said in stunned disbelief. I knew that was something he hadn't had for a long time, "Dylan-"

"Wait, wait, wait," I stopped him, "There's more. Ana, Bailey, Blake, you all have houses waiting for you and your families as well," Their eyes lit up with excitement. "But there's something else waiting for all of us as well," I smiled, ear to ear, barely able to contain myself.

"Some of you have never even been there, but so long as The Organization stays quiet for now… While we wait for our forces to build up again… the last semester of our senior year is waiting for all of us." I knew Ana was a bit too old to be in her senior year, and Alex was a bit too young, but I had fixed it so that we would all be together, "Ultimate normality!"

Laughs of excitement rose from my friends while tears came to the eyes of the three mothers in the room. "What about running the base?" Alex asked, reluctant to accept this as reality.

"We'll run it from under my dad's house, in the tunnels there, in the afternoons," I explained, "I made sure our classes are easy. We're mostly just going to school for the experience."

"There's gotta be a catch," Bailey said, having the same disbelief.

"Well, I guess there is one," I admitted, "The world doesn't know about powers, and I'd like to keep it that way. For now, powers stay a secret. We only use them in private or with helmets and uniforms while we're in Tullahoma."

"That's it?" Blake asked, "That's the only catch?"

"Yep!"

Everyone took another moment to be excited, then Mr. James spoke up, "There is one more catch. It affects Dylan."

We all looked at him with confused faces. Even I didn't know what he was talking about. Still, I was ready to accept whatever consequence to make this a reality. "What is it?" I asked.

"You don't have a legal guardian," he explained, "So they wouldn't let us register you for classes."

"What!" I said, aggravated, "We can't just fake that or something?"

"No," he shook his head, "I'm afraid not."

I scrunched my eyebrows in disbelief. I was sure I had thought of everything. Now my gift and hopes were ruined.

"But there is one thing we can do, if you'll let us," he continued after a moment of suspenseful silence.

"Well, what is it?" Blake spoke for me.

"Dylan, your father's will is clear," he smiled gently, "If you'll allow us to adopt you, the Vale name is yours."

A smile reappeared on my face. It took leading a war effort to get it, but the sole thing I wanted all those months ago, had finally come to pass.

"Yes!" I yelled.

"We thought you might feel that way," Mrs. Cassey said, "It's already been taken care of... Dylan Vale"

I looked over at Blake and he returned my excitement.

"Well," Mrs. Boone said, "It sounds like we have a lot to discuss! How about we discuss it over Christmas dinner?"

The room agreed with her and we headed for the dinner table, readied with ham, mashed potatoes, corn, and rolls. This would be the best meal we'd had in months, I thought.

We sat down and Mr. James offered to say grace. We bowed our heads, "Dear God, we thank you for this wonderful day, your birth, your death, your resurrection. We thank you for keeping us and for empowering us with your spirit to fight against evil. We thank you for each other, for allowing us to be brought together, and for making us one big family.

We thank you for your protection and your grace in allowing us to be here. And... Oh, yes, we thank you for the food too!"

There was a gentle giggle and a uniform "Amen" from the group and we began to eat.

All that filled anyone's mind was, not what had happened this past year, though just for me there would have been much to think about: my father's death, finding out my father's alive, and then, my father's death again. The takeover of The Organization and our victory in defending the base. Finding the crystal, finding out there are more crystals, fighting someone who wields one of those crystals. Still, that all sat at the back of my mind for now.

Most nights, that was all I could think about, that's what kept me awake. Rather, all I could think about tonight was the future. In a few short weeks, we would be back home. I would be safe and with the people I loved most. I would be back, attending services at my church. I would be able to hear the wisdom of my pastor once again.

The sun was finally beginning to rise as we came out of a long dark night. Surely the sun would set on us again, as is the way of things, but for now, the light felt amazing.

Hello, reader! I am pleased you made it this far. If you enjoyed what you just read, you're in luck! This is the first book in a series. Be on the lookout for:

The Crystal: Parts 4-6 - Releasing in Fall 2025

The Crystal: Parts 7-9 - Releasing in Fall 2026

Also be on the lookout for the "Legends" series which will follow the supporting characters of "The Crystal" series. Learn about their pasts, their flaws, and their skills in a new way as they become the main characters in their own stories. The first three in the series are as follows:

The Legend of Bailey Boone - TBA

The Legend of Daniel Sons - TBA

The Legend of Hunter Hogan - TBA

If you loved this book, please write a good review and tell all of your friends! Thank you so much for your support!

For the Nations!

J. A. Daniel